ECHO IN TIME

Also by C. J. Hill

Erasing Time

ECHO IN TIME

C. J. HILL

 KATHERINE TEGEN BOOKS

An Imprint of HarperCollins Publishers

Katherine Tegen Books is an imprint of HarperCollinsPublishers.

Echo in Time
Copyright © 2014 by C. J. Hill

Library of Congress Cataloging-in-Publication Data
Hill, C. J.
    Echo in time / C. J. Hill. — First edition.
        pages   cm
    Sequel to: Erasing time.
    Summary: Taylor and Joseph are part of a team sent to Traventon to destroy
the QGPs and, perhaps, Reilly, on a mission that could endanger Taylor's twin and
Joseph's girlfriend, Sheridan, but reunite them with Joseph's supposedly dead twin,
Echo.
    ISBN 978-0-06-212396-1 (paperback)
    [1. Time travel—Fiction.   2. Government, Resistance to—Fiction.   3. Twins—
Fiction.   4. Sisters—Fiction.   5. Brothers—Fiction.   6. Science fiction.]   I. Title.
PZ7.H547687Ec   2013   2012051732
[Fic]—dc23   CIP
                                                                              AC

Typography by Carla Weise
13 14 15 16 17   LP/RRDH   10 9 8 7 6 5 4 3 2 1
❖
First Edition

To my husband, Guy (AKA Techno Bob), who always comes up with the scientific terms and dialogue my engineering-type characters use. It paid off in so many ways to marry a rocket scientist.

To my kids, Asenath, Luke, James, Faith, and Arianna—thanks for being understanding when I have to put in long hours writing.

To my sister, Ginger Hunsaker, who stayed up late the night before my revisions were due to help me go over them. I probably should have put you in a dedication long before now.

And just so the rest of my family knows that I love them too: Hey, Mom, Dad, Erin, Gibbs, Stephen, and Brandon, I love you! You're an awesome family! Thanks for your support.

ECHO IN TIME

chapter hapter

1

Treason was becoming habit-forming.

When Joseph Monterro escaped from the city of Traventon, he'd thought he was done with his covert life, done with running, hiding, and sabotage. Done with deceiving people who trusted him. Things weren't ever that simple, though.

Joseph walked onto the grounds of Tranquility Park, scanning the grassy fields for his contact. He saw no sign of the man, but then, Joseph was a few minutes early. He headed toward their meeting spot at the lake.

Santa Fe had plenty of parks, most of them full of amusement equipment, skating pits, and places to hover-jump. Joseph liked this one for its old-fashioned feel. Ducks paddled across the lake, frogs hopped on rocks at its edges, and hummingbirds zoomed around flowering bushes. Even after being in Santa Fe for three weeks, he was still struck with a small jolt of wonder every time he saw an animal. The only animals in Traventon were in the virtual reality programs.

Another difference was the domes covering the cities. Traventon's had been opaque, making the weather invisible. Santa Fe's was clear. He still wasn't used to seeing clouds stalking through the sky like silent, watchful entities.

Joseph pulled his comlink from his pocket and brought up the QGP program on the handheld computer. It had been dangerous to copy design specifications from a weapons system, and it was even more dangerous to write subroutines to fix its flaws. But even if someone saw his screen, it would be hard to tell what he was doing, and besides, Joseph didn't have the time to be careful. Plans were already in motion.

A few minutes after Joseph reached the lake's edge, a man walked across one of the trails toward him. Abraham, his contact. The man was probably thirty years older than Joseph—fifty or maybe even fifty-five. A bushy beard covered a good portion of his face, and a black hat hid most of his dark hair. Joseph didn't know if Abraham was his real name, or whether he came from the Christian, Jewish, or Muslim sector of the city. According to his search of the city's data, all three groups claimed Abraham as an ancestor.

Joseph turned his comlink off, slipped it into his jacket pocket, and glanced around. A few couples were meandering around the park trails. Some children splashed and played in the swimming section at the other side of the lake. A group of teenage boys launched a light drone into the sky so they could target hunt. No one seemed to have taken note of Abraham walking up to Joseph.

Abraham nodded in greeting, turned so he faced the water, then opened the bag he carried. He reached inside, took out a handful of food pellets, and scattered them across the water in front of him. Dark shadows of fish rose through the lake's surface, mouths open to snatch the floating pellets. The water puckered with their darting movements.

Joseph kept his gaze on the fishes' twisting silver bodies. "The council asked me to go to its planning meeting this afternoon."

Abraham tossed more pellets onto the lake. "I told you they would. Who else is as qualified to go back to Traventon to destroy the QGPs?"

Fortunately, no one. Unfortunately, very few people were also in as much trouble with the Traventon government. The threat of capture, torture, and death had a way of sapping the fun out of a trip home.

Abraham turned to look at Joseph, to study his expression. "You understand what we expect from you in return for our help?"

Joseph nodded. "A life for a life."

Abraham turned back to the lake. "We'll need confirmation you made the kill."

"What sort of confirmation?" Joseph's mind flashed to a story from one of the books of scripture—a girl who had asked for the head of a man on a silver platter. *Not that*, Joseph thought. It was bad enough that he had agreed to kill someone. The last thing he wanted to do was carry a severed head around.

Abraham shrugged. "You have a while to think of something.

My sources say the team won't leave for two weeks."

Two weeks? "That's too soon." Joseph was barely getting any sleep now, and he was only halfway done writing the code that would allow the QGPs to work. He couldn't finish any faster. Especially if he had to spend a large chunk of that time in a virtual reality center acting out ways to break into Traventon's Scicenter.

Abraham dropped more pellets in the water, unconcerned. "Most of the council wants you to leave earlier, but the team needs to be trained and the engineering department says they still need two more weeks to finish producing those laser-box disrupters you designed."

Joseph frowned. "I'll need at least three weeks to finish fixing the program."

"Then you should have made your disrupter design more complicated so it would take the engineering department longer."

The design *was* complicated, and despite the fact that the council wanted to name the disrupter after Joseph, it was only partially his invention.

Ducks paddled in Abraham's direction, gliding over to see what sort of food he was offering. "You can find a way to delay the team's departure," Abraham said. "Shouldn't be a problem for a smart boy like you."

In other words, Abraham's group wasn't going to help Joseph any more than they had to. Joseph supposed he should have expected that. Help always came with a price. He watched the ducks pecking at the floating pellets. "When will you give me the signal-blocking bands?"

Traventon had one simple way to control its citizens. Every person had a crystal implanted in their wrist that constantly sent out and received signals from the city. If someone didn't have clearance to go into an area, they would only have a thirty-second warning—a tightening pinch in the wrist that got more painful every second—before the crystal sent out debilitating shocks that made movement impossible. The building's alarms would sound too, alerting the Enforcers of an intruder.

The shocks were stronger if someone tried to leave the city. Those didn't debilitate; they killed. Removing the crystals wasn't an easy or quick procedure. They were attached to the radial artery and programmed to explode if anyone tampered with them.

"The blocking bands aren't quite ready," Abraham said.

"But they will be in two weeks?" Traventon had made the crystal signals strong enough to penetrate not only the city's regular buildings but also high-security reinforced ones. Covering the crystals had always been impossible until now.

"Don't worry." Abraham flicked a handful of pellets to the waiting ducks. "The blocking bands are basically done already. You know how engineers are, though. They've got to triple test everything—make sure it works in high temperatures, low temperatures, underwater, with no water. I tell you, if Santa Fe's engineers had lived in Noah's day, the animals would still be lined up waiting for permission to board."

A few ducks waddled out of the lake, fixing their small eyes on Abraham. They weighed their hunger against the risk of danger and edged closer to the food. He tossed some pellets in front of them. "Do you have your list for me?"

"Yes." Joseph put his hand in his jacket pocket and felt for the piece of paper there. Paper was plentiful in Santa Fe. The people in this city didn't want to depend entirely on technology. They always left themselves another way to get things done. Paper, in this case, was essential for stealth. You couldn't hack into a computer to find a piece of paper. You couldn't capture it as it winged its way through the air as an electronic message.

Joseph hesitated before he gave Abraham the list. On one of the first days after Joseph's group had come to Santa Fe, Sheridan had written him a note. He wasn't sure if this was because she didn't know how to use the comlink the integration liaison had given her, or whether she knew a handwritten note would mean more to him. Whatever the reason, he had spent long minutes staring at the paper, tracing the lines of her words. They were so elegant, so effortlessly smooth and even. Just like her.

Joseph had handwritten a few things before. It had been a part of his studies as a historian. His writing was clumsy, though. Too large, too irregular. Anyone who saw this note would know it was the script of someone who had hardly ever practiced writing. They would know it had come from him.

He handed the list to Abraham anyway, passing it to him as they shook hands.

Abraham glanced at the paper, letting his eyes linger long enough to read it, then he reached into his bag, dropped the paper inside, and took out another handful of pellets. He scattered them on the lake, and the fish darted between the ducks, racing to gobble up the food first. "We agree to your terms. You'll need to tell President Mason privately that you want to take an extra man with you. We'll give you his name later. The council won't like you making additions to the team, but they don't have a lot of choices, do they?"

They didn't. Joseph not only knew the QGP system, he knew how to computigate through the Scicenter's restricted programs.

Abraham turned away from the lake to let his gaze lock on Joseph's. "You're sure you'll be able to complete the kill? When the moment appears, you won't suddenly decide that taking a life opposes your moral code?"

Joseph didn't look away from Abraham's scrutiny. "That's the benefit of being raised in Traventon. We don't have moral codes."

Abraham grunted in displeasure. "No one should be without a moral code." He tapped his finger against his chest. "You need to search in here and find one; but"—his finger raised in the air to make a point—"wait until after the mission to do that."

chapter hapter
2

Taylor Bradford walked toward the Council Hall building, wondering what the president wanted to talk to her about this time. Well, she didn't really wonder. It was always the same thing. It would have something to do with the QGP weapon. Questions about its capabilities, applications, and how to destroy it.

Large golden letters engraved over the building's doorway read LIBERTAS IN UNITATE EST—Freedom Is Found in Unity. Latin had been dead for thousands of years, but even here in 2447 people were still using it for mottoes. Everything looked more elegant and official in Latin, she supposed.

Taylor wasn't a native of the twenty-fifth century. She'd been born in the twenty-first century, and had been minding her own business like any other eighteen-year-old girl, when twenty-fifth-century scientists had sucked her and her twin sister, Sheridan, smack-dab into the city of Traventon.

Okay, maybe Taylor hadn't *just* been minding her own business. Sheridan liked to remind her, pointedly sometimes, that Taylor was partially responsible for the whole sucked-into-the-future thing because Taylor had invented the QGP: the quark-gluon plasma converter. It was a machine that changed matter into a timeless energy flux.

It didn't matter how many times Taylor insisted to her sister or Santa Fe's council that she hadn't meant for the QGP to be turned into either a weapon or a part of a time machine; there was still apparently a lingering cloud of responsibility hovering over Taylor's head.

Taylor had designed and helped build the QGP while working on her graduate degree at the University of Tennessee. The QGP transformed matter into energy and then retransformed it later in another location. The machine could have had applications for travel in space as well as on earth. It could have been used to transport medicine from one part of the planet to another almost instantaneously. It could have done so many good things.

Instead, Dr. Reilly, a physics professor at UT, had stolen the credit for the QGP. In what was either cosmic justice or really bad luck, Reilly then accidentally turned himself into an energy flux wave that didn't reconfigure until four centuries later. He'd wound up in Traventon.

Unable to build a working QGP for the Traventon government, Reilly had used Taylor's QGP to suck her and Sheridan into the twenty-fifth century so that Taylor could help him.

As if she would help him.

Yeah, up until the moment Taylor had found herself floating inside the Time Strainer, being a genius had seemed like a good thing. It had taken Taylor and Sheridan several days, and more than one close call, to escape with Joseph to Santa Fe.

Now Taylor walked up the steps of the Council Hall. Under the *Freedom Is Found in Unity* motto, a sculpted relief showed people from different cultures and religions walking, talking, and working together. The people were smiling, clearly happy to be so unified. The relief would have been more accurate if it had shown a few of the people scowling, one or two spying, and the rest competing against each other.

Santa Fe had been formed in the twenty-fourth century when the other cities passed a treaty prohibiting religion. The religious groups had put aside their differences to build this city, but it was clear their truce was only necessity deep. Even after ninety years, the city was strictly segregated.

The city's pro-unity signs were frequent targets of vandalism. Down the street on one that read, "Strength comes from peace," someone had scrawled, "Strength comes from a stocked armory." Another sign near Taylor's apartment said, "When we work together, we have everything we need." It was the object of constant editorial revision. "I don't need Christians" had been written on the bottom. The next day the word *Christians* had been crossed out and the word *Jews* was inscribed. Then it was *Hindus*. Over the next few days, every religion in the city had its turn at being unneeded. Finally someone wrote, "I don't need bigots," across the whole list. Actually, Taylor had done that, and she probably shouldn't have since she'd been living in Santa Fe for only three weeks, but really. A city founded by religious groups ought to be a bit more loving.

Taylor considered the phrase inscribed over the Council Hall doorway again. Maybe vandalism was the reason the council had put their motto in Latin. People didn't care about commenting on words they couldn't understand.

Taylor walked up the steps to the front doors, expecting them to slide open. Then she remembered she had to hold her ID card up to activate the door's scanner. A purple light ran over her, and the door finally opened.

She went inside and strode across the lobby. The whole room looked like it had been constructed out of glowing white marble. Golden veins fanned here and there, and as she walked past them, parts of the wall and floor sparkled. Coming here always made Taylor vaguely feel as though she'd walked into a jewelry box.

Joseph was leaning against the security desk, studying something on his comlink. He was a twenty-year-old genius who'd been one of Taylor and Sheridan's translators when they'd first been brought to this century. Genius incognito, that was. He'd hidden his computer abilities from the Traventon government by working for his father as a historian instead.

Joseph frowned at his comlink screen and for a moment reminded Taylor of a cologne ad from her day: a tall, ruggedly handsome guy with broad shoulders who was brooding for no apparent reason.

Well, he could have been from her day with one notable exception. He had blue hair. In this century people dyed their hair in the same colors people back in the twenty-first century had used for their clothes.

Joseph looked up from his comlink. "You're forty-five minutes late." Instead of speaking with a twenty-first-century accent, he used the modern one. Taylor was supposed to practice it.

"I was in the science district," she said. "I got lost."

Joseph cocked an eyebrow. His blue eyes were skeptical. "No, you didn't. I had the city map memorized three days after I got here. I doubt it took you much longer."

"Two days, actually." Taylor flashed her ID badge at the guard behind the desk. The badge projected a holographic image of Taylor in the air in front of her. "It doesn't matter if I'm late," she went on. "I've already told them everything I'm going to about the QGP. At this point they're just dragging me back here to annoy me."

The guard nodded and waved her on. Taylor headed toward the hallway that led to the council chambers. "Besides, you can't criticize me—you're not in there either."

Joseph fell in step beside her, rearranging calculations on his comlink. "They sent me to find you fifteen minutes ago. You might want to answer the messages on your comlink every once in a while, you know."

Whatever he was working on, he clearly wanted to be here even less than she did. "You don't have to translate for me anymore," she said. "The council can understand me." She'd practiced her accent enough that if she spoke slowly, she didn't have problems.

"I'm not here as a translator."

"Really? Why do they want to see you?"

He shrugged. "Probably my charm and good looks."

"Right," she said. "That's probably it." In truth, Joseph had enough of both. Taylor didn't let herself dwell on Joseph's looks though. A girl could get lost in his blue eyes, and that was something Taylor couldn't afford to do. Because Joseph was dating Sheridan. Which was just Taylor's luck. Joseph was the only guy she'd ever met who was as smart as she was, and he only had eyes for her twin sister.

Despite the fact that the hallway looked like it had been constructed out of blocks of white stone, Taylor's footsteps made no sound against the floor. She fingered the badge around her neck. She still wasn't used to having to wear it all the time. "Has the city council given you a decision about your work requests yet?"

"No."

A hesitancy in Joseph's voice made Taylor glance at him. He didn't seem to be telling the truth, or at least not all of it.

Taylor hadn't heard from the career department herself, but Sheridan had received a message on her comlink a week ago telling her she would be accepted into her choice of three of the city's colleges. She was given a list of books to read and computer courses to complete in order to be caught up with the incoming students when the next term started.

Taylor had expected to be assigned to a research lab right away. But then, maybe the city council was nervous about turning her loose with equipment. The last thing she'd invented could be used to kill people. Or change time.

Joseph and Taylor were nearly to the chamber doors. "So what did I miss in the meeting?" she asked.

"They're choosing who to put on the team to go to Traventon and destroy Reilly's QGPs. President Mason said the mission required the best-trained men in the city—"

"Which turned the selection into an Olympic event," Taylor finished for him. "So many sectors now want to send representatives, it will look like a parade is marching into the Scicenter."

"Exactly. So President Mason delayed that decision, and the council started debating whether the team should also assassinate Reilly."

Taylor inwardly groaned. *That* wasn't going to be a quick discussion. Really, she never should have let President Mason know she had invented the QGP. Prestige aside, being an expert sucked.

Joseph held up his badge to the council chamber's door scanner. A purple light swept over him, checking to make sure he was who his badge said he was; then the door slid open.

Taylor was supposed to do the same scanner check, but she followed Joseph inside instead. The room was almost completely filled by a huge, horseshoe shaped table, with about forty councilmen and councilwomen sitting around it. President Mason sat in a raised chair at the center of the curve. Screens hung on either side of his chair, used for showing video of whoever's turn it was to talk. Judging by the way the delegates were all fervently jabbing at their speaker buttons, the meeting was going to drag on and on. Taylor sighed. She should have come an hour late instead of only forty-five minutes.

"Reilly has already built nine QGPs." An older man with braided black hair spoke. His voice was slow but strong. "If Reilly gets even one of them to work, the Traventon government will need only the smallest amount of DNA to change a person into an energy flux wave. He'll never reconfigure those waves, never give anyone a trial. If anything, he'll use that energy to power more of his filthy inventions."

"Reilly doesn't have our DNA," someone from the table called out. "Why should we risk our people to kill him?"

A few people slapped their hands on the table in agreement.

"He may have your DNA someday," someone else called back. "And hiding will be nearly impossible. If a radio wave can find you—then so can the QGP's grasp."

Taylor followed Joseph toward a couple of empty seats in the experts' section of the table.

"We have operatives in Traventon," the old man said. "Are you willing to abandon them?" His dark eyes made a penetrating sweep around the table. "Have you forgotten the QGP could be modified to destroy large groups of people? It will be used on all of Traventon's enemies. And we are their enemies."

Even more table slapping followed this pronouncement.

The only empty seats in the experts' section were next to Pascal Chavez, the head of the science department. Her peacock-colored hair was twisted into a bun today. She smiled patronizingly at Taylor. After Taylor had refused to give Pascal any technical information about the QGP beyond the details needed to destroy it, the woman had treated Taylor coldly. Taylor, Pascal insisted, was casting aspersions on her character by refusing to trust her.

Taylor didn't care. Information about the QGP had already ended up in the wrong hands once. She wasn't taking any more chances.

Pascal leaned toward Taylor. "Sister Bradford, you finally decided to come and honor our invitation."

The citizens of Santa Fe addressed everyone except President Mason as either brother or sister. Being president apparently got you out of the family.

Taylor settled herself into her chair. "Yes, I did."

Pascal let out a small huffing sound and turned away from Taylor as though talking to her wasn't worth the effort.

A bowl of sugary nuts sat on the table in front of Taylor along with a glass of water. You knew a meeting was going to be too long when the council had to provide people sustenance just to get through it.

A man with a bushy beard was speaking now. He had on the usual clothes men in Santa Fe wore: long-sleeved tan shirts with colorful sashes that cut across their chests. The outfit had at first reminded Taylor of the sashes beauty-pageant queens wore, but after seeing them for three weeks, she liked them. Joseph looked particularly good in the blue ones he always wore. They brought out the color of his eyes.

Not that she let herself spend time thinking about him. Because once you got past his intelligence and good looks, Joseph wasn't her type. Too reserved and quiet. Taylor needed someone who was more spontaneous, more fun. And, most importantly, someone who wasn't dating Sheridan.

"Why send our people to destroy the QGPs," the bushy-bearded man asked, raising his hand and shaking it for emphasis, "if Reilly can build more? He *will* build more, and he'll find a way to keep us from destroying them next time."

The screen flashed to an older woman with apricot-colored hair. "If killing is wrong when Reilly does it, then it is also wrong when we do it. I wouldn't ask any of our team to murder someone. I wouldn't lay that burden on their consciences."

"Then don't ask them," the bushy-bearded man replied, even though he no longer had his speaker button lit. "I'll ask for you."

A round of table slapping erupted after that comment. When the noise faded, several people called out that they would not only ask, they would happily come along and do the job themselves.

President Mason tapped a lit square in front of him. "Delegates, please refrain from speaking unless you're lit." President Mason was a middle-aged man with kind brown eyes and too much gray hair. He'd probably gotten it from having to deal with the city council.

His two counselors sat in chairs that flanked him. One was a serious older man who wore a kaffiyeh on his head and always folded his arms like a sultan in judgment. The other was a Hindu woman with a piercing gaze that gave you the impression she might be able to read your mind. Taylor could never remember their names, so she simply thought of them as Counselor Number One and Counselor Number Two.

The Amish delegate stood up. He was easy to remember because he didn't use the technology in the room and he looked like he'd stepped out of the 1800s. "What sets us apart from the Traventon government," he said, "is that we don't wantonly kill our fellow man. Do we change our convictions now simply because we face a new threat? When have we not been threatened? We have flourished through peaceful means."

"We have flourished through stealth, intelligence, and courage," a woman at the end of the table called out. "We need to use those qualities in heavy doses now. We don't have to kill Reilly. We can capture him and bring him back here."

A nun sitting near Taylor shook her head so that her wimple swished back and forth across her shoulders. "It will be hard enough for the team to break into the Scicenter and do their job. How can we expect them to find, capture, and carry a prisoner out of the city? The QGP technology is unfortunately unavoidable." She sent Taylor a stern look indicating she thought Taylor should have known better than to invent the QGP in the first place. "Our scientists and engineers need to work on ways to shield our city from the QGPs' range."

President Mason broke in. "We're working on that already. However, we have no idea how long it will take to build an effective shield. Furthermore, we want our people who live or travel out of Santa Fe to be protected. Let's keep the discussion to the topic of assassination."

Taylor glanced at Joseph to see what he made of all of this. He was gazing at his lap. Most people wouldn't be able to see what he was doing, but since he sat beside Taylor, she could peer down at his screen. He was typing code, studying the syntax, then making adjustments.

It figured. He wasn't even paying attention to the debate.

The light went on in front of Counselor Number One. The president and his counselors could cut through the line of waiting speakers when they pushed their buttons, and it was a feature Counselor Number One took full advantage of. "I would like to remind everyone we have an important advantage where Reilly is concerned." He leaned toward the other delegates, and his voice took on the tone of a seasoned storyteller.

"Reilly is a cautious man, a suspicious one. A man who doesn't want to share his glory or his importance with anyone. Which is why Reilly has kept the knowledge of how to build QGPs in only one place."

Counselor Number One tapped his finger to his temple. "Reilly reasons that if no one else can build the QGPs, the Traventon government will have to keep him in charge and give him everything he wants. If we vote to assassinate him, we will destroy the knowledge with him."

It wouldn't be completely destroyed. The knowledge was still in Taylor's mind, although she didn't feel like pointing out this fact. Not when everyone was so assassination happy. Was that why President Mason had wanted her in the meeting—as a sort of veiled threat that she had better work with them because they already had ample reason to kill her?

Taylor glanced at Joseph again. He was running some sort of simulation with various inputs. She tilted her head to better read his screen. As she scanned the code, her stomach tightened. She recognized the QGP programming. It was almost like hers, but some things had been changed, shortened, or left out. It was Reilly's programming.

Joseph scrolled down to the next page, making some changes to one of the equations, a switch that would make a time range more powerful. Was he trying to figure out how to make a QGP work?

No, he couldn't be. Not while he was sitting in the council chamber next to her. Especially if he was even halfway paying attention to the assassination debate. She nudged her knee into his and whispered, "What are you doing?"

"Research." He didn't look up.

"Where did you get Reilly's QGP files?"

"I'm just checking some possibilities," he said.

"Yeah, I can see that," Taylor whispered. "Why?"

"To make sure the QGPs can be destroyed."

Taylor narrowed her eyes at him. Before they had escaped from Traventon, she and Joseph had broken into the Scicenter and used the Time Strainer to send a destruct message back through time to the QGP in the twenty-first century. "We've already destroyed one. We know the program works."

Joseph tilted his computer away from Taylor's view. "You can never be too prepared. At least that's what a sign near my apartment building says."

Taylor would have made a comment about that, but President Mason called her name.

"Taylor, can you tell us your thoughts on the matter?"

Her head snapped up. "Yes, um, after carefully considering the delegates' opinions, I think somebody should off Reilly." She held up a hand, already making amendments to her statement. "Usually I would think assassinating people was wrong—really, horribly wrong and a dreadful sin that you would all be held accountable for—but Reilly doesn't want to use the QGP for peaceful reasons; he wants to kill people."

Everyone stared at her in patient and not-so-patient silence. Taylor leaned forward and spoke more slowly to make sure she pronounced her words with the right accent. "I vote in favor of the assassination."

A couple of the leaders shook their heads in exasperation; a few more sighed. The rest kept staring. President Mason cleared his throat in a mildly reprimanding tone. "We suspended the assassination decision to discuss which experts to send on the team. Pascal believes Reilly will have placed safeguards on his QGPs that prevent the machines from taking your original self-destruct signal. We'll need people who can get around that sort of thing."

Oh. So that's where this conversation was heading—to her going along with the team. "I'm sure your city has many qualified programmers," Taylor said.

"We do." Pascal smiled condescendingly. "But you've refused to make them experts on the QGP."

President Mason looked firmly at Taylor. "You know the system the best."

Taylor shifted in her seat. "Hey, I'd like to help you, but the only way to send autodestruct signals to the QGPs is to use one of the classified computers in the Scicenter." She put her hand on her chest. "If I walk into the Scicenter, they'll recognize me."

Counselor Number One waved away her concern. "We can disguise you."

Taylor shook her head. She felt the weight of every delegate's stare on her, the weight of their expectations. "The last time I went to the Scicenter, I was caught and strapped to a chair, and Reilly hit me every time I denied knowing anything about the QGP." The only reason he stopped was that Sheridan told him she was the one who'd invented it. That memory still bothered Taylor, made her prickle with anger. "I'm the last person who should go anywhere near Traventon again."

Counselor Number Two pursed her lips. Her words came out in a slow, staccato rhythm. "You're the one who created the weapon. A person of honor would consider it her responsibility to destroy it."

President Mason's voice was gentler. "We'll send in a security team to protect you. We won't let you be captured."

Joseph pushed his speaker button. "You don't need to send Taylor. I can do it without her. I'm far better at splicing into Traventon's computers and I know the program she used to destroy the original QGP."

Taylor turned and stared at Joseph. "What?" she asked, blinking at him. Traventon's Enforcers weren't just looking for Taylor; Joseph was a wanted man too. "Do you have a death wish or something?" She turned back to President Mason. "Joseph is the second-to-the-last person who should go anywhere near Traventon."

"Joseph is a man of honor," Counselor Number Two said, aiming her words at Taylor. "He has already agreed to go on the mission."

So, Taylor had missed more than a debate on assassination. She turned in her chair to face Joseph. "I can't believe you're doing this. Sheridan is going to be so upset when you die."

He tilted his chin down as though Taylor was the one who was being unreasonable. "The QGPs have to be destroyed. You know that."

"But not by us." She looked upward. "Sheridan will be heartbroken. She'll cry for weeks."

"Who here in Santa Fe knows Traventon computers as well as I do?" Joseph asked.

Taylor let out a long sigh. "My sister will still be moping

around a year from now, and I'll be the one who has to deal with her."

President Mason steepled his hands and brought them to his lips. "We need people who can overcome anything Reilly has done." His brown eyes rested on Taylor. They seemed tired. "You'll be well paid. You'll receive a top-level year's salary in your account when you return."

If she returned.

Taylor swallowed hard. Her mouth felt dry, bitter. They couldn't make her go back. They couldn't force her to do this.

"Of course," Pascal added, turning a smug, catlike gaze on Taylor, "if Sister Bradford wanted to instruct someone else about the intricacies of the QGP, perhaps it wouldn't be necessary to send her. I'm brave enough to do the job."

Nope. Even as much as Taylor would like to wave a cheery farewell to Pascal, Taylor couldn't divulge more information about how the QGP worked. Instead of destroying the machine, Pascal might become Reilly's new assistant.

Taylor stared stubbornly at President Mason and didn't say anything.

Her expression must have spoken for her, because Counselor Number Two clucked her tongue disapprovingly. "Most people would feel a debt of gratitude toward the people who rescued them from Traventon, who took them in, who gave them clothes, food, and protection."

Counselor Number One waved a hand in Taylor's direction. "It's a year's salary for less than a week of your time. No one else in the city gets paid that well. I don't."

President Mason simply kept looking at Taylor, watching her with his kind eyes. "Please," he said.

Taylor groaned and rubbed her forehead. She didn't like feeling as though she owed these people something and was too cowardly to repay them. She didn't have a choice. Not really. "Fine," she said wearily. "I'll go."

chapter~~hapter~~
3

Taylor put her head down on the dinner table and groaned. Her muscles ached. She wasn't hungry. After she'd agreed to be on the QGP destruction team, Brother Hwan Choi, the head of security, had taken her and Joseph to a military-training virtual reality center. They'd been shown how to use gas masks, laser boxes, laser-box disrupters, laser cutters, boot speed boosters, comlink jammers, image scramblers, restorer boxes, and zip lines.

She and Joseph had gone through three different simulations of the mission to the Scicenter. He'd done fine. He already knew how to use most of the stuff. Despite having a "Joseph Box"—the laser-box disrupter Joseph had invented—Taylor had managed to get shot by Enforcers twice and killed by a gasbot the last time. The problem with the Joseph Box was you could use it only once. Its pulse was so strong that it not only disabled all laser boxes in a half-mile radius but also destroyed itself.

If more armed men arrived, you were toast. Granted, the laser boxes in the VR program didn't actually cut through you or explode your organs, but they still stung. And today was only Taylor's first day of training. She would have two more weeks of this.

Sheridan, who sat next to Taylor at the table, looked at Joseph with incredulous horror. "They can't send you to the Scicenter. You'll be captured."

The three had taken their dinner trays out of the cafeteria to eat in the courtyard, where it was less crowded. None of them was eating, though. Taylor had barely touched her salad. "I was guilted into going. Guilted into sacrificing myself for the good of humanity. If I die, make sure Santa Fe erects a really big statue of me."

Joseph ignored Taylor. "They're sending a security team with us, and we'll have help from their contacts in Traventon. We'll be fine. At least I will. Taylor may die from an overdose of drama."

Taylor pushed away a strand of her dark-purple hair. Sheridan kept her hair its natural color, red, but Taylor changed hers every time she got bored. "Make sure the city council inscribes something nice on my statue. And make sure they put it in Latin so no one vandalizes it."

Joseph reached over and took Sheridan's hand in his. "The longest part of the mission will be getting there and coming back. Two and a half days' trip each way. Taylor and I will only be in the Scicenter for a little while, maybe an hour."

He squeezed Sheridan's hand. She didn't squeeze his back. She was still staring at him in stunned disbelief. "It's not just Traventon's Enforcers who are looking for you. The Dakine are too."

The Dakine were a mob-like group who had killed Joseph's twin brother, Echo, nearly two months ago. Joseph was also on their hit list.

"Don't be mad," he murmured. "If the council asked you to risk your life to destroy a weapon like this, you'd do it. You'd be the first volunteer."

Sheridan blinked, looking tearful. "They didn't ask me, though. They asked the two people I care most about."

"And another thing," Taylor said, ignoring the love scene unfolding in front of her. "I want my statue to be facing Council Hall and flipping it off."

"Taylor—" Sheridan started.

Taylor didn't let her finish. "What? No one from this century knows what it means. You can tell the council I'm pointing upward to remind everyone of heavenly virtues."

Joseph let go of Sheridan's hand and turned to Taylor. "You don't have to go. If you don't trust Pascal with all the QGP information, you can tell it to me."

Taylor groaned and put her head back on the table.

Joseph watched her for a moment, then picked up the roll from his plate. "You don't trust me either?"

"I don't trust anyone," Taylor mumbled.

Joseph didn't comment about that. He ate his dinner while murmuring assurances to Sheridan. He could have saved his breath. Taylor knew her sister well enough to know three things would happen by the end of the night. First, Sheridan would call President Mason to try and convince him not to send Taylor and Joseph. Second, Sheridan would cry when President Mason wouldn't relent. And then, third, she would volunteer to go with the team.

While Taylor ate her salad, she messaged President Mason to let him know in no uncertain terms that Sheridan could not go on this mission.

Sheridan finished her dinner first, said she had things to do, and hurried off toward their apartment building. Countdown to comlink call.

Joseph didn't follow her. Instead he stayed with Taylor. "While we're in Traventon, there's something else we should do."

Something else? He wanted to add items to their to-do list? Taylor tilted her head. "Such as?"

"You know how we're supposed to sabotage the QGP data?" The council had asked Taylor to create a program that changed the data in any existing QGP files so that anyone building new ones would incorporate false data into their designs.

"Right," Taylor said, finishing the last bite of her salad. "While I was dead during the virtual reality programs, I wrote an algorithm for that and sent it to the council for approval. Everyone thought it was brilliant. Well, at least the two people who understood it did."

"We could give the false data program more run time if we disabled the rank program beforehand."

Taylor let out a slow whistle. The one thing Traventon citizens obsessed about was their rank. It was a number determined by a person's bank balance, age, job status, family status, and friend ratings—a popularity badge that changed daily, and that people willingly wore on their shirts. It was also one of the city's best-protected programs.

"If the rank numbers blink out," Joseph went on, "officials will be so busy dealing with the chaos, there won't be a programmer around who's looking at anything else. It will make getting away from the Scicenter easier too."

Taylor nodded in appreciation. "So simple in its utter diabolicalness."

"Project Misdirect. We just need to find a way to bring the rank program down."

Taylor considered the idea. "It won't be possible from the Scicenter computers. They don't have any way to connect to the rank computers." Which was true of most computers in Traventon. During one of the centuries—Taylor couldn't remember offhand which—countries had attacked other countries through the internet. They had wiped out each other's computers, leaving the population disconnected and vulnerable to incoming physical attacks. Traventon had kept tight control on its computers ever since. Most people didn't have access to computers with internet capabilities. Those who did were carefully monitored. It was the reason the team had to physically go to the Scicenter. The only computers that could give them access to the QGPs were a few high-security computers on the fourth floor.

The rank building had to be a veritable fortress.

Taylor took a sip of water while she thought it over. "As much as I hate the ranking system, we can't risk breaking in somewhere else before we go to the Scicenter."

"We won't have to. Both computers systems are linked to a common place."

"Then why not break in there instead of going to the trouble to break into the Scicenter?"

Joseph put his silverware on his plate, gathering his things together to take them back to the cafeteria. "Because that common place is the Dakine base."

"Ah," she said. "Well yes, that is a place we need to avoid."

When they had been back in Traventon, Joseph used some Dakine contacts to free Taylor and Sheridan from Reilly. In return, Joseph had promised the base leader that Taylor and Sheridan would become operatives.

The Dakine were understandably unhappy when the group fled from the base instead.

"The Dakine," Joseph went on, standing up from the table, "have paths to most government computer systems. That's how they do their espionage. The Dakine also have a path to the rank system, because selling rank is their biggest business."

Taylor picked up her salad bowl and stood up. "You think we can upload something from the Scicenter to the rank computer going through the Dakine base?"

"That won't be the hard part," Joseph said, heading slowly toward the cafeteria. "The hard part will be coming up with a virus that can get past the rank filters. We'll need extra time to work on it."

Taylor walked beside him, already going through possibilities in her mind. The rank program interfaced with the neurochips in people's crystals. It kept track of over seven million people, each a potential source for a virus.

"If we tell the council what we're doing," Joseph went on, "they should give us an extra week to work on it."

That meant they only had three weeks to find a weakness in a program Traventon had protected for decades. "You think we can do it that quickly?" Taylor asked.

"One of us should be able to." Joseph's voice curled off into a challenge. "Whichever of us is smarter . . ."

"You didn't just say that." She cocked her head at him. "How many machines did you invent that changed the world's view on matter?"

"And that are currently being turned into weapons of mass destruction? None." He smiled at her. "That's why I'm smarter."

chapter hapter
4

Joseph worked through more than one night, but on the evening before the team left, he finished his QGP program. It would simultaneously send instructions to three semifunctional QGPs, making them work together so they were capable of searching for people and transforming their matter into perfect energy flux waves. It was a thing of beauty. A thing of genius. A thing of infinite danger if the wrong people got ahold of it. Joseph didn't let himself dwell on that. He had to run the program through a few simulations to make sure he'd gotten the glitches out.

The front door chimed. He didn't even bother glancing at his bedroom wall to see whose name flashed on it. He wasn't expecting anyone. He scanned over the preliminary results. Good . . . good. . . .

Jeth, Joseph's father, yelled, "Sheridan is here!"

Sheridan? Joseph's gaze flew to the time display on his computer. *Sangre*. It was seven fifteen. He'd told her he would meet her in the apartment's dining hall at six thirty.

"Coming!" Joseph called back. He minimized and locked his screen. As he walked toward the front room, he heard Jeth say, "You *are* Sheridan, aren't you?"

A couple of weeks ago, Taylor had dyed her hair back to its original color and pretended to be Sheridan. Now Jeth was perpetually unsure which twin he was talking to. The trick shouldn't have bothered Joseph. He and Echo had done it often enough. It did bother him though. He knew Taylor had been testing Jeth and him to see if they could tell the difference. Joseph wondered what Taylor would have done if he hadn't been able to recognize her.

"It's me," Sheridan said. "I'm not staying. I just brought Joseph some dinner."

Jeth stood by the door, his maroon hair in an untidy ponytail. He gave an unhappy grunt at Sheridan's announced departure and didn't take the dinner box from her. He called over his shoulder, "Sheridan says she's not staying!"

Joseph had reached the door by then. "Sorry," he told her. "I didn't realize what time it was."

Sheridan wore a white formfitting shirt and a blue skirt with two rows of white buttons down the front. She always chose clothes that were similar to twenty-first-century styles. He liked it that way, liked that she was different. Her long auburn hair hung loosely around her shoulders, framing her fresh, beautiful face.

Joseph had expected Sheridan to be mad, to have that haughty look of superiority Taylor always got when she was angry. Instead Sheridan smiled and held out the box. "It's all right. I know you're busy. I didn't want you to miss dinner though."

Joseph took the box, then took her hand and pulled her into the room. "Sorry," he said again. "I haven't had much sleep and I was working on—" He didn't finish the sentence. Sheridan didn't know anything about programming and always assumed he was working on the rank virus. He didn't like lying to her, though. "I meant to meet you," he said.

Jeth retreated down the hallway to his bedroom, leaving the two alone. Santa Fe had strict chaperone rules, and whenever Jeth wanted to talk history with Sheridan, he claimed he ought to respect those rules. Joseph was glad this wasn't one of those times.

He led Sheridan toward the couch. It was a made of green gel and had tiny air bubbles floating around in the middle. Cheap but comfortable. "Why didn't you call me when I didn't show up?"

"You're getting ready for your trip tomorrow. You don't need distractions."

"Maybe I want to be distracted." Still holding on to her hand, he sat down on the couch. The gel molded around him to support his weight.

Sheridan sighed, looked back at the door, and didn't sit down. "I should go. I'll feel terrible if something happens to you because you didn't have time to program things right."

Joseph motioned to the spot next to him. "I'll feel terrible if something happens to me and I know I wasted my last night alive with a computer instead of my girlfriend."

She sat down, sadness gleaming in her eyes. He shouldn't have joked about this being his last night alive. Taylor routinely predicted both of their deaths, using an assortment of twenty-first-century slang: bite the dust, pushing up daisies, meet their maker, and something about being six feet under. Sheridan was soft in all the places where Taylor was hard. She couldn't joke about him getting hurt, didn't want to be reminded it was a possibility.

"I'll be fine," he told her. "I'm smart enough to do this." To do all of it.

She leaned into the couch, shifting the gel. "Sometimes being smart isn't the issue."

He undid the flaps on the dinner box. "Well, this time it is. You can get around almost anything with the right knowledge."

The box held a rice-and-bean dish, an apple, a protein twist, and two large cookies. She'd given him her dessert—something they got only once a day because they were still at refugee status. No jobs yet meant no credits yet. And the cookie was chocolate, her favorite.

She saw him looking at it. "I thought you'd want something good to eat tomorrow. Taylor says you're only getting nasty-tasting meal squares on the trip."

He smiled at her and then laughed.

"What?" she asked.

Joseph stood up, walked to the table, and brought her back a box. "I meant to make wrapping paper to go over it." From his studies, he knew it was taboo in the twenty-first century to give a gift without first hiding it behind special paper. Joseph followed Sheridan's customs as much as he could.

She looked at him curiously, then opened the box. She grinned at what was inside: five chocolate bars.

"You went without dessert five times?" she asked. "Now I feel cheap."

"One to eat each day I'm gone. That way you won't miss me too badly."

"Yes, because being with you and eating chocolate are about the same in my book."

In her book? He didn't ask. Instead, he leaned over and kissed her. "Good. Now you won't miss tonight's cookie."

Joseph took out his rice dish, not realizing how hungry he was until he started eating. Sheridan talked about her day—studying for her classes and volunteering at the stables in their district. As he listened, his mind kept drifting to the mission.

By this time next week, he would be back. Would he be a different person after killing someone? Maybe he was already becoming one. He hadn't told Sheridan about any of it.

Once everyone knew what he'd done, how would she react? Could a girl who was made of so much softness understand killing and subterfuge? Would she love him anyway?

Without wanting to, Joseph pictured Allana, his last—well, *girlfriend* wasn't the right term. She and Joseph had never been exclusive. She'd dated others, including Echo. Allana had been the last girl Joseph had cared about, though. The chairman of trade's daughter. Beautiful, rich, influential Allana.

Allana wouldn't have blinked at the news that Joseph had killed someone. In fact, she would have probably critiqued his methods and told him how he could improve the next attack. That was how the Dakine were. He just hadn't realized it back then.

Joseph leaned his head against the couch and concentrated on Sheridan. His eyes lingered on the sloping curve of her neck, her hazel eyes, the way her long hair fell across her shoulder. Everything about her was gentle and innocent.

He'd been quiet for too long. Sheridan considered him for a moment, then said, "I should let you get back to your work."

He took hold of her hand. "Don't. Let me look at you for a few more minutes." Right now she still loved him. There was no disapproval in her eyes, no sense of guardedness or withdrawal.

"Look at me?" she asked.

"So I'll remember everything about you."

Her eyebrows quirked up. "You're not going to forget what I look like. You'll be with my identical twin sister the whole trip."

He ran his thumb across the back of her hand. "Taylor doesn't have your smile."

"Yes, she does. We have identical dimples too."

"Your voice is softer, and Taylor tilts her chin down in an aggravated, superior way."

"Those are mannerisms, not differences. Can you really even tell us apart?"

"Of course," Joseph said, smiling. "Taylor's eyes don't glow like yours do."

Sheridan tilted her chin down in an exact impersonation of Taylor. "That's the difference? My eyeballs are shinier?"

He threaded his fingers with hers. "There are a few other differences too." He would have added to the list, but the wall screen chimed. Taylor's name flashed on it, announcing she was in the lobby and on her way up to the apartment.

"Taylor's here?" he asked.

Sheridan shrugged. "She's probably found a way to destroy the rank program, and she came to gloat."

As it turned out, though, Taylor hadn't come to gloat. She'd come to spit fire.

chapter 5

Taylor stormed into the apartment, accusations tumbling through her mind. She didn't yell at Joseph. Not yet.

Her father had been a minister. He hadn't been the kind of preacher who held a crowd's attention by raising his voice or pronouncing dooms of fiery torment. His voice always stayed calm, but he could pin you with a look. Taylor fixed one of those looks on Joseph.

"Project Misdirect," she said, and held up her comlink so he could see the code displayed on it. "Aptly named, I suppose, since the whole purpose of the exercise was to misdirect me, wasn't it?"

Sheridan and Joseph had both come to the door to let Taylor in, and they all stood in the entryway staring at one another.

Joseph didn't answer Taylor. He just sighed and ran a hand

through his shaggy blue hair. He looked tired, drained. And why wouldn't he? He'd been busy. Taylor didn't spare him any pity.

"You meant to keep me so focused on creating a rank virus, I wouldn't check on what you were doing."

"No," Joseph said, thrusting his hands into his pockets. "I actually want to bring the rank program down. It will make our job easier."

Sheridan's gaze bounced between Joseph and Taylor. "What's wrong?"

Taylor didn't answer her sister. Instead she squeezed her comlink so hard, several buttons beeped in protest. "These are the protocols for creating a time vector protection field!"

Joseph's expression hardened. His whole body seemed to go rigid. "How did you access that file? I didn't give you permission to snoop around on my computer."

"That isn't the issue," Taylor said, her hand still gripping her comlink. "The issue is that you're planning on tampering with the past."

Joseph narrowed his eyes. "I had a DNA block on that file. How did you get around it?"

Taylor ignored the question. "You're doing something that's illegal and dangerous."

"Illegal?" Joseph let out a scoff. "By whose standards? There aren't any laws about time travel."

Sheridan broke into the conversation, taking a step so she stood between Joseph and Taylor. "What are you talking about? What's a time vector protection field?"

Taylor wanted to wave Joseph's program at her sister and

say, "This!" But few people understood that sort of code. So Taylor explained it the long way—all the while slicing glares in Joseph's direction. "Any time you strain someone out of the past, you risk changing history's timestream to a point that you might not exist in the present. Even if you're not a direct descendant of the person you strained, there's no way to measure the effect one person has on a society. What would happen if you took the person who introduced Einstein's parents to each other? Or Hitler's?"

Taylor held up a hand to emphasize her words. "You might think you were doing the world a favor by preventing Hitler's birth and saving tens of millions of people who died in World War Two, but by adding those people back into the timestream, you would change the world so much that none of us would exist in the same way. If World War Two hadn't happened, how many men and women would have ended up marrying someone different? What mark would all of those new descendants leave on the world? One decision, right or wrong, could change everything."

"Okay, I get that part," Sheridan said.

"If you're going to mess around with the timestream," Taylor went on, "you have to find a way to keep yourself from being swept away in a rogue current. A time vector protection field protects people within its boundaries from changes in the timestream. Everything and everybody around you could change, but as long as you were in the perimeters of the field during the switch, you would remain unaffected."

"Which is why," Joseph said patiently, "it's important for us to have that technology. As long as Traventon potentially has the power to change the past, any of us are at risk." He took a step toward Taylor and held out his hand for her comlink. Probably to delete the information. "The next time you want to know what I'm working on, ask instead of splicing into my computer files."

Taylor was not about to give him her comlink or let him get her off track. She scrolled through the code on her screen. "I'm impressed you came up with something this sophisticated in such a short time. Really. I would have thought this sort of thing took years to invent."

"It did take years," Joseph said. "The Time Strainer scientists created it to put around the Scicenter. While we were there, I stole the information from their computer. I thought Santa Fe might want to study it and see if they could modify it for larger spaces." Joseph crossed his arms. "Now, are you going to tell me how you got through my computer's safeguards, or do I have to confiscate your computer and figure it out myself? We're both busy right now."

Taylor let out an angry groan. "Don't pretend you're not up to something. I can tell from your data that you're planning on using the Time Strainer to take someone from the past." She held up the next set of code for Joseph to see. "Who put you up to this? Who do they want?"

Joseph didn't answer, just clenched his jaw.

Sheridan looked from him to Taylor. "I thought the Time Strainer couldn't work without a QGP. You destroyed the only working QGP—the one in the twenty-first century."

Taylor paced over to Sheridan. "We destroyed the QGP two months after the date it strained us into the future. That means there's still a two-month window in the past that could be used to take people who were within the QGP's range."

Taylor had first tried to destroy the QGP on the date she and Sheridan had been taken from Knoxville. It hadn't worked. Apparently, the timestream was amenable to changes, but not paradoxes. Reilly had left the twenty-first century two months after Taylor and Sheridan had been taken. Destroying the QGP before the date of Reilly's departure would have kept Reilly from being transported to the future, which in turn would have kept Taylor from being taken in the first place. And since she wouldn't have been taken, she wouldn't have destroyed the QGP, which meant Reilly would have left the twenty-first century and the paradox would have looped endlessly through time.

Taylor had settled on destroying the QGP right after Reilly left.

"It's only two months," Sheridan said, still confused. "The Time Strainer can't pull people from a slot so small. It needs at least a year."

"The scientists in Traventon need at least a year," Taylor said. "Joseph, however, has been working on that too." She showed her sister the algorithms written on her comlink screen. "With these program amendments we're down to a slot of minutes—seconds maybe." She turned to Joseph again. "Who are you planning to take?"

Joseph still didn't answer, but Sheridan did. She was watching Joseph, reading the furrow of his brows as though he were a book. "It's Echo, isn't it?" she asked. "You want to save your brother."

Joseph's lips remained set in a tight, defiant line. His blue eyes darkened. Taylor could tell from Sheridan's expression, not Joseph's, that Sheridan's guess was right. Sheridan reached out, took Joseph's hand, and squeezed it. Her eyes brimmed with sympathy.

There was a crack in Joseph's expression then, a flash of pain he couldn't hide.

Taylor sighed, shut off her comlink, and slipped it back into her pocket. She had never been good at consoling people and hardly tried now. She was too relieved Joseph had been trying to save his brother, not change the past at the request of one of Santa Fe's factions.

Taylor kept her voice soft, apologetic almost. "For the Time Strainer to work, it has to be able to contact a working QGP. The QGPs in Traventon aren't functional now. They couldn't have been functioning when Echo was alive."

"I know," Joseph said. "I had to try anyway. If I could find a way to save Echo . . ." He looked away, unable to finish the sentence.

Sheridan let out an "Oh" of concern and wrapped her arms around him. Joseph returned the hug, resting his cheek on her hair.

It was up to Taylor to point out the painful truth. "Even if you could find a way to save your brother, you shouldn't do it. What would have happened to us if the real Echo had been time-strained out of Traventon before he told you to switch places with him? Or what if Echo's unexplained disappearance made the Dakine suspicious that you or your father knew things you shouldn't? They could have started watching you closely. Maybe they would have found out about the illegal laser disrupter you built."

Joseph released Sheridan. "I know." Taylor could tell he did know, but the steel in his eyes said he didn't particularly care about the risk.

"It isn't just our lives we have to think about," Taylor said more forcefully. "If the events of the past are changed, either one of us could end up being used as a tool by the Dakine or by the Traventon government."

"I know," he said again, this time with resignation in his voice.

Taylor let it go then. Certainly, Joseph realized he couldn't tamper with the past. All of these programs he'd been working on—they must have been an exercise in grief. "I'll see you tomorrow morning." Taylor turned to leave, then paused and turned back. "Oh, and I was able to download your data because your father thought I was Sheridan and let me in. Once I stole her ID badge, it was pitifully easy."

Sheridan put one hand on her hip. "You stole my ID badge?"

Taylor headed toward the door. "You never even missed it."

"My computer doesn't start without a DNA scan," Joseph called after her. "How did you get around that?"

"I didn't have to," Taylor said. "You left your computer logged on. Really, Joseph, you should get more sleep."

She was out the door before he could respond to that.

chapter chapter

6

Facing down death, Taylor thought groggily, really required a full night's sleep. Which was why President Mason should have let the team leave at, say, nine o'clock in the morning. But no, at six a.m., Taylor and Sheridan arrived at Santa Fe's western gate. Taylor had been up most of the night running simulations on her rank virus. It would work, she was sure about that, but it wouldn't work as fast as she wanted.

Her program would give dozens of users different parts of the virus that would then be uploaded from the individuals to the main system. By themselves, the virus segments were harmless. The rank filters shouldn't even detect them. After the virus segments uploaded into the system, they would compile and change the rank data. It would take hours though, maybe even a complete day for the virus to take effect. Which was too long.

The team would reach Traventon in two and a half days' time. Taylor had until then to figure out a way to make the virus work faster.

Taylor and Sheridan headed over to the group that had formed in front of the city gates. Sheridan had insisted on seeing Taylor off, although Taylor imagined her sister would have done that back at their apartment—without dressing up—if Joseph hadn't been leaving too.

In Traventon, the doors out of the domed city had been hard to spot. They blended in with the walls. Here the doors were decorated. A stone arch accented them, and the words *Freedom Lives Here* were engraved across the top. Even that sign had been vandalized. Underneath it someone had written, *Unfortunately this place is so crowded, Freedom has to share an apartment with Duty, Disillusionment, and Disrepair.*

A deluge of refugees had been finding their way to Santa Fe for the last several decades, which was something the original city planners hadn't taken into account while designing the city. The buildings in the middle of the city—those built during the founding years—were architectural artwork. An array of cathedrals, temples, shrines, and mosques glimmered, jewel-like, around the city center. The early apartment buildings looked like castles with spires, turrets, and regal towers made from curving stone.

Apartment buildings constructed during the last two decades were tall, straight, and built close together. They ringed the city in layers like giant dominoes waiting for a good push. Refugee rows, they were called, and even those were getting crowded.

Jeth and Elise, the other wordsmith who'd left Traventon with them, had come to see Taylor and Joseph off. They both stood near the row of airbikes, admiring the machines. The airbikes did look cool. Sort of like long motorcycles with wings. The team would ride them for the first day until they got near other cities. City scanners picked up nonbiometric signatures, and the team didn't want to risk being shot down. They would leave the airbikes at an outpost, spend the night there, and travel the second day by horseback. The team would stay the second night in a hidden, underground med clinic not far from Traventon and then walk the last three hours to the city the next morning.

Five days, Taylor told herself. Six if they had problems along the way. The mission wouldn't take long.

Taylor looked around for Joseph but didn't see him anywhere. One of the council leaders was checking packs, while two men in camouflage stood by. Taylor was also dressed in camouflage, complete with matching skin dye and hair dye. While the team traveled through the wilderness that separated cities, they needed to stay hidden from city patrols and the gangs of criminals, called vikers, who lived in the forests.

President Mason saw Taylor and waved for her and Sheridan to come over. Even though it was still early in the morning, he wore his business clothes, complete with black sash. Counselor Number One stood next to him, checking something on his comlink. Taylor didn't see Counselor Number Two anywhere. The woman was probably out guilting other citizens into doing her bidding. *Some people would feel a debt of gratitude toward the people who rescued them from Traventon, who took them in, who gave them clothes, food, and protection.*

Honestly.

President Mason nodded at Taylor. "Are you ready?"

"Ready enough."

While Counselor Number One tapped things on his comlink, he spared Taylor a glance. "I set up your salary payment. It will activate when you return."

The phrase shouldn't have bothered her, but it did. "I'm not doing this for the money," she told him.

"Why *are* you doing this?" President Mason asked. It wasn't a challenge. She could tell he wanted to know.

Taylor pointed to the words above the door. "Because freedom means paying off your debts. After this is over, we're even."

President Mason smiled tolerantly and didn't comment on her reasoning. The two men who were dressed in camouflage walked over, packs slung on their backs. President Mason turned to them. "Let me introduce your security team. This is Ren and Lee."

Taylor wasn't surprised President Mason didn't tell her their full names. One of the concessions he'd made to the council as he whittled down the contestants for the Olympic bodyguard competition was that the identities of the bodyguards would stay a secret. That way none of the sectors could claim favoritism.

Ren and Lee nodded and gave perfunctory smiles as their names were spoken. It was hard to tell much about their features under the camouflage. Each man was tall, seemed to be in his twenties, and had the physique of a Marine. Lee's hair was cropped short with spiky ends that stuck up a bit. Ren's shoulder-length hair was tied behind his neck. Both looked her over with dark-brown eyes.

"Ren and Lee," President Mason went on, "are experts on travel and combat. They've spent the last week scouting the area and learning about Traventon from our operatives there. They can get you in and out of the Scicenter."

Taylor nodded at the men. "I'm glad to have you watching my back." As soon as she said the phrase, she realized they had no idea what she meant. Ren and Lee's eyebrows both furrowed in puzzlement.

"That's a saying from the twenty-first century," Taylor explained. "It means I'm glad to have your help. You don't really have to watch my back. Nothing exciting is happening there."

She was babbling. This was not the best first impression, especially since the men had undoubtedly been told she was a genius. "I'm really tired," she added.

Joseph and another man walked up to the group, both out-fitted in camouflage. This was odd, because the council had decided to give her and Joseph only one bodyguard apiece. The council was afraid a group larger than four would make it harder for them to walk around unnoticed.

The new man was tall like most of the men here but had a leaner build than Ren and Lee. He looked older too, perhaps in his early thirties. He carried an extra-large pack on his shoulders, which shifted as he walked.

Ren gestured to the new man. "Who's this?"

"This," Joseph said, "is Xavier. He's going with us."

"What?" Lee cocked his head in disbelief. "You can't add

people to the team without council approval."

President Mason held up his hand to stop the flow of protests. "The council approved Xavier's addition. It became a necessity."

"Why?" Ren asked. The suspicion in his voice verged on hostility.

President Mason glanced at Joseph, at a rare loss for words. No, that wasn't it, Taylor realized. It wasn't that President Mason didn't know what to say; he was just waiting for Joseph to say it.

Joseph looked at Ren and Lee, not at Taylor or Sheridan. "I requested it."

"Why?" Taylor asked. "What's his specialty?"

Joseph glanced at Taylor, then quickly returned his attention to Ren and Lee. "I thought the team could use another person, and I wanted it to be Xavier."

Taylor put her hands on her hips. "That's BS." Which, judging from everyone's expressions, was another term that wasn't used in the twenty-fifth century. She thought about saying the real words, but it wouldn't make a difference. No one from this century would have any idea why she was suddenly talking about cattle poop.

"What's the real reason?" Taylor asked.

"That *is* the real reason," Joseph said firmly. "And it's the only one you're going to get."

Taylor gaped at him in disbelief. "You thought we were shorthanded, so you decided to go out and interview militant combatants in your free time?"

She'd spoken too loudly. The other council members were all staring at her now. Some drifted farther away as though she might turn her anger on them. The rest regarded her with the sort of strained patience they usually had when dealing with her. *She's one of those temperamental geniuses. Humor her.*

Ren stepped closer to Xavier, surveying him. "How can we trust this man when we know nothing about him?" Addressing Xavier, Ren asked, "What sector are you from?"

Xavier returned his gaze coldly. "That doesn't matter."

Ren let out a scoffing grunt. "You haven't lived here long if you think that."

See, Taylor wanted to say to the still-staring council members, *I'm not the only one who has a problem with this. Even the untemperamental ungeniuses are ticked off.*

Shaking his head, Lee walked over to President Mason. "This isn't what we agreed on."

President Mason calmly tucked his comlink into his belt. His casual stance said that he was used to dealing with quarreling children, and he expected them to play nicely regardless. "Plans always change," he said. "They're just changing earlier on in this mission than we expected. Your job remains the same: protect those under your care." His gaze swept over Ren, Lee, and Xavier. "Do I have your promise on that?"

"Yes," Xavier said.

A moment passed. Then Ren and Lee also gave a yes, although theirs sounded considerably more forced.

"Joseph," Sheridan said quietly. She stood next to Taylor but was watching him, waiting for an explanation. "Why are you suddenly keeping secrets?"

Suddenly? Taylor doubted that. Joseph had kept secrets from them back when they were in Traventon, and apparently the move here hadn't changed that habit.

Joseph looked at Sheridan, and the lines of tense defiance on his face softened. He walked over to her, took her hand, and led her away from the others.

Taylor watched them for a few seconds, then stormed over to join them. If Joseph was explaining things to Sheridan, he could explain them to her too. As she strode up behind Joseph, he said, "I can't tell you some things right now." He squeezed Sheridan's hand. "You'll just have to believe that I have a good reason."

Sheridan's face was upturned, trying to read more from his expression. "I believe you, but—"

"Why should we trust you," Taylor interrupted, "when you don't trust us enough to let us know why you're bringing Xavier along? Trust begets trust."

Joseph let out a breath of frustration. He didn't turn to face Taylor. "Well, those are words we can carve somewhere. We'll put them right next to your last quote about the subject: 'I don't trust anyone.'"

Taylor walked around Joseph so that he had to look at her. "Yeah, but I'm not the one who showed up here with an entourage."

Sheridan stepped between them, her hands raised and pleading. "Don't fight. Come on—you guys have to work together or this mission will fail before you even get to Traventon."

"It won't fail," Joseph said. "Despite Taylor's dramatics."

Dramatics? Oh, she would show him dramatics. The next time she hacked into his computer, she would add an irremovable tagline that went out with all of his messages. It would read, *Big sale today! Discount everything I say! With me, the truth is always half off!*

"Maybe," Taylor said slowly, "I should insist on bringing someone along too." She waved a hand in Sheridan's direction. "Maybe I'll demand to take my sister with me."

Sheridan brightened. "Really?"

"No," Joseph said, keeping his gaze on Taylor. "You won't put her in danger that way." It was as much a command as a statement.

Sheridan cocked her head at Joseph. "Why do you think I can't handle danger? I'm not a weakling, you know. I can face danger as well as either of you."

Taylor inwardly groaned. She never should have gotten her sister started on that subject again. Taylor gave Joseph one last angry glare, turned on her heel, and stalked back toward the airbikes. She didn't have any leverage to use against Joseph, and he knew it. Because the last thing Taylor wanted was to put Sheridan in danger.

chapter chapter
7

Taylor rode on the airbike behind Lee, straps across both shoulders keeping her secured to her seat. Joseph rode with Ren. Xavier flew on an airbike between the two. Taylor supposed that was so Ren could keep an eye on him. The group skimmed over a forest of oaks. Leaves and branches ran together in a green blur. Every once in a while they passed patches of land where nothing grew—not trees, not bushes, not grass. The earth there spread out in unusual brownish-red spots. Something toxic had penetrated the dirt.

The wind pushed against Taylor's ears noisily, and looking down made her dizzy. She shut her eyes and concentrated on the rank virus. Or at least tried to. Her lack of sleep and the dipping and swaying of the airbike soon put her to sleep.

When she woke up, they had landed on the ground and she

was leaning limply against Lee's back. She hoped she hadn't done anything embarrassing like drool on his pack. Pine trees surrounded the group, spreading out their welcoming boughs. The air smelled like Christmas. If she looked at the trees, just focused on them, she could pretend she was back in the twenty-first century. She could imagine that over the hill, shopping malls, fast food restaurants, and her family all waited for her—beautiful, ordinary life.

That was the sort of bandage that hurt when you ripped it off. She stumbled off the airbike, still sleepy, and crunched her way through the pine needles to the spot where the others were gathering. The sun hung midway through the sky, letting her know the day was half gone. "How much longer until we get to the outpost?" she asked.

"Five hours," Lee said. "This will be our only break."

Ren and Lee both had their comlinks out, checking the scanners for city scouts. After a few moments Lee said, "No one is near."

Ren kept checking his scanner, then said, "We're clear."

Lee raised an eyebrow. "I already told everyone that."

Ren slipped his pack from his shoulders. "And this time you were right."

Both sat down, keeping their packs close, as though they were worried someone would run off with them.

Great. This whole mission was going to be like a convention of the paranoid. Taylor slipped her pack from her shoulders, sat down on the ground, and pulled her meal square from her backpack. It looked like a brownie. Unfortunately the similarity ended there. Meal squares were dense and had an aftertaste like chewable vitamins. Square meals, she thought, weren't all they were cracked up to be.

As she ate, she noticed there were other trees mixed in with the pines, trees whose leaves were yellowing for fall. Grass and wildflowers tangled on the ground around large pieces of rock. No, on closer examination, what she had assumed were gray rocks were actually chunks of weathered pavement. This place had been a road once.

Had it been one of the plagues or one of the wars that had depopulated the area? Both had happened so frequently over the last four hundred years that the world's population had fallen to a fourth of what it had been in her time. The trees and flowers here were probably descendants of ones someone had planted in their yard.

Taylor reached out and ran her hand along a rough piece of pavement. "America was the most powerful nation on earth. How could it have been destroyed like this?"

Joseph calmly took a sip from his drink pouch. "It was also the world's biggest debtor. Eventually, other countries wanted to be paid."

"So they attacked?"

"They asked for payment in food, and they sent in armies to oversee the process. At the time, a fungus was attacking the world's corn and wheat crops. The bee population had already plummeted, so food was scarce anyway."

Bits of pavement came loose under Taylor's touch, dusting her fingers with black sand. "A fungus took down the country?"

"The fungus just caused people to starve," Joseph clarified. "The wars took down the country."

When Taylor had first arrived in the future, she'd read through information about the wars. They all ran together in her mind though. The regional conflicts seemed to involve almost as many countries as the Third, Fourth, and Fifth World Wars. And then there were the Second and Third Civil Uprisings.

"But America finally ousted the armies by pushing them into Canada," Taylor said, trying to remember.

Joseph shook his head. "The plague stopped the Third World War. It killed off so many people that no one had the resources left to fight anymore."

"The plague," Taylor said bleakly. "Nature's peacemaker."

Joseph bit into his meal square. "When you have famine, you're bound to get disease. Weakened bodies can't fight off microbes."

Lee let out a sigh as he ate. The camouflage dye on his face looked like mismatched puzzle pieces. The whole group looked that way, actually—like puzzles that had been put together wrong. "Plague and fungus," Lee said. "You two are great lunch conversationalists."

Ren was sitting beside Xavier. He motioned to Xavier's oversized pack. "What do you have in there?"

"Equipment," Xavier said.

Ren let out a bark of laughter. "Don't give us that freeze. We're out of the city. You can tell us why you came."

Joseph shifted and pine needles crunched underneath him. "He came to help. Just like you two."

Lee took a drink. His voice was light but had an edge to it. "Someone has made a secret addendum to our mission. What is it, who ordered it, and how is Joseph involved in all of it?"

"Xavier could be an assassin," Ren offered without any hint of humor. "Hired by one of the delegations to delete Reilly."

"No," Lee said. "That would be redundant. We've got you for that."

Ren smiled, the white of his teeth flashing against the browns and greens on his face. "Then Xavier must be sent to stop the assassination. But no, that's why you're here."

Lee stretched his legs out along the ground. "I follow orders, same as you."

Taylor took a drink of water from her pouch and eyed her bodyguards more closely. "So which sectors are you guys from?"

"We were instructed not to tell you," Lee said.

"Why?" she asked.

"Because everyone knows," Lee said with a smirk, "that Christians favor other Christians—at least when they're not arguing with each other."

Ren waved his hand in a motion of agreement. "And they try to convert everyone else."

Taylor couldn't tell whether they were poking fun at each other, at themselves, or just at her. Probably it was just at her.

"Fine," she said. "Whatever. I don't care what you believe so long as you can shoot straight."

Now Lee's tone was even, serious. Maybe with a bit of warning thrown in. "It's dangerous to ignore people's beliefs. Actions are rooted in belief."

Joseph sat silently finishing his square. He was always silent when it came to discussions of religion, although Taylor couldn't help reading more into his silence this time. He was keeping his secret from her too, and it ticked her off.

A breeze ran through the trees, making branches swing and shadows dart through pine needles and leaves alike. The movement kept drawing her eye—all the shifting shadows.

Ren turned to Xavier, his gaze calculating. "Does your mission have something to do with the new cities?"

Xavier shrugged vaguely. "Does yours?"

Ren scoffed and looked at the data on his scanner. "I'm here to make sure this mission is successful."

"What new cities?" Taylor asked.

The three men shared a glance, checking, she supposed, whether it was okay to answer her. At last Ren said, "Santa Fe is too crowded, so the city elders are building two smaller cities nearby, each with room for growth. The council is deciding whether to populate them with a mixture of religions as we've done in Santa Fe, or whether to move separate religions into each one so that eventually each group will have its own city."

A fly buzzed around Xavier's food and he swished it away. "It's the council's most-debated issue."

Taylor considered the matter as she nibbled off a bite of her square. "People don't want to stay together? What about the value of diversity and learning about one another's cultures?"

Ren leaned toward Lee. "You can tell she's a Christian. They're all for staying together. Just wait—next she'll try to convert us."

Lee checked his scanner before taking another drink from his pouch. "The problem with having so many different groups in one city is that the council can't make the simplest decisions without days of deliberation. Every request is bogged down. It's impossible to get anything done."

Ren finished off the last bite of his square and wiped the crumbs from his hands. "That's not true. Your people have been finding their way around the council for years. You just do whatever you want to, secretly."

"Consider your tongue carefully," Lee said, "or you may lose it."

Xavier leaned forward. "Perhaps the council sent me because it knew the two of you couldn't make it to Traventon without laser fire." His gaze went back and forth between Lee and Ren. "Just because you don't know who I am, don't assume I don't know who you are, Brother Lee and Brother Ren."

It was only when Taylor heard the names emphasized like this that she realized they were fake names. Brotherly and Brethren.

They hadn't even bothered coming up with something believable. She had been way too tired if she hadn't caught that before. "Okay," she said. "Enough with the secrets. Who are you all really?"

None of them answered. Not even Xavier, who had just admitted to knowing who the other two were.

"This is wonderful," Taylor said. "I'm on a mission with two guys who hate each other, some mystery man, and . . ." She waved her hand in Joseph's direction. "And the one guy I know won't tell me why he's brought the mystery man along." She stood up, brushing dirt and twigs off her pants. "If this mission goes wrong and I'm captured by the Traventon government, the first people I zap with my QGP are going to be all of you."

She grabbed her pack and stomped off toward the bushes—the only restroom available. Behind her she heard Ren say, "Idle threats. Christians never kill anyone."

Joseph spoke then. "You've obviously never studied the Crusades. And," he added in the same confidential tone, "you don't know Taylor."

TAYLOR DIDN'T QUESTION HER bodyguards anymore after that. There wasn't a point to it, and besides she needed to concentrate on her rank virus. That night when they reached the outpost, she still didn't have a solution. No matter what algorithms she came up with, it would take her virus a couple of hours before it infected the rank system. Anything that worked faster would be detected and blocked by filters.

Well, it didn't matter. She would still run the slower version. It was about time the citizens of Traventon stopped ranking each other.

The food at the outpost was good and the gel beds were soft. Taylor could have used a nice hot soak, but they didn't have baths. The people of the twenty-fifth century used a cream called sparkle that kept a person clean for nearly three weeks at a stretch. It would have been a charming invention except Taylor couldn't quite forget that sparkle was comprised of bacteria that ate dirt, sweat, and dead skin cells. She pictured them writhing on her skin, masses of furry, sausage-shaped microorganisms. It made being clean sort of creepy.

Ren, Lee, and Xavier kept tight control of their packs. They were never out of their sight, never even out of reach.

They probably slept on them.

The next day proceeded about the same way the first had. None of the group talked much, and Taylor stewed about the rank program. It was ironic, really. She could build a machine that changed time, but the popularity program had stumped her. Well, maybe it was more symbolic than ironic actually.

The group spent the night in the med clinic and woke up before dawn to get ready for the walk to Traventon. While everyone ate breakfast, Mendez came in. He belonged to the Santa Fe underground that lived in Traventon, a group called the DW. He was a hulking man, six and a half feet tall, with enough muscle that Taylor suspected he might bend steel rods for amusement. He looked considerably friendlier now than he had when he'd been her guide out of Traventon. He smiled as he sat down at the table across from Taylor and Joseph. "*Ete sen*," he said.

It was a common greeting at Santa Fe. At first Taylor had wondered if Thomas Edison had been memorialized in salutation form, which in some ways would have been cool. The phrase actually came from Ghana, though. It meant, "How is your soul perceiving the world?"

Without waiting for a reply, Mendez added, "Do you like Santa Fe?"

"I'm not sure," Taylor said, taking a bite of a muffin. "I've only been there six weeks, and the council is already trying to kill me."

"We're both fine," Joseph said.

Mendez nodded approvingly at Taylor. "You speak much

better than you used to. I couldn't understand you before."

She finished chewing. "Does that mean you'll answer my questions this time?"

He smiled again. "Probably not."

After breakfast, the group set off on foot. They all had laser boxes in case they ran into any vikers. Even Taylor had one, and she was a lousy shot. Between working on the rank virus and going through the rest of her training, she hadn't practiced much.

Laser-box pulses came in two settings. The kill setting sent a pulse that tunneled through a person's body, ripping up any nearby organs. It damaged only organic matter: people, animals, and plants. Everything else remained unaffected.

Taylor couldn't decide if society's switch from guns to lasers was practical or just chilling. People wanted to protect cars and buildings while they killed one another.

The laser box's stun setting sent out a pulse that tightened a person's muscles, making them unusable. Once a person passed out from lack of oxygen, the tightening relaxed enough that their heartbeat returned to normal and they could breathe again, but it generally kept the person stiff and unconscious for a couple hours. The only way to get muscle function back sooner was to use a restorer box. Its beams relaxed muscles, freeing them.

Three hours later the group was close enough to Traventon that Mendez blindfolded Taylor and Joseph. Ren and Lee led them by the hand toward the DW's secret entrance. Logically, Taylor understood the reason for the secrecy. The fewer people who knew the whereabouts of the DW's entrance and bases, the better. If she and Joseph were caught, they wouldn't be able to give the Traventon government any information. But it still irked Taylor. She was risking her life on this mission, and everyone was keeping secrets from her.

chapter hapter

8

Taylor let her eyes adjust to the light. The team stood in a large wardrobe room. Mirrors lined the walls, and bright lights shone down from the ceiling. A counter stood against one wall, filled with makeup pens, hair dye, face dye, brushes, combs, and hair shapers. Eyelash extensions lay in trays, looking like rows of sunbathing spiders. All sorts of hair ornaments were pinned to a black velvet panel.

An older woman with pink, wispy hair fussed with a pile of overalls, dividing them out by size. "After you take off your camouflage dye," she told the group, "change into the clothes I've laid out for you. They're made from laser-deflecting material, which means they're stiff. Try to move as naturally as you can, so you don't attract attention. You'll put on your Scicenter overalls in the car. That way it won't seem suspicious that five scientists are all in the beauty district together."

Scicenter personnel were required to wear blue overall uniforms now. This change had come about after Taylor and Joseph's break-in a month and a half ago. You had to love bureaucracy. *That* was what the building administrators had come up with to fight crime—blue overalls. Like no one would be able to think of a way around that regulation.

The woman with the pink hair gave out a few more instructions. Taylor sat down at the counter in front of the dye extractor, only half listening. She already knew what to do. She'd practiced the mission dozens of times in the VR center.

The team would go to the Scicenter during the first shift change. So many people would be coming and going from the building that the security guards—even if they were watching their monitors—wouldn't notice that five people in the crowd didn't have crystal signatures. The Time Strainer and its computers were all on the fourth floor, but since Joseph and Taylor's last break-in, the whole floor had been changed to restricted status. The elevator wouldn't take anyone to the fourth floor unless their crystal had been given clearance to be there.

Taylor, Joseph, and their bodyguards would get into elevators with the rest of the incoming scientists. If no one was getting off on the fourth floor, the team would go to the closest unrestricted floor and use laser cutters to cut their way through the stairwell. The walls and doors had an electric current running through them, and any break into the current would normally cause the building's alarm to go off. Santa Fe had developed a special type of laser cutter, though. While it cut, it rerouted currents in order to circumvent the alarms.

Once the team made it to the fourth floor, they'd use their scanners to find an empty room with computer access. If the team couldn't find an empty room, they would put on their gas masks, break into a room, and put the occupants of the room to sleep. Then the team would lock themselves in and run the program. Once Taylor destroyed the QGPs, the building's alarms would most likely go off. The group needed to escape quickly.

The team had sleeping gas to take care of pursuers in the hallway. At least the human kind. When sensors in the building detected sleeping gas, all doors in the area would automatically lock, and compartments in the walls would open to release gasbots, wolf-sized droids. Gasbots were programmed to shoot anything that moved.

In the training programs, the gasbots always freaked Taylor out. To get away from them, she had to throw out concealing gas that darkened the air and reflected the gasbots' sensors. It always made her feel panicky to grope blindly through a hallway while vicious machines whirred after her.

Taylor wiped a dye-extractor cloth across her face, making the patchwork of greens and browns disappear. It was odd to see Ren, Lee, and Xavier without camouflage. Ren and Lee, for all their jabs and mistrust, looked enough alike that they could have been brothers. Both had black hair, olive complexions, and strong, handsome features. At least they did until they redyed themselves. Then Lee had a palm tree painted in the middle of his face so that his mouth disappeared into the trunk and the palm fronds feathered across his eyebrows. Ren went for simplicity. He painted black and silver diagonal stripes from the corner of his temple to his jaw.

Xavier was attractive too. Most people here in the future were. In every city but Santa Fe, the governments chose what genes to pass on, and they chose attractive ones. But Xavier was handsome in a softer way. He had observant brown eyes, the kind you expected on scholars. He seemed like the type of man Hollywood would have cast as somebody's best friend or big brother.

Could he really be an assassin, as Ren had suggested? If Xavier was, what did he have to do with Joseph? Taylor had asked Joseph about it as they walked to Traventon, trying to get more information from him.

"Why can't you tell me?" she'd prodded.

All Joseph had said was "You didn't tell me the QGP data."

"That information is too important to share with anyone else."

"So is this."

Taylor doubted that, but had no way to argue with him about it. She could have demanded answers, threatened to abort the whole mission, except she knew the QGPs had to be destroyed. The issue was bigger than her or Joseph or whatever side deal he was running with some council faction.

When Taylor finished taking off her camouflage dye, she changed into her new outfit. People in Traventon decked themselves in bright, outlandish clothes, and hers were no exception. She wore tight-fitting spring-green pants that looked like they were made of individual silk leaves. Pansies peeked out here and there among the leaves, and glittering butterflies fluttered around the stitching every time she moved. The matching leaf, flower, and butterfly top also fit snuggly, and it had sleeves so long that the material came to points over the backs of her hands.

The wardrobe woman hadn't been kidding about the stiffness. Like the armor the Enforcers wore, the outfit was rigid everywhere except at the knees, elbows, and small sections of the waist. Those parts used normal material so that she could move. Corsets were probably more comfortable.

Next she put on green shin-height boots. The soles were thick due to the concealed speed boosters, and they made her a couple inches taller than she normally was. After that, she glued an image scrambler to her wrist. It looked like the crystals everyone in Traventon wore but actually sent out signals that distorted the images picked up by nearby surveillance cameras.

Although the council had promised Taylor a disguise, the DW wardrobe woman vetoed adding molding cream to change the contours of Joseph's and Taylor's faces. "The Dakine always use it when they commit crimes," the woman explained. "So the government has recently installed sensors in high-security places that detect molding cream. We can't risk you being caught that way."

Taylor felt the first flurries of dread then. She had to go into the Scicenter undisguised?

"I doubt anyone will recognize you," the wardrobe woman assured Taylor. "Drastic changes in hair and face dye can mask most people, but to make sure, I'll give you an irritant shot in the neck. It causes mild facial swelling."

So much for a high-tech cover. Her disguise would consist of *puffiness*.

Taylor decided to go heavy on the face dye. She circled her eyes with ready-made tattoos of pansies and leaves, then put trailing vines that grew up her neck, twisting along her jawline and onto her cheeks. For the finishing touch, she painted her lips pansy purple.

Men and women in Traventon both shaped and stiffened their hair in such odd arrays, Taylor could have formed her hair into a replica of the Statue of Liberty and she wouldn't have stood out. Instead she dyed it forest green and used hair clips to put it in a simple bun.

When she finished, she stood back and surveyed herself in the mirror. Butterflies glimmered on her shirt, fluttering up and down her torso. The flowers nestled between the leaves seemed to stretch and sway in an unseen wind. Basically she looked like Mother Nature in action.

The wardrobe woman came up beside her. "You're beautiful," she proclaimed with satisfaction. "Or at least you will be with this." She held up a white badge with a row of electronic numbers: 4,258. "As they say in Traventon, no one is ever truly attractive without the right rank."

Over seven million people lived in this city. A rank of 4,258 meant there were only 4,257 people who were wealthier, smarter, more powerful, or more popular than her. Automatic elite-class status.

The woman took a step closer to Taylor. "Use this rank if you need to pretend to be someone important, and use this one"—she pressed an unseen button on the top of the badge, and the number changed to 5,328,121—"when you want to be ignored."

Lastly, the woman got out the irritant shots. Joseph got his first. He wore an outfit that resembled a tuxedo with fringed shoulder pads and golden cording wrapping his chest. His hair was black, slicked at the sides so that it came to a sharp point at the base of his shoulders. He'd dyed the area around his eyes like a bandit's mask. Fitting, considering what they were doing.

A minute after Joseph got the shot, he seemed to gain thirty pounds. Well, at least his face looked like the face of someone thirty pounds heavier. His jawline wasn't as square, his cheeks weren't as defined. His eyes appeared smaller while his nose looked bigger and rounder.

The wardrobe women then turned to Taylor and poked her neck with the shot. Taylor glanced in the mirror and winced. Right before her eyes, all of her baby fat from fourth grade turned up again. She would have made a joke about it, would have teased Joseph about his appearance too, but she was still mad at him for his secrecy. If he wanted to act like they weren't friends, fine. She would too.

The group put their packs and overalls into large shopping bags. Then the wardrobe lady led them out of the room and into an expansive, brightly lit corridor. Life-size pictures of models covered the gleaming marble-like walls. As the group passed by them, the pictures moved, murmuring things about sales on youth treatments and specials on body sculpting.

"Have the calves you've always wanted," a lavender-haired girl cooed at Taylor.

Taylor rolled her eyes. "I've never even thought about my calves before."

She hadn't expected a response, but the lavender-haired girl turned and eyed Taylor with disdain. "You should. Trueness, everyone else thinks about your calves as soon as they see you."

The words startled Taylor so much that she stopped and gaped at the wall. The lavender-haired girl shook her head mournfully at Taylor's calves. "They don't have a perfectly smooth shape. Too muscular. For nine hundred credits the experienced staff at Glamouria can fix that."

Joseph took hold of Taylor's arm and pulled her forward to catch up to the rest of the group. "Come on," he said. "We don't have time to watch advertisements."

Taylor went with him, her mouth hanging open in indignation. "Did you hear that little trollop? She said my calves weren't smooth."

"It's just a computer program."

Taylor looked down at her legs anyway. Too muscular? Really? Then she groaned, angry at herself for checking. This place could give anyone a complex.

The wardrobe lady spoke in a hushed tone. "If you run into problems, you know who to contact."

Taylor nodded. They had all memorized Mendez's comlink number.

"It won't do any good to come back here," the wardrobe woman told them. "We only rented the room for the day. It's being packed up right now."

"We know where to go," Joseph said. Their contact place was the Fisherman's Feast restaurant. It was part of a mall-like area in the Traventon Plaza Recreation Center.

The group walked past a doorway that led to a beauty salon.

Men and women were standing in front of mirrors that reflected what they would look like with different hairstyles.

The wardrobe woman kept going down the corridor. "You know where to find your specials?"

Special was the code word for mobile crystals. The team couldn't take an unauthorized crystal into the Scicenter without setting off the building's alarms, so the DW had hidden mobile crystals in various places near the Scicenter where the team might end up. They would need a crystal to work a getaway car. In Traventon cars were government property, things you summoned when you needed and left by the side of the road when you were done. Anyone could signal a car with a comlink and the nearest available one would come, but in order to give the car directions, they needed a working crystal.

"We know where they are," Ren said.

Satisfied, the wardrobe woman led them out of the building. A white opaque dome stretched across Traventon where the sky should have been. It made Taylor feel like she was inside a gigantic mall. All sorts of stores clustered around the courtyard, and crowds of vividly arrayed people milled in between them. No bushes. No trees. No insects buzzing around.

A woman passed by them wearing a hat shaped like a miniature merry-go-round. Another woman had two mechanical birds dangling from her ears. They chirped out a tinny melody.

Don't stare, Taylor told herself. *Act like you belong here.* The group strolled into the courtyard's parking garage, out of sight of most of the shoppers. No one paid much attention to their group, and the people who did glance at them lost interest quickly. With rank badges set in the five millions, they were social pariahs. The only people with worse ranks were probably old, poor people.

There was something vaguely unsettling about parking garages in the twenty-fifth century. Granted, they were clean and well-lit, and had designs on the floor that reminded Taylor of kitchen floors. But all the identical beige, egg-shaped cars—rows of them, staring back at you like an evil car clone army that was waiting to spring to life—Taylor could do without those.

The group climbed into the nearest car, and once they were seated, the wardrobe woman leaned inside and pressed her crystal to the car's control panel. "The Scicenter," she said, and leaned back out quickly before the door shut on her. She mouthed a farewell to the group, then turned back the way she'd come.

A map of the city appeared on the car's control panel, showing their location and their route to the Scicenter. The car headed out of the parking garage, humming along the rails that ran down the middles of the streets.

Cars didn't move fast here, only around twenty-five or thirty miles an hour. The cars still got places quicker than the ones from the twenty-first century though. They never stopped at intersections. The cars' programming timed their crossings to avoid collisions with other traffic.

Taylor pulled her overalls and pack from her shopping bag. She felt like she should be humming a James Bond theme song with all the gadgets she had in her pack: a lock disabler, a laser disrupter, a restorer box, a zip-line shooter, a laser cutter, gas vials, and a gas mask. The gas masks from Santa Fe weren't bulky like they'd been in her century. A small flexible bowl fit over a person's nose and mouth with a snoutlike filter in the middle. The edges had gel that stuck the mask to the face, creating an airtight seal.

After Taylor had pulled on her overalls, she put the mask in her front pocket and clipped her electronics onto the underside of her belt. Carrying everything there made her waist look thick, but she supposed it would match her face . . . and her calves.

Stupid advertisements.

Ren and Lee had more equipment in their packs. Besides the things Taylor carried, they had holographic cameras, syringes of tranquilizers, and comlink jammers. They also had canisters that shot out sticky black goo to cement an Enforcer's armor joints, and knives with moving serrated edges to slash through armor. The last two items were for protection in hand-to-hand combat. Other Enforcers carried them in case they had to deal with Dakine, who wore laser-proof armor.

Ren and Lee both clipped their packs around their middles and put their overalls on over them.

Xavier had the biggest pack. From it, he pulled out four already-filled smaller packs. He handed two to Joseph and strapped the others to his waist and stomach. Joseph did the same. When they pulled on their overalls, both of them looked overweight.

Ren shook his head at them.

"What?" Xavier asked.

"When was the last time you saw a fat person in Traventon?"

Xavier tapped his rank badge. "My stomach explains the reason my rank is in the five millions. I'm too poor to buy fat reductions and not vain enough to exercise. What's your excuse?"

Ren snorted. "I ride around with low rankers like this guy." He gestured to Lee.

Lee switched his badge to display a high rank. "Oh? Now I'm too superior to talk to any of you. So I'll ignore you and amuse myself by listening to the city announcements."

As soon as the car had started, a woman's silky voice came over the car speakers, spouting city propaganda: "Friendships can end in a moment, but your government will always support you. Always support your government by reporting any suspicious behavior your friends display."

Taylor looked out the window. They were nearing the government headquarters sector. Each building had a digital display on the upper walls that flashed mottoes and videos of happy workers contributing to the city. Driving through the streets made Taylor feel like she was winding her way through a forest of gigantic TVs. The Birth Department building showed a white-clad worker supervising monitors on tanks of growing embryos. The words underneath the video stated, "We create perfect children for a perfect society."

If it was perfect, how come it felt so disturbing?

Taylor turned her attention to the map on the car panel. They were almost to the Scicenter. Only a few more minutes.

She tapped her foot nervously on the floor. It would be

fine, she told herself. They had been trained. Things would go smoothly. She might not even see a gasbot. Probably wouldn't even hear that menacing whirring in the darkness.

Finally the car pulled up to the Scicenter—well, not actually to the front of the Scicenter—a row of cars twenty deep rimmed the walkway. Their car sensed the line, slowed to a stop at the end, and opened the door.

This was it, then.

Ren got out of the car first, and everyone else followed. The building loomed in front of them, thirty-five floors high, with eight more floors underground. It was white, like some mammoth bone sticking out of the ground. Except for the top ten floors. Those showed a video of scientists studying code on a 3D clear computer monitor. "The immortality tax is working," the motto underneath the video proclaimed. "We're closer than ever to finding the cure for death."

Yeah. They were also one day closer than ever to dying. All these stupid mottoes made Taylor think longingly of Santa Fe. The citizens there would have added some good commentary to these buildings.

Fountains of light sizzled on either side of the Scicenter front door, symbols of the light of knowledge piercing the darkness of ignorance. A pale cement courtyard spread out in front of the building, offering benches to workers waiting for cars.

Taylor had gone into the building in every virtual reality simulation she'd done. This time the doors seemed mouthlike, gaping open to swallow the stream of people heading inside.

Ren had his comlink out, pretending to make a call while he checked the scanner function. He nodded. That meant a mobile crystal was where it was supposed to be—taped under the bench closest to the right side of the door. Everything was a go. Taylor walked, heart pounding, with the rest of the crowd slowly making its way to the Scicenter's entrance.

chapter 9

Joseph had been to the Scicenter a lot over the years, usually to get dating on an artifact. The last time, when he'd snuck in with Taylor, he hadn't had bodyguards or many electronics. He hadn't even had much of a coherent plan. He was twice as nervous now, though. More was at stake.

Joseph moved along with the crowd, keeping his gaze fixed on Taylor, on her shiny green hair twisted into a bun on the top of her head. He wouldn't let himself look around as though he had a reason to worry.

The security guards at the front desk didn't even glance at Joseph as he went by with the crowd. He sauntered toward the elevator, his senses on alert. He forced himself to walk casually, even though he could feel the adrenalin pouring into his system. Xavier kept pace beside him, talking about problems on a nonexistent project. It was unlikely the entire team would make it into the same elevator, but Joseph needed to make sure he and Xavier weren't separated.

Ren headed into an open elevator, following two women. A group of three men slipped in, and Taylor and Lee joined them. By the time Joseph and Xavier had walked over, the elevator was full and the door slid shut.

Another elevator door opened. Joseph hurried to it, and he and Xavier were the last ones inside before the doors shut. Joseph checked the lit floors, pretending he was about to add his to the directory, then stepped away from the panel as though his floor was already marked. And it was. Someone was going to the fourth floor.

That could be a bad thing. Not many people were allowed on restricted floors, so the workers were more likely to know one another. If he and Xavier got off on the fourth floor, the person who had clearance to get off there might ask who they were and where they were going.

Joseph let his gaze slide left and then right. The men at his side didn't look familiar. He couldn't be sure about the men behind him. It would be horrible luck to get off the elevator with one of the scientists who knew he'd translated for Taylor and Sheridan.

The elevator stopped. Third floor. The door slid open and a man in the back corner pushed his way to the front. It might be safer for Joseph and Xavier to get off on the third floor, too, and cut through to the fourth.

Xavier sent him a questioning look. Joseph shook his head. He didn't want to take the extra time. The door slid closed.

Joseph felt a short electric pulse shoot into his hip and then smelled a lemony scent. He had put his comlink on silent, and this was the comlink's way of letting him know he had a message from Taylor. No one else smelled the lemons. It was a trick of electronics sending messages to his brain.

He glanced down at the top of his comlink. The number 3 appeared, which meant Taylor's group had gotten off on the third floor.

The elevator door slid open again. Fourth floor. Joseph and Xavier stepped out and headed left toward the largest room on the floor, the Time Strainer bay. Joseph pulled out his comlink as he walked and replied to Taylor's message with a number 4. He resisted the urge to turn his head to see who had gotten off the elevator behind them. Out of the corner of his eye, he had seen two men step out, but he hadn't gotten a good look at either. Joseph listened for footsteps and heard a set following them. They were uneven, unnatural sounding.

A man behind them spoke. "You'll have the test reports to me before lunch?"

Joseph recognized the voice. Carver Helix. Everything the science chairman said was barked out in a disapproving tone, indicating he thought himself mired in a sea of incompetence.

Sangre, Joseph silently swore. *This was going to complicate things.*

The last time Joseph and Helix had met, Helix had ended up bleeding and unconscious. Joseph doubted Helix would ever forget Joseph, and Helix would undoubtedly recognize him even with a puffy face and black dye. How had Joseph missed seeing the science chairman by the elevators?

The man walking with Helix spoke. "I'll show them to you as soon as I have the results." It took a moment for Joseph to place the man. Anton something, one of the Time Strainer engineers.

Joseph kept walking slowly, didn't alter his pace. He bent his head over his comlink. With luck, Anton and Helix would walk around him and Xavier without looking at them. He typed a one-word message to Xavier: *Helix*.

"Make sure you review them before you send them," Helix said, his voice still sharp. "Last time, one of the simulation code summaries was missing. It was worthless."

"The simulation code summary wasn't missing," Anton said. "We deleted it when Reilly decided to change the event time horizon."

Helix's voice rose. "I approve all modifications. Not Reilly, not the mayor. Me. If you didn't get my approval, don't make the change."

"You were in the med clinic at the time," Anton pointed out weakly. "We didn't know if you would live. Reilly had to take command."

Even though Joseph and Xavier were walking slowly, Helix and Anton hadn't overtaken them. Helix was walking even more slowly than they were. Joseph realized what the uneven footsteps meant: Helix was limping.

"Reilly isn't in command," Helix growled. "I expect you to undo any modifications you've done without my consent."

"But you haven't seen them yet," Anton protested. "Don't

you want to examine the modifications before you make that decision?"

"No. You will give me hourly reports until you've undone anything I didn't agree to."

Well, that pretty much explained why Reilly hadn't made more progress on his projects. Helix wasn't trying to build anything but his own personal empire.

Joseph and Xavier turned a corner, and the huge double doors of the Time Strainer bay came into sight. Up ahead in the hallway, two men and a woman had reached the bay doors. The woman pressed her crystal to a panel on the wall, unlocking the door. It slid open and the workers walked inside.

The problem with reaching the fourth floor so soon—besides the fact that Helix was right behind them—was that Joseph didn't know how many more scientists and engineers were on their way to the room. Ideally, Joseph and Xavier would be the last ones into the Strainer bay, and then they wouldn't have to worry about disabling any stragglers still arriving for their shift. If any of the scientists called for help on their comlinks, he and Xavier could easily be surrounded and trapped.

Joseph fingered the comlink jammer on his belt. He couldn't use it yet. If he jammed signals now, Taylor wouldn't know where he was or how to reach him.

The door loomed up ahead. Joseph's comlink sent a tingle of energy into his hand, and he smelled the scent of baking bread, Xavier's identifier. Joseph checked the screen, already worried it would show a number 111, the code for "fight." The number 0 glowed on the screen. That meant "bluff."

Xavier murmured something to Joseph about needing to transfer some part IDs, stopped in the hallway, and fingered his comlink. Joseph stopped as well, turning his body to keep his profile hidden from Helix. If Helix didn't recognize Joseph as he passed by, there would be no need to fight. Not yet.

Joseph didn't breathe. Didn't look. Just listened to the shuffling sounds of footsteps.

Helix and Anton walked by, with Helix still going on about unauthorized modifications. Neither man paid any attention to Joseph or Xavier. Which, now that Joseph thought about it, he should have expected. Helix wasn't the type who cared about his subordinates enough to notice people in the hallway. And Anton was so nervously focused on Helix, he probably wouldn't have noticed if Taylor herself stood in the hallway wearing her twenty-first-century clothes.

Still, it wasn't until the men were nearly to the Time Strainer bay doors that Joseph glanced up for a better look. He hadn't recognized Helix in the elevator because the man had changed his hair. The long black-and-gray stripes were gone. It was short now, a spiky bronze flecked with blood red—like someone had exploded near him and he hadn't bothered to clean off the mess. Helix was thinner too, and he walked not only with a limp but with his shoulders slouched.

Turning his back to Helix and Anton, Xavier unzipped his overalls so he could get into his pack. "Tell me when they've gone inside the bay," he whispered. Xavier took out a vial of sleeping gas, then pulled out his mask.

Joseph unclipped his laser box from his belt and watched Helix's limping progress through the bay doors. When they slid shut, Joseph said, "They're in."

Xavier read his comlink screen. "Taylor's group is in the stairwell. They'll be here soon."

They couldn't hesitate then. Joseph put on his gas mask, and he and Xavier hurried to the bay door. When they got there, Joseph put his lock disabler to the door panel. The panel let out a spark, a small electric protest against the invasion. The disabler fried the lock's original components, then added new ones so that the door didn't sound an alarm. It slid open more slowly than normal, fighting the command. Before it had opened more than a few centimeters, Xavier threw the vial of sleeping gas inside. A tinkling crash sounded.

Someone called, "What was that?"

But no one answered. By the time Joseph and Xavier stepped inside, the gas had saturated the air and the scientists were stumbling, eyes glassy from the drug.

The door slid closed behind Joseph. A man in the farthest corner was the only one still standing upright. He frowned at Joseph in confusion and then fell face-first onto the floor.

"That's going to hurt when he wakes up," Joseph said. He kept scanning the room, laser box drawn.

The room looked the same as the last time Joseph had seen it. Back then he'd been brought here with his father to translate twenty-fifth-century English to the time riders. Joseph hadn't thought the Time Strainer would actually work and had stood stunned and speechless when the light cleared and two unconscious girls floated in the Time Strainer chamber. Since then, not a day ended that he didn't think about the machine and all of its applications.

The Time Strainer stood in the center of the room: five meters high with cables trailing from its top. A glass chamber stuck out of the middle, like an elevator that had been fused to a short building. Computer terminals and equipment stations were scattered around the room, lights blinking as the machines waited for input. Joseph stepped over a couple of unconscious men to get to the command terminal.

Xavier made his way to the Time Strainer chamber, checking the room for anyone who might have escaped the effects of the gas. Once he was satisfied that all the scientists were on the floor, he unzipped his overalls and unfastened the packs around his middle. Joseph did the same, tossing his packs in Xavier's direction.

Xavier caught them and glared at Joseph. "Careful with the equipment. It's expensive."

Joseph didn't answer him. He'd reached the main terminal. If one of the scientists wasn't already logged on, it would put the whole mission at risk. Joseph was good, perhaps the best in the city, at splicing into computer programs, but success was never certain, and he didn't have much time.

One glance erased his worries. Programs were running. Now he just had to access the right one and put his transfer stick into the port. Both took him only a few moments. While the computer downloaded his program, he strode over to Helix. The man lay on the floor, eyes staring upward blankly.

Joseph never would have thought running into Helix was a good thing, but it was about to credit them with some time.

Joseph took Helix's comlink from his belt and tapped out a message: *I'm in a meeting in the Time Strainer bay. Don't bother me or anyone in this room until I give you clearance. Anyone who ignores this order will face a questioning.*

That ought to keep people away for a while.

Joseph went back to the command terminal and sat down in front of the computer. His download had finished. The computer would now run from orders on his transfer stick. One of his programs deleted the computer stations' recording functions. Another program synched up the QGPs. Using the functioning parts of three units, they would work together to transform matter into an energy flux wave.

Joseph's comlink sent him an electric prickle and he smelled lemons. Taylor. He was too busy to answer. He searched through the timestream data on the computer, searching for the exact moment he needed to snatch his brother out of the past.

From over by the Time Strainer, Xavier called, "Taylor's group is on the fourth floor."

"Understood," Joseph called back. He kept his attention on the computer screen, couldn't think about Taylor right now. The timestream data was longer and more complicated than he had expected. He had pictured it like an actual stream, data layered on top of each other. Instead, it was like cords that twisted together to make a rope while all of it whipped and wriggled in a strong wind. He could barely keep track of the piece he needed, let alone *control* any of it.

Then he laughed at himself for ever believing it would be easy. Time wasn't one of Sheridan's horses—a beast who ignored its own power and would let you ride on its back. Time was a snake slithering unnoticed and uncaring until you grabbed hold of its tail. Joseph had grabbed that tail, and now he had to control it before it turned and sank its fangs into his hand.

chapter

10

Taylor hurried down the hallway, Lee by her side, Ren behind them. Her insides churned with fear and anger. Why in the world had Joseph chosen to go to the Time Strainer bay—the most important room on the fourth floor? Five other rooms had the computer equipment she needed to destroy the QGPs. Five. All of them were better strategic locations than the Time Strainer bay.

If a scientist or two found one of the smaller rooms locked when it wasn't supposed to be—well, it wouldn't automatically be cause for alarm. It might have been hours before someone noticed. But the Time Strainer bay—how many people did Joseph have to knock unconscious to take that room? People would notice when a large group of scientists went AWOL.

Taylor rounded the corner in the hallway, and the Time

Strainer bay doors came into sight. The hallway was empty. That was good, at least. They didn't have to shoot anyone and drag them into the bay.

Ren and Lee had already put their gas masks on. Taylor put on hers as well. Ren jogged to the door while Lee turned around, laser box drawn, watching for anyone who might come into the hallway. Ren could have called Joseph and asked him to open the door from the inside, but it was just as quick to use a lock disabler.

The door slid open and the three slipped inside.

Taylor hadn't thought about this room since she'd been carried out of it a month and a half ago, nearly unconscious. It seemed larger without the crowds of scientists gawking at her. The Time Strainer stood in the middle of the room. Equipment stations surrounded the huge machine, looking as though they were peasants paying homage to their monarch.

Joseph sat in front of the main computer terminal. Xavier was kneeling next to a fallen scientist, bending over him. She didn't bother to ask why. Her mind was focused on the computer programs and everything that had to be done. Ren and Lee took up their positions near the door, guarding it against anyone who tried to enter. Which would probably happen soon, because Joseph had chosen the worst room possible.

She wouldn't criticize him for that now though. She didn't want to get Joseph off track while he hacked into the Time Strainer's programming. Judging from the furrow of his brow, it was harder than he'd expected.

She strode over to the main computer terminal, her transfer stick already in her hand. She would send the QGPs self-destruct signals and run the programs to change the QGP data that the Scicenter had already recorded. She had invented a brilliant algorithm that would change each test result, each parameter by random degrees. The numbers would remain close enough to the original to not be easily caught, but far enough from the actual result to mess up anyone who used them.

It should . . . Taylor suddenly felt a wave of sleepiness engulf her. She peered at Joseph's computer screen to figure out how far he'd gotten already. She couldn't make sense of the data. The numbers and symbols were blurring around the edges.

Joseph stood up and took her arm. "Lie down before you fall." His edges blurred too.

"I feel . . . ," she started, but couldn't get the rest of the sentence out. A crash sounded near the door. She looked over and saw Lee lying on the floor. Ren sagged down the wall, losing consciousness.

Something was very wrong.

Her gaze went to Xavier, and she realized the form he bent over wasn't a scientist who had passed out; it was empty clothes. He was arranging syringes and metal tools into piles next to them. What was going on?

"Lie down," Joseph told her again. "You'll be fine."

That was when she noticed the filter at the end of Joseph's mask. It fluttered with each breath he took. Hers gave only a limp wave. The mask had a hole somewhere, and with every breath she took, she was inhaling sleeping gas. She slowed her breathing rate. "Someone sabotaged my mask."

Joseph showed no surprise, no concern. She realized what his expression meant, and her stomach twisted. He had known

92

all along. That was why he kept telling her to lie down.

She struggled to keep conscious, to reason with him. Everything around her swayed. "Don't try to strain your brother," she mumbled. "None of Reilly's QGPs work."

He kept hold of her arm, steadying her. "I wrote a program to fix that."

"Don't do it," she said, knowing he wouldn't listen to her. She sank to her knees, dizziness overcoming her. Her vision was going black. "How did you puncture our masks?" she asked. "Ren and Lee never left their packs."

"I didn't puncture them," Joseph said. "You brought them from the city that way."

Someone on the council had helped with the betrayal. It was a bitter sting, and the last thing Taylor felt before darkness overtook her.

chapter hapter

11

Echo walked alongside Joseph. The length of Plymouth Street stretched out in front of them: stores flashing advertisements, a few people here and there strolling down the walks, cars gliding by on the rails. Echo barely saw any of it. He was sifting through details in his mind, searching for anything he might have missed. He kept his voice low as he spoke to Joseph. "Everything I know about the Dakine is in the file I just gave you. Memorize it before you talk to any of them. Especially the signs and oaths."

Joseph's face had gone so pale, the blue crescent moon on his cheek stood out like an angry slash. "I won't let you die in my place. We'll go to the Enforcement office. We'll tell them the Dakine ordered an assassination on me."

Echo shook his head. "That would only get both of us killed. The Dakine have people who work as Enforcers."

Joseph's voice rose in frustration. "We'll go to the Enforcer chairman then. If you give her information on the Dakine, she'll protect us."

"For how long? Weeks? Months?" Echo shook his head again. "The Dakine would find a way to kill us and Jeth too. And they'd probably make it spectacularly slow and painful, to send a message to everyone who's ever thought about informing on them. It's better this way. You know how to pretend to be me. You can fool everyone and live."

Joseph quickened his pace. His footsteps beat out an angry rhythm on the walkway. "We'll find a way out of the city then."

"And that would be a better life—fighting with the vikers until starvation or bad weather kills us?"

Joseph let out a groan and clenched his hands as though he wanted to hit something. "There has to be a way out of this besides death. We'll get to a safe place and think of something."

It wouldn't do any good. Did Joseph think Echo hadn't already considered every answer to this equation?

Joseph pulled his comlink from his belt and pressed the car-call button. "We'll need laser boxes. We'll also need to build or buy a signal-jamming detector." That was how Dakine members kept from being tracked when they broke the law. They had jammers that kept sensors from picking up their crystals' signals. Only important government officials had signal-jamming detectors. No one else had advance warning when Dakine assassins approached.

Joseph kept hold of his comlink. "We probably already have most of the equipment we need to build a signal-jamming detector, and I can splice into specifications somewhere."

They wouldn't have time for that. Echo knew he'd be dead

before the day ended. He didn't stop his brother from listing things, though, from planning. Joseph always felt better when he had control of a situation. Echo wouldn't take that away from him now. He'd already taken too much from Joseph: his freedom, his identity, maybe even his life. Who knew how long Joseph would be able to pretend to be Echo before the Dakine found him out? Any little forgotten phrase or conversation might reveal him.

The thought cut through Echo, as sharp and painful as a laser burn. He could face his own death, but not his brother's. It was ironic he felt this way now when he'd spent all last night cursing fate for giving him a twin brother.

Echo had always been forced to share everything with Joseph. His parents, his friends, his appearance, his identity, and then Allana too. That had been the hardest, being in love with her and knowing his brother was his competition.

Echo stared at the thrumming lights twirling around one of the stores and told himself not to think about Allana. His mind kept returning to the bitterness of what had happened anyway.

Echo had joined the Dakine because Allana had asked him to, because she'd said they could be together if he was a member. Then she'd chosen Joseph over him, had deemed him better. Just like their father had favored Joseph. And their caretakers had too.

Last night when Allana had cut her relationship with Echo, he might have been able to shrug with nonchalance and pretend it didn't matter. He'd gotten good at that. But she couldn't leave things that way.

Joseph noticed Echo's silence. "I'm not going to let you die in my place," he insisted. "This is my fault too. I never should have told you what Allana said."

Allana had gone to see Joseph last night, to tell him she wanted to be exclusive with him. It probably never occurred to her that Joseph would turn her down. He knew how much Echo cared about her. Joseph had told her it would hurt Echo too much.

So Allana told Joseph he didn't know the real Echo—didn't know the one who had joined the Dakine. She told Joseph she knew Echo had joined because she recruited him.

Had she really been trying to sway Joseph, or was she just being spiteful? Echo supposed it didn't matter. Joseph had found Echo and spent the rest of the night berating him. How could you join the Dakine? How could you be so stupid?

How could *Echo have been so stupid?*

"None of this is your fault," Echo said now.

Echo had been the one who wanted to hurt Allana, who had been so saturated with anger that he told Lobo, their Dakine base leader, what she had done. Echo expected to see her censured. He never imagined Lobo would order her death for revealing a Dakine membership and order Joseph's death for hearing it.

Echo had sent a message warning her, and then had found Joseph and asked to switch identities with him. Echo hadn't told Joseph why until a few minutes ago.

Joseph pushed the car-call button on his comlink again. "If we change coloring so we both look the same—"

"No," Echo told Joseph. "One of us would still be killed. I won't let it be you."

Neither of them suggested going inside to talk. It was safer to be out in the open with crowds. Dakine hit men usually waited until their targets were alone. They didn't like witnesses. They didn't want to risk hitting bystanders. Too messy. The Dakine wanted people to feel they were safe as long as they did what the Dakine wanted.

Joseph let out a shaky breath. "I'll get us out of the city. Give me time to figure something out."

"Think of Jeth," Echo said. "He can't lose both of us. You should be the one to live. He loves you more."

"No," Joseph said, and his voice caught. He didn't say more. Maybe he couldn't deny the claim.

Cars were slowly passing by them; their darkened windows acted as mirrors, warping Echo's and Joseph's reflections as they went by. Echo had walked down this street a thousand times. He couldn't imagine not seeing it again. That was the thing about death—it was so unimaginable.

While studying different periods of history, Echo had read legends about death.

One story said death came to claim people dressed as a hooded farm worker, carrying a scythe. Others said winged spirits called angels carried souls to a place with doors made of pearls. The ancient Egyptians believed people went to live in an afterlife where gods with animal heads ruled. The walls of their tombs were painted with instructions for traveling through the land of the dead.

Echo wondered if any of the stories were true. He should have studied those tomb paintings better, just in case. This meant Joseph was right about one more thing—he always told Echo he needed to study more.

Joseph ran his hand through his newly blue hair. It was like looking in a mirror, seeing Joseph after they'd switched identities. "Isn't there any way you can reason with the Dakine leaders? Isn't there any sort of bargain you can make with them?"

Echo let out a short laugh. "The Dakine don't bargain much."

Echo couldn't help noticing that Joseph hadn't once mentioned Allana, hadn't talked about saving her life. More irony. Echo was the one who cared about saving her and he'd caused her death.

A little way down the sidewalk, a strange light swirled and grew. He didn't pay attention to it. It was probably an advertisement of some sort.

A car stopped in the street ahead of them. Echo turned to it, expecting it to be the car Joseph had called. Then two more cars pulled up behind the first and stopped. That never happened on a regular stretch of street—three people all wanting and reaching the same destination at the same time.

It meant assassins. It meant the Dakine were sending a message and didn't care that bystanders would see the execution. It meant Echo had no time left.

"I want you to live, not fight," Echo told Joseph quickly. "Live your life for both of us now."

Joseph stared at the cars, too stunned to move or speak. The doors slid open.

"I love you," Echo said, then he turned and ran, putting as much space as he could between Joseph and himself.

The light on the sidewalk was bigger now, brighter. Echo had assumed it was far away, but it was close, a growing electric whirlwind of energy.

He heard Joseph scream, "No!" and Echo glanced back to look at his brother. The car doors were open and several men emerged, laser boxes outstretched in their hands. The men wore the dark suits of Enforcers, helmet shields covering their faces. They were Dakine, though. Echo was sure of it.

The sizzle of shots filled the air. One hit his left shoulder. The *burning pain made him stumble. He held out his hands to break his fall and saw the whirlpool of energy had grown even larger. It pulled at him so that instead of falling to the ground, he tumbled toward it, swallowed in its brilliance.*

Had anyone else seen this light? Or did only Echo see it because it had come for him?

Echo's last thought was that all the historical documents were wrong. Death didn't come carrying a scythe or wearing wings. Death was a light.

ECHO'S NEXT SENSATION WAS a sharp, throbbing pain in his shoulder. The air smelled of antiseptic and something awful. Something burning. He heard voices, the words so jumbled he couldn't understand them. He opened his eyes. Colors and shapes bled into one another like a bad picture feed. He squinted and the colors coalesced for a moment, then drifted apart. A cold sensation ran through his shoulder and he fell back into darkness, his consciousness fading out.

When Echo awoke the second time, he felt groggy, drugged.

A voice near him said, "The air is clear. We can take off our masks."

Echo opened his eyes. Someone who resembled Joseph knelt beside him. His face was swollen, and his hair was dark and slicked back. Two black ovals surrounded his eyes like a nineteenth-century bandit mask. None of it made sense.

Joseph peered down at him. "Can you hear me?"

Echo glanced around. He was lying in a room with a large machine, computer equipment, and an assortment of people lying unmoving on the floor.

"How do you feel?" Joseph asked. He put his hand on one of Echo's arms. "Say something."

Echo squinted, then blinked. "This isn't at all what I thought death would be like."

Joseph smiled and gave his arm a squeeze. "Death will have to wait. I told you I would find a way to get us out of the city."

Echo looked around the room again. "Where are we?"

"Technically we're still in the city. In the Scicenter, actually. But we have a way out of Traventon once we make it out of the building."

"What?" Echo asked. He tried to sit up and realized his left arm was taped to the floor. His shirt had been cut away and his shoulder looked like a mass of charred flesh. That was what the burning smell had been. Him. His shoulder. He'd been shot. A med of some sort poked around the wound with lighted medical equipment.

Echo didn't feel anything. The med must have given him a pain eraser. "How much damage is there?" Echo asked.

The med kept working on the wound. "Not nearly as much as there could have been. I've stopped the bleeding and I'm repairing the major blood vessels. You won't have full use of your arm until your muscles regrow. I'll reattach the ones I can."

Echo went back to studying the room. "How did I get here?"

Joseph smiled again. "Determination and luck. Also there was some time travel involved."

Well, it was nice to know Joseph could joke around after an assassination attempt. "Right," Echo said. "I don't know why I didn't think of that option first."

Joseph opened his mouth to say something, then stopped.

"It's going to take a while to explain everything. The important thing is you're safe. For the moment."

His safety had never been the issue. Echo wanted *Joseph's* safety, Jeth's safety. Hadn't Echo already explained that? He let out an exasperated sigh. "The Dakine are looking for both of us now, aren't they?"

Joseph didn't answer. He checked the time on his comlink and stood up. "I'll tell you everything after I'm done computigating."

Echo gritted his teeth in aggravation. "It doesn't do any good to save my life if the Dakine want to kill both of us now." He forgot his arm was taped down and tried to sit up again. "You never listen to anything I tell you!" Echo yelled.

Joseph disappeared behind a computer terminal and didn't reply.

Echo laid his head back down, noticing again the men and women lying on the floor around him. "What happened to all these people?"

No reply from Joseph. That meant the answer was bad news.

"*Sangre,*" Echo swore. "You did something really foolish and really illegal, didn't you?"

Still no answer. Echo heard Joseph's fingers tapping at the computer's controls.

Echo groaned. It must be worse than he thought.

The med tugged at something in Echo's wound. "All the scientists will be fine. We put them out with gas, then stunned them before it wore off. They'll be asleep for another hour."

"This is unbelievable," Echo said. "Absolutely brilliant. Why have only the Dakine trying to kill us when we can have the government join in too? You don't need to fix my shoulder. None of us are going to make it out of this room alive."

"I've missed you for the last two and a half months," Joseph called over. "Don't make me rethink that."

Two and a half months? Had Echo been in coma? But then why was his shoulder wound fresh? He was about to ask when he saw one of the scientists moving, waking up. She rolled over, and the green bun on the top of her head flopped sideways.

"Joseph," Echo called. "Your stun didn't last as long as you thought. One of them is getting up."

Joseph peered around the terminal, then went back to his work. "That's not a scientist. That's Taylor. She's a friend."

"You gassed a friend?" Echo winced as the med tugged something in his arm especially hard. "You know, it's time we had a talk about your social skills."

Taylor pulled herself to a sitting position, peered around, then ripped the gas mask from her face. She was younger than Echo had first supposed. Mildly pretty. A ring of flowers and leaves framed her eyes. They made her look fairylike.

She threw her gas mask on the ground and glared in Joseph's direction. "I will kill you for this, Joseph."

Echo let out a short laugh. "You'll have some competition for that job."

chapter ~~hapter~~
12

Taylor stared at Echo with growing disbelief. Joseph had done it. He'd gotten Reilly's QGPs to work. She would have been impressed if she weren't so furious.

Taylor's gaze turned to Xavier. He was a surgeon. That was why Joseph had brought him along. Joseph had snatched Echo from the past during the assassination and knew he would need medical help.

Her mind felt muddled from the gas. She tried to put the pieces together. The council had agreed to let Xavier come. Had they known what Joseph planned to do? "Who set this up?" she called to Joseph. "Who helped you sabotage our gas masks?"

The tapping at the keyboard didn't diminish in speed. "While you were passed out, I took your transfer stick," Joseph said calmly. "I've already uploaded your rank virus. The computer is running the algorithms to change the QGP data. You can send the destruct signals to the QGPs whenever you're ready." Without looking up from the computer, he added, "I used Helix's comlink to announce he's in here and doesn't want to be disturbed. So far no one has."

Taylor stood up. Her legs didn't feel sturdy and her mind still wasn't clear. What had President Mason said about Xavier during their send-off? The memories were disjointed, didn't make sense. She remembered pointing to the sign above the city gates and telling President Mason, "Freedom means paying off your debts. After this is over, we're even."

Another memory looped through Taylor's mind too. She had stood in that same spot by the gates and President Mason put his hand on Taylor's shoulder. "Have faith," he told her. "Prayers are never said in vain."

Wait, when had that happened?

Taylor shook her head as if she could shake away her confusion. Right before they left Santa Fe, Sheridan had asked Joseph about Xavier. Taylor could picture herself striding over to the two of them. "Maybe I should insist on bringing someone along too," Taylor had said to Joseph, throwing the words at him in a challenge.

But Taylor had another memory of those same moments. That argument hadn't taken place. Sheridan wasn't even there. Taylor had only halfheartedly protested Xavier's addition. She was too eager to leave to say anything that would delay the team.

Which of the memories had actually happened? It was like holding water in her hands; the images kept slipping away.

She shut her eyes, concentrating. Taylor recalled walking

over to the airbikes. "Let's go," she'd told Ren and Lee. "Every moment we stay here is a moment that—"

With a razor-like pain to her chest, Taylor realized what all of this meant. The white walls of the Time Strainer bay seemed to be collapsing, pressing in on her so that she couldn't move. She forced her still-weak legs to take her to the computer where Joseph sat.

"How could you mess with the timestream?" she asked, clenching her hands together. "Do you realize what you've done?"

"Don't worry," Joseph said without looking at her. "A time vector protection field covers the entire building. Changes can't affect us."

"Sheridan . . ." The word only came out as a whisper. Maybe he didn't hear her.

"Anyone outside the building won't remember the old timestream. They won't know a change even happened. Although taking Echo during the assassination was such a small change in the timestream, I doubt—"

Taylor interrupted him with a sound that was half growl and half wail. This mistake had to be undone. Had to. "It changed everything for Sheridan!"

Joseph stopped typing.

"I have two sets of memories now," Taylor said. "An old one and a new one. And in the new one, Sheridan never escaped from Traventon with us."

chapter 13

chapter

Joseph felt as though the room had lost its oxygen. He couldn't breathe. His lungs refused to work right. Between Echo's arrival and getting the programs uploaded, Joseph hadn't thought about the past. As soon as Taylor said Sheridan's name, he remembered it all. A new set of memories joined his old ones, forking off into a different reality.

Joseph and Caesar, one of Echo's Dakine friends, had driven to the back entrance of the Scicenter. They were waiting to meet the Dakine operative who'd agreed to free Taylor and Sheridan. In the new memory, they hadn't been able to rescue Sheridan.

A man dressed in Enforcer armor brought Taylor to the car, then leaned in to talk to Caesar.

"We can't get the other girl," he said. "They moved her to an

antistraining chamber somewhere."

"*What?*" Caesar asked. "*What's an antistraining chamber?*"

The man straightened. "*I don't know, but I can't get there.*" The man turned and left, striding back to the Scicenter. The car door slid shut and Caesar reached over to the control panel, typing in the address of the Dakine base instead of speaking it. Taylor looked from Caesar to Joseph, panic growing in her expression. "*Where's Sheridan? We can't leave her.*"

The car moved forward, humming along the rails, gliding away from the building. "*We'll get her later,*" Joseph said, hoping it was true. "*The important thing now is to take you somewhere safe.*"

Taylor stared out the window back at the Scicenter. "*How soon can you get Sheridan?*"

"*I don't know,*" Joseph said.

"*It has to be soon.*" Taylor turned to him, piercing him with the intensity of her gaze. She gestured to the bruises on her face. "*What do you think Reilly will do to Sheridan when she can't tell him what he wants to know?*"

Joseph was keenly aware of Caesar watching them, straining to understand the twenty-first-century accent. It was a good thing he couldn't. He would ask questions about Taylor that Joseph didn't want to answer.

"*I care about Sheridan too,*" he told Taylor. "*We'll find a way to free her.*"

They hadn't, though. They had escaped from the Dakine base and met up with Elise, the other wordsmith Joseph and Jeth worked with. Joseph had hoped Elise's DW contacts could help them rescue Sheridan. Instead the DW had immediately sent Taylor and the wordsmiths to Santa Fe. They said it was too dangerous for Taylor to stay in Traventon.

Joseph remembered other events from the new reality too. They rushed at him in a scramble of images: Dakine assassins converging on Plymouth Street. Echo had fallen, caught by laser fire, and then had vanished. The only proof he had been there was the splatters of blood on the pavement.

Streetcams had recorded the whole event, and the footage blasted through the newsfeeds. Experts analyzed, theorized, and bemoaned the Dakine's new weapon: a laser box that vaporized victims. People talked about it for days afterward.

The Enforcers questioned Joseph for their criminal report, which was normal procedure. Then Joseph and Jeth had been brought into the Scicenter and questioned by a panel of scientists and government officials, which wasn't normal procedure at all.

The panel was seated in raised rows on a dais. Jeth and Joseph sat on white medical chairs that threw a constant stream of statistics into the air by their knees. Heart rate, respiration rate, brain activity, everything that might help the panel determine whether someone was lying. Helix sat in the front row on the largest chair like a king on a throne. "Do you know why anyone might have use for Joseph in the future? Was he important somehow? Did he have any special abilities?"

A dark-haired man leaned forward in his chair. "Was he poised to make some contribution to society?"

Jeth nodded and blinked away emotion. "Of course, Joseph was important. He was smart and kind and lived a life of honor. Everyone who knew him respected him. He was . . ." Jeth broke down and couldn't say more after that.

The scientists eyed Jeth, clearly disregarding what he'd said as the words of a grieving parent. An impromptu eulogy, one Joseph found excruciating to listen to. He hadn't been smart enough to save his brother. He hadn't been honorable or kind enough to refuse Echo's sacrifice. He had let his brother die in his place.

The scientists then turned their attention to Joseph, demanding the same information from him. "Was Joseph special somehow?"

"No," Joseph said. "There was nothing extraordinary about Joseph." He had felt a hard bitterness at this truth. He wasn't important. He was only unlucky.

One of the scientists tapped his armrest and a computer screen flashed in front of Joseph. It showed his school grades, the scores of his computigating tests back before he realized it was better to hide that skill. "He had an extremely high IQ and an obvious gift for programming."

"He didn't want to be a programmer," Joseph said, which was the truth. The Dakine went after programmers and pressured them to join their organization. "History was Joseph's main interest."

This led the scientists to speak to one another in hushed tones, murmuring things about history. He heard them mention Joseph's translation skills with twenty-first-century English. "This is bad," one said. "We can't have anyone interfering with our time period. Who will they take next? One of us?"

Joseph hadn't understood their questions back then, but now he did. They had suspected Echo was strained into the future. It made them careful. It made them create an anti-straining chamber. And when Sheridan told Reilly she was the physicist he wanted, Reilly put her in it.

One other memory pressed itself to the surface of Joseph's

mind. When they had first met the DW, Taylor refused to leave Traventon without Sheridan. "We have to help her," Taylor had pleaded. "They're probably torturing her."

Joseph had literally dragged Taylor, crying, out of the city. "I care about Sheridan too," he'd said over and over again. "I'll come back for her. I promise."

Now the words bit at him. It was his fault Sheridan hadn't been rescued. His fault because he had cared more about saving his brother than keeping her safe. His fault.

Joseph felt a grating sickness that started in his stomach and spread through his entire body.

Taylor gripped the side of the terminal desk, anger vibrating from her eyes.

He swallowed. It was difficult to speak. "We'll rescue her. I promise."

Taylor drew her hand back and slapped him hard. "Sheridan was safe until you changed the timestream! We don't even know if she's still alive."

Joseph didn't flinch from the slap. Didn't argue. With numb fingers, he minimized the QGP data screen and flipped back to the screen that operated the Time Strainer. "We'll strain her here. You have the same DNA, so we'll use yours to find her DNA energy signal. We'll take her before they put her in the antistraining chamber."

"It won't work," Taylor said, rubbing her temples. "They put those shielding chips into us as soon as we stepped out of the Time Strainer."

With a lurch to his stomach, Joseph remembered that new memory too. The scientists had not only created an antistraining chamber, but they had also designed chips that created a field to scramble energy signals from a person's DNA. One of the scientists had injected them into Taylor's and Sheridan's necks as soon as they reconfigured in the Time Strainer.

And all this had happened because Echo's disappearance warned the scientists that people could be snatched from this time period.

Joseph let out a groan of disbelief, of pain. He wanted to hit the terminal, to break something. Instead he went through the computer's files until he accessed the detention logs. "They wouldn't have killed her. They want her to help them with the QGP." He scrolled through names of prisoners. "I'll find her. The antistraining chamber was in the Scicenter. She might be in the building right now."

"What if they gave her a memory wash?" Taylor turned and paced the floor behind him. She gripped her hair as though she wanted to rip it out. "Reilly threatened to erase her memory if she didn't help him."

Lee and Ren were both on their feet now, peeling off the useless gas masks. Lee turned his mask over in his hands, checking it. Ren lifted his laser box and scanned the room.

Joseph didn't speak to them. He skimmed through the detention logs, his thoughts spinning and scattering like shattered glass. He needed to find Sheridan's information among the lists of criminals.

Instead of walking over to the computer where Joseph sat, Ren and Lee strode over to Xavier. He was still working on Echo's shoulder. "What in the name of darkness happened?" Ren demanded. "Why didn't our gas masks work?"

"Who shot you?" Lee asked, and then added, "Why did you change hair and face colors?"

Echo looked up at them placidly. "I have no idea who either of you are."

Ren's mouth dropped open. "He has amnesia too?"

Joseph didn't explain anything. He tried, unsuccessfully, to block them out and concentrate on finding Sheridan's location.

Taylor paced over to them. "That's not Joseph. That's his twin brother, Echo. Joseph is over there."

Ren's and Lee's gazes went from Echo to Joseph, taking in their similarities.

"I thought Echo died months ago," Ren said.

Joseph remained silent.

Taylor let out a grumble. "He did."

Echo lifted his head. "It's just a shoulder wound. The med is fixing it right now."

Taylor went on, spitting her words out angrily. "Joseph discovered a way to combine Reilly's QGPs to create a functioning one. He used them to change time and save Echo's life."

"He did what?" Lee demanded.

Xavier finished brushing artificial skin over the top of Echo's wound. "We've brought you back to life at a great price. Remember that and live accordingly."

"I hate to disagree with everyone," Echo said, finally able to sit up, "but I think I would remember being dead for months."

Lee marched over to Joseph. "Who in the council knew what you were planning? What did you exchange for Xavier's help?"

Ren stormed over to Joseph as well. "Did you destroy the QGPs already?"

"Would someone," Echo called out, "please explain to me what is happening?"

Xavier pulled out a pair of shoes and some clothes from one of his packs. He handed the clothes to Echo. "These are laser deflecting," Xavier said. "I'll help you put them on."

Ren looked over Joseph's shoulder and scanned the names on the computer screen. "Who are these people? What are you doing?" He turned to Taylor. "Have you destroyed the QGPs?"

"No," she said, still pacing back and forth between the Time Strainer and Joseph's computer terminal. "We can't destroy them yet. If I can think of a way to get around the shielding chips, we can use the QGPs to save Sheridan."

"Sheridan?" Lee asked, and Joseph could see the realization hit Lee and Ren, the fact that they now had two separate memories of the events leading up to this moment. In one, Sheridan had seen them off, standing somberly with the council members as they left the city. In the other she was never there and Taylor had been anxious the entire trip to Traventon. She had kept pressing everyone to go faster, hadn't even wanted to stop to sleep. In that one, part of the mission had been to rescue Sheridan.

The council had promised Taylor that after she destroyed the QGPs, Ren and Lee would meet with a DW contact and try to free Sheridan. It had always been a vague promise. What, Taylor had asked them more than once, constituted "try"? The council wouldn't give her or Joseph any details, though. They said that doing so could endanger their contact.

"Fine," Echo called over again. "No one has to tell me what's going on. Apparently I've been dead for months. What's another few minutes of complete confusion?"

Lee put his hand on his forehead, rubbing at the space between his eyes. "Which memory happened? Which is the truth?"

"It doesn't matter," Ren said, raising his voice. "Saving Sheridan was never our primary mission." He waved his hand at Taylor to emphasize his point. "You can't save one person if it means letting countless others die. You need to destroy the QGPs and make sure this government never rebuilds one."

Joseph didn't join the discussion. He had found Sheridan's file. "Taylor," he called, and didn't have to say more. She hurried to the terminal. He clicked on Sheridan's name and skimmed the information. She was at Detention Center Thirteen, a high-security prison about ten kilometers from here. Several interrogations were reported. Each listing brought a sharp pain to Joseph's chest. What had happened in those meetings? What tactics had Reilly used? It was Joseph's fault she was there. His fault.

He skimmed the details until he reached the end. The last thing listed was a memory wash order. Sheridan was scheduled to have her memories wiped clean tonight.

chapter 14

Taylor read the words *memory wash* in Sheridan's file with numb horror. Right now Sheridan was alive and knew who she was. She remembered Taylor and their life in the twenty-first century. In a few more hours, that wouldn't be the case. The sister Taylor had known would be completely gone. "We have to rescue her now," Taylor told Ren and Lee.

Ren looked upward in exasperation. Lee was still rubbing his forehead as though he had a sudden, persistent headache.

"I won't go back to Santa Fe without Sheridan," Taylor said. She could hear the panic in her voice but didn't care. "If that means delaying the QGPs' destruction, so be it."

Joseph said nothing. He had accessed layouts of the detention center and was copying them onto his comlink.

Ren's dark eyes fixed Taylor with a stare. "Destroy the

QGPs now." He gestured in Joseph's direction, piercing the air with his forefinger. "If Joseph found a way to combine the QGPs' energy to make them work, the government can too. They'll use that power to kill innocent people."

Taylor shook her head. "Joseph is smarter than anyone the government has working for them. They won't be able to figure it out." Even as Taylor said the words, she wasn't sure it was the truth. Reilly was smart enough that he'd managed to build a time machine. She turned to Joseph. "You didn't leave any record of Echo's reconfiguration on the computer, did you?"

"No," Joseph said.

Ren didn't appear to be reassured. He stalked off toward the Time Strainer, switched into a language Taylor didn't understand, and let out a stream of angry-sounding words. Probably cursing her. Lee switched to another language as well. It might have been the same one or a different one, but the two of them clearly agreed about something for once.

While Xavier helped Echo dress in his laser-deflecting clothes, he gave Echo a brief rundown of what had happened—including the fact that his rescue had rearranged events so that Taylor's sister was in a detention cell. Echo shot a few sympathetic looks in her direction then, which Taylor ignored. Echo looked so much like Joseph that she couldn't help but be angry at him too. Or maybe that wasn't why she was angry at him; maybe it was because his life had cost Sheridan's freedom. At any rate, he could keep his sky-blue eyes and model-perfect face to himself.

Ren turned to Lee and spoke in English again. "We know

the QGPs' probable locations. We can set explosives and take out those rooms."

"Are you sure you can destroy all of them?" Taylor asked pointedly. "If they aren't destroyed simultaneously, the scientists will protect the remaining ones. The only way to be sure you get them all is to send signals from the system they're linked to. You need me for that." She folded her arms resolutely. "In the new timestream, it's part of your mission to rescue Sheridan. All I'm asking is that you do it sooner than you were supposed to."

Lee raked a hand through his hair. "The new timestream is only a blur in my mind. I don't remember what our contact's name is or where we're supposed to meet to rescue Sheridan. The orders I remember—those take precedence. Destroy the QGPs, and then we'll figure out what to do about Sheridan."

Lee didn't remember their contact's name? The dread tightening around Taylor's stomach constricted into a painful, jolting knot. She turned to Ren. "Do you know the contact's information?"

Ren ran his fingers across his eyes, thinking. "Her name started with a P. We're supposed to meet her near the detention center somewhere." He scowled, unable to retrieve more information. "After you destroy the QGPs, we'll go to the detention center. Maybe seeing the building will congeal our memories."

Maybe. It was as vague as the council's promise of "try." Too easy to get out of. Taylor had only one piece of leverage to save her sister, and she had to use it. "If you won't rescue Sheridan right now, then I'll go to the detention center and do it myself— and it's your job to protect me."

Ren let out a growl and strode back over to Taylor. His

muscles were as taut as if he was about to go into battle. He seemed bigger, more menacing than he had before. "No. My job is to see that you destroy the QGPs and then keep you from being captured by either the government or the Dakine. Now you want me to help you—without any sort of workable plan— break into a high-security detention center?"

"Yes," Taylor said.

Ren lifted his hands in a gesture of disbelief. "I was given orders to kill you if your capture looked imminent. I don't see how you can break into a detention center without it looking like your capture is imminent."

Taylor drew in a sharp breath. "You would kill me?"

Ren lifted his hands again, trying to show her the logic. "If I thought it wasn't possible to rescue you, death would be better than letting someone torture you into using your knowledge to kill others."

Taylor took a step back from him, indignation pressing her mouth into an open circle. "The council said your orders were to protect me."

"Yes, well, we all have our secrets." Ren shot her an impatient look. "Taylor, destroy the QGPs. Then, while Lee gets you out of the city, I'll rescue Sheridan."

"I can't," Lee said. He stood nearby, arms folded, watching Taylor. "As soon the QGPs are destroyed, my orders are to find and assassinate Reilly."

Everyone turned and stared at Lee. Ren raised an eyebrow.

Lee shrugged. "As you said, we all have our secrets."

Taylor glared at both of them. "I heard you promise President Mason—"

"To protect those under our care," Lee finished for her. "We are. You can't hold us to orders from the new timestream. We only partially remember them."

Joseph stood and came around the computer terminal, his comlink in his hand. He took Lee's comlink so that he could transfer the detention-center schematics to it. "Help me rescue Sheridan first, and then I'll help you kill Reilly. I made that bargain with one of the sectors in Santa Fe. If Xavier saved Echo, I promised to make sure Reilly was no longer a threat."

Ren shook his head in amazement. "You see, Brother Lee, this is the problem when factions don't communicate—a redundant team member. You didn't need to come along after all."

"Oh, I needed to come," Lee said with a forced smile. "Someone has to ensure the mission is a success."

Ren still shook his head. "After all your father's talks about peace being a way of life, you're willing to kill Reilly?"

"You're willing to kill Taylor," Lee countered. "Which is worse?"

Echo walked to the computer terminal, a pair of the blue overalls covering his other clothing. "I'd like to point out that I'm not planning on killing anyone. I find that ironic since I'm the one with the Dakine membership." He sat down in the chair Joseph had vacated and switched the screen back to Joseph's program. "Tell me again why you can't strain Sheridan?"

"QGPs identify people by their DNA's energy signal," Joseph explained. "The government inserted a chip into Sheridan that's shielding her energy signal so that the QGP can't pick it up."

"How does it do that?" Echo asked.

120

"I don't know." Joseph handed back Lee's comlink and then turned to get Ren's. "I haven't had time to study it."

"And you don't have time now," Ren said, but he let Joseph transfer the detention schematics to his comlink.

Taylor walked over to the computer terminal and studied the screen over Echo's shoulder. "Can we strain Reilly in here? We could leverage his life for Sheridan's."

Lee let out a grunt. "Two of us came here to kill Reilly. That's not going to give you much leverage."

"We don't have Reilly's energy signal," Joseph told Taylor. "And even if we did, he probably has an antistraining chip in him."

Ren pointed his scanner at the bay door. "Eventually, someone isn't going to care if Helix is in here, and they'll want to come in. The QGPs need to be destroyed by then, or we'll have given our lives for nothing." He gestured to the computer. "Run the destruction program. We'll take an oath to try to help your sister."

Try to help? This from the guy who had just admitted he would kill Taylor rather than let her be captured. What sort of help did he have planned for Sheridan?

Taylor looked at the Time Strainer. Purple and white lights blinked at its sides. It let off an electric sort of hum, waiting for further commands. "You all have your own agendas," Taylor said. "I have mine too. I won't destroy the QGPs until my sister is safe. That way I know you won't just *try* to rescue Sheridan. You'll do it."

Lee turned to Joseph. "You can destroy the QGPs, can't you?"

Joseph's eyes met Taylor's. He could. He had seen how she'd done it the first time.

"No," he said. "Only Taylor knows how."

This, she knew, was his attempt to make things right between them. Joseph wouldn't take away her only bargaining chip.

Joseph turned to Ren and Lee. "If you can't remember the plan to rescue Sheridan, we'll come up with a new one. The DW will help us." He held up his comlink screen so that the others could see the schematics he pointed to. "Sheridan's cell is right here. If we can get inside the detention center dressed as Enforcers, we can bring her out before her memory wash is scheduled."

Xavier had finished packing up his medical equipment and walked over to join the group. He took four gas masks from one of his packs. Working ones, Taylor supposed. He handed them to Ren, Lee, Echo, and her. "How were you planning on killing Reilly?" Xavier asked Lee.

Lee examined the mask as though he didn't quite trust it. "Reilly has an apartment here at the Scicenter. After the mission, I'll wait there until he comes home."

Xavier took out his comlink and switched on the tracking function. "Men with Reilly's rank have more than one apartment. It could be days until he shows up."

"I know," Lee said. "I'm patient."

Xavier tapped through the screens on his comlink. "You don't have to be. Joseph and I have a way to find him."

Lee stepped closer to him and peered at his comlink screen. "Were you able to locate Reilly's crystal signature?"

"No." Xavier scrolled through the data on his screen. "My source has never even seen him. But I know the crystal signature of one of Reilly's assistants. Which means I can tell you that right now Reilly is in the detention center."

"He's probably with Sheridan," Taylor said dully. "Interrogating her." Memories flashed at Taylor. Reilly's face leering over her as he hit her.

"Help us rescue Sheridan," Joseph told Lee, "then I'll help you kill Reilly."

Lee nodded, resigning himself to the new plan. "Agreed."

The knot in Taylor's stomach finally unloosened a bit. "Good. I'll go with you."

"Absolutely not," Joseph said, at the same time Xavier and Ren added *no*s of their own.

Lee sent her an apologetic smile. "I would hate to see Ren shoot you."

"Stay here with Echo," Joseph told her. "I'll message you as soon as we have Sheridan so you can destroy the QGPs. Then we'll meet up at our contact spot."

The Fisherman's Feast restaurant. At least, Taylor hoped that was still the spot the DW had designated. Memories from the new timestream were dreamlike, with huge gaps.

Ren checked over the weapons on his belt. "We can't leave Taylor here unprotected. One of us needs to stay with her."

"Well, it's not going to be you," Taylor told him. "If Enforcers break in here, I know who you'll shoot first."

Ren rolled his eyes. "Yes, the Enforcers. Killing you would be a last and desperate option."

"I'll stay," Xavier said. "I should be here anyway in case

Echo has any medical problems."

"You're a surgeon," Ren pointed out. "We can't trust Taylor's safety to you."

Xavier tilted his chin down condescendingly, his expression reminding everyone that he was the oldest one in the group—the most experienced. "I'm a paramilitary surgeon. I can shoot as well as the rest of you."

This seemed to satisfy Ren and Lee. Lee pointed his scanner toward the bay door again, checking how many people were in the hallway. "We can't risk going outside through any of the building's exits. If the guards notice we don't have crystal signatures, they'll lock down the building."

Ren switched his comlink to scanner function as well. "We'll find an empty room on the ground floor, cut through a wall, and then head to the mobile crystal on Charles Street. We'll figure out how to get into the detention center while we get a car." He didn't have to explain why he'd suggested using a crystal that was farther away. He was leaving the closer mobile crystals for Taylor's group to use.

"The hallway is clear," Lee said, heading to the bay doors. "Let's go."

Ren turned to Xavier. "If something goes wrong . . ." He shot a meaningful look in Taylor's direction.

Taylor bristled.

Xavier nodded. "I'll make sure she makes it back to Santa Fe."

Joseph took Taylor by the arm to get her attention. He kept his voice low and spoke to her in the twenty-first-century accent so that the others wouldn't understand. "I'll do everything I can to save Sheridan, but you need to destroy the QGPs as soon as we walk out the door. The last time Sheridan protected you, she told you not to let her sacrifice be for nothing. I'm telling you the same thing now."

Then he turned and followed Lee and Ren out of the room.

chapter 15

hapter

Taylor walked toward the computer, feeling as though her insides were unraveling. Joseph was right. She needed to destroy the QGPs now. Every second she didn't was a moment she was gambling with danger. But then again, if a chance existed, however small, that she could find a way around the government's antistraining chip . . . She should at least try to think of something first.

How could she get through the chip's scrambling mechanism to get to Sheridan's DNA energy signal? Taylor's mind was blank, washed white by panic. Why—when she needed the whole genius thing to kick into overdrive—had her brain stopped functioning?

Xavier stood by the door, laser box in one hand, checking his scanner. Echo sat at the computer terminal, still looking over Joseph's program. The entire time Taylor had argued with Ren and Lee, she'd hoped Echo would call out, "I've found a way to turn off Sheridan's chip." But he hadn't.

Taylor should just destroy the QGPs, and trust Joseph's team to rescue Sheridan. Taylor walked to the terminal, stopped short, and paced back over to Xavier. A glance at his scanner showed the hallway was empty. Apparently nobody wanted to be anywhere near the room where Helix was. She still had some time. Could she remotely disable the antistraining chip? Could she jam a jammer?

Instead of focusing on this, her mind went to Joseph, Ren, and Lee. What if she had sent them to do something impossible? What if they all died?

She forced herself to think of the problem at hand. Would an electromagnetic pulse knock out the antistraining chip? Was there any way to send one through the detention-center walls? The building probably had safeguards against that.

Taylor walked over to the computer terminal to see if Echo had made any progress. He was flipping through screens, taking in data and code with the same ease Joseph always had. "Having any luck?" she asked.

Echo didn't take his attention from the screen. "Luck is only part of computigating if you don't know what you're doing." More tapping. "Which in this case applies. So let's hope so."

"Do you have any ideas about overcoming the shield?"

"No, but I'm about to try something else." He got up and went over to a nearby equipment station. This one had a clear tray and a scope that reminded her of a magnifying glass. Echo pulled something from his pocket, slid it into the tray, then tapped some numbers on its monitor.

Taylor watched him. "What are you doing?"

"This is a DNA scanner," Echo said. He headed back to the computer terminal.

"What did you put in it?"

He didn't answer, just sat back down at the main computer terminal and typed in commands.

"What are you doing?" she asked again, making sure to emphasize the modern accent. As soon as she repeated herself, she realized it was pointless. Echo had studied the twenty-first-century accent with Joseph. He could understand her either way.

"Back in the twenty-first century," Echo said, keeping his gaze on the monitor, "*parejas* had the custom of exchanging rings, didn't they?"

Parejas? That was one of those Spanish words the twenty-fifth-century English was now sprinkled with. Taylor had taken a crash course on the new Spanish vocabulary when she'd first arrived at Santa Fe and now translated most of it without thinking. This word escaped her. "*Parejas?* What's that?"

"You don't know what a *pareja* is?" He shook his head. "You must have lived a secluded life."

"I don't know what the term means," Taylor clarified. "I probably know the concept."

"Couples," Echo said. "Boyfriends and girlfriends. People in love."

"Okay, so people exchanged rings when they got married. What does that have to do with DNA scanners?"

"People here exchange rings too. Not only when they get married. Anytime they're in love. The first ring you exchange is usually braided from your hair."

That was either charmingly sentimental or creepy. "What does that have to do with Sheridan?" Taylor asked.

"Nothing."

Taylor stepped closer to the monitor, this time searching it in earnest. Echo had it open to the Time Strainer control panels. Why? Before she could ask, the Time Strainer let out a humming noise that startled Taylor so much, she whirled to look at it. A light at the top of the cubicle glowed. Xavier left his position at the door and edged toward the strainer, laser box in his hand. "What's happening?"

Echo didn't answer. Instead he got up and walked over to the Time Strainer chamber.

"What have you done?" Taylor demanded.

He still didn't answer. Which meant it wasn't a good thing. Taylor sat down in front of the computer, watching data flash onto the screen. Graphs showed the fluctuating levels of energy, matter, and time. Then she noticed the tab of archived news stories on the bottom of the screen. She opened it and found a report on Allana Arad, murdered by Dakine assassins.

She inwardly groaned. Great. Just wonderful. The Time Strainer had now become a way to reunite the lovelorn. Joseph hadn't cared about ripping apart the seams in the fabric of time; why should Echo?

Taylor scanned the Time Strainer commands again. Was there a way to stop it? The light at the top of the chamber grew brighter, threw sparks shimmying downward along the length of the booth. She cursed herself for ever leaving Echo alone with the controls. Who knew how much damage he'd done, what he had changed now.

Jaw clenched, she slid her chair closer to the computer. It was her fault for not destroying the QGPs sooner, for hoping she might discover a way to retrieve Sheridan.

Well, Taylor wouldn't wait any longer. While light from the Time Strainer chamber filled the room, flashing out pulses like a lightning storm, Taylor uploaded her QGP destruct command into the computer. Right before she left the room, she would navigate through Reilly's program, forcing the Time Strainer to send signals to the QGPs that instructed them to turn their own casings into energy. They'd be destroyed in the process. Immediately after that, the Time Strainer would update its signal settings, saving the corrupted data so that it couldn't contact QGPs in the past anymore.

Each keystroke felt painful; each was the death of the hope that Taylor could reorder time for Sheridan. Taylor had wanted to spare her sister all the pain Reilly had delivered and the emotional trauma accompanying it.

Now it would be unalterable. This was the timestream they were all stuck with.

chapter 16

chapter

Joseph, Lee, and Ren made their way to an unused room on the first floor without anyone paying much attention to them. Joseph felt numb as he followed the others inside. He felt detached from this building and everything he was doing. His mind reeled between worry and grief. What had Reilly done to Sheridan in the last month and a half? All the time Joseph and Sheridan had spent in Santa Fe together—it was gone. In the new timestream, she didn't even know he was Joseph and not Echo. Back when she'd been captured by the Traventon government, everyone thought he was Echo.

Lee and Ren chose a room with an exterior wall that faced away from the street. There was less chance anyone would see them emerging out of the side of the building that way. Once they had locked themselves inside the room, Ren drew an oval on the wall. Each of them thrust their laser cutters into the outline to cut the hole. Unfortunately the steel interlacing in the wall kept diffusing the lasers' energy and made cutting the hole slow work.

Ren and Lee immediately turned it into a contest, each straining to pull his laser cutter faster than the other. Ren was winning. "So your leaders favor assassination after all," he said, gloating at Lee. "That's typical. You wave the banner of peace with one hand and carry a dagger in your boot."

Lee pulled harder. The veins in his neck stood out, and a line of sweat formed at the base of his short-cropped hair. "I don't see why you're complaining. Your leaders favored assassination all along."

"Yes, but my leaders agreed to abide by the council's rule. I thought yours did too."

Lee's cut was now slightly farther ahead of Ren's. He let out a laugh. "The council voted not to order an assassination. That didn't mean nobody else could order one."

"Be careful," Ren said. "If you twist your word too often, it will break apart."

Joseph didn't comment. From his perspective, it was a good thing the council leaders kept secrets from one another. If Abraham's group had known one of the bodyguards was planning on killing Reilly, they might not have offered Joseph their help saving Echo.

Lee turned his attention to Joseph. "How did you figure out who Reilly's assistant was? My sources couldn't locate any personnel files." He nodded toward Ren. "The only reason Ren's leaders didn't give an assassination order is that they couldn't find any information about Reilly."

"Not true, Brother Lee," Ren said, huffing as he pulled. "We know Reilly used to date your mother. Have you ever considered your resemblance?"

Lee wiped the sweat off his forehead before it dripped into his eyes. "Watch your insults. Remember, I carry a dagger in my boot."

"Coffee," Joseph said, hoping that rerouting the subject would end their argument.

"What's coffee?" Ren asked.

"A drink from the twenty-first century." Joseph's laser cutter's handle was heating up and he had to shift his grip on it. "It had a mild but addictive stimulant in it. Reilly still has the habit. Taylor smelled the coffee on his breath when he questioned her. When we got to Santa Fe and she realized coffee wasn't available, she told me about it." Joseph adjusted his grip again. The handle felt so hot, he was afraid it would overheat and stop working.

"The Agrocenter in Traventon has several coffee plants to keep Reilly supplied. Xavier's contacts found out the beans are delivered to a man named Tariq. They planted a receiver on one of his shoes and found out he's Reilly's main assistant. Brings him everything. They've been tracking Tariq's crystal ever since."

A memory came to Joseph, unbidden.

He and Sheridan were sitting on the couch in his apartment. Her long red hair spilled over her shoulders in gleaming waves. She watched him, her large hazel eyes showing their interest in everything he said. Joseph had just learned about Tariq and had

*told her about him. "Reilly's assistant brings him whatever he
wants: women, food, and a whole assortment of pleasure drugs."*

"No wonder Reilly has trouble finishing his project," she said.

"Right," Joseph agreed. "Women are a big distraction."

*Sheridan nudged into him, playfully upset. "How would you
know? I never distract you."*

*He dropped a kiss on her lips. "You distract me all the time. You
and thoughts of you."*

Thoughts were all he had left now.

Joseph forced himself back to the present, back to the conversation. "When Tariq isn't fetching things, he stays close to
Reilly. Reilly doesn't go a lot of places. Mostly he stays in the Scicenter, and . . . ," he said with a pang, remembering the reports
from the new timestream, "and the detention center."

Joseph hated the way his memories kept shifting, how painful ones overshadowed the happy ones. All of the time he and
Sheridan had spent together in Santa Fe—it was gone, as unreal
as if he had imagined it. Now he had memories of sitting in
front of a computer in Santa Fe, not only working on the program to save his brother but also studying the detention center's
layout and computer systems.

He had checked in on Taylor daily, mostly to remind her she
had to eat if she wanted to be strong enough to go on the mission. He'd also gone to see her because looking at her was like
looking at Sheridan. He had wondered every day what Reilly
was doing to her, had imagined horrible things.

Joseph gave his laser cutter a particularly strong pull. He
would find her today. And he wouldn't even flinch when he
killed Reilly.

They had almost finished the hole when Joseph's memories shifted again and he realized what had happened. He let go of his laser cutter, left it there, while he leaned against the wall, heart pounding. He took a couple of shallow breaths.

Lee paused and scanned the room. "What's wrong?"

"Nothing," Joseph lied, and made himself return to his laser cutter. It would be too complicated to explain that the past had just altered again. This latest change didn't affect what they needed to do right now—get to Sheridan. But he would have a long talk with his brother about it when they met again.

A new memory bloomed in Joseph's mind.

He was sitting at the meeting with the scientists who had questioned him about Joseph's disappearance.

Helix eyed him with particular suspicion. "You were dating Allana Arad?"

Joseph swallowed, trying to hide the fact that even hearing her name made him feel like hitting something. He unclenched his fists. "Yes," he said. "Her and a few others. It wasn't serious."

"Do you see it as coincidental that both your brother and she disappeared?"

"People who get on the wrong side of the Dakine often disappear. That's not coincidence. That's their policy."

Helix shook his head, making his black-and-gray-striped hair shiver. "When the Dakine are through with people, we find their remains somewhere." He pointed to the crystal on his wrist. "These surface eventually."

Joseph thought about saying, "You're right. It's the government that makes people disappear." Over ten years ago, Joseph and Echo's mother had joined the Traventon army and disappeared on a defensive patrol against San Francisco. *The government said she had been permanently reassigned to one of the out-city posts, but Joseph knew it wasn't true. She was dead. The government didn't like to admit that any of its war measures were unsuccessful.*

Joseph hadn't pointed out this fact to Helix. Instead he said, "Perhaps Allana's crystal will surface somewhere."

Helix let out a grunt, and his eyes narrowed as though he was certain Joseph was withholding information. "You've seen the street-cam's recording. She wasn't taken somewhere. She vanished—was swallowed up in the air."

"I don't know what happened to Allana," Joseph said, more firmly.

But now he did.

Echo had strained her. She was in the Time Strainer bay.

chapter ~~chapter~~

17

Echo pulled Allana from the Time Strainer chamber and laid her gently on the floor. His shoulder burned at the effort. He'd been so intent on saving her, he'd forgotten about his injury. He ignored the throbbing pain shooting down his arm and checked her for laser wounds. He didn't see any. Her face, smooth and perfect, looked nothing like the waxy one he'd seen in the news-feed. No streaks of blood covered her metallic silver hair. Her eyes were shut, her lips open, drawing in breaths in a normal rhythm.

Relief washed over him. He had managed to take her before the Dakine assassins got to her.

Allana's crystal went off, the low, scolding buzz already changing from warning mode to the ever-loudening restriction alarm. He turned to call Xavier and found him already standing there, peering down at Allana.

"That's not Sheridan."

Echo gestured to her wrist. "She needs a crystal blocker."

Xavier knelt down beside her and opened his pack. "Who is she?"

"It's Allana," Taylor called over from behind the computer terminal. "Because that's what we need right now. More Dakine."

"Allana?" Xavier pulled a blocking band from his pack and clamped it around Allana's wrist. He pinched the ends together, activating a glue that melded the band in place. His motions were swift, angry. "You didn't have permission to take anyone from the past."

Taylor stayed seated at the computer terminal. She was viciously tapping out something. "Oh, that has a lot of weight coming from you. Using the Time Strainer has become one big party for the dead, hasn't it?"

"And how did you get here?" Echo called back to her. "Shouldn't you have died a few hundred years ago? Welcome to the party."

"That's different," Taylor said.

Echo squeezed Allana's hand to wake her up. "I had to save her."

"You realize," Taylor called over, biting into each word, "Allana is the reason you were killed in the first place."

Allana moved her head, lolling it from one side to the other. Echo squeezed her hand again. "It wasn't her fault. She didn't realize what the Dakine were like any more than I did."

"Hmmm," Taylor said, still typing. "I'm not sure all of your memories returned after you reconfigured. Do you happen to remember, for example, that Allana dumped you for your brother?"

That memory hadn't been lost. It was there in Echo's mind as vividly as if Allana had just finished scraping her words across his heart.

Last night, he and Allana had been in a car on their way home from the VR center. It had been like a dozen other dates they'd been on. Better, really, because this made two times he'd been out with Allana this week to Joseph's one. Echo kept track of those sorts of things.

Allana pushed her hair off her shoulder, a silver wave that reminded him of polished steel. She leaned back in her chair and let her gray eyes rest on him. There was a smirk in her expression, a look that said it was her right to be adored. "It's time we redefined our relationship," she said softly.

He grinned at her. "Fine. I'm ready to upload something new."

She ran her brightly colored fingernails along the seat fabric between them. "I've been thinking about becoming exclusive with someone. . . ."

He nodded. He knew she was going to tell him that if he wanted her to give up her other boyfriends, he would have to give up all his girlfriends.

Echo dated several girls, although since he and Allana had started matching up, he saw the other girls less and less. Funny how that happened without him even noticing it. He always said he wouldn't get attached to one girl until he was old and boring, and here he had already snipped the other ones away. He wouldn't tell Allana that. Not yet.

Still giving him a coy look, she said, "I've decided I fit best with Joseph."

It took Echo several seconds to process the words, to make sure he had actually heard his brother's name in that sentence. "With Joseph?" Echo repeated.

"You understand, don't you?" Allana asked, only mildly apologetic.

No, he didn't. He didn't understand how she could sit there with that sultry pout on her lips and tell him she wanted his brother. Echo felt the ring on his finger, twined from her silver hair and given to him on the day he agreed to join the Dakine. His throat felt tight. "You told me," he said slowly, "you had never met anyone you were so effortlessly synchronized with—"

"That's the problem," Allana said. "You and I are too much alike. If we stayed together, we would dare each other into more and more trouble. We need to be balanced with the responsible kind, the kind that can clean up our indiscretions. For me, that's Joseph."

Echo didn't argue with her, wouldn't submit to that sort of beggary. He put his crystal to the car control panel and said, "Stop."

The car slowed to a halt. The word stop, *his own word, kept reverberating in his mind. Stop. Stop. Stop. He couldn't stop Allana's decision. Couldn't stop the anger he felt building inside him. The anger at her. At Joseph. At himself. If he had been better somehow—more like Joseph . . . But no. Echo wasn't Joseph, and no matter how much he looked like him, he would never be him.*

Allana leaned toward him. "You're not going to tell me goodbye?"

"I'm bad with good-byes." The door slid open, and Echo stepped from the car without taking another look at Allana.

"Echo," she called after him. "It might not always be this way. Things might change."

He didn't answer. The door slid shut behind him and the car moved on. He wished he could ignore her last comment, just forget everything about her, but it cycled through his mind. *Things might change? Did she expect him to plug himself somewhere and wait for her to reconsider? Was she playing a new game—one in which she claimed Joseph and then expected Echo to pull her away? Neither was going to happen.*

He took out his comlink and deleted her information. She was gone to him. Gone. He fingered her ring, the one braided from her silver hair. He meant to fling it onto the street. He didn't, though. Couldn't. It represented that moment in time when she had given a part of herself to him.

Now he stroked the same silver hair away from her face. "Allana," he murmured, desperate to see her wake up, to know she was all right.

Her eyes fluttered open. She blinked at him, confused. Not seeing him at all.

"Your vision will clear in a moment," he told her.

After another blink, her eyes focused on him. "Assassins . . . ," she whispered. "They're coming for me. They were waiting. . . ." She turned her head, took in her surroundings.

He knew what she was feeling. That odd sensation of being ripped from the street and finding herself somewhere completely different. "You're safe for the moment." He didn't say more. He didn't know how long they would be safe.

Allana let out a breath so heavy with relief, it seemed to ripple over her entire body. She sat up, shaking, and flung her arms around Echo. She pulled herself to him, laid her cheek against his chest, and let out muffled sobs.

He wound his arms around her, murmuring assurances into her hair. He hadn't completely forgiven her for choosing Joseph, but holding her this way felt like forgiveness. She clung to him so tightly, so completely. Had facing the void of death made her realize she loved him?

Echo was aware, vaguely, that there were other people in the room. Xavier still stood near them, shaking his head. Taylor sat at the computer tapping out commands. It didn't matter.

Xavier went back to his post by the door, reading his scanner again. Taylor stopped typing. Echo didn't check to see where she had gone or what she was doing. Allana pulled away to gaze into his eyes. She looked vulnerable, fragile, like she wanted to cling to him forever. "I was on my way to see you, to warn you. I thought we would have more time, and then I saw the cars—the assassins." She gulped hard, finally noticing the Time Strainer beside them. "How did you get me here?" She sat up straighter. "Where are we?"

"Those questions will take some explaining."

She sighed and rested her cheek against his chest again. "That's fine. All that matters is we're safe and we're together." The last part of her sentence was a question, an invitation.

Echo hesitated, then ran his hand along the curve of her back. "Yes," he said. "That's all that matters."

Allana pulled away from him again and gave him an admiring smile. "I should have known you would find a way to save me, Joseph. No one is as smart as you are."

Joseph. She thought he was Joseph. In Echo's urgency to save

Allana, he had forgotten he'd traded places with his ⟨...⟩ He'd cut his hair and changed it back to blond. He'd e⟨...⟩ his crescent moon and replaced it with Joseph's blue star. C⟨...⟩ course Allana had mistaken him for Joseph. That had been the idea.

Slowly, Echo peeled her arms from around him.

She stiffened at his sudden coldness. "What's wrong?"

"I'm not Joseph."

Her mouth opened and shut in surprise. She flushed, gulped. "Echo . . . what are you . . . why would you . . ." Then she understood. Her hand flew to her mouth and her eyes went wide. "You meant for the Dakine to shoot you?" She looked around the room again. "Where's Joseph?"

"He left." Echo stood up, a tightness running through his whole body. "I saved you, Allana. Joseph didn't take the time to do that. But you were right about him being the smartest—that obviously isn't me."

Echo turned from her and saw Taylor leaning against the terminal. She had seen the whole thing, watched his and Allana's love scene turn into a farce. Taylor didn't look at him with any pity though, just icy anger.

"We need to get a few things clear," she said. "I know you're Joseph's brother and he loves you, but I will shoot you and leave you with the scientists if you pull another stunt like that."

Echo stared at her in puzzlement. He'd understood the bulk of the threat, but the part about getting things clear— what needed to be cleared? Was there still gas in the room?

Allana got to her feet and stood beside him. "Who is that girl? What did she say?"

Taylor strode over to Allana, staring her down. "I am your boss." She annunciated the words clearly. "And you had better not give me even two seconds of grief, because I already want to shoot you."

Allana's gaze fixed on Taylor's rank badge. 5,328,121. Most people hid that sort of rank. "Really?" Allana drawled. "When did people in the five millions become the bosses of anything?"

Taylor pulled a laser box from her belt. "That's it. Your two seconds are up."

Before Taylor could fire, Allana let out a shriek and darted behind Echo, using him as a shield. Well, he thought bitterly, why shouldn't she use him to block laser fire?

Echo lifted his hands. He had seen enough historical feeds from the twenty-first century to know it was their sign of surrender. "You don't need to shoot anyone," he said. "Allana will do what you say."

Allana didn't comment about that, so Echo looked over his shoulder at her. "Won't you?"

Allana made a huffing noise that might have been agreement.

Taylor reluctantly lowered her arm. Her expression was firm. "She'd better."

Echo lowered his hands as well. "Taylor is a friend of Joseph's," he told Allana. "We need her help. We're in a restricted section of the Scicenter, and if anyone finds us, we'll face a questioning. Taylor and Xavier will take us out of this building to . . ." He hesitated to tell her they were going to meet up with the DW. Most Dakine members hated the DW. They were the only group in the city the Dakine couldn't intimidate. It was better to hold off telling Allana that news. "We'll go someplace where the Dakine won't find us."

Allana glanced over at Xavier, then peeked around Echo, casting Taylor a suspicious look. "Joseph didn't have such low-ranking friends. Where did these people come from?"

"While we're on the subject of rank," Taylor said, "you might want to hide yours."

Allana looked down at her badge and let out a second shriek. Her badge was blank, devoid of numbers. The screen showed nothing but the same dull gray that badges had when someone died and the government turned off their crystal for the funeral.

She pulled her badge from her shirt and clutched it, tight fisted. "What did you do to my rank?"

The blocking band on Allana's wrist not only hid her crystal's signal from the building sensors but obviously blocked it from the rank program too. Echo unzipped his overalls enough to see his own rank badge. Blank. Just like a funeral. Seemed fitting. Since his scene with Allana, a part of him felt dead.

Allana jiggled her badge as though she could shake numbers into it. "It's illegal to tamper with badges. Fix mine right now or I'll report you to the Enforcers."

Taylor lifted her laser box back up. "You're bothering me again."

Allana let out a third shriek and darted back behind Echo. He had never seen her like this—without her calm confidence. She was being not only foolish but irritating too. Didn't she realize you shouldn't antagonize someone with a laser box?

Allana gripped the back of Echo's shirt. "That girl is

neurofailed. Make her leave or take me somewhere else."

"Or," Echo said slowly, "you could always do what she says, and then neither of us will be shot."

Allana didn't reply. Taylor didn't lower her box. "Well, Little Miss Dakine, what will it be? Are you going to follow my orders?"

Allana let out an offended scoff. "I'm not Dakine," she said, as though the suggestion was ridiculous. "You shouldn't accuse people you don't know."

Echo hadn't noticed before how easy it was for Allana to lie. No, that wasn't true—he had always known she lied convincingly and hadn't cared because he had been part of the lie too. Belonging to the Dakine had been their secret, their bond that Joseph hadn't shared.

But there was something pathetic about lying to people who already knew the truth.

Taylor wasn't amused. "That's it," she said, and pressed the button on the laser box. A beam of light winged by Echo's shoulder, narrowly missing Allana's head.

Allana let out shriek number four.

Taylor didn't lower her box. She squinted, sizing up Allana to take her next shot. "I knew I should have spent more time practicing with this thing."

Echo raised his hands again. "Yeah, about that—you nearly hit me, so until you've got better aim, could you not shoot your laser box off randomly?"

Taylor still didn't lower her box.

"Remember," Echo went on, "I'm Joseph's brother and he

loves me. You wouldn't want to tell him you shot me, would you?"

Echo heard footsteps coming toward them and then Xavier's voice behind him sounding worried. "Taylor, what are you doing?"

Taylor gave Xavier a calm smile. "Just having a talk with our new friends about mission expectations."

Echo turned to Allana, frustration making his words short and low. "Use a gram of sense and agree to do what they ask. They're trying to help us."

For a moment Allana didn't say anything. Her gaze slid between Xavier and Taylor. "All right," Allana finally said. "I'll follow their orders."

"Good." Taylor clipped her laser box back onto her belt. "We need to get out of the building and find a place to lie low until the others rescue Sheridan."

"Lie low?" Allana asked. "What sort of activity is that?"

"We'll go somewhere safe," Taylor clarified. "A park or shopping center where we can blend in with the crowd."

Xavier's features grew stern. "What about the QGPs?"

"I already queued up the my program. I'll take care of the QGPs when we're ready to walk out the door." Taylor held out her hand to him. "Give me your comlink. That way I know you won't tell the rest of the team when it's done."

Xavier unclipped his comlink from his belt, disappointment flashing in his eyes. "You really don't trust anyone, do you?"

"I can't afford trust," she said, her hand still out.

He put the comlink into her outstretched palm. "Have

you ever considered that perhaps you can't afford *not* to trust people?"

She clipped the comlink onto her belt. "Not since a physics adviser stole the credit for my invention. That pretty much cured me of trust."

Taylor walked over to where Xavier's packs lay on the ground. She knelt down, sifted through the contents, and pulled out a gas mask. "Our first problem is that we don't have enough gas masks. No one brought one for Echo's girlfriend." She gave Echo a quick look. "I mean ex-girlfriend. Sorry about that."

Echo took his gas mask out and noted how it attached. "Allana and I can share one. In between, we'll hold our breath."

Xavier shook his head. "Once gas is in the air, each time you put the mask to your mouth you'll capture some of the gas inside. The mask won't be able to filter it out before you breathe it in."

Allana finally stepped all of the way out from behind Echo. "Why can't Echo and I just leave? We didn't do"—she gestured around at the scientists sprawled on the floor—"whatever it was you did to these people. We're not with you."

"Fine with me," Taylor said. "Once we go out those doors, you can go wherever you want. But Echo comes with us."

"Why?" Allana asked, wary.

"Because my sister's imprisonment isn't going to be for nothing." Taylor turned to Xavier. "What about the faulty gas masks? Is there a way to fix one?"

"If we can find the leak." Xavier walked over to where Taylor's old mask lay on the floor. He picked it up and turned it over in his hands, examining it. She went to look at it with him.

Allana tapped her rank badge with disgust, then slipped it into her pocket and fingered the band over her crystal. "How do I get this off?"

"Don't," Echo told her. "If you take it off, you'll trigger the building alarm."

She kept fiddling with it, clearly not understanding the seriousness of their situation. He stepped over to her and pulled her hand away from the band. "You need to leave that on until we're out of the city."

Allana's head jerked up. "Out of the city? We can't leave Traventon."

"If we don't, the assassins will find us again. We'll be killed." Echo didn't add that he had already seen it happen, that he had watched a newscast of her being carried, limp and bloody, to the morgue collector. "Xavier and Taylor can take us to another city."

"No," Allana said, twisting at the band on her wrist again. "We can't leave our friends, our jobs—our rank."

"I can." Rank didn't seem so important anymore. Echo waited for Allana to ask if Joseph would be going with them, braced himself for the question. He didn't want to see the relief on Allana's face when she found out Joseph would be there too.

She didn't ask. Instead she kept yanking at the band over her crystal. "I can't leave all my things." More yanking. "My father will find a way to protect me." She let go of the band and reached for her comlink. "I'll call him and tell him what's happened."

As soon as she pulled her comlink from her belt, Echo reached over and snatched it from her hands. "Allana, you need to understand this: If you stay in Traventon, the Dakine will kill you. Your father couldn't protect you the first time assassins came for you, could he?"

She frowned, then set her jaw. "That's because he didn't have time to get a signal-jamming detector for me. I'll get one though. A bodyguard too." She stepped toward Echo and reached for her comlink, trying to take it from his hand.

He held it away from her. "Then the Dakine will find another way to kill you. They always do. As soon as the signal on your crystal is unblocked, they'll know where you are every second of every day."

Allana's hands drooped back to her sides. He could see the fear clicking through her gray eyes as she considered his words.

"Are you going to trust the waiter in the next foodmart you eat at?" he went on. "If he's Dakine, he might get an order to poison your food. And you'll have to be careful about when and where you call for a car. One could show up with explosives attached to it."

Allana took several deep breaths and composed herself. It was almost like seeing her put on a persona. She smiled at Echo, suddenly calm, and stroked the edges of the band. "Then I'll keep this bracelet on so my crystal stays blocked."

"You can't," he said. "Someone would notice. Besides, how would you use food dispensers or cars without a crystal?"

Allana put her hand on Echo's arm, her face raised hopefully. "You could figure out a way to make things work for us. Your mind—Echo, it's special. You sprint where others crawl."

Now that she needed something from him, he was special again. She had said the same sort of thing when she'd asked him to join the Dakine. He wondered if it had always just been manipulation.

He brushed her hand off his arm. "I'm leaving. You can stay behind if you want. Maybe the government will believe that you didn't have anything to do with this. Should we tell Xavier and Taylor you don't need a gas mask after all?"

Allana hesitated, grimaced, and looked around at the unconscious men and women on the floor. She let out a grudging sigh. "Fine. I'll go with you."

Echo smiled, relieved, but didn't give her back her comlink. He slid it onto his belt, then turned and walked over to where Xavier and Taylor had taken the gas mask. Xavier was holding the mask up to a light, turning it one way and then another. "I can't see a leak," he said, "and I don't have a sensor that identifies gear failures."

Echo let his gaze sweep over the equipment in the room. "They must have one of those around here." His eyes stopped on Taylor. She had dumped out a container of tools and was filling it with water from a dispenser. "What's Taylor doing?" Echo asked Xavier.

Xavier glanced at her, and his brows drew together, puzzled. "I thought she was looking for a sensor."

Taylor straightened and waved to Xavier. "Bring the mask over here."

He did, eyeing the container full of water. "Thirsty?"

Instead of answering, she took the mask and plunged it into the water.

Xavier stared, incredulous. "What are you doing?"

Echo cocked his head, watching as she held the mask down.

"She must be cleaning it. In the twenty-first century, people used water to wash everything. Clothes, dishes, themselves."

Xavier kept staring. "Dirt isn't the problem."

Taylor's arms were immerged up to her elbows. "Sometimes the simplest method is the best." She lifted the mask out of the water, her finger pressed to one of the folds in the breathing tube. "Here's the hole." She handed the mask to Xavier. "I followed the trail of air bubbles."

"Ah," Xavier said, and nodded. "That would be an equally good way of finding the leak." He headed to his pack, his finger over the hole. "I'll put some artificial skin on this. That should patch the hole."

Taylor shook the water off her hands and motioned to Echo. "Help me get a pair of overalls off one of the scientists for Allana." She walked past the nearest one, and went to a man with short-cropped bronze hair. It took Echo a moment to realize it was Helix, the science chairman. Taylor's eyes narrowed at him with clear dislike. She knelt beside him and, without any gentleness, undid his belt and dropped it to the ground beside him. Then she worked on his overall fasteners.

Echo knelt by Helix's feet, pulling the man's boots off. "Do you know Helix?"

"He tried to kill my sister. Nearly succeeded, too." Taylor stopped herself. "I guess that didn't happen in this timestream. Who knows what he's done to her in this one."

Echo watched Taylor for a moment, noting the hard edge in her expression, which seemed a contradiction to the soft curves of her face. He'd never seen Sheridan, wouldn't have known her if he passed her in a hallway, but he felt responsible for what had happened to her anyway. "I'm sorry," he said.

Taylor yanked one of Helix's arms out of his overalls. "Not as sorry as I am."

Echo pulled Helix's other arm out and then turned the man on his side so that Taylor could slide the overalls off his legs. Helix had the skinny, wrinkled legs of an old man. "This," Echo said, "is not a sight I want to remember."

Once the overalls were free, Taylor threw them at Allana. "You got a promotion. You're the new science chairman."

Allana caught the overalls and sullenly put them on.

Taylor gestured to Helix's rank badge. "You're in luck. It comes with an awesome rank."

The overalls were too big for Allana, and she had to fold the sleeves under so they didn't hang past her hands. "We'll all get memory washes if we're caught," she said.

"Which is why we can't get caught." Taylor strode over to the computer, sat down, and went to work on her program. Navigating around code barriers usually took a while, but before long Taylor stood and headed toward the door. "The deed is done."

Echo didn't know what a deed was although he vaguely recalled it had something to do with buying property. Still, he knew what she meant. The destruct signal had been sent. He headed to the door behind Xavier and Taylor, gas mask in hand.

Each of their shirts came with a hood, one that not only covered the head but had a clear flap inside that could be pulled over the face. Xavier and Taylor had already put theirs on. As Echo grabbed his from the back of his shirt, he told Allana, "Stay behind the rest of us. Our clothes deflect laser fire."

Allana gripped her gas mask. "But no one gave me any

protection? How nice."

Xavier paused, unfastened his overalls, and pulled off his shirt.

"What are you doing?" Taylor asked in disbelief. "You need that."

He handed his shirt to Allana. "Let no one say I protected myself instead of protecting an innocent woman."

"No one would say that." Taylor fluttered a hand in Allana's direction. "She's not innocent. Did you forget she's Dakine?"

"Lies and libel," Allana said, glowering as she pulled the shirt on. "There are laws against defamation."

Taylor ignored her and hit the button on the door panel. "You know what people will say, Xavier? They'll say you're foolish. I'm already saying it."

Before the door opened, Helix's comlink went off. Almost simultaneously another scientist's comlink chimed. Then more went off, a discordant symphony that filled the room. Outside, a buzzing alarm sounded in the hall.

Xavier placed his gas mask over his face. "The front entrances will be blocked," he told Echo and Allana. "Follow the wall to the stairwell. We'll escape off the roof." He stepped out into the hallway, laser box drawn and gas vials in his hands.

"The roof?" Allana repeated in disbelief. "How are we going to get off the roof?"

No one answered her. There wasn't time.

chapter chapter
18

Joseph, Ren, and Lee walked quickly down the street. Getting out of the Scicenter had been easy enough. After they'd gone through the hole, Ren had reached back inside, grabbed the edge of an equipment station, and pulled it against the wall to hide what they'd done.

From the outside, the hole had been much too noticeable— an uneven oval standing out against the smooth, white surface of the building. So Lee had pulled a small hologram camera from his belt and taken a picture of an intact portion of the wall. He left the button-sized projector sitting on the ground where it could project a flawless holographic picture of the wall to cover the ruined spot.

Hopefully no one would realize what they had done until Xavier, Taylor, Echo, and—Joseph didn't even like thinking her name—Allana had left the building.

Allana. Joseph clenched his teeth, angry that his brother had brought her here, and angry at himself for not realizing beforehand that Echo might do it.

This was just what they needed now when the mission had already become impossibly hard: a Dakine member to drag around and protect. Hadn't Echo already learned that he couldn't trust her?

Ren checked the scanner on his comlink to make sure nobody had rushed out of the Scicenter to come after them. No one had.

The walkway wasn't too busy. A few people strolled by. Other people stood at the edge of the street waiting for cars.

In a few more minutes, Joseph, Ren, and Lee would reach the mobile crystal on Charles Street. They would need a car to meet with the DW and need one to get to the detention center. Lee kept his stride casual and he smiled, as though the three of them were talking about the latest light-ball game. "How come none of us remember the plan to free Sheridan?"

Joseph had his own comlink out, looking at the detention-center layout. "We were in the protection of the Scicenter's time vector field when the past switched, so we didn't change. We still remember the old timestream even though a new one replaced it. But our brains aren't designed to deal with two different realities at the same time. Our minds are mixing them together, rejecting the new memories."

Joseph turned his comlink to a video feed and tapped in Mendez's number. Mendez had a secret comlink, one he used only for DW business. He would know what to do and how to help them rescue Sheridan.

Mendez's face appeared on the screen. As usual, his expression was stern and unreadable. "Yes?"

"We have a problem," Joseph said. How could he explain this in a short time? "We need help with the detention center. Is there somewhere we can meet?"

Mendez's eyes narrowed. "Who are you? How did you get this number?"

Joseph stared at him, not wanting to hear what he was hearing. "Mendez, it's me. Joseph . . ." Even as he said the words, he knew they wouldn't matter. The timestream had changed, and apparently in the new one, Mendez wasn't their contact. After a moment's thought it made sense. Sheridan had found Mendez in the old timestream, and he'd been their contact ever since. In the new one, someone else had the job. Joseph searched for that memory and could vaguely picture a man—an unassuming older man you normally wouldn't notice in a crowd. Joseph couldn't remember his name or comlink number.

Mendez gave Joseph a scowl to show he didn't like being bothered. "I don't know who you are. You must be mistaking me for someone else."

"No," Joseph said. "While I was working with the QGPs, I inadvertently changed time. That's the problem. We need to rescue Sheridan from the detention center, but I don't remember how we planned on doing it or who our contact was."

Mendez shook his head. He looked like he was about to turn his comlink off.

"Wait," Joseph told him. "Ask about it. Someone in the DW knows what I'm talking about. We have a contact there."

At the mention of the initials *DW*, Mendez's eyes turned into cold slits. "Is this a joke? You call up a stranger and accuse him of belonging to the DW? I wonder if the Enforcement Department would think that was funny?"

The screen went dark. Mendez had ended the call.

"Great," Lee said. "That went really well."

Ren's pace was faster now, angry. His dark ponytail swished across his shoulders with every step he took. "Didn't you realize this might happen before you changed time? Didn't you make contingency plans?"

Joseph stared at his comlink, unwilling to clip it back onto his belt yet. "I knew Taylor and I would be safe. . . ." He couldn't finish the sentence. The pressure he'd felt earlier was there again, pushing against his chest.

"Maybe Mendez will call back," Lee said. "You told him to ask people about what you said. Some of them know about our mission. Somebody will understand what has happened."

"He's not going to call back," Ren said, his words coming out in a sharp rhythm. "It sounded like a trap. Strangers claim to know someone in your organization, although they can't remember who. Mendez probably thought his comlink was compromised, and he's incinerating it right now."

Ren was right, Joseph knew. Not only was their mission damaged, but he had also messed up their way back home. Were they even supposed to meet at the Fisherman's Feast restaurant when this was all over? If not, where were they supposed to go?

Joseph searched his memory but could only think about the night before he left Santa Fe. He'd forgotten to meet Sheridan for dinner. How could he have forgotten? How could he have messed everything up this badly?

"So what do we do now?" Lee asked.

"We do what we have to," Joseph said. "You have para-military training, and I can figure out a way to outsmart the Enforcers. We'll find a way to rescue Sheridan by ourselves."

chapter
19

As Taylor rushed out into the hallway, she braced herself. She knew what would happen, had gone through it during training. Enforcers. Darkness. Gasbots shooting at them.

Everything happened quickly. Doors in the hallway opened; people walked out. She saw the surprise on their faces, the fright. Most rushed back into their rooms. Two Enforcers dressed in the black laser-deflecting armor rounded the corner. Both lifted their laser boxes to shoot.

Xavier threw down two vials—the sleeping and concealing gases. A black cloud exploded into the hallway, instantly darkening the area and masking the group.

The Enforcers shot anyway. Slivers of light cut through the cloud, arrows in the roiling darkness. Taylor lunged against the left wall. She hoped Xavier hadn't been hit. She wanted to call out to him and tell him to use a disrupter. She didn't speak for fear it would give away her position. She pushed forward along the wall, hurrying toward the stairwell. More shots cut past her. She felt the heat of one hitting her back.

She knew why Xavier hadn't used his laser-disrupter box. It would destroy their own laser boxes as well as the Enforcers', and he didn't want to lose those weapons. He was gambling that the Enforcers wouldn't be conscious long enough to hit any of them. A dangerous gamble for him since he'd given his shirt to Allana.

With one hand on the wall, Taylor hurried down the hallway. A voice from the building's speaker repeated, "Air toxicity is high. Evacuate the corridor immediately." Colored spots of light flicked on the wall, pointing the way to the elevators. She reached the bend in the hallway. The gas had arrived there first, a wave of darkness that covered everything she could see. It wouldn't last long though. Three or four minutes. The building's air filters were already working to clear it.

Taylor heard noises in front of her. Footsteps, an Enforcer calling for backup, people coughing. She couldn't tell where anyone from her group was. For all she knew, everyone else had been captured.

Even if she got separated from the rest of the group, Taylor had been trained to continue on with the escape plan. She would use a lock disabler on the stairwell door, go to the roof, and zip line to the building just east of the Scicenter. From there, she would use another zip line to go to the building behind that one—the courthouse. The idea was to get far enough away from the Scicenter to avoid the Enforcers converging on and searching it. Once she made it to the courthouse roof, she would take off the scientist overalls, use a laser cutter to get inside the building, and then blend in with the streams of people who were coming and going inside. The DW had taped a mobile crystal underneath a bench outside the courtyard. She would use it to take a car to the Traventon Plaza Recreation Center, then go to Fisherman's Feast.

It was one thing to complete a mission alone during training; it was another to consider that possibility in a darkened hallway surrounded by people who could kill her. The voices in the hall stopped, replaced by the thumps of people hitting the floor. Where was the stairwell? Shouldn't someone on the team have reached it by now?

Taylor heard the clicking sound of doors being locked. The building's sensors had realized that anyone who hadn't passed out by now was wearing a gas mask—was an intruder. In another moment the gasbots would come out. They wouldn't be able to locate movement through the black cloud, but they would still shoot randomly into the hallway. The group needed to make it to the stairwell before then. Xavier wasn't protected.

The next sound was the twang of small doors springing open to release gasbots.

Had she missed the stairwell somehow?

A rectangle of light flashed a few yards ahead of her. Xavier had gotten the stairwell door open. His profile was visible against the outline of light.

"Run!" he yelled to the others. If they could all make it through the doorway before the gasbots reached them, they could lock them out.

Taylor sprinted toward the door. She heard footsteps behind her. Echo and Allana. She also heard the whir of the gasbots moving down the hallway. The ripping sound of laser fire filled the air. Streaks of silver light cut past her.

Seconds later, Taylor ran through the door. Allana followed her, gasping so quickly that the air filter in her gas mask flapped back and forth like a trapped butterfly. Echo came in last and pounded the button to close and lock the door. Taylor was fairly certain Echo could have outrun Allana. He had kept behind her to shield her from laser fire.

Xavier had already turned on the speed boosters in his shoes. Taylor and Echo reached down and turned on theirs as well.

Allana looked up the stairwell, still gasping. "Why are we going up?"

"Because they'll expect us to go down." Xavier motioned for Allana to come over to him. "Hold on to my back. You won't be able to keep up otherwise."

Allana groaned out a protest. Taylor didn't wait around to hear more of Allana's complaints. She bounded up the stairs, the boosters in her boots hissing as they rocketed her upward. It was like jumping on a trampoline. She took the steps four at a time, could have even done more, but leaping that far made it hard to turn in the stairwells.

The sound of the group's jumping steps echoed all around. Could anyone outside hear them? Had the Enforcers figured out where they'd gone? Every time she made a turn in the stairwell, she expected to see black-clad Enforcers careening downward toward them. She looked for their dark forms, for the helmets that made them seem inhuman.

Echo passed Taylor, and then a floor later, Xavier passed her too. His movements, even carrying Allana's extra weight, were precise and athletic. Every time he landed, Allana jostled against his back and let out a small *ooof!* sound.

When the group reached the nineteenth floor, Xavier's boosters began to burn out. Echo switched places with Xavier then, carrying Allana on his back. Xavier took the lead, even though his boosters were only half strength. "I'll go ahead and get the door open," he said, and disappeared around a stairwell bend.

Just past the thirty-first floor, Echo's boosters ran out. They weren't designed to carry two people.

"I can't carry her," Taylor said. Her boosters were getting low too, and Allana weighed at least as much as Taylor did.

"Go," Echo told Taylor. "It's only four floors. We'll run up the regular way."

Allana looked put out by this news, which irked Taylor. Boosters or not, the rest of them had sprinted up twenty-seven flights of stairs. Allana hadn't done anything but hang on to men and pretend they were her personal ponies. Still, Echo took Allana by the hand, murmured words of encouragement, and pulled her up the stairs.

Taylor gritted her teeth as she left them. Allana had dumped Echo and then broken Dakine rules so that assassins had hunted him down. And yet Echo still treated her like she was a damsel in distress. What sort of sign did he need that it was time to move on? A literal knife sticking out of his back?

When Taylor reached the top floor, Xavier was leaning

against the doorframe and getting his zip-line shooter from his pack. Taylor told him Echo and Allana were on their way, then took his place in the doorway to keep it open. While she waited, she pulled the gas mask off her face and shoved it into her pocket. Xavier, soundless as a cat, padded over to the far edge of the building to set up the zip line.

Echo and Allana finally appeared. Allana was red-faced and out of breath. Strands of her silver hair clung to her neck in sweaty tendrils. She must have never exercised a day in her life.

Taylor motioned for them to follow her. "We need to go to the side of the roof. Be quiet, quick, and stay near the building's edge so the people on the floor below don't hear us."

Taylor went that way, carefully placing each foot on the roof. It felt like there should be a breeze up here so high. Instead the air felt stagnant, trapped against the opaque dome that covered the city.

Behind her, Allana panted out the words, "Couldn't you have come up with an escape plan that didn't involve running up stairs?"

Taylor ignored her. She'd reached the edge of the building and picked up her pace. "Hurry," she told the others.

"*Sangre!*" Allana cursed. "We shouldn't be so close to the side of the building. I can't . . . *sangre* . . . This is too dangerous."

They weren't that close. The edge was a sidewalk's width. Taylor went faster, just to show she wasn't afraid. "We don't want the people down on the street to notice us and report us." The team was counting on the fact that people down below on the streets were used to ignoring the videos that played on the tops of buildings. Their gazes wouldn't be drawn up here because of movement.

Echo's voice was gentle and coaxing as he spoke to Allana. "You won't fall. Here—hold on to my belt and watch my back."

Taylor laughed and looked over her shoulder at Echo. "If you want someone to watch your back, I think you chose the wrong person."

Allana took hold of the back of Echo's belt. "What's that supposed to mean?" she snapped.

Taylor never explained the twenty-first-century figures of speech and didn't plan on starting now. She kept walking along the ledge. The trick was not to look over the side of the building.

"It's an old saying," Echo told Allana. "When men went to battle and fought by hand, they could only see the enemy in front of them. They needed comrades to watch their back. The term came to mean anyone who protected you."

Taylor turned around to face Echo, going backward as she did. "I'm impressed you knew that."

"I'm a historian," he said.

"So are Joseph and Jeth, but their knowledge of past slang is pathetic."

"Oh," Allana said, her tone changing from frightened to condescending, "you're one of Joseph's historian friends. That partially explains your rank, I suppose."

Echo didn't pay attention to Allana's commentary on his profession. His attention was riveted to Taylor and her backward progress. "You're the one who needs to watch her back, or you'll go off the edge. You do realize how far down it is, don't you?"

"I'm fine," Taylor said. She was; she could judge where to put her feet by seeing where she'd come from. Still, she turned around. Her comlink pulsed out a tingling sensation and she smelled pine trees, the signal that Joseph had messaged her. While she walked toward Xavier, she looked at the message.

It read, *Have you destroyed the QGPs yet?*

She used the speech-to-text function to send a message back to him. "Have you already rescued Sheridan? How is she?"

A moment later she got another buzz and a whiff of pine. *Be reasonable*, the message read. *Think about what Sheridan would want you to do.*

"I am. Sheridan would want me to rescue her." And then because Taylor was still angry at Joseph, she whispered into the comlink, "By the way, Echo used the Time Strainer to save Allana. Lovely girl, except I'm afraid she'll jeopardize the whole mission. Do you have any messages for her?"

It took only a moment for the scent of pine to wash over Taylor. *No*, Joseph wrote back, *but tell Echo the next time I see him, we're going to have a long talk about that choice.*

Taylor let out an incredulous grunt that her comlink wrote as *Chuuu!* She erased it, and said, "That's the pot calling the kettle black."

Tingle. Pine. *What does that mean?*

Taylor had reached Xavier. He'd already set up a stand, a thin rod about six feet tall.

"You tell me," Taylor said into her comlink. "Then I'll know you have Sheridan and her memories are still intact."

Xavier aimed his zip-line shooter and shot. A nearly invisible cord zinged across the distance between the buildings, connecting somewhere on the other building's roof. Xavier pulled the line tight.

Another tingle and whiff of pine. *Mendez isn't our contact anymore. Do you remember who is?*

Taylor let out a stream of swearwords, which the comlink did its best to phonetically transcribe. Frustration gripped her. She didn't know the new timestream well enough to be able to retrieve those sorts of details. "How are you going to rescue Sheridan without outside help?"

We'll do it, Joseph wrote back. *If you remember our contact, message me. Otherwise we'll meet at the old rendezvous place.*

The Fisherman's Feast restaurant was still run by DW. That wouldn't have changed. Taylor and Joseph could go there and ask to speak to the chef. He could check up on their story.

"I've got to go," Taylor said into her comlink. "Let me know when you have Sheridan." Taylor shoved her comlink back onto her belt.

Xavier had attached the line to the stand, then used his laser cutter to slice the line from the gun.

Taylor peered over the edge of the building. The ground somehow seemed farther away than it had in the VR programs. The Enforcers' cars converging around the building were tiny. She could make out several rail-jumpers zooming along the streets that led to the Scicenter. Most Enforcers used cars like everyone else, but in emergencies they called elite Enforcers who rode rail-jumpers. The high-speed bikes could jump over the slow-moving cars in front of them. From here, they looked like little leapfrogging toys.

Xavier attached a handle and two slender rope harnesses to the zip line. During training, Taylor had argued against using the harnesses because they took longer to get into and out of, but Joseph had told her the council wanted every safety measure possible to protect her. Now she realized the harnesses were for Echo as much as they were for her. Joseph hadn't known how injured Echo would be after his transportation into the future.

Xavier unbuckled the first harness. "Two people will have to share." He eyed Taylor, calculating. "I'll wrap the harness around you and Allana. It won't be comfortable, but it will work."

Allana took a look over the side of the building and then backed up, gasping. "We can't go over that. Are you neuro-crashed? We'll all die."

Xavier motioned for her to come over. "The equipment will hold. We've tested it."

Allana stared at the meager pole that held up the zip line and shook her head. Her silver hair swayed around her shoulders. "That thing will come loose."

Echo took hold of Allana's arm and tugged her forward. "We don't have time to argue about it. It won't take the Enforcers long to figure out where we went."

Allana planted her feet and pulled her arm away from Echo. "You can't trust these people. You don't even know them."

"You're right," Echo said patiently. "Joseph knows them, and I trust him."

Allana still didn't move. She swallowed uncomfortably and

fidgeted with her crystal band.

"Don't you trust Joseph?" Echo asked her.

Allana peered at the zip line and didn't speak.

Honestly, it was like some sort of soap opera. It was bad enough the group had to take Allana along, readjusting things at every step and risking themselves for her. Taylor was not going to let herself be taken prisoner because Allana was having second thoughts about their escape plan.

"Do it," Taylor said.

Allana gave her a scathing look. "I don't take orders from you, Ms. Five Million."

Taylor yanked her laser box from her belt. "Your two seconds are *so* up."

She fired at Allana's throat. This time, Taylor didn't miss. Allana let out a whine, stiffened, and toppled backward.

Echo caught her shoulders before she hit the roof. He stared at Taylor incredulously. "Did you even check your laser-box setting before you shot?"

Taylor made a waving motion in Xavier's direction. "Get her into the harness."

Echo half dragged, half carried Allana toward the harness, all the while staring at Taylor. "You didn't, did you?" His blue eyes swirled with anger.

Taylor clipped her laser box onto her belt. "It's been on stun since we got to Traventon."

Echo helped Xavier thread the harness around Allana's arms. "Every time laser boxes turn on, they reset themselves. You're always supposed to check the setting before you shoot. Next time you get impatient, you could kill one of us."

"All right then, how about next time you don't give me reason to shoot one of you."

Echo didn't reply to that. They were done with the harness, and Allana hung, mannequin-like, near the building's edge. Her eyes looked blankly upward at the white opaque dome.

Xavier surveyed her, then the second harness. "I should go first; that way I can catch Allana on the other roof. After I go, push her off, then wrap the harness around you and Echo."

"Go," Taylor told him. "I can take care of it."

Xavier grabbed hold of the handle he'd attached to the zip line, took a running start, and leaped off the edge. He flew through the air, zooming toward the other building. It would take him only a minute to reach it. Taylor slipped the harness over Echo's injured shoulder. While Echo slid the other side of the harness on, Taylor took hold of Allana and towed her to the edge of the building. Taylor gave Allana a kick in the seat of her pants, which toppled her off the roof and set her swinging back and forth as she slid down the line. Silver hair streamed out behind her like a metallic flame.

Echo walked forward, holding the harness buckles out to Taylor. The straps weren't big enough to fit around both of them. "And now?"

Taylor snapped the buckles together across Echo's chest and held on to the strap that went over his uninjured shoulder. "Now we jump."

Echo didn't move toward the edge. "I don't want you to slip. We'll figure out—"

"We don't have time for that." Taylor looked over at the door they'd come through. "Go. I'll be fine." She gripped the strap tighter. "Unlike your last girlfriend, I know how to hold on to a guy."

A hint of a smile lifted Echo's lips and he wrapped his good arm around her waist. "All right. Let's fly." They took running steps. One, two, and the roof disappeared. Gravity jerked them downward. Taylor held her breath, then the line caught them, and they glided through the air, dangling from a line so thin it seemed to vanish along the way. The wind rushed against her face, knocking off her hood and tugging at her bun.

Allana reached the next building. Xavier grabbed her arm as she went by, yanking her to stop her. It sort of worked. She only partially hit the roof.

"Ouch," Taylor said.

Echo made a grumbling sound in his throat. "I still can't believe you shot her." He turned his head to consider her. "There weren't laser boxes in your time. Who taught you to use one?"

"Joseph."

"Joseph? When did he learn to use one?"

"After you were killed."

Echo didn't reply to that because they reached the other building. Both concentrated on the approaching roof. "Lift your feet up," Echo said.

She did, and Echo landed on the roof, running to slow his momentum. He didn't stumble, didn't even jar much. He set her down carefully.

"You're pretty good at this," she said.

"It's like a VR adventure program—well, except for the threat of actual death. That's new."

Xavier had already unhooked Allana's harness from the zip

line. Taylor unhooked Echo's, then Xavier pushed a button at the base of the zip line, which sent a heated pulse through the rope. A white flash went along its length and it disintegrated. Bits of ash fluttered downward. When the Enforcers found the stand on the roof, at least they wouldn't be able to use the zip line to follow.

Fast paced, Xavier, Taylor, and Echo carried Allana toward the other side of the building. When they reached the edge, Xavier shot a zip line to the next building, tied it to a rod, and cut the line from his shooter. Taylor helped him attach Allana's and Echo's harnesses to the line. Xavier went first, Taylor pushed Allana off, and then she and Echo stood on the side of the building. "You still know how to hold on to a guy?" he asked.

She grabbed on to his harness strap. "I won't let you go."

He leaped and they sailed through the air. Now that she knew what to expect, there was something exhilarating about flying through the air this way. "This would be fun," she said, "except for, you know, that threat-of-death thing."

"Yeah," he said. "You'd be surprised at how many activities that ruins."

She laughed, and then she felt bad for laughing, for enjoying this moment. She shouldn't enjoy anything until Sheridan was free. And depending on what Reilly had done to Sheridan, maybe not even then.

chapter 20

chapter

Sheridan paced the length of her gray metal cell. Six steps forward took her past the bed that lay against one side of the room and the sink and toilet that stood on the other. She pivoted at the door and took six steps back to the wall. She did this exercise without thinking now, hours on end sometimes, so that her muscles wouldn't atrophy. She would need to be in shape when she escaped. *When*, she kept telling herself, not *if*. She wouldn't let go of *when*.

Two things were constants in her life now. The first was the piped-in propaganda that played all day long. A velvety-voiced woman extolled the virtues of Traventon and expounded on the roles of citizens. Sometimes the voice even got philosophical about how to best achieve happiness. Happiness always had something to do with being loyal to the city.

Still, Sheridan appreciated the voice. Listening to it gave her a chance to practice her accent. Sheridan repeated sentences to get the rhythm of the language, the cadence of words that only resembled the words she used to speak.

"Traventon's policies," the voice purred, "have made our people the most elite group in the world. The governing committee will continue to achieve this excellence—by choosing the best genes to generate our society, by deleting anyone who poses a threat, and by controlling information to ensure everyone is educated in the area they're most fit for."

Sheridan repeated the words like an acolyte in prayer. When she escaped from here, she needed to speak like everyone else so that she could blend in. *When*, not *if*.

The second constant in Sheridan's life was hunger. Her guards weren't starving her. They gave her three nourishment bars a day. The bars didn't even taste that bad, at least not after you got used to them. But Sheridan still ate sparingly.

At first, she didn't eat because she was afraid the food might be drugged. She reasoned that if she ate only a little of each bar, she could judge if it had any ill effects on her before she consumed the whole thing. Later she kept herself hungry on purpose as a way to gauge whether she was in a virtual reality program or not. Reilly liked to do that—switch around her reality in an attempt to get information from her.

After Sheridan practiced her accent each morning, she picked one of the novels she'd read in her English classes and tried to recall each event, chapter by chapter. She wasn't sure how many of the classics still existed here in the twenty-fifth century. Maybe none. Jeth and Echo had told her that only the literary committee was allowed to write novels now. If Sheridan remembered the stories she'd read, she could rewrite them once she got out of here. That way they wouldn't be completely lost, even if her writing would be a sorry substitute for Dickens, Shakespeare, or Cervantes.

Today her novel was *Pride and Prejudice*.

She was Elizabeth playing the piano for Lady Catherine while Mr. Darcy stood by watching. Proud, silent, handsome Mr. Darcy. He kept looking like Echo. He shouldn't. Echo had blue hair, and if he hadn't dyed it, it would have been blond. Didn't the story say somewhere that Darcy had brown hair? She couldn't remember. So many details had slipped her mind.

Sheridan shut her eyes and tried to remember images from the movie. Images came, but not of the movie. Reilly had shown her so many images since she'd been here that she was beginning to have a hard time distinguishing which were real, which were dreams, and which were virtual reality programs. The only thing she was sure about were the memories. Those were easy. They were the happy ones.

She wondered, not for the first time, if Reilly wanted her to lose her sanity. Was it easier to extract information from a person after you'd broken their mind into pieces?

She didn't want to think about Reilly. Sheridan let her thoughts center on Echo, seeing the lines of his face, remembering his smile. Echo's features were like the words of a poem. You couldn't exactly say why they went together so well, what made his chin or nose or cheekbones better than anyone else's. But placed all together like they were, they created something beautiful. Something you wanted to stare at.

The light panel on the ceiling flickered and then went out, plunging the room into complete darkness.

Sheridan held her breath, waiting for the light to come on again. It couldn't be night already. She'd been up for only a couple of hours. The propaganda was still playing. Someone down the corridor—another prisoner—yelled something. It was too muffled for her to understand what. A few seconds later someone in the opposite direction shouted something too.

Sheridan couldn't decide whether it was comforting or not that sometimes she heard the other prisoners. It was nice to know she wasn't alone, and it was also horrible to know she wasn't alone.

At any rate, the prisoners should have realized by now that crying out only made things worse. It let the guards know they were getting to you. They planned these power outages, she was sure. They wanted everyone to wonder if it would ever be light again.

Sheridan stood stock-still, breathing in the darkness. *Nothing is silently coming into my room*, she told herself. Nothing was creeping toward her. She would have heard the door swish open. Unless it swished open while one of the prisoners was yelling.

The lights flickered back on, dimmer this time. That was another thing the guards did. Each day the light in the room seemed weaker. Or maybe that was a by-product of being here—the way things grew darker. It was enough to make her wish for a virtual reality program that took place outside somewhere in the sunshine.

About a week after Reilly had captured Sheridan, and it had become clear to him that bribery, threats, and bouts of slapping weren't going to get her to cooperate, she was operated on. Reilly told her afterward that the surgery had only been to implant the crystal in her wrist. She had one now like every other citizen of Traventon. She should be proud of that fact, he told her. It meant she belonged.

Sheridan knew Reilly had done something else to her though, put something in her brain. A small scar had appeared on her left temple, a tiny place that felt bumpy. Whatever Reilly had put into her, it didn't tell him her secrets. He still didn't know Taylor built the QGP, not Sheridan.

When Sheridan had gone to bed the first night after her surgery, she found herself transported back to Knoxville. One moment she was drifting off to sleep in her cell; the next she was sitting in a twenty-first-century office.

Wooden bookcases lined two walls, filled with books with worn covers. A ceiling fan slowly spun overhead. A middle-aged man sat behind a large oak desk typing something on his computer. He was heavy-set, with graying hair at his temples and pronounced bags under his eyes. He wore a tweed jacket over a bulging stomach, and his collar was undone, as though he couldn't be bothered to button it. He stopped typing and looked at her with mild amusement. "You fell asleep again, didn't you?"

Sheridan straightened. "What?" Instead of the tan shapeless overalls she'd worn in prison, she wore the shirt and jeans she'd had on when she was taken from the past. "What's happened?" she asked. "Why am I here?"

The man lowered his reading glasses so that he could see her better. "Those are questions for philosophers, not physicists. Although I'll be the first to admit that the two fields overlap quite a bit."

When Sheridan didn't answer, the man leaned back and laughed. "You must have had quite a dream this time. I hope you weren't stuck on the moon again." He slid his glasses back onto the bridge of his nose. "I'll tell Mr. Swap that due to its unpleasant side effects, we can't endorse his pill." The man turned to the computer on his desk and typed in something while he shook his head. "A pity too. If the pill had been able to unlock more of a person's innate intelligence without the unfortunate side effects of temporary psychosis, it could have done the world a tremendous amount of good."

Sheridan let her gaze sweep around the room again. The desk was cluttered with papers, mail, and pencils. A box of paper clips sat on top of his computer. A coffee mug had left a ring on a manila envelope. One of the shelves on the wall held a picture frame that showed two young boys. Grandchildren maybe. Everything looked so twenty-first century. So normal. And yet completely unfamiliar.

Sheridan regarded the man warily for a moment. "What are you talking about?"

The man turned back to her, peering over his glasses. "The genesis pill. You agreed to be one of the test subjects. It does indeed increase intelligence, but unfortunately it produces vivid paranoid episodes beforehand—waking dreams in which people believe all sorts of things are out to get them." He smiled tolerantly. "Don't worry. It should be mostly out of your system by now."

Sheridan noticed diplomas hanging on one of the walls and stood up to take a closer look. The name on them read Perry Branscomb. Branscomb. He'd been Taylor's graduate adviser at UT, the man who had gotten the funding to create the first QGP.

This wasn't real at all. "Reilly killed you," Sheridan said.

Dr. Branscomb raised his eyebrows in tolerant surprise. "I guess better me than you. Isn't something bad supposed to happen to you if you die in your dreams?" He stood up and tugged his jacket into place. "Let's go to the lab. I'm eager to see how the pill has affected your mental prowess. Perhaps we'll even be able to finish the QGP."

Sheridan walked to the door without answering him. Reilly had re-created this place to trick her. If she could get away . . .

Sheridan flung the door open and ran into a hallway. She rushed past milling college students, all dressed in jeans and T-shirts. None of them tried to stop her. They just gave her curious glances as she wove around them.

She ran down a flight of stairs, saw an exit sign, and headed toward it. When she pushed open the door, she realized where she was. A perfect replica of the UT campus spread out in front of her. She'd come out of the Nielson Building. The colonial-looking Ayres Hall reigned over the quad, its flag standing at attention.

She stopped running and took in the buildings, grass, trees, the bright blue sky overhead. How had Reilly created a place this big? The answer came to her as soon as she thought of the question. The future had virtual reality centers. She was inside some sort of computer program.

Reilly had worked at UT, so he'd been able to replicate it. Sheridan doubted the ruse would have worked on Taylor, but it at least it would have had a chance. Maybe it was easier for a person to believe they'd had a psychotic, paranoid reaction to a drug than to accept they'd been snatched out of their time period by future scientists.

Sheridan had come with Taylor to campus enough times to know her way home. She headed that way at a fast pace. She wanted to see how far this virtual reality program could go. Reilly knew what the physics buildings and labs looked like, but he couldn't have known what the inside of her house was like. He couldn't have reproduced her family or friends. He hadn't known Taylor back in the twenty-first century.

Dr. Branscomb caught up to Sheridan and took hold of her arm. "What's wrong? Where are you going?"

She pulled her arm away from him. "This isn't real. I know what you're doing."

His brows furrowed together in concern. "The drug might not have completely worn off yet. Let's go back to my office so you can rest."

She wanted to run off again, but didn't. She couldn't escape, not when she wasn't in a real place to begin with. Sheridan looked around at the buildings. The detail was amazing. There was nothing like this in the computer games from her day. "You must have used old pictures or video of this place to reproduce it so well."

"Ah," he said, remembering something. "You were supposed to eat as soon as you woke up. That's probably why you don't feel well. I was instructed to give you this. . . ." He patted one pocket of his tweed jacket, then another, and then finally pulled out two cellophane packages containing oatmeal cookies. He handed them to her.

Curious, she opened one. She sniffed the cookie, put it to her teeth. It smelled authentic. It felt right. She had eaten only half of her last meal bar, and her mouth was already watering. She bit into the cookie and tasted the familiar flavor. She took another bite, savoring it. "Taste, smell, and feel," she said. "You're good. Are you accessing the memories I already have or are you able to duplicate them somehow?" She took another bite. "Actually I don't care. Either way, I'm eating both cookies."

Dr. Branscomb took her gently by the arm. "Come back with me. You'll feel like yourself again soon."

She shook him off and kept walking. "Since this isn't real, it doesn't have any calories, does it?" She took another bite and munched it happily. "This is probably the twenty-fifth century's best invention."

Dr. Branscomb took her arm again, slowing her. "I can't let you go off when you're not in your right mind. You're liable to hurt yourself."

A breeze ruffled through her hair. It felt so natural. She could hear the chatter of the students around her, the thud of their footsteps.

"Come back with me," Dr. Branscomb said more firmly, "or I'll have no recourse but to call campus security."

"I'm sure you will." She stopped then and looked around. "It doesn't matter though. I can't escape. I'm still back in my room, aren't I?"

"You ate food," he said in exasperation. "Doesn't that prove to you this is real? You don't taste things in dreams."

"Can we go to Smokey's? I'm craving a cheeseburger."

He hesitated, didn't answer.

"You told me I'm supposed to eat. I'll think much better after I have a cheeseburger."

Dr. Branscomb forced a smile and let go of her arm. "Very well. I've got my wallet with me."

They started toward the University Center and Sheridan ate both her cookies without feeling full, which she supposed was a drawback to the VR programs. She reached out and touched the smooth, delicate leaves on the bushes. She ran her fingertips over the *cold metal of the lampposts they passed. Those felt real enough, but the program couldn't take away what she already felt—hunger.*

"Did you make this place for me or for you?" she asked Dr. Branscomb.

"What do you mean?" he replied, although she imagined he already knew.

"It's so complete. It must have taken a really long time to program all of these things in. I bet you're lonely for Knoxville, aren't you? You made this before I got here."

He laughed and it seemed good-natured, not like the laugh of a person who wanted to hurt her. "I shouldn't be surprised at anything you say. Marion Jensen—you know him, he's one of my graduate students—he took the pill and was convinced the CIA was trying to kill him." Another forced chuckle. "You'll be embarrassed by this later."

"You probably come here a lot," she went on. "You can program in every girl who ever dumped you, and they all love you now. The Nobel Prize committee stops by to tell you that you won, and you can kill off Dr. Branscomb and everyone else who ever ticked you off."

Some of the humor dropped from his voice. "Those are the sorts of statements that make meds think you're unbalanced. You wouldn't want to be taken in for an evaluation, would you?"

She kept walking. "The twenty-first-century term is doctors, *not* meds. *And you forgot the dirt."*

He looked at her grimly. "What are you talking about?"

"The parking lot," she said, pointing to one they were passing. "It's been so long since you've seen a parking lot, you forgot what they're like. See how clean that is? No cracks, no litter, no oil stains

or bird droppings. Which reminds me, you forgot the birds too. They should be chattering in the distance." She turned her attention from the pavement to his clenched jaw. *"That's probably why you can't get your QGPs to work. You overlook the importance of the little details."*

Dr. Branscomb sent her a venomous glare, and then she was back in her cell again, groggy, half asleep, and without the taste of oatmeal cookies in her mouth.

It felt like that first virtual reality trip had taken place a long time ago. It hadn't, though. She was losing track of time. It was hard to keep the days straight when you went to bed in one reality and woke up in another one. It was hard to keep anything straight.

Sheridan heard footsteps in the hallway outside her cell. It happened often enough. Usually the footsteps kept going by. This time they stopped, and her cell door slid open.

chapter 21

hapter

Allana lay on the roof of the second building, staring vacantly upward. She looked younger that way, Echo decided. He was so used to seeing her with expressions of coyness or sophisticated disregard, she hardly seemed real without them. Xavier held the restorer box over her, shooting out beams to relax her muscles. She blinked, grimaced, and let out a small moan.

Echo's first impulse was to help her up. He didn't, though. He didn't have that role anymore. He finished peeling off his overalls and left her to Xavier.

"You'll need to take off the science uniform," Xavier told Allana, unfastening her harness. "When we go inside this building, we need to blend in with the crowd."

She sat up, looking around. "Where are we?"

"On top of the courthouse building," Xavier said. He'd

taken off his overalls and slipped Echo's old shirt on. He took a bag from his pack, one lawyers might use to carry evidence. He put everything else inside it.

Unsteadily, Allana got to her feet. "The courthouse building?" she repeated incredulously. "Why did you take us here? There are kilos of Enforcers in the courthouse."

Xavier helped her with her overall fasteners, hurrying her to get rid of them. "The Enforcers here were probably the first ones called to help out at the Scicenter. Hopefully most of them are gone."

Echo dropped his overalls on the roof. Taylor had already shed her pair, and he couldn't help notice how nice she looked out of them. Butterflies glimmered across her shirt and tight-fitting pants. The flowers around her eyes matched those tucked underneath the leaves of her clothes. Wearing that outfit, she reminded him even more of one of the woodland fairies he'd read about in historical documents.

He watched her pull her hair from its holder and shake it loose. It fell around her shoulders in emerald-green waves. It made him happy somehow that Taylor was pretty. It was as if the universe was reminding him that Allana wasn't the only woman to be admired. Taylor was attractive, intelligent, and from the twenty-first century, which made her intriguing too. If she hadn't been so quick to shoot people, she would be a good candidate for helping him get over Allana. Out of the corner of his eye, he noticed Allana staring at him. She'd seen him smiling and had followed his gaze. Her eyes narrowed at Taylor.

Allana stepped toward Taylor angrily. "You *stunned* me."

Taylor took her belt from her overalls and rethreaded it

around her pants. "I admit it. I'm a stunning sort of girl."

Echo laughed. Allana didn't. She turned and glared at him.

"*Stunning* used to mean 'gorgeous,'" Echo said.

Allana pulled off the rest of her overalls and threw them to the ground. "How nice. You can talk in code." She scowled at Taylor. "Where did you come from, anyway? You have a weird accent."

"Someplace you've never heard of." Taylor took the rank badge from her overalls and pressed down on the top; the number changed to 4,258. She stuck the badge on her shirt, nestling it under a fluttering butterfly.

Allana gaped at the new number. "Those are fake rank badges."

"Brilliant," Taylor said. "I bet you get your rank points from your IQ."

"If anyone stops us," Xavier said while he changed the number on his badge, "hopefully our ranks will make them think twice about detaining us." He took a badge out of his pack and handed it to Echo. It read: 1,091.

Taylor bent down and picked up Helix's rank badge from Allana's discarded overalls. She tossed it to Allana. "Look, now you're good enough to be with the rest of us."

Allana put the badge on her shirt. "What's your real rank?"

"It doesn't matter," Taylor said.

Echo could tell she meant it, and he somehow found that the most attractive thing about her. She was confident enough about herself that she didn't need a number to prove anything.

"You know, *rank* used to be an adjective," Taylor went on. "A fitting one."

Allana didn't say anything, probably because she didn't know what Taylor meant. Echo thought about it and laughed. *Rank* had once meant that something smelled awful.

Xavier motioned for everyone to follow him, and the group headed quickly along the edge of the building toward the roof's maintenance door. "Once we're inside," Xavier told Echo and Allana, "we'll go down a hallway to the stairwell. If no one is there, we'll take the stairs to the ground floor. If someone is waiting for the elevator, I'll decide whether it's better to ride with them or to pretend we forgot something and don't need the elevator after all. Once we're outside, we'll pick up a crystal. . . ." Xavier felt along his belt for his comlink, then realized he didn't have it anymore. "Taylor, call for a car, then check the sensor to see if anyone is near the other side of the maintenance door. We can't let anyone see us come in this way."

Without breaking stride, Taylor took out her comlink and did both tasks.

"Where are we going after this?" Allana asked, panting again.

Xavier craned his head to see the scanner results on Taylor's comlink. "To the postmission contact spot." He added under his breath, "Hopefully it's the same place in this timestream."

"We're not going there yet," Taylor said. "Not until I hear from Joseph and he's told me what I want to know about pots and kettles."

"What's a kettle?" Xavier asked.

Taylor didn't answer. She went back to checking the sensor. Echo answered for her. "A kettle was a twentieth-century device for boiling water. Don't ask me why Taylor wants to talk to Joseph about them."

"She's neurofailed," Allana said.

Definitely not. Anyone who could do the programming he'd seen at the Scicenter had a mind that was half computer, half art.

They'd reached the maintenance door. While Xavier used the disabler to unlock it, Allana adjusted the heel of her jewel-encrusted shoe. "These aren't styled for running," she muttered. "*People* aren't styled for running. We're all going to be shot, and the only thing that will have changed is that now I'm sweaty and tired."

Had Allana always been this whiny? Echo ignored the impulse to ask her if she had better escape plans.

Xavier opened the door, and they went down the ramp to the top floor, slowing their pace to a casual walk. Echo tried to breathe normally. His chest still rose and fell too fast. Everyone's did.

The hallway looked like a typical office walkway. In between the rows of closed doors, the hallway displayed building announcements, newsfeeds, city updates, and message links. He saw a flashing evacuation notice for the grounds around the Scicenter. The building was in lockdown, and any people found in the area would be immediately stunned. No notices about this building were posted. The Enforcers must not have realized yet that the group had left the Scicenter.

All the office doors on this floor had high-security locks, which meant this wasn't where the public usually went. The building's alarms weren't sending out a warning that unclearanced people were in the hallway, but if anyone saw them, they might still be questioned.

Up ahead, a couple of people walked from one room to another. Echo could hear the murmur of voices coming from a few open doors. Any moment someone would look over and see them. What sort of story had Xavier and Taylor prepared if they were stopped? If Taylor spoke, people would know she wasn't from Traventon.

Against his will, Echo began adding up the criminal offenses he was now guilty of. Even if the government never connected the Scicenter break-in to this group, they could still be charged for blocking their crystals, being on an unauthorized floor, having weapons—*sangre*, even having a comlink with a scanning sensor was enough to make the city give them memory washes. With the other things added in, the sentence would be death— probably the public kind to set an example.

At a cross point in the hallway, Xavier motioned to the right. "This way."

Wordlessly they followed him down the corridor. The group hadn't even made it around the first corner when they ran into a man and a woman walking the other way. The two were talking about a case, but they stopped when they saw the group coming toward them.

The woman looked them up and down with disapproval. "Do you have an appointment with someone?" Without waiting for an answer, she added, "Where is your escort?"

Xavier didn't slow down. He tapped his rank badge. "I *am* the escort."

The woman swallowed, stepped aside, and let them go by.

Echo waited for someone else to call after them, to come after them. The only footsteps he heard were their own. The group passed a couple of men. Both of them openly appraised Taylor. Not all that strange, Echo supposed. She was pretty and walked with a confident stride, the swagger high rankers always had. That was bound to bring attention, but neither man said anything to the group.

They came to the elevator just as the door slid open for a man waiting there. Echo looked to Xavier to see what he would do. Was it safer to make up an excuse not to take the elevator or to ride with the man?

The man was in his thirties, with the untoned physique of someone who spent too much time sitting in meetings. His curly blue hair sat on top of his head like a pile of bubbles. Not much of a threat.

Xavier followed the man into the elevator. Good; this would be much faster than the stairs, and Echo wasn't in the mood to hear any more of Allana's complaints.

He shuffled into the elevator with the others. Allana's face was still flushed and sweaty, making it look like she'd added splotchy red patches to her makeup. She pushed her hair away from her face and looked around with annoyance. Before, he had only seen her in situations she controlled. Now that they were in danger, her faults were compiling into an unignorable list. She was ungrateful. Unhelpful. Uneverything.

The man lifted his crystal to the control panel, and Echo silently willed him to choose the main floor. Instead the man chose the eighth subterranean floor. Not only a restricted floor, but one eight stories underground.

The man waited for someone in Echo's group to choose a floor. Xavier smiled at him blandly. "We're going to sub eight too."

The door slid closed. As soon as the elevator began to move, Xavier made a slight motion to Taylor, a flick of his hand. She had positioned herself behind the man and now unclipped the laser box from her belt.

Echo knew what they were planning. They would stun the guy, then use his crystal to choose the ground floor instead.

The man didn't notice Taylor. He was surveying Echo. "You look familiar. . . ." His gaze went to Echo's rank badge, then back to his face. "We've worked together on a case, haven't we?"

Echo gave an apologetic smile. "No."

Taylor pushed the button on her laser box. It clicked but didn't fire. She pressed it again. Nothing happened.

Odd. That shouldn't happen unless—it was only then that Echo noticed the red blinking lights rimming the elevator— unless the courthouse had installed his laser-disrupter design inside the building.

Sangre. Today was going to be filled with ironies. Joseph had told Echo that if he ventured into disabling engineering, he would regret it one day. Echo had known his brother was right; he just never figured today would be that day.

The Prometheus Project had been Echo's assignment from the Dakine, the assignment that would guarantee him enough credits to set his rank for life. It was named after the Greek god who stole fire, because that's what the Dakine wanted to do— steal the Enforcers' fire. Or at least keep their laser boxes from firing. Dakine engineers had been working on a disabler for the last two years and hadn't succeeded.

Echo hadn't exactly wanted to make the disabler work for the Dakine. That would have been foolishly dangerous, but he had wanted to make it work for himself. He had wanted to prove he could do it, that he could figure out the invention without Joseph's help. And Echo had wanted to have a disabler to protect himself from Enforcers. After all, if they found out he'd joined the Dakine, he would be given a memory wash.

Besides, how could Echo resist the opportunity to read through two years of research, testing, and trials? Then, like every other invention Echo had ever worked on, he hadn't been able to keep from asking for Joseph's help. Echo knew if he could brainstorm design theories with someone who understood the more intricate parts of physics, math, and engineering, he'd be able to come up with solutions.

And together, they had. They'd come up with not one but two different ways to shut a laser box down. Joseph favored a blast that would destroy a laser box's inner mechanisms. Echo's way was more refined: a field that temporarily absorbed the laser box's energy and left the box itself intact.

Echo hadn't told the Dakine he had figured out a way to make the Prometheus Project work. He'd enjoyed the Dakine lifestyle, knowing he had another year or two before the Dakine became frustrated with his lack of progress. And in a couple of years anything could change.

When the Dakine ordered Joseph's death, Echo took the Prometheus files that he'd hidden on his home computer, and he sent them to the mayor's office. It had been Echo's only way of taking revenge on the Dakine for his assassination.

It seemed like he had sent those files only this morning. He hadn't though. It happened two and a half months ago, and those red lights rimming the elevator told him the government had tested, built, and installed a Prometheus shield in the courthouse. It made a horrible yet logical sense. This was the building where criminals were sentenced. More than once assassins had come in during Dakine trials and shot the judges. The government was making sure laser boxes wouldn't work here anymore.

The man in the elevator was still staring at Echo. He tapped his finger in the air as though shaking something loose. "It's computing now—you look like that guy, the one the Dakine vaporized. It was on all the feeds. . . ."

Taylor pushed her laser-box button again and then gave Xavier a helpless, panicked look. *What now?* her expression said.

Xavier drew his own laser box from his belt. He stood in front of the man, so it wasn't at all subtle when he turned, aimed, and didn't fire.

The man saw the laser box, let out a startled gasp, and reached for his comlink. Echo grabbed for it at the same time, all the while watching the floors pass by. In a few seconds the elevator would stop, and they would find themselves eight floors underground. If the man yelled for help when the elevator opened, they'd be caught.

The man swung at Echo. Echo let go of the comlink to avoid the blow, then issued a punch of his own. His hand smacked into the man's temple. The man staggered sideways, hit the wall, and then slid unconscious to the floor.

Xavier grabbed the man's wrist and dragged him to the

control panel. Taylor turned her laser box in her hand, checking for damage, some reason it hadn't fired. "Stupid technology."

Echo shook his hand, trying to wave away the pain of impact. "As you said, sometimes the simplest methods are the best."

The elevator came to a halt. Xavier hadn't managed to cancel the first destination in time, and the door slid open. An older woman took a step toward the elevator and then stopped, noticing the scene before her. Xavier held the man's limp wrist to the floor controls, frantically pushing the button for the ground floor.

The woman let out a gasp. "Is that Frankos Doddard?" Another gasp. "What are you doing to him?"

Xavier pushed the override button so that the sensors wouldn't keep the door open, waiting for the woman to get on. The doors began to slide closed.

"He passed out," Echo called to the woman. "We're taking him to the meds."

He doubted she believed the excuse. Xavier looked too guilty. The elevator whirred again, moving upward.

Allana let out a low hiss of curse words. "We'll all be killed."

A helpful commentary.

Xavier dropped the man's hand and examined his laser box. "Why did these stop working?"

Echo pointed to the red lights above them. "The government installed a disrupter shield in the building. Our laser boxes won't work as long as we're inside. The problem is," Echo continued calmly, "that means the Enforcers here will be armed with other weapons . . . chemical spray, projectile shooters . . .

probably sword saws." He could tell by Taylor's expression that she knew what those were—a sword–chain saw combination capable of ripping through people.

"Have your gas masks ready," Xavier said, getting his out of his bag. "Head straight to the front door and go to the nearest car."

Allana fumbled with her mask. "When did the government get a laser-disrupter shield?"

Even though Taylor had already signaled for a car, Echo signaled for another. "We've been gone for two and a half months.

"Impossible," Allana said.

Echo unclipped her comlink and held it in front of her long enough for it to flash the date. "I saved you by turning you into an energy flux wave and reconfiguring you two and a half months later." He put her comlink back on his belt. He still didn't trust her enough to return it to her, which was just one more fault to hold against her. Untrustworthy.

The elevator was slowing. They were almost to the main floor. Allana narrowed her eyes at Echo in suspicion. "The government wasn't anywhere close to having that technology."

He shrugged. "Maybe Joseph invented it while we were gone. You know how smart he is."

Allana's eyes stayed fixed on Echo as though she knew what he'd done.

The elevator slid open. Echo could see the entrance doors across the sprawling lobby. Crowds of people were coming and going, crisscrossing the floor. Some stood in lines at the information booths; others checked screens for courtroom numbers. Xavier stepped out of the elevator and Echo followed, his gas mask clutched in his hand. Maybe, he thought hopefully, the woman didn't report them. Maybe they would walk out of here without any problems. And then he saw two Enforcers emerge from one of the hallways and head straight toward them.

chapter
22

The front entrance was in sight for a few seconds. Taylor could even make out the shape of a row of cars waiting in front of the building. Beautiful, beckoning freedom.

Then two Enforcers came out of a hallway.

"Gas masks," Xavier hissed. It was all the warning he gave the group before he threw two vials to the ground. A cloud of darkness immediately enveloped them and ballooned out across the lobby.

Taylor kept her hand on her gas mask, pressing it to her face. The building's walls let out a scolding buzz that nearly drowned out the crowd's sudden panicked yelling. She hated hearing the fear in their voices, the confusion. It made her feel like a criminal.

Someone jostled into Taylor from behind, knocking her

sideways. She put one hand out in front of her and kept heading toward the exit. The shouts began to fade, replaced by the thumps of people falling to the floor. In a moment she would have to worry about tripping over people.

Silence came. It was quickly replaced by the click of small doors opening. Gasbots whirred into the room.

As Taylor pushed forward in the darkness, with the sound of wheels and gears echoing through the foyer, she wondered how she had ended up like this. *Let me review my life*, she thought, *to see where I went wrong.* Going into physics had probably been a mistake. Thinking that she could make a difference in the world—yeah, that hadn't turned out at all like she'd expected. She had made a difference, and she was still paying for it.

She heard twanging sounds and saw bursts of light like camera flashes. She didn't realize what they meant until a fiery object zoomed by her shoulder. As she jerked away from it, her foot caught on something. She pitched forward, fell, and found herself sprawled on top of someone.

She stumbled to her feet. Her laser-deflecting clothes weren't going to stop whatever the gasbots were shooting. She needed to get out of here, fast. She stepped over the person lying on the floor and found herself falling again. She'd stepped over one body and onto another.

She noticed the light beams then. They went through the darkness around her, fingers of light sweeping the area. As they filtered through the darkness, the whole area brightened. The gas grew less dense.

With a jolt to her stomach, Taylor realized what was happening. Some sort of device was clearing the concealing gas, making it possible for the gasbot sensors to find them. She pulled herself to her feet again. *Move forward*, she told herself. She knew which direction the door was, had kept it in her mind even when she was toppling over people. She moved more slowly now, taking tentative steps. She didn't want to fall again.

A figure in front of her faded in and out of darkness. Allana. She was ahead of Taylor, standing still as though she didn't know where to go. The area went black again for a moment and then Xavier appeared next to Allana, taking her by the elbow to lead her toward the door. Which was just like him—coming back to help Allana. Honestly, if he got shot because he helped her, Taylor would never forgive her.

The fingers of light swept past Taylor again. The gas was thinning. In a few more moments it would be useless. The front doors wavered in and out of darkness. She caught sight of Echo standing there, looking behind him as he searched for everyone else.

Taylor would be the last one out. She picked up her pace, sidestepping another body. In a few seconds she would be able to see well enough to run.

"Taylor!" Xavier called. He stood a little ways in front of her.

She looked up. Through the darkness, she saw a gasbot whirring between her and the door. A barrel mounted on its top swung in her direction.

And then Xavier stepped in front of her.

She heard the impact of something hitting him. He took a stumbling step backward. Before the gasbot could get off a second shot, Echo came up behind it. He'd picked up a trash incinerator from the lobby and swung it into the gasbot, sending the machine smashing into a wall. Xavier kept moving forward, staggering now. "Run!" he called to Taylor.

She sprinted forward and caught up to Xavier. "Go," he told her. "Escape."

She took hold of his waist to propel him forward. They were nearly to the door. Echo ran back to her. He wrapped his arm around Xavier and with powerful strides hauled him outside.

Allana already sat in a car, waiting with the doors open. "Hurry!" she yelled.

Before the courthouse door closed, another shot whizzed by Taylor. She felt the wind from it brush by her head. Then the door shut. The gasbots wouldn't come outside. They were programmed to stay in the area they were protecting.

As Echo hefted Xavier into the car, Taylor sprinted to the bench third from the courthouse doors. She felt along the bottom of the bench for the mobile crystal. Nothing. No crystal. Had changing the timestream changed the locations where the mobile crystals were left? Had the group gone through all that just to be caught now? Then her fingers found it. She yanked it off and ran to the car.

Xavier was slumped in his seat, pale, limp, and with his hand over his chest. Blood seeped between his fingers.

Taylor threw herself into the car and reached toward the front. Allana sat by the control panel. She took the crystal from Taylor and pressed it to the right place.

"Traventon Plaza Recreation Center," Taylor said loudly, making sure to pronounce the words perfectly so that the car's computer would understand her. They would go to the DW's restaurant. Someone there would be able to help Xavier.

The door slid shut and the car hummed away from the walkway and into the street traffic. It joined the other cars gliding peacefully along the rails.

Taylor glanced out the window to see if anyone was chasing after them. No one had come out of the courthouse. The doors were peppered with holes, places where the gasbots had shot at them.

Taylor turned her attention to Xavier. He was leaning back against the seat, his hand still pressed against his chest. His breathing had gone shallow. Blood bloomed on his shirt.

Taylor scooted next to him. "How bad is your injury?"

Echo pulled Xavier's hand away from his chest. She couldn't see the injury for all the blood. "Bad," Echo said. "It's bad."

chapter
23

Joseph, Lee, and Ren were nearly to the bench that held the mobile crystal. Joseph wanted to run, to stop wasting time, but that would draw attention. So the group strolled along, passing multicolored government office buildings. Every once in a while a car swished by on the rails. A few people ambled along the walkways, most of them focused on their comlinks.

Joseph, Lee, and Ren all had the detention-center schematics on their comlinks and were discussing the security systems. It was a grim list. Most buildings in the city depended on the crystals to make sure people didn't go where they weren't wanted. The detention center had extra methods. An electrically charged wall surrounded the building. Anyone who touched it would be instantly killed, which was why the detention center also had a razor fence surrounding that wall—so that nobody accidentally touched it.

Even if Ren and Lee had been able to cut through the fence and disable the electric wall without setting off every alarm system in the detention center, the detention center's outer walls were made of titanium over hyperdiamond rods. They would be almost impossible to cut through.

Lee gestured upward at the opaque dome covering Traventon. "We could scale the inside of the dome, then drop down on the top the building. That would get us past the fences."

"The roof has motion detectors," Joseph said. This whole conversation had a déjà vu feeling to it. In the new timestream, he had studied all this. He had known some of the information before he even looked at the detention-center schematics.

Ren motioned to Joseph. "You're a computigator. Can you splice into the detention center's computer system and turn off the security features?"

"The computers are inside," Joseph said. "They aren't connected to any other systems, so there's not a remote way to splice into them."

The group fell silent as two women walked by. The women appraised them with interested smiles, then noticed their rank badges and looked away. Everyone, Joseph thought wryly, became less attractive when their rank passed five million.

"The Dakine get people out," Ren said after the women had gone. "How do they do it?"

"Easy," Joseph said. "They have people who work as Enforcers. They just use the exits."

Detention Center Thirteen was large enough that it had four entryways. Each had a guard station that cars had to pass through. Sensors at the stations showed guards information from people's crystals—names, photos, any criminal charges.

Ren scrolled through the schematics on his comlink. "Do you still have any contacts in the Dakine?"

"Only ones who want to kill me." And unfortunately Joseph had too many of those. "Do you have any memory of where your contact planned to meet you? Was it at one of the guard stations?"

Ren shook his head. "It wouldn't be there. Station guards need thirty years' enforcing work before they're assigned there. None of the DW agents work as Enforcers that long."

Joseph scowled, frustrated. "I would think a covert group would have as many people as it could get working as Enforcers."

Lee changed the magnification on his comlink so that he could zoom in on Sheridan's wing. "That's because you're not thinking about what Enforcers do. They don't just find and arrest thieves and murderers. They arrest people who look at the wrong information or believe something they shouldn't. Would you work as an Enforcer if you knew you would have to shoot people you agreed with?"

Joseph didn't concede the point. "When I shot, I would make sure I missed."

Ren lowered his voice. "Miss too many times, and you get a memory wash. We've lost more than one agent that way. It makes the job a lot less attractive."

They had almost reached the spot where the mobile crystal was hidden. Joseph could see the bench sitting empty by the street.

"We have no other choice," Lee said. "We've got to go through an entrance."

Ren let out a dismissive laugh. "I admire your courage, Brother Lee. It's almost enough to make me take back all the things I've said about your people. The guard stations are equipped with laser boxes, car-piercing missiles, gas, heat-seeking exploders—am I forgetting anything?"

"I meant dressed as Enforcers," Lee said. "That had to be our original plan. It's the only thing that could work."

Ren nodded. "But now we can't remember the contact who was going to give us Enforcer armor. . . ."

Joseph switched his comlink to search mode. His pace picked up. So did his mood. "I know where we can get armor." A moment later he'd brought up one of the city's dating databases. "Log onto a matching site and help me find two male Enforcers who are asleep during this shift. Two in the same apartment building would be best."

"Why?" Ren asked.

Joseph's mind was working so fast, sprinting ahead to plan out the details, that he almost didn't want to take the time to speak. He kept his explanation concise. "We'll drug a couple of Enforcers and take them in our car. We don't have crystals with clearance to get in, but they do."

"You want to take drugged Enforcers in the car with us?" Ren repeated. "You don't think the detention guards will find that suspicious?"

"The seats in the cars are hollow," Joseph said, bringing up an information page on one of the dating sites. "The Dakine use them to smuggle things sometimes. We'll use them to smuggle the unconscious Enforcers. When we pull up to the detention center, the guards' sensors will show two enforcers bringing in"—he gestured to the nearing bench—"whoever that crystal says. And that's also what they'll see in the car. Two Enforcers. One prisoner."

Ren considered this. "Wouldn't it be better to be three Enforcers? That way there isn't a chance one of us will be thrown into a cell."

Joseph shook his head. "We need an excuse to go to the detention center off our shift. Anything else will seem suspicious."

They reached the bench, and all three sat down. Ren casually ran one hand along the underside. He peeled off the mobile crystal hidden there and slipped it into his pocket.

Lee was already filling out profile information on one of the matching sites. "I'm a twenty-five-year-old woman with a high rank who enjoys adventure programs, light ball, and dartys . . . Must have same shift."

Ren turned to his comlink, bringing up the same dating site. "Try to find Enforcers who look like us."

Lee nodded. "That means I'm looking for a handsome man with a chiseled build. . . ."

"And I'm looking for someone," Ren said, typing in information of his own, "with an ultrachiseled build."

"*Ultrachiseled* isn't even an option," Lee said.

"Should be," Ren muttered.

Joseph scanned over the descriptions of men on his site. It wouldn't be hard to find Enforcers. They always had a way of bragging about their jobs. "The men won't look enough like you to fool the guards. We'll have to depend on the holocameras for that."

"Career preference: Enforcer," Lee murmured. "I like all types of foods. . . ."

Ren stopped typing. "What do you think—do I want a serious relationship?"

"No," Lee said. "Because Enforcers never do."

"All right," Ren said, returning his attention to his comlink. "Just fun and more fun . . ."

A few minutes later Ren and Lee had enough names for Joseph to start plugging them into his comlink's address database. It didn't take long to locate two men in the same apartment building. Then Joseph pushed the car-call button.

Ren took the mobile crystal from his pocket and kept it hidden in his palm. "How are we going to get past the elevator security?"

Nonresidents had to check in with the lobby guard and tell him who they were visiting. The guard would message the resident to make sure it was legitimate.

"We stun the guard," Lee suggested.

"Too many witnesses," Ren said. Apartment buildings had foodmarts on the ground floor, and people were always coming and going to those. "We'll have to do it the Traventon way. Find some women at the foodmart, flirt them up, and get them to invite us to their apartments. Once we're in the elevator, we stun the women and go to the Enforcers' rooms instead."

Lee nodded. "Easy enough. The hard part will be finding a way to drag unconscious Enforcers to our car without people reporting us. How are we going to do that?"

A car slid to a stop on the rails in front of the bench. Its door opened, waiting for someone to get in. Joseph stood up and headed to the car. "I've got the plan figured out already. I'll explain on our way to the building."

Lee followed Joseph. "Does it involve flirting with women? I thought that was a good idea, and I don't usually say that about Ren's suggestions."

"Sorry," Joseph said. "Mostly it involves scaling the building."

chapter 24

Taylor stared at the blood on Xavier's chest, dread gripping her. *He's going to die*, she thought, and then, *No, I won't let it happen.*

She took his pack of medical supplies and opened it. "Xavier, tell me what to do." She sifted through syringes, bottles, electronics. "What do I need to fix the wound?"

"About two years of medical training," Xavier said, and put his hand over the wound again.

Taylor gripped the pack harder. "I'm serious. How do I stop the bleeding?"

He didn't answer. His breathing was jagged, shallow.

She turned to Echo. "Help me. Take his shirt off so I can see the wound."

Echo reached into the pack and took out a small white box.

He held the box over Xavier's chest, watching it glow and flash out a diagnosis. He read it and sighed. "His heart is damaged. We can't fix it."

"We've got to try." Taylor's voice spiraled upward. A sense of panic wrapped around her. "We can't just let him die." She fumbled through the items in the medical kit, spilling some in her hurry. There were surgery tools in here. Things to fix major damage. Xavier had been prepared to work on Echo in much worse condition.

She vaguely heard Echo telling Allana to look for something to soak up the blood. It didn't need to be soaked up; it needed to be stopped. Allana took Xavier's other pack and went through it.

"Xavier," Taylor said. "Tell me which instruments to use and what to do." She could hear the hysteria in her own voice. It was almost as though someone else spoke. "I'm a genius, remember? I don't need two years of medical school. Just tell me what to do."

He opened his eyes. They were rimmed with pain. "I promised I would keep you safe. I kept my promise."

The panic grew and spread inside Taylor. Xavier was going to die, and not because of Allana. It had been Taylor's fault. She'd been too slow getting out of the building.

She grabbed items from the pack, held them up, but couldn't concentrate enough to read their labels. Her hands were shaking. She threw things back, spilling several onto the floor. "You saved my life," she told Xavier. "I've got to save yours."

Xavier had gone pale. His skin looked colorless, like plastic. Blood had soaked through his shirt and onto his pants. Allana dabbed at it with medical sponges, but it didn't do any good. Blood dripped on the seat, the floor, everywhere.

"Don't worry," Xavier said, his voice going weak. "God has me in his grasp."

"Well, God can just ungrasp you. We need you here." Taylor knew she sounded petulant, unreasonable. But how did a person reason with death?

Xavier's chest rose, fell, then didn't rise again.

"No," Taylor said. "You can't give up. You can't—" Her words choked off and her vision blurred with tears. She pawed uselessly through the things in his medical kit. More spilled onto the seat. "I don't know what any of these do. Why didn't they train me to use these?"

Echo took her hand, held it in his. He had streaks of Xavier's blood on his knuckles. "He's dead, Taylor. I'm sorry."

"You're not!" she yelled.

"He saved my life too," Echo said, so softly it was almost a whisper. "Don't you think I want to save his?"

Taylor gave in to her tears then, let them overcome her. When Xavier had given Allana his shirt, Taylor had pointedly thought that Allana's life wasn't worth Xavier's. Now a voice in Taylor's mind asked if her own life was. Xavier had come on this mission to save Echo. He'd helped Allana. He'd gotten them all out of the Scicenter and through the courthouse. It shouldn't have cost him everything.

Taylor lowered her head, bitter tears coursing down her cheeks. She didn't try to stop them; she couldn't. Nothing had gone right. Sheridan was being held in a prison, tortured probably. Joseph, Lee, and Ren were undoubtedly in danger somewhere, and now Xavier was dead.

Without a word Echo pulled her to him, gently putting his arms around her, "I'm sorry, Taylor."

"And I'm sorry to interrupt you two," Allana said, with more ice in her voice than Taylor had thought possible, "but we have to get out of the car. It's rerouted itself to take us to a med clinic. We'll be there in less than five minutes."

Taylor lifted her head. "Will they be able to help Xavier?"

"No," Echo said. "And Allana's right. We've got to get out before the car reaches the meds. We'll be taken in for questioning otherwise." He moved away from Taylor and bent over Xavier, hurriedly taking items from his belt. He flipped the laser cutter on, examining it.

Taylor tried to concentrate on what needed to be done next. They needed to get out of the car. Then they needed to find somewhere safe to go. Xavier probably had a wife and kids. How was Taylor going to tell the council he had died saving her? How could he have traded his life for hers?

Allana sat in the front of the car, arms folded, with a petulant look on her face.

"Aren't you going to stop the car?" Taylor asked.

"I can't," Allana said. "Once a car detects an emergency, it won't stop until it reaches the med clinic."

Echo knelt by the car door and turned the laser cutter on. "We'll have to jump."

It still didn't make sense to Taylor. "How does the car know Xavier needs a med clinic? I thought a person without a crystal was invisible to the sensors. He doesn't have a crystal."

An orange light as long as a knife blade protruded from the

213

laser cutter. Echo used it to puncture a hole through the car wall. "A large amount of blood is leaking onto the floor. The car's sensors are programmed to react to that."

Slowly, Echo cut a square big enough for a person to go through. When it was done, he kicked the broken square outward. It bounced onto the street with a metallic crash. Wind gushed into the car, sounding like a scolding roar.

"The edges are sharp," Echo said. "Be careful not to cut yourself."

Allana made her way to the hole, muttering things. She grimaced, then leaped out. Echo motioned for Taylor to go next. She turned back to look at Xavier. She didn't want to leave him here. It didn't seem right to abandon him that way, to let the people from Traventon find him. What would they do with his body?

Echo stepped over, took Taylor's hand, and pulled her forward. Toward the hole, toward whatever happened next. She felt numb, horrible. Outside, the street whizzed by. The car seemed to be going faster than normal. Perhaps vehicles sped up during medical emergencies.

Taylor took a breath and jumped onto the street. As soon as her feet hit the pavement, she knew it wasn't going to end well. She lost her balance, pitched forward, and tumbled across the ground in a dizzying blur of pain and colors.

When the world finally stopped moving, she lay on the street and wondered if her lungs still worked. She couldn't breathe. Her head hurt.

"Taylor!" Echo called. She didn't turn to him. He was going to ask her if she was okay. She wasn't sure if she was. The sting in her back and the heavy feeling that pressed against her lungs were subsiding. She could breathe now. That was good at least.

"Taylor!" Echo called again, more frantic this time, and getting closer.

He's afraid I'm dead, Taylor realized, and lifted her head to reassure him. It was then she saw the car heading toward her. It was coming fast, and she didn't have the strength to move out of the way.

It will stop, Taylor thought. The cars were programmed for safety. They had sensors that prevented them from running over people.

She struggled to get up. The car didn't slow. And then she realized why. Cars here were programmed to recognize people's crystals. Hers was a fake. The car couldn't tell anything was in its way.

chapter 25

When her cell door slid open, Sheridan expected to see Tariq. He was the guard who usually came in.

She had first met him about a week and a half after she'd been imprisoned here. The Enforcers who brought her food always followed the same schedule. One came inside, put the day's nourishment bars in an alcove by the door, said, "Visual check complete," and then left.

It seemed an odd routine. The detention center could have engineered a way for the food to come in without sending a guard in. Every time a person walked into a cell, they risked an attack. Perhaps the guards wanted that. Perhaps it was some sort of test. Five more guards probably waited outside.

Sheridan had tried talking to the guards who brought her food. One was a burly man who flatly ignored her questions.

The other was a woman with a pinched face, who always told her that guards weren't given information about prisoners.

Tariq was different from the start. He was younger than the other guards, mid-twenties probably. And he was handsome. Unlike most of the people in Traventon, he hadn't used his face as some sort of doodle pad of personal expression. Even through the smoky visor Enforcers wore, she could see his features clearly. They were smooth and strong. He had warm brown eyes, and a smile that was all the more brilliant for its contrast against his tanned skin.

Or maybe it seemed more brilliant because smiles were so rare here. None of the other Enforcers ever smiled at her.

On the first day Tariq came into Sheridan's cell, he set her food in the alcove, said, "Visual check complete," then took off his helmet and stood by the door, watching her. The black hair she'd only caught a glimpse of before was thick and shiny, mussed.

He hadn't needed to run his hand through it to make it look good, but he did. "Hello," he said, and gave her a lopsided grin. "I'm Tariq, your new guard."

Sheridan kept her distance. She spoke slowly to enunciate the modern accent. "What do you want?"

He gave her another smile. "For starters, I want more women to ask me that question."

She raised an eyebrow at him, not sure if he was serious. The other guards never joked with her. Humor didn't appear to be part of their job.

Instead of making demands or leering at her, Tariq turned his helmet upside down and spun it on one finger, the way Sheridan had seen people twirl basketballs. It didn't work quite as well. She kept a cautious eye on him.

"You're special," Tariq said. "Do you realize that?"

"Well, my mother always told me so, but I suspect she was biased."

"You warrant a personal guard outside your door twenty-four hours a day. All the other criminals on the floor just get the usual precautions. Impenetrable walls, sensors that keep track of you, that sort of thing. You get nonstop personal attention."

"Hmm," she said, still keeping her distance. "I do feel special now."

Tariq's helmet toppled off his finger. He managed to catch it before it dropped to the floor. He put it back on his finger, twirling it again. "Eight hours a day, five days a week, I get to stand outside your door. It's dead boring out there, so I have a request: if you're going to escape, can you do it soon? I'm already tired of waiting."

"Sorry," she said. "Maybe if you gave me weapons and an escape plan, I'd be quicker."

He let out a short laugh and spun his helmet faster. "I can't help you there. I'm bored, not suicidal."

"You think I'd kill you?"

"Not you. The warden."

Sheridan shrugged. "Then I guess you'll have to be bored."

Tariq's helmet tilted off his finger again. This time when he caught it, he tucked it under his arm. "Boredom is part of a guard's job." He leaned against the wall casually. "The government pretends enforcement is exciting, but the truth is the prisoners walk around inside the cells, and I walk around outside of them. Do you know what the three biggest differences in our lives are?"

"Besides artillery?"

"Your meals are free, your clothes are more comfortable, and the warden yells at you less."

Sheridan laughed. It felt good. She hadn't realized how much she had missed laughing until right then. "I imagine you get to go home at the end of the day."

"That's another difference," Tariq said, gesturing around them. "Your room is bigger."

"Really?" she asked.

He let out a chuckle. "All right. That's an exaggeration. Still, with what the mayor pays us, it's not much of an exaggeration. You'd think keeping the city safe would be worth enough credits to buy more than a small apartment, but no." He let out a sigh. "I'm not sure who should feel the insult more—me, you, or the good citizens of Traventon."

Sheridan didn't want to like Tariq, didn't want to smile. She knew full well he was the enemy. He would hurt her if Reilly told him to. But it had been so long since someone besides Reilly had talked to her that she smiled anyway.

"So what city are you from?" Tariq asked. "I've never heard your accent before."

She hesitated. He would probably think she was crazy once she answered. She told him the truth anyway. "I'm from the twenty-first century. Your scientists created a time machine and brought me here."

Tariq let out an amused cough. "Sangre. They must be getting serious about erasing crime if they're looking for it in other centuries."

"I'm not a criminal," she said.

He looked her over thoroughly, let his gaze linger on her. She wondered which was harder to believe—that she'd come from the past or that she was innocent. He probably thought she was lying about both.

"Well, you can't be much of a criminal," he said. "The real criminals—the good ones—they always have someone to get them out of this place. It's the ones without influential friends who're forgotten here."

Sheridan didn't comment about that. She felt forgotten, friendless. She wondered, not for the first time, if Echo had managed to rescue Taylor. Taylor was the important one, not Sheridan.

Sheridan didn't let the thought stay. Echo had kissed her, had chosen her over Taylor. If Echo had been able to, he would have saved her and Taylor both. He wouldn't have left her here.

Of course, Echo hadn't known how smart, how important Taylor was until she'd asked him to help her destroy the QGP. Maybe he had changed his mind about who he liked after that.

Tariq must have seen Sheridan's expression darken. He took a step toward her; his humor was replaced by concern. "You've got a reprieve, you know. At least a short one. You're not scheduled for any more interrogations for the next two weeks."

"Really?" she asked, hopeful and then cautious. "What am I scheduled for?"

"Nothing. That man who interrogates you—the one the warden whisks in and out of here like he was the mayor himself—he won't be back for at least two weeks. I heard him tell the warden he's not allowed to do anything with you until then."

"That's good news," Sheridan said, genuinely relieved. A part of her knew she couldn't trust Tariq, knew it might not be the truth, but she wanted to believe it. And why not let herself feel relieved *instead of worried? Worry was a prison in and of itself.*

Tariq took another step toward her. "And as long as we're just spending our time walking around the same wall, I thought we could play a game." He reached into his pocket and took out two small paddles. "Do you know how to play tryst?"

"Trust?" she asked, not sure of his accent.

He laughed and held up the paddles for her to see. "Tryst," he repeated. "Because in the game we knock the spheres into each other."

He threw a paddle to her. She caught it and turned it over in her hand. It wasn't much bigger than a playing card, and nearly as thin. The only thick part was the handle, and it felt like it was made of bumpy plastic.

Was there any way she could turn this into a weapon? She felt a flash of guilt. Tariq was being friendly, and her first impulse was to sharpen this paddle into a knife and use it against him.

Tariq pressed the end of his handle, and a ball of light appeared, hovering above his paddle. "When it's my serve, I send my ball to a wall. If you intercept it with your ball before it comes back to me, you get a point." He flicked his paddle, and his ball flew to the wall. It silently hit, bounced against the floor, and returned to his paddle. He gave Sheridan another smile. "It's tryst. Trust is a game that takes much longer to play."

It was. And he excelled at that game too.

This time when Sheridan's cell door slid open, the burly guard who had a face like iron marched inside.

Her stomach did a twist, momentarily replacing the sensation of hunger with fear. She called this guard The Tough One because he wouldn't ever talk to her. He hardly even acknowledged her when she spoke. At first she'd thought he couldn't understand her, but she had practiced the accent since she got here and had it down pretty well now. He still wouldn't speak to her. It was never good news to see him.

"How are the wife and kids?" she asked him. She kept hold of the hope, however vague and wispy, that if she got him to see her as an actual person, he might treat her better. Maybe he would even look the other way when she escaped. Not *if*—*when*.

The Tough One held a laser box loosely in one hand and motioned for her to come. "You have a visitor."

An interrogation, more likely.

"Everything is good at home then?" Sheridan went on. "Everyone is happy and healthy?" She took a small step toward the door.

The Tough One stared at her coldly.

"I bet I remind you of your daughter, don't I? She's probably charming, smart . . . helpless against men with laser boxes."

He didn't answer, just motioned again for her to come.

She took another small step. "I bet you don't like the guys your daughter dates. Do you do the big bad Enforcer routine to scare them off?"

He glowered at her. "I can stun you and carry you out. I get paid the same."

"You'll never get grandchildren that way."

Apparently The Tough One was touchy about grandchildren. He raised his laser box and shot her.

chapter

26

Taylor knew she needed to roll over, to get away from the car that barreled down the street toward her. She jerked to the right—or tried to anyway. Her boot was hooked underneath the rail. She pulled at it. The boot was stiff and wouldn't bend enough to free her.

Great. She was going to die because of a fashion choice.

The ground beneath Taylor vibrated as the car neared. She twisted her foot, uselessly trying to release herself.

She felt hands grasping her underneath her arms, lifting and yanking her backward. She knew it was Echo even though she hadn't seen him run over. His grunt of determination turned into a yell of aggravation. He hadn't seen that her boot was caught, and now it was too late for him to bend down and free it. All he could do was let her go and get out of the way.

She waited for him to drop her. He pulled harder. The fasteners that ran up the length of her boot broke and popped open. Her foot slid free, and both she and Echo tumbled backward. Taylor hit the ground again, this time landing on Echo's chest. The car whizzed by them, sending out a breeze that fluttered strands of hair into her face. And then it was gone. She was safe. Alive. She went limp with relief and lay there, motionless, feeling Echo breathe in deeply.

He shifted, moving her off him so that he could look at her. "Anything broken?"

"Maybe my ankle."

"Sorry about yanking you like that. It's easier to heal a broken foot than a severed one."

Taylor's gaze went to the rail. Her boot lay in a limp, shredded heap several feet farther down the street than it had started out. That shredded heap had nearly been her foot. The thought made her feel nauseous and dizzy.

Echo glanced around. Several people on the walkway had stopped and were staring at them. "Car malfunction," Echo called to them. "She'll be fine."

Most of the people turned and went on their way, perhaps embarrassed to be caught staring. A few others kept watching them. No one offered to help.

Echo lowered his voice. "We need to get out of here."

Taylor wasn't sure if she could walk. And now that she wasn't in fear of being run over, she noticed her hands were throbbing. Both palms were scraped and bleeding. A flap of skin on one hand hung loose. The knee on the right side of her pants was ripped, and a stream of blood trickled down her leg. She looked at her injuries with a sinking feeling of despair. How could she have let this happen to herself now, when she needed more than ever to be in control of the situation?

Echo scooped her up in his arms. Taylor wanted to protest and tell Echo he shouldn't carry her when he had a shoulder injury. She could walk. She didn't say anything, though. She wasn't sure she actually could walk.

Echo headed off the street toward Allana. She stood on the side of the road, shaking her left hand as though it stung.

"I've got Xavier's med pack," Echo told Taylor. "I'll work on your injuries as soon as we get into another car."

When Echo got to Allana, he set Taylor on her feet, keeping his arm around her waist for support. With his free hand, he pulled out his comlink and signaled for a car. He looked up one side of the street and down the other.

Taylor slowly tested her weight on her hurt foot. Pain shot up her leg. Not a good sign.

"So"—Allana eyed Taylor, taking in her injuries—"you had trouble with your jump. Did you stumble over that massive sense of importance you carry around with you?"

"Shut up," Taylor said.

Echo kept gazing around. "Did you see anyone reporting us?"

"No," Allana said.

People were still staring at them, although now most were just cutting them curious glances as they walked by. A few people were talking on their comlinks, but those didn't seem to be paying attention to them at all.

"Hopefully a new car will get here soon." Echo clipped his

comlink back onto his belt and held his hand out to Allana. "Give me the crystal."

"The crystal?" she repeated, blinking.

"The mobile crystal," he said, hand still out. "The one you used to program the last car."

Allana swallowed uncomfortably. "I . . . I didn't take it with me."

Echo stared at her, his expression growing grim. "Why would you do that when you knew we needed another car?"

"I forgot about it," she said, then added defensively, "It wasn't my fault. It's not normal to have to carry around a crystal."

Echo raked his hand through his blond hair. His voice came out sharp, like someone chopping things into pieces. "What part of this day has been normal? Running into assassins? Escaping off the roof of the Scicenter? Being shot at by gasbots? Maybe those things should have clued you that we left 'normal' a long time ago."

"I'm sorry." Allana folded her arms and pouted, reminding Taylor of one of those sullen magazine models from her day. Beautiful, haughty, and perpetually in a bad mood. "I guess we'll have to call someone for help." Allana lifted her chin challengingly. "I suggest my father. He'll come himself to get us."

"And bring Enforcers with him," Echo said. "He'll never let us leave the city, and Taylor . . ." He didn't finish; instead he turned to Taylor. "Call your contact."

Taylor put weight on her injured foot again, this time enduring the pain without flinching. If she could do this, she could walk. She wasn't helpless. "I can't let my contact know we already destroyed the QGPs. Joseph's team might not rescue Sheridan if they know."

Echo let out a low-sounding growl of frustration. "Joseph said he would rescue her. Trust me, he'll do everything he can."

Taylor shifted more weight onto her injured foot. She willed it to support her, to let her walk. "But Ren and Lee might not, so I can't let anyone know where we are until Sheridan is safe." The throbbing pain in Taylor's ankle became so intense, she gasped and put her weight back on her uninjured leg.

Allana peered around the street, perhaps hoping to see someone she knew. When she didn't, she huffed out a sigh of exasperation. "If you won't let us call anyone, then one of us will have to take off our blocking band so we can use a car. We can't walk to the Recreation Plaza. It's fifteen kilometers away." The look she sent Echo made it clear she thought he should be the one to do it. "I'm sure the laser cutter could take your band off."

"Yeah," Taylor said. "I'm sure it could take his hand off too."

Allana crinkled her nose at Taylor. "I wasn't suggesting he use the surgery tools."

Echo leaned closer to Taylor's ear. "Laser cutters," he explained softly, "are programmed not to damage skin cells."

He didn't speak softly enough. Allana raised her eyebrows, incredulous that Taylor didn't know this information. Allana didn't comment on it, though. She turned to Echo, her pout back. "Please. We can't stay here, and Taylor can't walk. We need a car."

"Don't," Taylor told Echo. "The Dakine will find us." The

palms of Taylor's hands burned. She wanted to go somewhere, anywhere. How could she though, when she couldn't even walk a few steps?

Allana stepped over to Echo and whispered, "If it's really been two and a half months, the Dakine stopped searching for our signals long ago."

"Really?" Taylor said. It was a statement more than a question. "Are you an expert on the Dakine or are you guessing?"

Allana ignored Taylor. "The Dakine must have assumed we left the city. What would be the point of searching for us months later?"

Taylor wasn't sure if Allana was being manipulative or just stupid. "Wouldn't the Dakine have some scanning program that automatically searches for wanted people? And wouldn't that program notify someone if a fugitive suddenly popped back up in the city?"

Allana sent Taylor a razored look. "You don't know anything about it."

Taylor's hands were throbbing worse than ever, and drops of blood dripped from them. She looked like she had stepped out of some sort of horror film. "I can walk," she said. "The DW left more than one mobile crystal around. We'll have to get the nearest one. Where are we?"

Echo brought up a city map on his comlink and showed it to Taylor. Most of the crystal locations were close to the Scicenter, and that was the last place she wanted to go. She pointed to a spot on the comlink. Marshal Street. "That's our safest bet."

Allana peered over Taylor's shoulder at the map. "That's four kilometers away."

"Right," Taylor said. "We can walk that in less than an hour. If Joseph calls me before that, we'll have him come pick us up."

"I could call a friend," Allana suggested. "Or if you don't trust my friends, have Echo call someone he knows. His father. Or that silly little wordsmith who was always in the way. Either of them would help us."

Echo's gaze circled around the street again. "Jeth and Elise both left the city. Everyone knows the Dakine and the government are looking for us. They probably both have rewards out for our capture." Done searching the street, Echo turned to Allana. "I don't trust my friends with that sort of temptation, and I'm not about to trust yours."

Allana gave an almost imperceptible stamp of her foot. "I can't believe you're being so paranoid."

Echo tightened his grip around Taylor's waist but kept his eyes on Allana. "If you don't want to spend the rest of your short life worrying about assassins, you need to come with us. Otherwise, I'll give you back your comlink now and you can call anyone you want."

Allana stared at him, nostrils flaring, her lips bunching in and out of an angry line. It was clear she wasn't used to being given ultimatums and didn't like this one now. She didn't answer.

Echo waited for another moment, then pulled Allana's comlink from his belt and tossed it to her. "Good-byes just got a lot easier for me." He turned away from her. "Good luck, Allana."

With one quick motion, Echo picked Taylor up and strode down the walkway with her in his arms.

Taylor shouldn't have felt relieved they were parting ways

with Allana. What Echo had said was undoubtedly true. If Allana stayed in Traventon, sooner or later the Dakine would kill her. Probably sooner.

Still, Taylor was relieved. This meant Echo wasn't so in love with Allana that he was going to throw away his life doing her bidding. This meant Sheridan wouldn't have to deal with Allana throwing herself at Joseph when they made it back to Santa Fe. And this meant Taylor wouldn't have to keep worrying about Allana doing something stupid that got the rest of them shot or captured. If Echo died again because of Allana—how would Taylor explain that to Joseph?

Echo turned off the main walkway that followed the road and headed down one that led to apartment buildings.

"Where are we going?" Taylor asked.

He nodded toward a tall yellow building. "We'll go inside there so I can take care of your foot. Once you can walk, we'll go for the crystal."

"You shouldn't be carrying me," Taylor said, remembering his injury. "You'll hurt your shoulder."

"It's fine." He shifted her in his arms, holding her so that his damaged shoulder carried less weight. "Put your arms around my neck and giggle. Act like we're in love and this is a game. We'll be less conspicuous that way."

Taylor adjusted her pant leg to hide the rip. "I'm not really the type of girl who giggles."

Echo gave her a warm, intimate smile, the type you gave to someone you were flirting with. She knew it was fake, and yet it still managed to make her insides flutter. His blue eyes had a way of catching a person's attention and holding it. "Come on," he murmured, "arms around my neck. If people know you're injured, they'll wonder why I'm not taking you to a med clinic. They'll remember us. Every once in a while demand I give you your boot back."

"I'll get blood on your shirt," she said, and gave him a sultry look. "Darling."

He leaned his forehead toward hers. He smelled of something fresh, woodsy, like the outdoors. She missed the outdoors; that was why she was breathing so deeply.

"People won't notice blood splatters," he whispered. 'If they see a smile on your face and a kiss waiting on your lips, they'll think it's just red dye on your hands."

A kiss waiting on her lips? She supposed that was a saying from the twenty-fifth century and not a poetic moment from Echo. Taylor carefully wound her arms around his neck. With his square jaw and perfect features, he really was unfairly handsome. She couldn't help but notice how muscular he was. He had such strong arms. "Where have you been all my life?" she asked, and then leaned over and nuzzled his ear. "Oh yeah, you weren't born for most of my life, and then you were dead."

"But I'm here now," he said, and his voice turned soft and silky. The kind of voice a girl could lap up. "That's the important thing—showing up eventually."

He put his lips against her temple, a touch that sent an electric sensation skittering down her back. That wasn't supposed to happen. This was all pretend.

His lips made a soft trail down to her cheek, then he lifted his head. "How much do you love me?" The question was for the benefit of a couple of women who were passing by.

Taylor forced a laugh. "As much as you love me."

Echo grinned, and it seemed genuine, amused. Could he tell her heart was beating faster? Was she blushing?

They were nearly to the entrance of one of the buildings. People were coming and going, their clothes brilliant splashes of color against the beige walkways. A group of benches circled the courtyard, and several people sat there eating and talking.

It was nice resting against Echo's chest, Taylor decided, easy to nestle in his arms like this. He leaned his head so that his lips brushed against her hair. "You're beautiful," he said. "The first time I saw you, I wanted"—he paused, stiffened—"your laser box."

Taylor almost snorted. "Okay, as romantic lines go, that one is lacking." She glanced up at his face. He wasn't looking at her anymore. He had turned to see who was running up behind them.

Taylor heard the footsteps then, too late to grab her laser box. She peered over Echo's shoulder and was relieved to see it was just Allana, hurrying to catch up to them. Echo turned back around and kept walking forward.

Taylor smiled at him again, but Allana's arrival had changed everything. She could feel the tension in his body now. "Go on," Taylor told Echo. "You were telling me how beautiful I am."

Allana reached Echo's side and slowed down to keep pace with him. Breathlessly, she said, "I decided to come with you."

Taylor looked upward. "Suddenly I'm feeling a lot less romantic."

Echo spoke to Allana without looking at her, didn't act like she was with them at all. "What's wrong? Couldn't you get ahold of any of your friends?"

"It's not that." Allana tossed her silver hair from one shoulder to show the suggestion offended her. "I was deciding who to call—who I could trust—and I realized you were right. Any of my friends could turn me over to the Dakine. Most of them would. Even my father won't be able to keep the Dakine away." Her voice turned soft. "The only way I can be safe is by staying with you."

Taylor couldn't tell if Allana's words had the effect she wanted. Echo's expression was emotionless. "Give me your comlink."

Allana unclipped it from her belt and held it out to him. He set Taylor down and took the comlink. He pushed a few buttons on the side, checking the call history. Then he tapped in some command functions. Judging from the computer code, he was going through the internal history to see if Allana had deleted anything.

Allana knew what he was doing. She folded her arms, and her model pout returned. "You don't trust me," she said, sounding hurt. "I told you I didn't call anyone."

"And now I have the proof you didn't." He tucked the comlink back into his belt. "So I can trust you. If you had called your father, every Enforcer in the city would be looking us."

"We just gassed the courthouse lobby," Allana pointed out. "They're already looking for us."

"No," Echo said. "They're looking for four unknown people. Xavier and Taylor's image scramblers blurred the surveillance cameras." Echo picked up Taylor again, wincing this time. His shoulder was bothering him more than he let on. "Keep behind us," he told Allana. "Taylor and I are pretending we're in love."

He headed toward the building, smiling at Taylor again. "I believe," he told her in an intimate sort of tone, "you were telling me how wildly attractive you think I am. Go on. . . ."

Taylor laid her head against his neck. She caught another whiff of his sensual outdoorsy smell and wondered if he used a special type of sparkle to keep himself clean. Did bacteria come in aftershave scents? "I'd find you more wildly attractive if your ex-girlfriend wasn't following us." Taylor sighed playfully. "But then, the course of true love never did run smooth."

"Shakespeare," Echo said, as though answering a trivia question. "*A Midsummer Night's Dream.*"

Taylor straightened in his arms a bit. "People still read Shakespeare here?"

"No, but historians do. Shakespeare is the most-quoted writer in history. He added over seventeen hundred words to the English language."

Taylor leaned her head against Echo's neck again. "I find that incredibly attractive."

"Do you mean Shakespeare is attractive for creating all those words or I'm attractive for knowing about it?"

"You," Taylor purred. "I've never been crazy about Shakespeare's hair."

When they were nearly to the apartment building's front entrance, Echo whispered, "We'll be able to find someplace private on the ground floor. Security guards only check people's crystals if they want to use the elevators. For all the guard knows, we're here to use the building's foodmart. Act happy."

As Echo carried Taylor through the front doors, she tossed back her head and managed a laugh that she hoped sounded carefree. The lobby was large and hotel-like. A security desk stood directly in front of a line of elevators, a store and a restaurant were visible to the left, and doors to several hallways circled the rest of the room. Computer-graphic flames lined the bottom of every visible wall, churning and crackling like one gigantic fireplace. It was probably supposed to look cozy, but it made Taylor want to reach for an extinguisher.

As Echo carried Taylor across the lobby, he gave her a rakish grin. He was very good at those, actually. He must have had a lot of practice doing that look. "I won't put you down until you tell me you love me," he said.

The bored-looking man at the security desk barely noticed them. Echo walked toward one of the hallways, passing groups of people coming or going. A few people glanced over at them. Most ignored them altogether.

Bless human nature. People in the twenty-fifth century were as obliviously unconcerned and unobservant as those in the twenty-first.

Echo walked past closed doors, and some that were open too. In those, groups of people sat on gel couches watching programs on monitors, eating, and talking. The rooms were like public living rooms.

Allana followed behind Echo, far enough to look as though she was a stranger who happened to be walking in the same direction. Even now when everything had gone wrong, Allana's walk had a strut to it, a confidence in her beauty and power.

Right before Echo found an empty room, Allana's gaze connected with Taylor's. Allana's eyes were cold, hard, and glittering with jealous hatred. There was a challenge in that look, an assurance. She might as well have said the words out loud: *I will get Echo back. He'll always love me. And in the end, he'll do what I want.*

chapter ~~hapter~~
27

Sheridan woke up from the laser stun by degrees, drifting in an odd sort of dream state, one that felt almost like a memory. She was in a living room with Echo, sitting on a green gel couch.

He leaned his head against the back of the couch, giving her a look that was both sleepy and intimate. "Don't go yet. Let me look at you for a few more minutes."

"You want to look at me?" she asked, amused, flattered.

"So I'll remember everything about you."

And then the dream was gone and she was staring at the gray metallic ceiling of the detention center.

She blinked, trying to hold on to the images as they faded. Maybe it was one of those psychic twin bonds she'd always heard about. Perhaps she had caught a glimpse of what Taylor was doing.

The thought brought her no comfort.

"You're awake," a voice behind her said. "Good. Your visitor has been waiting."

Sheridan recognized The Tough One's voice before she turned to see where she was. She lay on the metal floor of an observation room. A chair sat nearby waiting for her. The Tough One stood behind her next to the door, his laser box held loosely in his hand. Visitors were never a good thing. Hesitantly, Sheridan got up from the floor and sat in the chair.

A glass wall divided the room in two. Taylor stood right on the other side it. She looked almost the same as the last time Sheridan had seen her—white hair, blue swirls on her cheeks. Her eyes were red and there was a catch to her voice, as though she'd been crying. She pressed her hand to the glass wall. "Sheridan," she said, "you're all right."

That depended on your definition of *all right*. Sheridan was alive, mostly sane, and suspicious. Would there be fingerprints on the glass once Taylor moved her hand? Was that the sort of detail Reilly had started paying attention to?

Taylor was probably just a projection, a hologram of some sort. Reilly had used those before. She'd been visited by the images of Elise, Jeth, and Echo, all of whom looked through her instead of at her. That was why the Enforcers kept Sheridan behind the glass. You couldn't touch holograms. Still, Sheridan's hand automatically stretched toward the image of her sister.

Taylor gulped, chest heaving with emotion. Her words came out in a broken rush. "They said they would kill me if you didn't help them. They said they would torture me first." Taylor blinked back a new set of tears. "I told them that if they let me

238

talk to you, I could get you to agree to work with them."

Footsteps sounded from the hallway on Taylor's side of the room, someone walking toward the door behind her. Taylor looked over her shoulder, then back at Sheridan. Her eyes were desperate. "You're going to help them, aren't you? Don't let them hurt me anymore." She moved her hand away from the glass. No fingerprints.

Sheridan sighed. "You're not my sister."

The door behind Taylor opened and an Enforcer walked inside. Taylor took a couple of nervous steps across the room, backing away from him, shaking now. She shot a quick look at Sheridan. "You've got to help me. Please."

"You're not real," Sheridan said, more firmly.

"Don't let them take me," Taylor wailed. "Please, Sheridan, you're the only one who can help me."

Sheridan shut her eyes. She didn't like seeing what would come next, even though she knew it wasn't real. She had nightmares with these images. Taylor's wailing grew louder. The Enforcer yelled, and then a smack sounded through the room. He was a hologram too then. Otherwise his hand would have gone right through her.

More wailing penetrated the room. Whoever had programmed the hologram didn't know Taylor very well. The real Taylor would have showed some attitude somewhere in all that. The real Taylor would have given Sheridan some sort of message.

Sheridan hummed to block out the sounds as best she could. All of this was good news, she told herself. Reilly could have only one reason for not using the real Taylor in any of these scenes. He didn't have her anymore. Somehow she had escaped.

Sheridan liked to think that Taylor had outsmarted them all and figured a way out of her prison, that maybe someday Taylor would find a way to rescue her too. Sheridan didn't let herself consider, at least not for long, the possibility that Taylor was dead. It was an outcome too horrible to think about.

The wailing stopped. The door slid closed.

Sheridan kept humming. Were they still playing the soundtrack of Taylor screaming in the hallway? Or was that only in Sheridan's mind, a sound that wouldn't go away?

The door behind Sheridan slid open. She turned and saw Reilly strolling in.

He was in his sixties and shorter and heavier-set then any of the other men she'd seen in the twenty-fifth century. Sheridan supposed that was due to the genetic breeding Traventon did now.

Wrinkles sagged across Reilly's face, and he had jowls that hung down like fish gills at his neck. His thick green hair was probably real, but it reminded her of an artificial-lawn toupee. Really, he'd been here too long if he thought it looked anything but ridiculous. Ditto for his green lips and bushy green eyebrows.

He strode across the room to her with the same air of self-importance that always accompanied him. His rank badge read 42 today—up one from the 43 it had been every other day she'd seen him. She wondered if he'd had one of his rivals killed off.

Reilly shook his head in disapproval. "You're not a very loving sister, are you? Do you even care that Taylor was dragged off to be tortured?"

Sheridan forced a smile. "Don't get me wrong. I'm completely against the torture of holograms. It makes me wonder what you're going to beat up next. Fairies? Leprechauns? I'd hate to see Ronald McDonald getting roughed up."

"Still so flippant." Reilly walked over until he stood next to her. He casually reached out and ran his hand across a strand of her hair. His breath smelled like coffee. "Do you think I'm a hologram too?"

She eyed him. "You could be. A real person wouldn't purposely do his hair that way. Must be a computer malfunction."

Reilly slapped her so quickly that she didn't have time to brace herself beforehand.

"Real enough?" he asked her. "Or do you need more proof?"

Sheridan's cheek stung. She tasted blood in her mouth. This was probably a good time to shut up, and yet she didn't. She'd grown reckless here in prison. Somehow it seemed worth it to make him angry even though she knew it would cost her. "Do I need the proof or do you? Do you believe you're real?"

He stared at her without answering.

"Why should people believe in you," she said, "when it's clear to everyone else you don't believe in yourself?"

He hit her again. This time she expected it and flinched. Taylor had done this, resisted him. Taylor hadn't cried. Sheridan could be as strong as Taylor.

Sheridan shut her eyes. "Go away and send me another hologram. How about a hot guy from our century? Can you do a young Harrison Ford? Make him look like Han Solo. I might tell Han Solo everything I know about the QGP." *It wouldn't,* she thought wryly, *even be a long conversation.* She didn't know much about physics.

Technically Reilly had already tried the hot-guy informant trick on her, was still trying it on her. The two weeks that Reilly had been gone, Tariq had spent hours every day talking, playing games, and flirting with Sheridan. He'd brought her real food: strawberries, peaches, and cookies. Even though it was hard to keep her appetite at bay, she never ate enough to completely fill her. If she landed in a VR program again, she wanted to have a way to tell.

On the last day of Reilly's absence, Tariq sneaked her out of her cell and took her to the top floor of the detention center, to an apartment the warden used for entertaining visitors. "Enforcers," Tariq told her confidentially, "use it when the warden doesn't. It's my turn to have it tonight."

The room looked as though it belonged on a spaceship. The walls and ceiling were black with stars twinkling everywhere. A three-dimensional moon glowed on one wall. A swirling nebula pulsed on another. Saturn hung down in the middle of the room, providing light as its rings turned. Slick black couches faced each other over a silver coffee table.

What held Sheridan's attention the most was a dimly lit glass case that stood against the nearest wall. Food sat on its shelves. Bowls of fruit, sandwiches, and pieces of cake in puddles of chocolate. Some of the dishes she didn't recognize. They still made her mouth water.

Tariq stood behind Sheridan. He put his hands on her shoulders and leaned near enough to whisper in her ear. "It's beautiful, isn't it—how the rich people live."

She pulled her attention away from the food. "Where I lived, everyone used to be able to see the stars. Although"—she gestured to the glowing planet hanging from the ceiling—"Saturn was a lot smaller."

He took her hand and led her toward the food. "What do you want to eat?"

All of it. Especially the chocolate. *A fork sat on the side of each plate, beckoning to be used.* "Won't the warden notice if food is missing? I don't want to get you in trouble."

As soon as Tariq stopped in front of the glass case, the door slid open. "Don't worry. The foodmart workers will make more. They overlook our indiscretions, and we overlook theirs. Choose something."

Sheridan told herself to take something she could resist, something that wouldn't fill her up. She reached for the chocolate cake anyway. It was in her hand before she could finish reminding herself to protect her hunger. She couldn't help herself. Chocolate tasted like home.

Tariq took a raspberry pastry, then motioned for her to follow him over to the couch. "Have you ever had a massage?"

Was he asking for one? A part of her was still afraid of Tariq, wary of what he would do next. He was her guard, and he might expect something in return for his gifts.

Sheridan took the fork from her plate. It was light, plastic-like. Not much of a weapon. "Everyone has had a massage, haven't they?"

Tariq sat down on the couch, and it shifted and reshaped underneath him, supporting his legs like a recliner. He leaned back and took a bite of his pastry. "I love these."

Sheridan sat down on the opposite end of the couch and then realized Tariq's love was directed at the couch, not the pastry. Not only did the couch shape shift around her, but warm jets of air kneaded into her back, massaging the muscles there. She melted into the couch, relaxing. "Civilization has made progress after all."

As they ate, Tariq told her about other things the warden had in his apartment: 3-D action games and programs people could watch or take part in. "He doesn't have to go to a virtual reality center and spend credits on it like everyone else. He's got his own equipment."

Sheridan took slow, savoring bites of her cake. She told herself every bite would be her last but somehow ate the whole thing anyway. Chocolate, her Achilles's heel. This would mean she couldn't eat any of her meal bar tonight. She needed her hunger.

The couch's pulsing massage faded into a warm, soothing sensation. Tariq took her plate and her fork and placed them on the floor. "Music," he said. "Twenty-first century."

At first Sheridan had no idea what he meant. Then a melody from The Nutcracker filled the room.

Tariq moved over next to her, and the couch automatically shifted to accommodate the change. He slid his arm around her shoulder. "Do you like this?"

Sheridan's heart began to pound, beating out a warning. "The music? Yes. But it's not twenty-first century." She leaned away from him to put more space between them. "I mean, we had The Nutcracker in the twenty-first century, but it was written in the nineteenth. At least, those are the sorts of clothes the people in the ballet wore." She was nervous and babbling.

Tariq smiled at her, amused that she was flustered. "I meant, do you like me putting my arm around you?" His fingers wound through her hair, teasing the skin at the nape of her neck.

"Oh." She didn't move closer to him. "Sorry. I guess I'm not one for doomed romances."

"Are you sure ours is doomed?" He leaned over so that his breath brushed against her cheek, then his lips brushed there as well.

"You're my guard," Sheridan said slowly. "Sooner or later you'll have to take me in for a memory wash. That's pretty much the definition of a doomed romance."

His lips slid from her cheek to her earlobe. "It doesn't have to end that way."

"Right. Reilly could order me executed instead."

"Or I could help you escape."

A shiver of hope went through Sheridan. She turned, pulling away from Tariq enough to see his eyes and gauge their sincerity. "Are you offering?"

His fingers continued to stroke the hair at her neck. "I read your file. I had to find out if what you'd told me about coming from the past was true. I know why you're here. I know about the QGPs."

"Are you going to help me escape?" she asked again.

He hesitated, deciding how much to say. "You have to under-stand—it's not something I can do by myself."

The shiver of hope turned to a tremor. This was real. She had eaten cake and it had made her less hungry. Tariq was actually here talking about helping her.

He dropped his hand away from her neck and turned to look at her squarely. "I belong to a group called the DW. At first they weren't interested in helping you. It's dangerous for them, and you're not a member. But after I told them about the QGPs, once they understood you've refused to help Reilly because you don't want to hurt people, they agreed."

Sheridan knew who the DW were. Elise had told her they had ways to get out of the city safely.

"The DW's engineers," Tariq went on, "want to build machines that counter the QGPs. The problem is we don't have the schematics. We have to know how the QGP works so we can figure out how to stop it."

Well, that would present a problem since Sheridan didn't know the schematics. Still, if Sheridan took Taylor with her, Taylor would be able to help them. Taylor already knew how to destroy QGPs. "Can they free my sister too?"

"We can try. Her guards aren't my friends. It will be harder to get Taylor away from them."

Sheridan didn't want to keep feeling the glow of hope inside her, the lifting of her heart. It would make her careless, and she needed to be cautious. Tariq's plan could be an attempt to get information from her. Tariq could be working for Reilly, using honey instead of vinegar to get what he wanted.

Tariq kept his gaze locked on Sheridan's. She saw no deception in his dark eyes, only eagerness. She wanted so badly to believe him.

He put his hand on top of hers, weaving his fingers into hers. "Are you willing to give the DW information about the QGPs?"

Sheridan didn't answer, just kept watching Tariq's eyes. They were chocolate brown. Hard to resist.

"If I could, I would free you by myself," Tariq emphasized, giving her hand a squeeze. "I need their help, though."

Sheridan's mind spun. How could she ensure freedom without risking her sister? What could she tell them?

When Sheridan didn't answer, Tariq slid his hands around her waist. "Our romance doesn't have to be doomed," he said again, and *leaned over and kissed her. His lips were soft against hers. Gentle and coaxing.*

She felt a flash of guilt for kissing him. Echo loomed in her mind, his piercing blue eyes watching her. What would he think if he knew she was kissing her guard?

She pushed the thought away. Tariq was trying to help her. He might be her only way out of this prison. She needed a piece of hope to hold on to. As she kissed him back, her mind went through different possible ways to handle the DW, safeguards she would need in order to protect herself and Taylor.

Finally Tariq lifted his head. He took her hands in his and smiled. "Is there something about the QGP that you can tell me—anything that will show the DW you're going to cooperate?"

No, actually there wasn't. She let out a long breath. "I have to be sure about the DW's intentions before I tell them anything. I can't risk the QGP falling into the wrong hands."

Tariq ran his fingers up her arm. "It won't fall into the wrong hands. The DW only want the information to save lives."

That was when Sheridan realized, with an icy shudder in her stomach, the mistake Tariq had just made—had been making all along without Sheridan noticing. He never questioned the twenty-first-century idioms Sheridan used. If she had used the phrase I can't risk it falling into the wrong hands *with Echo, he would have said, "We won't drop the QGPs. That would damage them." Or at the very least, he would have given her a questioning look while he figured out what she meant.*

Tariq took in most of her slang without confusion. Without question. Which meant he had heard the slang phrases before and already knew their meaning.

The coldness spread from Sheridan's stomach into her chest, went through her limbs like ice water. She nearly shivered. The only person Tariq could have heard twenty-first-century slang from was Reilly. And it wasn't something a person would pick up all at once. Tariq must have spent months, years maybe, with him.

"What's wrong?" Tariq had seen her expression change. He took her chin in his hand and tilted her face so she was looking at him.

Sheridan gulped and did her best to keep the fear from her voice. "The QGP is a dangerous machine. I'm responsible for it. I can't forget that."

Concern flashed in Tariq's eyes, sympathy. "You're not responsible for what other people do."

He seemed so sincere. Was there a chance, however small, that what Tariq was offering her was legitimate? Just because Tariq had been around Reilly didn't mean he was in league with him. Tariq might be a double agent for the DW. He might be telling her the truth.

But then why would he pretend he didn't know Reilly? Tariq acted like he hadn't even seen Reilly until he became Sheridan's guard.

Tariq dropped another kiss on her lips, still gentle and coaxing. The kiss of someone who cared about her. Perhaps Tariq had a reasonable explanation for not telling Sheridan he'd been around Reilly. Or . . . perhaps she was a fool who was unwilling to let go of a string of hope once it had been handed to her. There was so little to cling to in this place.

When Tariq lifted his head this time, Sheridan said, "Tell the DW I'll only cooperate with them after they help both Taylor and me escape from the city and go someplace safe. I won't give them *any information until then."*

Looking back, perhaps it had been a mistake to ever propose that deal. It led to a series of virtual reality programs. Each time Sheridan woke up now—whether it was in the morning or in the middle of the night—she didn't know if what she experienced was real or the work of a computer program. Sometimes Tariq came to rescue her. A few times it was Jeth, Elise, Echo, other guards, even strangers. Once her cell door malfunctioned and she escaped on her own.

Usually during the escape programs, the rescuer told Sheridan that Taylor was already free and they would meet up with her later. Other times Taylor was with them but so sick, injured, or dazed she couldn't talk much. Taylor always had a reason for not acting like herself, a reason she couldn't answer Sheridan's questions.

Sheridan escaped into various safe houses in the city. One time she even escaped out of the city. That experience had been especially strange. Tariq had smuggled Sheridan in a stolen garbage-transport vehicle through one of Traventon's outer doors.

As soon as the transporter had gone outside, Sheridan had known what she would see: the wreckage of a ruined city, jagged pieces of cement stacked on one another, rebar reaching from the ground, and everything covered with gray dust.

The landscape was exactly how Sheridan had pictured it. Even the outline of the wreckage seemed familiar.

How had she known? Had Reilly put this image in her mind before? No, she was sure he hadn't. It was new, and yet she recognized it.

The déjà vu added one more layer to the odd surrealness that had become her life.

Every time a new escape started, Sheridan hoped it would be real. She carried that hope around, cradled and protected it while she waited to eat. Her hunger never diminished during the escapes. In fact, it grew worse. Her mind expected food and every single bite left her emptier. Still, with every new escape she hoped. She hoped until she began to hate hope itself. It lifted her up, just to let her fall. She was tired of being crashed and broken.

Sheridan always let the programs play out until someone insisted she give them information. Then she tried to escape. That usually led to her being shot or killed. Which might not have been so bad except that the pain, like the taste of food, was authentic.

Sometimes Sheridan would wake from one program just to plunge into another—to someone opening her door and motioning to her that it was time to go. It was like dreaming you had woken up. She lost track of time, events, couldn't remember how many days she'd been here. Everything felt unreal and unhinged. Even pacing in her cell and practicing her accent had a surreal quality to it.

Now Sheridan looked at Reilly steadily. "You don't have my sister anymore, do you?" She liked asking him this question. It made him angry, and that was as good as reassurance.

Reilly put his hands behind his back. The wrinkles between his bushy green eyebrows deepened. "I'm losing patience with you."

"We had a secret handshake, you know. All twins do. I'll always be able to tell it's not her."

"We have new ways to torture people now," Reilly said

slowly, injecting each word with menace. "I can strap electrodes directly to the pain region of your brain. It's very efficient."

Sheridan didn't answer him.

He leaned closer to her and smiled. "Of course the old methods work well too." He picked up her left hand and caressed her wrist. "In the Middle Ages, the Normans used to cut off limbs as punishment for crimes." He turned her hand over, examining it. "How many fingers does a person actually need?"

Prickles of fear jabbed into Sheridan's chest. She wanted to yank her hand away from him. She didn't though. She'd played poker with Taylor enough times to know how to bluff. "You can torture me if you want. We both know I'll eventually agree to help you. But then while we're working on the QGP, you'll have to wonder whether I'm really helping you or whether I'm sabotaging you. How sure are you that you'll be able to tell the difference?"

Reilly squeezed her hand, each moment applying more pressure until she gasped out in pain. "Fine," he spit out. "Have it your way. I've already scheduled a memory wash for you." He flung her hand back at her, left it throbbing in her lap. "You have an hour to willingly cooperate with me. After that, your mind will be wiped clean, you'll be reeducated, and you'll be taught to work with us anyway. Think about that."

He turned and stalked out of the room.

chapter ~~hapter~~
28

Echo's hands were gentle as he slid the medical scanner over Taylor's foot. She watched his progress with a growing sense of dismay. Even though she was lying on the couch with her foot elevated, it was already so swollen, it looked like she didn't have an ankle. She wasn't going to be able to walk on it any time soon.

Allana sat on a gel chair not far away. The wall in front of her doubled as a large computer screen, and she flipped through updates from the city's news channels. She looked bored and beautiful, and kept running her fingers through her silver hair absentmindedly.

Taylor felt an electric tingle from her comlink and smelled pine. Joseph. She unclipped her comlink and read the message. *We have a plan in motion to break into the detention center.*

Have you destroyed the QGPs?

Speaking into her comlink, Taylor said, "I have a plan in motion to destroy them. Let me know when you have Sheridan." Taylor wanted to tell him about Xavier, and yet at the same time dreaded it, couldn't do it. She put her comlink back on her belt.

Echo took his attention from the medical scanner long enough to give her a penetrating stare. "You know, sometimes you have to trust people."

"If you never trust anyone, you'll never be disappointed."

He went back to checking her foot. "But you'll never be happy either."

Taylor let out a short laugh. "Right now, I'll settle for cynicism and my sister's life."

The medical scanner beeped and Echo read its diagnosis. "Your ankle isn't broken. You need a shot for swelling and one that reconnects torn ligaments" He put the scanner down and rummaged through the medical bag. Every once in a while he pulled out a vial to check the label. "It will still be—I don't know—maybe an hour before you'll be able to walk."

He was clearly discouraged by this fact, but it seemed miraculous to Taylor. An hour wasn't that long. And they needed to be hidden out of the way somewhere until Joseph had rescued Sheridan. This place was as good as anywhere else.

Echo found the vials he was looking for. He attached needles to them and then used the scanner to tell him where the medicine needed to go. Taylor's foot already throbbed so much, she barely felt the needle pricks.

"We'll need to find some shoes for you," he said.

"When you say 'find,'" Taylor asked, "do you mean 'steal'?"

"Probably," he said.

Taylor sighed. She just couldn't seem to stay on the right side of the law in this city.

Echo took the needle out of one side of her ankle and put it into the other. "You can't walk four kilometers with only one boot."

Allana clicked on a report about an attempt to disrupt courthouse rulings. The wall showed blurry pictures of the group walking down the hallway on the top floor of the courthouse.

"Enforcers are matching DNA from the scene," a plaid-haired newscaster said smugly, "and will issue arrest warrants soon."

Allana scoffed. "Which means they know nothing. Hundreds of people go through that building every day. They're not going to find DNA that will help them."

Echo jabbed a needle into a particularly tender spot on Taylor's ankle. She winced. "Is it good news or bad news that the newsfeeds aren't mentioning what happened at the Scicenter?"

"Neither," Echo said, finishing up the shot. "They won't report damage to equipment that they don't want people to know about. They'll try to figure out who we are and how to find us without letting the public know anything about it."

Finished with her ankle, Echo scooted down the couch to examine Taylor's hands. He gently turned them over. Streaks of blood ran from her palms to her fingertips, some still fresh. One thumb was swollen. He pulled the lid off a flesh-colored tube, revealing a tip that looked like a paintbrush. "Artificial skin," he told her. "It will sting." He dabbed the liquid along her palm.

It didn't sting; it burned like fire. The stab of pain made Taylor want to jerk her hand away. She didn't, though. She left it there, trembling, cradled in his hand. "Stinging has apparently become a lot more painful through the centuries."

He moved the brush to her finger, gliding streaks of pain in that direction. "Did you know," he said conversationally, "that your fingertips have some of the densest areas of nerve endings in your body?"

"I didn't," Taylor said, "or I would have caught myself with my elbows."

Another finger. More pain. "That would have been tricky," he said, "but it wouldn't have surprised me. Not from a girl who walks along ledges backward." He was trying to distract her from the pain with small talk. She wished it worked better.

"How old are you?"

"Eighteen."

"Eighteen?" He glanced up at her, surprised. A flash of intrigue went through his eyes.

Taylor realized she shouldn't have told him anything about herself. He already knew she was from the past and that she and Joseph had come back to Traventon to destroy the QGPs. But he didn't know that she had also created the QGP and that both the government and the Dakine wanted to capture her.

Echo went back to applying the artificial skin. "You computigate pretty well for an eighteen-year-old."

"You're only twenty," she pointed out. "And you know a lot more about computigating than I do."

"Yeah. That's why I know how hard it is to learn." He finished with her first hand. The pain had already subsided along her palm; it felt almost normal.

Echo looked up at her and did a double take. Then he stared openly at her.

"What?" she asked.

"Your face," he said. "You look different. You look . . ."

For a moment she was alarmed, and then relaxed when she understood what had happened. "I took a shot to make my face puffy. It was supposed to help disguise me. The shot in my ankle must have gotten rid of the swelling in my face too."

Echo kept staring at her. It made her feel self-conscious. She wondered if she'd been mistaken and he was staring at her for some other reason.

"What?" she asked, touching her cheek tentatively. "What's wrong?"

"Nothing," he said, and smiled. "I just didn't realize before how beautiful you are."

She felt herself blushing and didn't know what to say.

Taylor had forgotten Allana was in the room until she called out, "Echo, I need your help too. Look." She held up her left hand to show him. A small scrape ran along her palm. It wasn't deep, only pink with flecks of blood.

Without glancing at Allana, Echo moved to the scrape on Taylor's knee. He stroked the brush across the wound. It felt like a burning slash. "Taylor's injuries are worse than yours. I want to make sure there's enough artificial skin to cover them."

Allana let out an irritated huff. "You didn't even look at mine. How do you know hers are worse?"

"I know," Echo said calmly, "because if you were hurt worse than this, you would have told us about it repeatedly."

Allana let out another huff, this one sounding offended. "The medkit has to have more than two tubes of artificial skin."

The tube Echo had been using ran out. He tossed it onto the couch and opened the second one. "The rest of them fell out in the car."

That had been Taylor's fault. She'd spilled things out of the medkit when she was trying to help Xavier.

"Are there pain erasers?" Allana asked.

"If there were, don't you think I would have given one to Taylor before now?" Echo straightened and took Taylor's other hand in his. She flinched before he even touched her with the brush. "Are you all right?" he asked patiently.

She nodded. "Just give me a second to catch my breath."

Allana turned in her chair, coldly surveying Taylor. "Catch your breath?" She laughed in a way that was more mocking than amused. "Is it running away from you?"

"I like the phrase," Echo said. "It's either poetic or a very intriguing activity." He gave Taylor a knowing smile. "You'll have to show me how to do it sometime."

He was flirting with her. She wondered if that was solely for Allana's benefit—Allana had hurt Echo by rejecting him for Joseph, so Echo flirted with Taylor to make Allana jealous.

The strategy was working perfectly. Allana sat tight-lipped on her chair, chin tilted in that angry haughty-couture way.

Taylor smiled back at Echo but didn't feel it. She didn't like being used, didn't want to be discarded after Echo decided he'd punished Allana enough.

"Breath caught?" he asked her.

Taylor nodded. She wasn't going to flirt back. She would pretend Echo was Joseph and therefore off-limits.

As soon as Echo ran the tube across her hand, pain flamed through her palm. To block it out, she focused on Echo's face, on the expression of concentration in his blue eyes. The smooth planes of his cheeks. The square jaw. Such a handsome face. Not that she was attracted to him. She was only making an observation. Some people were gorgeous.

Echo glanced at her. She was embarrassed to be caught staring and had a sudden irrational worry that he could read her thoughts. She shifted her weight. "How did you manage to keep from falling when you jumped out of the car?"

"Practice," he said. "I do a lot of VR adventure programs."

"Oh." Taylor took a couple of quick breaths to push away the pain. "I guess I should have spent less time writing computer code and more time flinging myself from moving vehicles."

He chuckled and leaned over to better see her hand. "People who are smart enough to write computer code generally avoid flinging themselves out of cars. They know too much about force and acceleration principles."

"It's not the acceleration that's the problem," Taylor said. "It's the friction that accompanies the sudden deceleration."

Allana let out a disgusted grunt. "First arcane sayings and now physics discussions. You're positively the girl version of Echo, aren't you?"

"I wouldn't say that." Echo still didn't look over at Allana. "I was just thinking that Taylor seems like the responsible type, the kind who can clean up indiscretions."

Taylor wouldn't have described herself that way. The words meant something to Allana though. She narrowed her eyes angrily at Echo, then turned away and busied herself by flipping through more news updates.

When Echo finished, he put the lid on the artificial-skin tube and tossed it to Allana. "Give it back when you're done. I got nicked by some flames in the courthouse." He turned his arm to check on the wound.

Until then, Taylor hadn't noticed that one of Echo's sleeves had a tear. He gingerly pushed the material aside, revealing an inch-long raised welt above his wrist. Not bad, but it had to hurt like crazy. Burns always did.

While Allana, grimacing, spread artificial skin on her wound, Echo unbuckled Taylor's remaining boot. She felt oddly like a reverse Cinderella.

"I'll need this," Echo said, referring to her boot, "so I can find the right size shoes for you. I'll also need your lock disabler. One of the apartments upstairs must have something you can wear."

Allana blew on her hand to make the artificial skin dry faster. "How are you going to get past the elevator guard?"

"I'll find a way." Echo set the boot down, then sifted through the pack that lay open on the couch. "I might need a sleeping shot."

"And no one will notice the guard slumped over his desk." Allana stood up with a martyred sigh and flounced over. She held her hand out for the boot. "Let me do it. I know how to get around elevator guards. I'll not only get Taylor shoes, I'll find some clothes we can change into."

Echo hesitated. His gaze cut over to Taylor. "What do you think?"

"I think you should have given Allana the boot a long time ago."

Echo smiled, letting her know he'd gotten the double meaning. "All right," he said, and handed Allana the boot and the lock disabler.

She slipped the disabler onto her belt, examined the boot, then tossed it onto the couch. "This will take a half hour— maybe an hour." She headed toward the door. "I always chat with the lobby guards for a while before I ask them for favors." As she went out the door, she shot Echo one last insincere smile. "And sorry about your burn. The artificial skin ran out. I guess you shouldn't have used so much on Taylor."

Then she left.

Echo stared at the door. His jaw looked tight, like he was clenching it.

"Does your burn hurt a lot?" Taylor asked.

"No," Echo said. "I'm just worried she'll borrow a comlink and call someone."

"Then why did you let her go off by herself?" Taylor fluttered her hand toward the door. "Go with her. Keep an eye on her."

Echo shook his head. "I'd rather know right now if we can trust her than find out later when it's more dangerous."

Taylor straightened. "I'm injured, we only have two laser boxes, and it won't take a lot of Enforcers to trap us in this building. How is it going to be more dangerous later?"

Echo kept staring at the door, considering. "Later Joseph and Sheridan will be with us. Their lives will be at stake too."

Taylor let out a sigh. He had a point.

chapter
29

From the doorway of the parking garage, Joseph watched Lee and Ren march up to the side of the Rico Estates apartment building. They had been lucky to find two Enforcers who lived not only in the same building, but also on the same side of the building.

Ren and Lee had taken off their face dye and science over-alls as soon as they'd all gotten into the car. Now they wore the bright clothing typical of Traventon. Lee had on lime-green checkered pants, a silky red shirt, and a hat with red horns that curled upward at the sides. Ren wore puffy orange pants, a striped blue shirt, and a yellow hat with tassels that swung around his cheeks. Distinctive. That was important.

Without hesitation, Ren and Lee took zip-line shooters from their belts. Lee squinted up at the curved windows that dotted the side of the thirteen-story building, judging the windows' distance. "Think you can make it with one shot?" he asked Ren.

"I know I can," Ren said. "If you're not sure, you'd better shoot first. Once I go up the building, people will notice us."

Lee let out a laugh. "I'm going to miss your arrogance once Santa Fe splits." He held up his shooter, taking aim. "Actually, I'm lying about that. I won't miss it at all." He pressed the button, and his wire whizzed toward a window on the ninth floor. The hook connected right above the third window over. Lee grinned. "One shot," he said, "and I was humble about it."

Ren didn't answer, just took aim and shot his wire. It flew in a nearly imperceptible line up to the building. It connected above an eleventh-story window, four windows over. Ren smirked at Lee. "One shot, and my target was farther away. What's the point of being humble when you're as good as I am?"

Lee hooked his shooter back onto his belt, connecting himself to the wire. "I'm also going to miss your competitiveness." He put his hands on his belt near the wire, steadying himself. "Actually, I'm lying about that too." With a press of a button, the wire drew in, pulling Lee upward and toward the building.

Ren joined him a moment later, and the two were half flying, half running up the building's outer wall.

Joseph held his breath, watching, hoping the plan went as flawlessly as he'd envisioned.

Several pedestrians on the walkway between the buildings stopped and gaped as Ren and Lee skimmed up the wall. Joseph walked over to the gathering crowd, pretending to be a bystander so that he could listen to their comments.

"What are they doing?" a woman asked her friend.

"It's probably part of an advertisement," her friend replied.

"Maybe they're fixing something on the outside wall," a man farther down the walkway said. He didn't sound like he believed his own explanation, though.

A couple of teenage boys edged nearer to the building; both held their comlinks out, recording the event. It was just like teenagers to record the climb—as though the streetcams wouldn't do a better job. This might make the newsfeeds if nothing more interesting happened in the next hour. "Riotsweet," one of the teenagers said, then yelled up, "Where did you buy those brilliant lifters?"

"Lifters are illegal," a woman near Joseph muttered. She wrinkled her nose disdainfully. "Those men are probably thieves or assassins."

"They can't be assassins," someone else said. "Assassins aren't that obvious, and they always give themselves a way to escape. How are those guys going to get away unnoticed?"

A man pulled his comlink from his belt. "They're DW," he said. "Once they reach the top, they'll unfurl a banner on the side of the building." He fingered a couple of buttons on his comlink. "I'm calling the Enforcers."

Even though Joseph had known this would happen, his stomach still constricted. *Hurry*, he thought, staring at Ren and Lee. They were almost to the right windows now. In a few more moments they'd be inside.

A woman just joining the group let out a disappointed sigh. "You shouldn't have called the Enforcers so soon. I want to see what their banner says."

"They all say stupid things," another woman said. "Freedom

of knowledge, freedom of belief. Freedom to hang tacky banners where they're not wanted."

Lee reached his window. He stopped in front of it, feet planted on the wall, and pulled his laser cutter from his belt. With one swift motion, he jabbed the laser cutter into the glass.

"What's he doing now?" one of the teenage boys asked. He stepped closer to the building.

The man with his comlink out had gotten ahold of someone at the Enforcement Department and was reporting the situation. "One is wearing green pants, a red shirt, and a red hat. The other man has orange pants, a blue shirt, and a yellow hat."

Joseph swallowed hard. *Hurry*, he thought, *hurry*.

By the time Lee finished arcing the laser cutter around the window, Ren had reached his window and started the same procedure.

Lee put a suction grip on the top of the cut glass and nudged the bottom with his foot. A large section of the window gave way. He pulled it out and let it drop.

The crowd stepped back, gasping. No one wanted to leave the spectacle, but they didn't want to get hit by falling glass either. Joseph took a few steps back toward the parking garage.

The window hit the ground and broke into pieces. Chunks shot upward like a small explosion. He hadn't expected that. Window glass was supposed to be shatterproof. But then again, at terminal velocity, any solid would— Joseph stopped himself. This wasn't the time to be calculating physics.

Lee slipped inside the hole he'd created, disengaging his wire as he did.

"They're thieves," a woman said with disgust. "They'll be in and out of the building before Enforcers can get here."

"They might be assassins," one of the teenage boys said. "I give it odds they push people out of the window."

At that pronouncement, two more people unclipped their comlinks.

The woman who had pronounced them thieves looked around at the crowd. "Someone will have to stop them when they come back down."

The man who'd called the Enforcers shook his head. "They might be Dakine."

A wave of murmuring went around the group, either for or against taking action against the criminals "The Enforcers will be here soon," Joseph said, and hoped his voice sounded normal, unconcerned. "They'll catch them."

Ren finished his hole. He put a gripper on the glass, pried it away from the window, and let it fall to the ground. This time the crowd stepped even farther away from the building.

Joseph didn't stay around to see how many chunks the glass broke into. He slipped back into the garage. Using the mobile crystal, he climbed into the nearest car, turned it on, and told it to wait at the garage entrance.

While he waited, he pulled his laser cutter from his belt and sliced a careful line along the side of the seat where the cushion met the car's side. He kept glancing at the clock on his comlink. Five minutes had passed. Then six. He finished cutting the top off one side of the seat, then started on the other.

What if Ren and Lee hadn't been able to hit their targets with sleeping darts? Enforcers were trained to be more careful, more aware than the average person, and they had weapons.

What if Ren and Lee had been shot as soon as they'd gone through the windows? What would Joseph do then? What *could* he do? Maybe this hadn't been a brilliant idea. Maybe it had been a miserable plan from the start.

Joseph gave the laser cutter a hard tug. Overconfidence. That had been his problem all along. He was smarter than most people, and so he thought his ideas would always work. He got caught up in applauding himself for his intelligence instead of paying attention to the details that could rip his plans apart.

He had saved his brother's life, and it had cost him Sheridan. Details like that. Now he might have just gotten Ren and Lee killed.

When he finished slicing the seat cushions, he sat down next to the car's control panel and held the mobile crystal to the map. "Wait in front of the Rico Estates building."

The car glided outside, following the rail to connect with the main rail out front. Joseph glanced at the clock. It had been twelve minutes since Ren and Lee had gone inside, and there was no sign of them.

If they didn't hurry, they would run into Enforcers. Joseph didn't see any cars besides his waiting in front of the building, but Enforcers might have parked on the other street. They might be inside already.

The crowd stood around still, watching and talking.

Another minute went by. Joseph growled and fingered the laser box on his belt. This had been a stupid, stupid idea.

How long should he wait until he went inside searching for them?

Then the building's doors slid open. Two black-clad

Enforcers strode outside. One half carried, half dragged the limp form of a man with lime-green pants and a silky red shirt. His hat perched at a crooked angle, hiding most of his face. Behind him, the other Enforcer carried the second man. His orange pants were crinkled, and the blue shirt was no longer tucked in. His hat had been smashed down over his eyes. The tassels swayed back and forth with every step the Enforcer took.

The crowd turned when they saw the Enforcers emerge from the building. The teenage boys let out whoops of approval, and a couple of the women clapped. Several other people held out their comlinks, recording the event.

"Finally," the man who'd reported the break-in said. "For once the Enforcers got to a crime in time."

The Enforcers ignored the crowd and walked straight toward the car. Joseph watched them, every muscle in his body tense. When they got close, he pushed the button to open the door.

The Enforcers climbed into the car, pulling the unconscious men with them. It was only then, when Ren and Lee were close enough that Joseph could see their faces through the Enforcers' smoky visors, that he let out a sigh of relief.

Before the door had even shut, Joseph held the mobile crystal to the car's control panel. "Detention Center Thirteen," he said, then dropped his hand away from the panel. "It took you long enough. If the real Enforcers had been faster, they would have run into you."

"Sorry," Lee said. "It's harder to dress an unconscious man than you'd think."

Ren straightened his belt. "I'm just glad I found my guy's

suit. His place was as messy as a viker camp."

The car turned onto another street, and Joseph lost sight of the dispersing crowd. They'd done it. They'd gotten away.

Lee looked upward and laughed. "I can't believe that worked."

Joseph sat back in his seat, satisfied. "I'm brilliant. Have I mentioned that already?"

"A few times." Ren pulled the holographic camera from his belt. "Let's hope the rest of the plan goes as smoothly."

For the next few minutes, Ren and Lee fiddled with the computer on the camera, trying to get a holographic picture of the Enforcers' faces that looked normal. Even with their eyelids propped open, the Enforcers' stares were vacant, expressionless, and the computer could do only so much to fix that.

"It's good enough," Lee finally said. "The guards will probably just wave us through."

Ren kept adjusting the image. "They'll ask us why we're here off-shift. We can't look like the dead when we answer."

"Yes, we can," Lee said. "Everyone knows Enforcers give up their souls when they take the job. They all look dead." Stooping, he pulled off the top of his seat. "Help me move our friends to their new sleeping accommodations."

Ren relented, and together the three of them hefted the drugged Enforcers into the hollows of the seats. When the car pulled up to the detention center, the crystal scanner would show that two Enforcers were coming in with a prisoner.

Everything would seem routine.

At least, that was what Joseph hoped.

chapter hapter
30

It took Echo longer than he wanted to scout around the perimeter of the building. The base was L shaped, it had three exits, and the only windows on the bottom floor were in the restaurant. He was tempted to take Taylor and leave while Allana was gone. That way he wouldn't have to worry that Allana was actually calling her father or contacting one of her friends—trying to find an alternative to leaving the city.

One moment Echo was convinced she would do something stupid; the next he was just as convinced she would be sensible. She had to realize she wouldn't ever be safe in Traventon. If Echo took Taylor and left Allana, he would be leaving her to a death sentence.

So he would trust her, but he was also making an escape

route. If Allana called her father, it would take Enforcers a few minutes to arrive. They would assemble by the building's three exits to trap Echo and Taylor inside, then they would move in. Echo needed to find an inconspicuous place where he could cut a hole in the outer wall without anyone noticing.

The area in the crook of the L shape would work the best. Checking the scanner on Xavier's comlink, he saw that some of the rooms on that side were empty. Good. He and Taylor would move to one of them.

He walked back to the closest entrance, still reading the scanner. He didn't see any groups of people congregating at the exits. The DW scanners listed the name of every person in the building. He didn't recognize any Dakine names.

Echo went back inside, going over details in his mind. Taylor's ligaments should have healed enough by now that if he helped her, she could make it down the hallway to another room. He would have to use a holocamera to hide the hole. Fortunately, that had been one of the items Echo had taken from Xavier's belt.

As Echo drew close to the room where he'd left Taylor, he saw the door was open. Why had she opened it and left it that way?

He quickened his pace and went inside. The room was empty.

His heart slammed into his ribs in a burst of panic. Who had taken Taylor? What did he do now?

He grabbed his laser box and checked the scanner, hoping it would give him some clue as to who had her.

Taylor came up behind him. "Good," she said. "You're back."

She stepped into the room, hobbling a bit. He let out a long, relieved breath and stared at her. Even with a limp, she reminded him of a fairy maiden from an ancient story. Her long green hair cascaded past her shoulders in smooth waves. Pansies and butterflies shimmered around her. It was more than her clothes, though. Her hazel eyes had a mischievous and magical look to them, as though she knew all sorts of secrets she had no intention of telling.

Taylor turned to him, and he saw she held a large glass in one hand.

Echo's relief immediately changed into anger. "Where did you go? I told you to stay here."

"Yeah, but you're not in charge of this team. I am."

He shut off the laser box and shoved it back onto his belt. "You're injured, and you don't know your way around this city or this century. Right now, I'm a better leader."

"Sorry," she said. "I'm not stepping aside."

"You shouldn't be stepping anywhere for another forty minutes." He strode over to the computer screen on the far side of the room and left a message for Allana, telling her to call his comlink from this computer. "Besides," he said as he walked back to Taylor, "Joseph will never forgive me if I let anything happen to you. So consider this a mutiny. From now on, you do what I say."

"Not likely," she said.

"It's a mutiny. You have no choice." He put his arm around her waist to help support her. "Lean into me," he told her.

She put one arm around his waist and kept hold of the drink with her other. Slowly, they made their way out of the room and down the hallway.

"Where did you get that drink from, anyway?" He let out a huff of exasperation as he considered its most likely source. "Did you go to the foodmart and flirt it off some guy?"

Instead of getting defensive, Taylor laughed. It wasn't the coy and sophisticated sort of laugh Allana had. It was natural sounding, happy. She smiled at him, clearly amused by the idea. "If you were sitting in a foodmart and I limped up and asked for your drink, would you give it to me?"

"Yes." Echo glanced over his shoulder to see if anyone was watching them. "And I wouldn't let you walk off without getting your name and number." This was another reason why he shouldn't have left Taylor alone. She had no idea what guys were like in this century.

"Really?" Taylor asked him. "You would try to pick me up?"

Echo tightened his grip on her waist. "Do you need me to carry you again? Are you having trouble walking?"

"No," she said. "Picking someone up is a twenty-first-century way of saying that, you know, you're hitting on someone."

Hitting on someone? Before he could ask about that, she said, "I mean, you want to hook up with them, hang out. . . ." She must have seen the blank look on his face. "It means you're interested and you want to date them."

He lifted his eyebrows. "That all sounds so violent. What exactly did you do on dates in the twenty-first century?"

"Never mind," she said. "A lot of our slang didn't make sense, and I have no idea why we said any of it. Your father has already spent the last month and a half interrogating me about it."

"Yes," Echo said.

"Yes what?" Taylor asked.

"Yes, I would pick you up . . . hang you on a hook, whatever the phrase was."

"Oh," she said, and smiled. It was a soft, knowing smile, one that had encouragement all over it. It warmed Echo in a way he hadn't expected.

Not this. Certainly not here. He and Taylor had other things to concentrate on. They were running for their lives. This wasn't the time to start thinking of matching off with someone new.

But then another part of him asked, *Why not here? Why not now?* Who knew if either of them would even live until tomorrow? This might be the only time they had.

And besides, when would he ever meet another girl from the time period he'd studied for the last five years—a girl who was smart, beautiful, and effortlessly made Allana seem like an outdated version?

"I left the room," Taylor said, as though he'd been brooding over that, "because you took so long that I got worried. I peeked out into the hallway to see if you were around, and I noticed a couple girls leaving a room. One of them left her drink on the table, so I walked over to see if it had ice. And it does."

That didn't sound nearly as bad as eyeing up interests in the foodmart. Echo relaxed his grip a little. "Why do you need ice?"

"For your burn."

It didn't make sense to him. "What does my burn have to do with ice?"

"If you put ice on a burn, it takes away the pain."

He looked at her skeptically. "Right. How could ice erase pain? It's just water."

Taylor reached into the cup, strained out an ice chunk, and put it on his arm.

The pain vanished. Immediately. He stared at it, trying to make sense of what had happened. He knew the chemical formula of water. Two hydrogen atoms covalently bonded to an oxygen atom. It couldn't . . . And then he understood. "The ice is numbing my skin."

"Yeah, we ancients knew a few tricks."

"Sorry," he said. "I just never thought about numbing wounds. I've always had something around that cures them."

She lifted her chin with mock offense. "I don't think I should let you be team leader anymore. I'm mutinying back."

They'd reached the new room and went inside. Once the door shut, Taylor took a wrap from Xavier's pack. It was meant to hold broken bones in place, but she used it to keep the ice on his arm. Her fingers brushed against his skin quickly, efficiently, as she secured the wrap in place.

"First the gas mask and now this," he said. "Is there anything you can't fix with water?"

"A few things."

He helped her over to the couch, noticing things about her that he probably shouldn't have—how small her waist was . . . the curve of her neck . . .

He went to the eastern side of the room and plunged his laser cutter into the wall. Slowly, he pushed the laser cutter downward. After a couple minutes his shoulder began to ache and he had to stop to rest. He glanced over at Taylor. She had her comlink on scanner function, but instead of looking at it, she was watching him.

He smiled at her. "Are you staring because you think I'm gorgeous, or is it some social custom of yours?"

"I'm trying to figure you out."

"Ah. I wish you success. Then you can explain me to me." He turned from her and pulled the laser cutter sideways to make the top of the hole.

Taylor made her way over to him, limping less now. "People aren't complicated if you know what motivates them." She took hold of the laser cutter, helping him pull. "Helix, for example, is motivated by power. Reilly is motivated by an intense desire to prove he's brilliant—it's his own special brand of egotism."

The laser cutter handle was made for only one set of hands, so Taylor had put her fingers around his. It was easier to move the laser cutter now, and he liked the feel of her fingers against his.

"Joseph," she went on, "is motivated by learning but mostly by love. It's why he chose to work with your father, why he changed time to bring you back, why he's trying to rescue Sheridan right now."

Echo nodded. "That's Joseph."

Taylor turned her head to survey him. She was so close, she only had to whisper to be heard. "But you're harder. . . ."

"Well, you only just met me."

"I only just met Allana too, but I can tell she's motivated by power."

"Power?" Echo shifted his grip on the laser cutter, then

pulled again. "Vanity, yes. Comfort, luxury, all those things. If she wanted power, she wouldn't have chosen Joseph for a boyfriend. She would have wanted someone important, a leader in the government or in the Dakine."

"She went after Joseph," Taylor said as though it was obvious, "because bringing him into the Dakine would give her more power. She'd already gotten what she wanted from you, so she dumped you and went to work on him."

Echo paused. He'd never considered this before. "Joseph wouldn't ever have joined."

"Yes, but Allana didn't know that. She got you to join easily enough. She probably thought Joseph wouldn't be much harder."

Echo went back to pulling the laser cutter through the wall. They were nearly done with the hole, but he didn't see it. He saw Allana coldly calculating Joseph's worth to the Dakine.

"The only thing I can't figure out," Taylor went on, "is whether Allana wanted to become more powerful than her father as some sort of ego thing, or whether he was involved in the Dakine too and she was just taking up the family business. Did your Dakine leader order her execution because he was actually that strict about the laws? Or was it his way to undercut a rival?"

"Wait, wait," Echo said. "I'm still back on the fact that you think Allana didn't care for Joseph. What sort of proof do you have?"

They'd finished the cut. Echo handed Taylor the laser cutter, and he used his good shoulder to push the wall piece outward.

Taylor stood back and surveyed their work. "Guys are

so blind. You'd think after all these centuries, you would have, I don't know, devised some program that alerted you to when a girl is playing you." The top part of the cut piece didn't come loose, so Taylor pressed against it. "Allana is so concerned about rank that she doesn't want to leave the city, even though she knows she'll be executed if she stays. Do you think a girl like that really wants to date a historian word-smith? Joseph didn't have any ambitions to rise in rank. Is that Allana's type?"

Echo took in her words, each of them bluntly truthful. He had given so much of himself to Allana, done things he shouldn't have, and now it all seemed pitifully stupid. "You're right," he said, and gave the wall an extra-hard shove. The piece came loose and toppled to the concrete outside. "I'm so used to everyone liking Joseph better, I never even considered that Allana might be gaming him."

Taylor clipped the laser cutter to her belt. "Everyone likes Joseph better? That's hard to believe."

"My father always favored Joseph."

"I doubt that."

Echo didn't argue the point. Glancing through the hole to make sure no one was around, he went outside. He quickly took a picture of a spot of undamaged wall, set up the holocamera to project the same image over the hole, then dragged the fallen piece of concrete back inside. Taylor was sitting on the floor by the hole checking the scanner. Without looking up, she said, "After the Dakine assassination, Jeth defended you to everyone, even though he knew you were involved somehow. He left the city and everything he'd worked for, just to be with you."

"To be with Joseph," Echo corrected as he pulled the wall piece behind a couch.

Taylor looked up then. "No, with you. He thought Joseph died."

"What?" Echo let out an incredulous cough. "He didn't realize Joseph was alive? He couldn't tell the difference?"

She shrugged. "Jeth isn't all that observant."

"Yeah, but still . . ." Echo straightened and wiped wall rubble off his sleeves. "My own father?"

"Besides," Taylor went on, "Elise told me that girls always favored you."

It was mostly true, but Echo wasn't about to concede the point. "Our caretakers always liked Joseph best." Echo walked back over to Taylor and helped her to her feet. "By the first month of school, I usually had a detention schedule and he was appointed captain of the young soldiers' team. If we hadn't traded places once in a while, I would have never led a recess offensive."

Echo put his hand around Taylor's waist to help her walk to the couch. It seemed a natural thing to do, as natural as her putting her arm around him for support.

"Teachers," Taylor said, "like whoever causes the least trouble. I somehow doubt that was you."

They reached the couch. He eased her onto it and sat down beside her. She shifted, sitting so close to him that their legs touched. Taylor checked her scanner again. "You don't have to compete with Joseph. It isn't a contest."

Echo tilted his head back and looked at the ceiling. "Joseph and I," he said slowly. "You can't understand—can't know what it's like to have only half a claim on your own identity."

"Did I mention," Taylor said, taking her attention away from her comlink, "that Sheridan is my identical twin sister?"

Echo blinked at her in surprise. "You're . . . No, really?" It seemed unbelievable, and yet why else would she say it? Her expression made it clear she wasn't joking.

"You would think," Taylor continued, "that my parents would have been thrilled to have a genius daughter, but my dad was a pastor, so he was more concerned about his children being good than being smart. Guess which one of us was naturally kind, charitable, and so tenderhearted you couldn't take her to a sad movie?"

Echo smiled. "Not you?"

"Sheridan cried so incessantly, strangers in the theater felt compelled to come over and comfort her."

Echo laughed. He couldn't help himself. He'd thought he would never meet a person who could really understand him, and yet here in the most unlikely of places he'd found one. If he had set out to design the perfect girl for himself, he couldn't have accomplished it as well as Taylor was doing naturally. Even if Allana hadn't cut things off with him, he would still be attracted to Taylor, would still be sitting here marveling at how right she was for him.

Taylor misinterpreted his laughter. "You wouldn't think it was so funny if your father had constantly quoted you scriptures about love and charity. He might as well have come right out and said, 'Why can't you be more like Sheridan?'"

"Could he tell the two of you apart?"

"Yes, which means Sheridan couldn't even switch places with me to get me out of trouble." Taylor paused, then grimaced. "Until we came here." Her jaw tightened, and everything about her stiffened. "She told Reilly she was me. That's why they have her. They want information from her that I have."

"I'm sorry." Echo put his hand on top of hers. Back in the Scicenter he had wanted to find a way to strain Sheridan and had been frustrated by the impossibility of it. If he'd had days to study it and weeks to work on it, he might have found a way around the scientists' barriers. But he had wanted to strain Sheridan only because Joseph wanted it, because Echo could tell by the panic in Joseph's eyes how much it meant to him.

Now Echo wished he'd been able to do it for Taylor. He wished it because a tenderhearted girl who looked like Taylor was sitting in a detention cell somewhere.

"She can't make it through a sad movie," Taylor said, and her voice wavered with emotion. "How on earth could she survive a month and a half of government torture?" Her fingers unconsciously curled around Echo's. "That was supposed to be me. It should be me."

Echo gave Taylor's fingers a squeeze. "If Joseph doesn't rescue her, we'll find a way to do it."

Taylor's gaze went to Echo's, testing it for sincerity. He must have passed. She nodded and then seemed to realize that she still had hold of his hand. A slight blush crossed her cheeks. She let go of his fingers and returned her attention to the scanner.

He leaned over to see her screen. The courtyards around the building were mostly clear. "I don't see any Dakine from my base. . . . No, wait; there's one. But that could be coincidence."

Taylor arched her eyebrows. "In a city of seven million?"

Echo hesitated, frowned. "If we leave Allana, the Dakine will kill her. We have to be certain it's not a coincidence."

Taylor let out a frustrated sigh.

He could have gotten Xavier's comlink out, but it was faster to lean over and use Taylor's. He enlarged the scanning parameters and scrolled through more names. "It's only one Dakine. . . ."

Their foreheads were nearly touching. Taylor kept watching him, didn't move her head away from his. "Are you sure you're not letting your feelings for Allana color your judgment?"

He wondered what color Taylor thought his judgment was. "Yes," he said.

"What will happen if Allana wants you back?"

"Then she'll be disappointed."

Taylor kept hold of his gaze. Her hazel eyes were an interesting color, a mix of greens and browns. The city hardly ever used genes that produced hazel eyes anymore—which was clearly an oversight. Hazel eyes were beautiful.

"Do you need proof I'm done with Allana?" he asked.

"Proof is always good."

Echo reached over and ran his fingers through a strand of Taylor's hair, gauging her response. She looked at him steadily, waiting.

"I've learned a lot about Allana today," he told her. "A lot about myself too. Thankfully, I've also learned a lot about you." He leaned toward her.

She put her hand on his chest. "Don't you think this is a

little fast? I mean, how long has it been since you and Allana were a *pareja*? Ten minutes?"

"Two and a half months."

Taylor tilted her head, making her hair spill to one side of her shoulder. "I don't think it counts if you were dead for most of that time."

Echo kept running his hand over the strands of her hair, twining them around his fingers. "I think it counts double the time. Dying gives you a perspective about life." Echo didn't know what sort of perfume Taylor wore. He'd never smelled it before, but it made him think of the color gold. Rich. Strong. Warm to the touch. He leaned in closer, taking it in. "I don't recommend dying for everybody, of course. It doesn't always work out so well. . . ."

Taylor didn't move away from him. She didn't move toward him either. His fingers left her hair and ran down the length of her cheek, caressing it. She had such soft skin. His hand trailed to her neck and then to her chin, tilting her face closer to his.

She still looked at him cautiously. "It seems like you've had a lot of practice at this. How many girls have you kissed?"

"One less than I want to."

She laughed, a sound that was light and amused. He wanted to capture that laugh, to taste it. He wanted to make her laugh again. Instead he brushed his lips against her cheek.

"Incredible," she said. "Do the girls usually swoon at this point?"

"Just wait. It gets better."

She laughed again and shifted away from him. Had he just thought he wanted to make her laugh? Well, that had been stupid. He didn't like it now, didn't like that she was shaking her head as though this was a joke.

She picked up the scanner and held it up for him to see. "Have any more Dakine popped up?"

He skimmed the list of names. "No."

She went back to studying it. "I guess that's good news."

"Taylor," he said.

She glanced up at him, her eyes guarded.

He kept his voice serious so that she would realize this wasn't just more flirting. "I don't know all the twenty-first-century customs or how guys back then let girls know they were interested." As he said this, he tried to remember details from films he'd studied of that era. "I'm supposed to buy you meals, and men gave certain kinds of flowers." He recalled something about folded pieces of paper with pictures on the front. Cards, they were called. No, wait. Cards was a game people played. The papers must have been called something else. "I can do whatever I have to, but in case it turns out we don't have time— well, I want you to know how I see you."

He expected her to smile or to move away—some sort of reaction. She just kept watching him, judging something. He didn't know what.

"Gardenias?" he asked.

"Roses," she said.

"Roses," he repeated. "They probably grow them in Santa Fe."

She didn't answer. She was still watching him. He hadn't meant to try and kiss her again. In fact he'd told himself he wouldn't. Not until Santa Fe. Not until he knew her customs and they knew each other better. But there was some underlying emotion in her gaze, a longing in her expression that made him lean forward again. This time when his fingers found the back of her neck, she leaned toward him and shut her eyes. His lips brushed hers, softly, waiting for a response.

She kissed him back for two seconds, then suddenly pushed him away.

The action was so unexpected, he looked around the room to see what had startled her. "What's wrong?"

Taylor shook her head, wouldn't meet his eye. "Sheridan is in prison because Joseph brought you back. If I kiss you, it would be like saying I'm glad it happened, like I don't care they've been hurting her this entire time."

Echo took a deep breath and considered this. He wanted to point out that he hadn't asked Joseph to save him. He hadn't purposely changed the timestream. And Echo had just told Taylor he'd help her rescue Sheridan if Joseph couldn't do it.

It didn't matter. In Taylor's mind, Echo would always be connected with Sheridan's pain. He nodded, already feeling the bitterness of this fact taking hold.

chapter 31

The car was nearly to the guard station. Joseph clenched and unclenched his fingers, reassuring himself again that the cuffs weren't real. He'd cut the backs off them and could slip out of them easily. Perhaps too easily. It would be just his luck if they fell off in front of the real Enforcers.

Ren and Lee were talking about Santa Fe's split, had been for the last ten minutes. The debate had moved from mostly friendly banter to not-so-hidden accusations. "Your people," Lee said, "only want a split so they can declare war on my people."

Ren waved away his words. "Why go to the trouble of moving then? If we wanted to declare war on you, it would be easier to do it beforehand. We know where your sector is."

"You can't do it beforehand," Lee said slowly, "because the rest of the city would turn against you."

"And they wouldn't turn against us if we were in separate cities? They only care about you now because you keep the roads clean in a middle district?"

Lee shook his head. "You wouldn't care what the other sectors thought if you had your own city."

Ren leaned closer to Lee. "I'll tell you a secret. We don't care now. We know that if the rest of you didn't breathe the same air we did, none of you would mind if someone radiated us."

Lee broke into a language Joseph didn't understand. Its rhythm was angry and harsh. Ren seemed to understand, though. He answered in the same language.

"What you both need to learn," Joseph said in a voice louder than the other two, "is we're on the same side. All of us. It's time to trust one another."

Ren waved his hand in derision. "Those are platinum words. You're the one who gassed us so you could change time. Where was your trust then?"

"You're right," Joseph said. "I did what I wanted without thinking about anyone else." His voice grew quiet. "Now Sheridan is paying for it." He gestured to the detention center, a gray citadel visible in the distance. "Those are our enemies out there. If we fight one another, there won't be anybody left to fight them."

Ren and Lee looked at each other sourly. "If I die during this mission," Lee said, "because Brother Ren didn't help me when I needed it, make sure you tell the council."

"If I die," Ren rejoined, "because Brother Lee didn't help me, you won't have to tell the council. They already expect it."

Well, so much for Joseph's talk on unity.

He watched out the window as the detention center loomed larger and larger ahead of them. Four floors of the building peeked over the fifteen-foot electrified wall. Most of the detention center was underground. What Joseph could see looked like a gigantic gray box covered with hundreds of insect eyes. No windows, just multiple cameras, twitching on their perches as they surveyed the doings inside and outside the complex. Joseph understood why the Enforcers used the articulated cameras instead of fixed ones. There was something chilling— something that made you cautious—when you saw a half dozen cameras swivel your way and train their lenses on you.

Joseph's cuffs had come loose while he'd pointed to the building. He straightened them. "Has either of you remembered anything else about the contact who was supposed to help us at the detention center? A comlink number or a name?"

"It started with a *P*," Ren said.

"It's one of those names that isn't really a name," Lee added. "Like Plentiful or Paradise."

"Plentiful?" Ren repeated. "That's not it. When was the last time you met someone named Plentiful?"

Lee didn't answer. They were nearly to the guard station. Ren and Lee turned on the holographic projectors clipped to their collars. Immediately, their faces vanished, replaced by the faces of the Enforcers who were hidden in the seats. Ren pulled out his laser box. "Are my lips synced up to the hologram?"

There had been a slight lag. Hopefully not one the guards would notice. "Close enough," Joseph said. It was suddenly hard not to think about all of the things that could go wrong with this plan. What if the holographic projectors malfunctioned? A freeze of only a second could give them away.

As the car pulled up to the guard station, Ren pushed the button on the control panel that lightened the car's darkened windows. An Enforcer peered at them and then at his computer screen. He was clad in a silver uniform instead of the usual black. That meant he was an officer. The feed from his microphone was automatically piped into the car. "Enforcers Dawkins and Stern, isn't this your sleep shift?"

"Should be," Lee said, "but when we got a find on this guy, we knew we had to bring him in. He was talking to a group in a foodmart about how the mayor should be voted out. Several witnesses heard him."

The man looked at Joseph. Joseph stared at his hands. *Just wave us through. Send us on our way.*

The man held up a face scanner and pointed it at Joseph. His stomach clenched. When had they started using those at the guard stations? Crystals had always been the only ID tags Enforcers cared about.

The man's eyes widened in surprise. "Echo Monterro," he said, reading his screen. "Wanted for questioning. Class two."

It wasn't surprising the scanner had matched Joseph's face to Echo. Most everyone in the city thought Joseph had been vaporized during a Dakine hit. Anyone in Traventon who saw him would think he was Echo.

The guard kept staring at Joseph. "He's a class two. The warden will want to see him right away. I'd better bring him in personally."

"We'll take him," Ren said. "No need to leave your post."

The man stepped out of his booth. "I said I'd take him."

Great. Echo was such a catch that random Enforcers wanted to lap up some of the credit for his capture. Joseph half expected the man to get into the car and evict Ren and Lee. Instead, the man climbed onto a rail-jumper. He stayed in front of their car the entire way to the processing entrance, an escort to let everyone know someone important had been captured.

Joseph fingered the hole in his cuffs. Would the silver Enforcer check and see if his cuffs were secure?

Ren and Lee were talking in lowered voices. "We follow our silver friend," Lee said, "and when he's alone, we stun him."

The only way to take down an Enforcer was to hit an unprotected area at the joints—the knees or the elbows. Those weren't large targets.

"You'll have to get a full stun on the first shot," Joseph told them. "You can't give him time to call for help. If someone sounds an alarm, we'll never get to Sheridan."

Ren let out a scoffing grunt and turned to Lee. "He doesn't think we can shoot the Enforcer on the first shot."

Lee joined in the scoff. "I can shoot your eyelashes off from ten meters." Lee motioned to Ren. "And he can do it while you're blinking."

"Good," Joseph said, and then added, "While we're inside, if you ever have to choose between rescuing Sheridan and saving me, rescue Sheridan."

The car stopped. They'd reached the detention-center processing entrance. Ren climbed out first, laser box drawn as though he expected Joseph to sprint away as soon as he stepped from the car.

Joseph got out reluctantly, and Lee followed him, his laser box drawn as well. All around the building entrance, dozens of cameras rotated to peer down at Joseph. He saw himself reflected in their gaping lenses.

The Enforcer in the sliver suit used his crystal to open the processing door, then gestured with a flick of his laser box for Joseph to walk inside. Joseph did.

The room didn't look that different from other lobbies Joseph had been in. City updates flashed on the walls. Security guards sat at a desk with built-in computer screens. A row of chairs stood in the middle of the room. The difference was that these walls were titanium over a hyperdiamond core. The chairs had hooks that attached to handcuffs, and the people milling by the desk wore Enforcer uniforms.

The room was free of cameras, just as the schematics said it would be. Enforcers didn't record what went on inside their buildings. That way lawyers couldn't ask for video feeds of how prisoners were treated.

The silver Enforcer motioned to the desk while he spoke to Ren and Lee. "You can report out now. I'll be sure to mention your names to the warden."

Right. As if they didn't all know that by the time Silver Guy got to the warden's office, it was going to be a one-man capture event.

Ren and Lee followed Silver Guy across the lobby. "The warden should know certain details about the capture," Lee said.

"What details?" Silver Guy asked.

Joseph eyed the Enforcers at the desk. None of them gave

him more than a glance of interest. They were laughing about something on a monitor.

Lee said, "Some of his friends were acting suspiciously."

"How?" Silver Guy asked.

Joseph walked faster than he normally would have. In order for Ren and Lee to shoot Silver Guy, they needed to get out of the lobby and to a private place.

Lee said, "His friends scattered as soon as they saw us."

"And," Ren added, because running from Enforcers wasn't an impressive crime, "I wasn't picking up crystal signals from any of them."

"Probably Dakine," Silver Guy said. "Why didn't you bring them in too?"

"We couldn't catch them all," Ren said. Joseph noticed that his words weren't exactly synched up to his lips. "We decided it was more important to concentrate on this one."

Fortunately the silver guy wasn't paying attention to Ren's face. He looked at Joseph with a threatening sort of calculation. "Mr. Monterro will give us their names. I'll pass along the information to the warden." It was a dismissal, and they weren't even out of the lobby yet. Joseph walked faster.

"A particularly peculiar girl was with him," Lee said, drawing out the sentence so that he had to explain what he meant in the hallway. The corridor smelled strongly of cleaning detergent and something else. Probably despair. It was completely plated with a tin-like metal. Their blurred reflections followed them as they walked.

"How was the girl peculiar?" Silver Guy asked. He still

didn't sound concerned. He'd taken his comlink out and was putting in data.

"I'll wait until you're done with that," Lee said, as though it was the polite thing to do.

Silver Guy mostly ignored him and kept tapping things into his comlink. The hallway wasn't crowded, but it was too close to the main entrance. The Enforcers in the lobby might hear if someone yelled. Then again, people most likely yelled a lot in this place. The Enforcers probably expected it.

Halfway down the corridor, the silver Enforcer motioned to Joseph to turn left into another hallway. Only one other Enforcer was in this one: a man walking toward them. Not too many to fight. If Ren and Lee waited until the Enforcer passed them, they could turn and shoot him before the man knew what was happening. Joseph stretched his fingers, curling them around the edges of the cuffs so that he could slip them off quickly. He gave Ren and Lee a meaningful look and nodded at the approaching Enforcer.

Silver Guy put his comlink back onto his belt. "So what was peculiar about the girl?"

"I could tell she favored me," Lee said.

"She favored you?" Silver Guy repeated blankly.

"Well, that's not the peculiar part," Lee said. "Most girls would favor me over a historian, don't you think?"

Ren shrugged. "It depends on how picky the girl is."

The other Enforcer was nearly to them.

"What is your point about the girl?" Silver Guy asked. His voice was clipped now. It was clear he didn't like anyone wasting his time.

"The point is," Joseph said, to let Ren and Lee know he was ready, "you should leave her alone."

The other Enforcer walked past them without even a glance.

"No one asked you anything," Silver Guy barked out. "You'll have enough—"

Joseph turned around, the cuffs already swinging in an arc to hit Silver Guy's face. Enforcers wore helmets. The cuffs wouldn't do any damage, but the surprise would give Ren and Lee the time they needed to shoot him.

Silver Guy moved faster than Joseph expected. In one smooth motion he stepped away from the cuffs, lifted his laser box, and shot Joseph. If the shot had hit Joseph's clothing, he would have been protected. Joseph took the blast in the face though.

He felt his muscles stiffen, harden like stone as the stun took effect. He fell and couldn't stop himself. All he could do was bend his head forward before it completely stiffened. That way his back would hit the ground first, not his head.

Ren fired at the Enforcer who'd passed them. Joseph saw the man flinch from the shot and throw his hands forward. Joseph hit the floor himself then. A slap of pain went through his shoulders, knocking the breath out of him. He rolled so that he faced Lee and the silver guy. Lee stood, laser box outstretched while the silver Enforcer fell, an expression of fury frozen on his face. He hit the ground with a thud, eyes staring at Joseph.

Joseph's lungs ached to take a breath. He couldn't. Without help, he would pass out before his lungs regained function.

Ren hurried to him, taking his muscle restorer from his belt.

294

Lee stood nearby, scanning the hallway, laser box still drawn. "That was some precise shooting," he told Ren. "Eyelashes everywhere are trembling with fear."

Joseph's vision was darkening around the edges.

Ren pointed the restorer box in Joseph's direction, and it shot out beams to reverse the stun. "Good shooting on your part too. Now I know why that girl favored you."

At last, Joseph's muscles relaxed. Warmth spread throughout his body and he breathed in giant gulps of air.

"Are you all right?" Ren asked. He took hold of Silver Guy's arms, ready to drag him off somewhere.

Joseph propped himself up on one arm, still breathing deeply. "Yeah."

Lee picked up Silver Guy's legs. "Get your scanner out. We need an empty room to put our friend in."

Joseph unclipped his comlink. As he got to his feet, he scanned the rooms around them. An empty one stood down the hallway to their left. Unfortunately he also picked up a nearby Enforcer signal. Someone was turning the corner and walking into the hallway right now. He looked up and saw the Enforcer, laser box already drawn and pointed directly at them.

chapter 32

Sheridan was pacing the length of the observation room when the door slid open. Three guards came in. The Tough One, Tariq, and a woman Sheridan didn't recognize. The Tough One carried a pair of metal cuffs in one hand and his laser box in the other. The woman held a small computer.

Tariq pointed his laser box at Sheridan too. His voice was emotionless, but his eyes were apologetic. He didn't want to do this. "You have one more chance to cooperate. Read over the schematics and correct them. If you refuse, we're to take you to the medroom for a memory wash."

Sheridan backed up. Her gaze ricocheted between the guards. "Real physicists don't deal in absolutes. Reilly should know that."

The Tough One raised his laser box. "I'll take that as a no."

"Don't," Tariq said. "Reilly wants her conscious for this."

The Tough One lowered his laser box and clipped it back onto his belt. "Fine. I can do it that way." He walked forward, flexing his hand into a fist as he smiled at her. He wanted her to fight back, she realized. He was looking forward to forcing her into cuffs.

Sheridan took two more steps backward until her heel hit the glass wall that divided the room in two. She was trapped. Her mind whirled, searching for some way to stop this from happening. She couldn't bluff her way through QGP schematics. If she even attempted it, they would realize she had no idea what any of it meant. And this might be another virtual reality program. She'd woken up in this room and she hadn't eaten since then. "Raise your arms," The Tough One snapped.

She didn't. Her gaze went to Tariq. If she were to bolt, would he shoot her? But even if he didn't, the woman would. She had a laser box out now too.

"Raise your arms," The Tough One barked out again.

Sheridan knew he meant out in front of her, but she raised her hands over her head. She was giving herself time to think, weighing her options.

"Dirty viker." The Tough One swung one of the cuffs at her, aiming to strike her across the face.

She turned her head and dodged the blow, which only made him angrier. He let out another string of names and swung his fist at her, full force. It was done in anger and without much thought. Either that, or he'd forgotten the glass wall stood behind her. She sidestepped the blow and The Tough One's hand collided into the wall with a loud smack, a noise that indicated several of his knuckles had cracked. The wall didn't even vibrate from the impact.

The Tough One yelled and shook his hand as though trying to dislodge it from his body. Even through his darkened visor, Sheridan could see the rage in his eyes. He was going to do something horrible to her.

She darted around him and ran toward the door.

Tariq stepped in her way and raised his laser box. His face was calm, his movements precise. She only had time to gasp before he fired.

The shot went over her shoulder. She heard the thump behind her and turned to see The Tough One stiffen and topple to the floor. She automatically looked for the woman guard but didn't see her. And then Sheridan noticed her sprawled out on the floor, eyes staring vacantly upward. Tariq must have shot her while The Tough One was practicing his boxing skills.

Tariq took hold of Sheridan's hand and without a word pulled her from the room. No one else was in the hallway. It loomed like a silver tunnel in front of them. Tariq broke into a run, still holding on to Sheridan. Their footsteps clanked noisily on the floor.

So this was another VR program, another escape that wouldn't lead her anywhere. At least, it probably was. There was always a chance—wasn't there?—that it could be real this time.

Stupid hope. It wouldn't leave her alone. She began looking for clues, for details that would give away the false reality.

"Where—"

"Shhh," Tariq told her. "Don't speak yet." They'd reached an intersection in the hallway. Tariq slowed to a walk in case any other guards saw them. A metal cart hummed down the center of the corridor, self-propelled, but no guards were around. Tariq pulled her into that hallway. They ran down it, their footsteps clattering in the silence. All around her, her reflection wavered. She was a blurred form in tan overalls next to a black shadow.

They passed by doors. She waited for an Enforcer to open one of them and step out to see why they were running. She didn't slow down though, didn't suggest it. She wanted to get out of this place.

Tariq came to a stop in front of a door. He put his crystal to a panel, and the door slid open. Instead of an exit it was another prison room, nearly identical to her own. Small, dim, and hopeless. He pulled her into the room. She turned around, taking it in. Why had he brought her here? It wasn't as though she could hide. As soon as someone tracked her crystal, they would find her here.

Tariq stood with his hands on his hips, catching his breath. He took his helmet off and tossed it onto the bed.

"This is where I'm escaping to?" she asked. "Another cell? I hate to point this out, but it's not much of an improvement."

"No one will look for us for a few minutes, and I need to talk to you."

Oh, they were talking first. That was different. "Okay," she said.

Instead of talking, he paced back and forth, thinking, clearly agitated. She kept glancing at the door, waiting for it to open. Listening for footsteps hurrying by.

"Was there something in particular you'd like to say?" she prompted.

"I care about you, Sheridan. I really do."

"That's sweet, Tariq. But can you get me out of the building now? I think escaping would be easier that way."

He stopped pacing and faced her. "Why won't you trust me?"

"What are you talking about?" she asked. If he could pretend the other virtual reality programs hadn't happened, so could she.

He held a hand out to her as though showing her something. "You won't tell me anything about the QGP. You won't cooperate at all."

"I thought I was supposed to tell the DW about the QGP. Why do you need to know about it?" She tried to make it sound like a real question, but it came out as an accusation.

She expected him to say something about how the DW needed proof that she could work it.

Instead he stared at her, aggravation making his lips thin into tight lines. "Reilly isn't a patient man. You should know that by now."

"How do you know anything about Reilly?"

Tariq took hold of her shoulders. His dark eyes turned pleading. "Listen to me. You could have everything you ever wanted, everything *we* ever wanted. Doesn't that mean anything to you?"

She tried to step away from him. His grip was too firm. He pulled her forward so that she had to look at him. "Do you want to stay in the detention center? Do you want a memory wash? You could have freedom. Just say you want it."

Freedom. She did want it. She wanted it so badly, she nearly forgot she couldn't give Reilly what he wanted anyway. She opened her mouth. No sound came out.

"Just say it," Tariq urged, "and everything will be all right. I'll make sure everything is all right."

She needed to fight him, to end this feeling of vulnerability encircling her. Because part of her wanted to throw herself on Tariq's mercy and hope for the best. That part was growing more insistent with every second that passed. "You're working for Reilly," she said. "You always have been."

There. She had told him. Now he couldn't pretend he cared about her anymore.

Tariq didn't deny the claim, didn't even flinch at it. His eyes held the same warmth they always had. "That doesn't mean I don't love you, Sheridan. I do. I want to help you. We've both been playing games. It's time we start trusting each other." His hands slid from her shoulders and he took hold of her hands. His fingers felt strong against hers, comforting. "Can you do that?" he asked. "Can you show me I have your trust? I promise I'll help you get out of here if you'll promise to tell me the truth."

Freedom. Freedom. Freedom. The word repeated in Sheridan's mind, growing louder each moment. If Tariq knew the truth—that it was Taylor who had the information he wanted—would he still offer his help? And if he did, could she be happy, tucked away somewhere under Tariq's protection? Could she be with him, knowing he worked for Reilly, knowing he wanted to complete a weapon that would kill so many people?

Her gaze drifted to Tariq's chest. He took her chin and lifted her face. "I love you, Sheridan. You believe that, don't you?"

Could he? But even if he did, he would still use Sheridan to try to get to Taylor, wherever she was. Sheridan couldn't let that happen, and yet this was perhaps her only chance for freedom—trusting Tariq.

A voice in her mind said, *Why shouldn't you turn this whole mess back over to Taylor?* Taylor was responsible for this problem. She was the one who had invented the QGP. Why shouldn't she be the one who dealt with the consequences?

Sheridan had been here so long—she was so tired, so broken—and all the while Taylor was probably off someplace flirting with Echo.

Tariq ran his thumb across her cheek. "Sheridan?"

She shut her eyes, imagined freedom, thought about what it would be like to wake up without being afraid. The thought didn't make her happy. When she had told Reilly she'd invented the QGP, she had lied not only to save Taylor, but to save people from the weapon. How could she live with herself if her freedom caused their deaths? Which was worse: waking up with fear or with guilt?

Sheridan took a step away from Tariq. "You want me to tell you the truth—I will. The truth is I'm not . . ." She swallowed hard, took a deep breath. "I'm not someone who'll help Reilly kill people." She kept her gaze on Tariq, asking him to understand. "If you're that type of person, I don't want to be with you."

The warmth in Tariq's eyes immediately drained away, leaving them hard and cold. The change was so sudden and so complete that she couldn't draw her attention away from his face. She didn't see that Tariq had pulled out his laser box until he pointed it at her. "Good-bye then," he said, and shot her.

chapter
33

Joseph reached for his laser box, knowing as he did how grim the situation was. Ren and Lee had already dropped the silver Enforcer to the ground and pulled out their laser boxes. Lee, Joseph could see from the corner of his eye, had pressed the comlink jammer to keep the new Enforcer from pushing her alarm button.

But it didn't matter that they outnumbered the new Enforcer. She wasn't giving them a target to shoot at. She dropped to her knees and held both hands straight, leaving no gap at her joints. And she already had her laser box pointed in Joseph's direction. Not only would he be shot again, but if she yelled for other Enforcers, the group would be surrounded. Even if Joseph used his laser disabler, they'd still never make it through so many Enforcers, so many security devices.

Ren shot, but not his laser box. He used his zip-line shooter. The cord zinged across the hallway and attached to the Enforcer's laser box. Ren immediately reversed the line, and the box flew out of the Enforcer's hands, back across the hallway to Ren.

Joseph expected the woman to call for help. Instead her gaze zeroed in on him. "Joseph?"

"Yes?" he replied, shocked she knew his real name.

She slowly stood. "Why didn't you tell me you were here?" Her voice was low and irritated. "I wouldn't have known at all if I hadn't seen Echo's stats just come in."

Joseph stared at her. "You are . . ."

"Patience," she said. Their DW contact. She had found them.

Relief poured over Joseph. Their chances of rescuing Sheridan had just gotten a lot better.

As Patience walked over to them, Joseph saw her features better. She was a tall woman with dark hair and skin. Black marks swirled across her face. She bent down to grab hold of the silver Enforcer. "Let's put them in that room." She gestured toward a door in the hallway. "Use his crystal to open it."

While Joseph and Patience picked up the silver Enforcer, Ren and Lee took hold of the other. They quickly dragged the men over to the room. "Patience," Lee muttered. "I can't believe neither of us could remember Patience."

"It's not surprising," Ren said. "We've never been good at patience."

Joseph held up the silver Enforcer's crystal to the door panel. It slid open. "You can help us free Sheridan?" he asked Patience.

She nodded. "I'll take you to the high-security wing."

When they were through dragging the men into the cell, Ren gave Patience her laser box back. Lee took the comlinks of the unconscious Enforcers. That way even after they woke up from the stun, they wouldn't be able to call for help.

Joseph put the fake cuffs back on, and the group walked through one hallway and then another. No one gave them more than a passing glance. New prisoners were brought in every day. It was all routine.

When they came to the high-security wing, Ren got out his lock disabler. Patience waved it away and used her crystal to open the door. "It's better not to take chances you'll set off an alarm," she said as the group continued on its way.

"Will you get into trouble for opening the door?" Joseph asked. The door would record whose crystal had opened it.

She shook her head. "I'll stun myself after you leave. That way it will look like you used my crystal."

"You're sure there aren't cameras anywhere in the hallways?" Ren asked, scanning the area where the wall met the ceiling.

She shook her head again. "It would be too easy for some undercover reformer to splice it to a public feed. The warden doesn't want the public to know what happens here."

The words made Joseph's stomach lurch. He automatically walked faster. What had they done to Sheridan? What would she be like when he reached her?

Joseph didn't expect her to forgive him when she found out what he'd done. It was his fault she'd been through all this. He deserved her anger, just as he deserved Taylor's. But he hoped with every footstep he took that she wouldn't be hurt too badly, that anything wrong could be fixed.

Finally, the group stopped in front of a cell. Joseph had to keep himself from shouting out Sheridan's name. He wanted her to know they had come to rescue her, that everything would be all right now.

Patience opened the door. He looked around the room, then looked around the room again. It was empty.

"Where is she?" Joseph asked.

"It's the wrong room," Ren said.

Patience put her crystal to a screen by the door. It brought up notes on Sheridan: when she last was given food, the time she was logged out of her cell. She'd been taken to an interrogation in observation room six. He hadn't finished reading through the list when Patience moved her hand away and the notes disappeared.

"Tariq took her early," Patience said. "She's being prepped for a memory wash right now."

Joseph felt the blood draining from his face. Patience had to be wrong. "No," he said. "That wasn't supposed to happen until tonight."

"Yes, well, sometimes those schedules get moved up."

Joseph turned away from the cell. "We need to find her."

"Are we too late?" Lee asked.

"No," Patience said, thinking. "But this will make things harder." She eyed Joseph. "I'll get you an Enforcer suit and some weapons you can use on armor. You're about to become a guard."

chapter 34

hapter

Echo scowled at his scanner. One Dakine member arriving at this building could be a coincidence; two Dakine members from his old base definitely wasn't. "Call your contact," he told Taylor. "See if they have someone close by who can pick us up on the street."

Taylor had messaged Joseph asking for an update. He'd answered with three words. *Busy. Destroy QGPs.*

Taylor hesitated, fidgeted with her comlink.

"We don't have a choice anymore," Echo told her. "We need help."

"My contact won't know who I am," Taylor pointed out. She'd already told Echo that Joseph had changed the contact when he changed timestreams.

"Convince him," Echo said. He didn't say more because his

comlink beeped. Video feed of Allana appeared on the screen. She was calling from the computer in their last room. "Allana's back," he told Taylor.

Taylor tapped in a number, then held up her comlink so that it could get a picture stream of her face. She smiled into it. "*Ete sen*, Mendez; it's me, Taylor. Do you know who I am?"

A small gruff voice from her comlink said, "Of course I know who you are—you just told me your name was Taylor. Should I know you for some other reason?"

Echo checked his scanner to make sure Allana was alone, then answered her video call with directions to the room. It was possible someone had recognized Allana and called the Dakine to report her whereabouts. They could be closing in on her. Then again, it was also possible she'd done something stupid to alert them where she was.

Echo stood up to go out in the hallway. "Be ready to leave quickly," he told Taylor.

She fluttered her fingers at him to show she'd heard but was busy talking into her comlink. "Maybe you'll want to know me after you know what I've done. I've just been at the Scicenter working on the QGPs and giving the rank program a virus. Rank is about to go down in a big way. Then I made a dramatic exit from the courthouse. You might have heard about that from the newsfeeds. Are you interested now?"

Echo went out the door and didn't hear the rest. He stood in the hallway watching his scanner until Allana strode up. She had changed into a tight miniskirt and a shirt made of lace and ruffles. She'd also spent time on her hair. It flowed down her back in curly waves. That had always been his favorite style.

She carried a bag of clothes looped around one wrist. "Why did you switch rooms?" she asked, and then added, "Where's Taylor?"

"She's inside." He opened the door and tossed the bag of clothes to the couch where Taylor sat, then pushed the door panel to close the door.

Allana looked into the room to get a glimpse of Taylor. "Why did you change rooms?" she asked again.

He checked the scanner. All the signals he'd been keeping track of had stopped moving. They were stationed around the building's three exits. "We changed rooms in case you told the Dakine where we were and they decided to come by for a visit."

She didn't flinch at that accusation. Instead she just raised an eyebrow in vague amusement. "You have my comlink," she pointed out.

"You're resourceful."

He didn't mean it as a compliment, but she smiled and leaned against the wall next to him. She was the old Allana again. Confident, in control, and oozing sensuality. "Why are you suddenly so suspicious?"

Echo turned his comlink so that she could see the screen. "Xavier's scanner is more advanced than the ones here in Traventon. It can still pick up crystal signals even when the Dakine are jamming theirs. I wasn't in the organization long, but I'm good at remembering names. I'm also not bad when it comes to breaking into encrypted personnel files. That's quite a gathering forming at the doors."

A faint blush crossed Allana's cheeks. She didn't seem surprised that Dakine had blocked off the exits, which meant she had been the one to call them. He turned the scanner back around. "Ah, Lobo himself has come—the base leader who ordered our assassinations. You didn't see a problem with letting him know our location?"

Allana put her hand on Echo's arm, a gentle, teasing caress. "Everything is going to be fine. I made a deal with him. Lobo is willing to cancel his execution order against us and against Joseph. That's why he came here. So you would know it was a legitimate offer."

Echo hadn't realized there *was* an execution order against him as well as Joseph. His brother must have done something interesting while he had used Echo's identity. Echo didn't ask about it. Instead he pulled his arm away from Allana. "And what do we have to do in return for the cancellation?"

Allana shrugged as though it wasn't anything troubling. "I told Lobo about Taylor—how she destroyed that program in the Scicenter. It takes a lot of computigating skill to do that. You said so yourself." Allana's eyes flashed eagerly. "The Dakine know about her and they want her. If we give them Taylor, they'll let us live."

"What?" Echo felt a wave of sickness pass over him. Allana had used his words to sell Taylor, and now Allana stood here telling him about it as though he would actually consider the deal. Was that the type of person she thought he was?

"The government wants Taylor too," Allana went on happily. "Something to do with her sister. It's made the Dakine consider her a peak commodity. We'll never get this lucky again. We give her to Lobo, and we can go back to our old lives. Everything will be like it was." She ran her hand across the front of Echo's shirt, leaning in to him. "Exactly how it was before I stupidly chose Joseph. I should have chosen you, Echo. I'm choosing you now."

Gently but firmly, he peeled her off of him. "It's not your choice anymore."

Allana barely seemed to notice his rebuff. She took a small laser cutter from her bag and swiped it across her blocking band. "I forgot to tell you the best part. As a bonus, Lobo took ten thousand off my rank." With a grunt of satisfaction, she pulled the blocking band off her wrist.

Echo reached out and took it from her. He didn't want the Dakine to end up with it, and now he chided himself for not considering that possibility beforehand. So many things had happened so quickly, he'd overlooked that detail.

While he tucked the band into his pocket, Allana took her rank badge from hers. The gray screen fluttered back to life, flashing as it picked up a signal. She clipped the badge to her shirt. "I'm in the twelve hundreds now. Can you believe it? Lobo guaranteed I'll stay under five thousand for the next five years. He'll guarantee under ten thousand for you."

Feeling even sicker, Echo reached over and took the badge from her shirt. Allana not only thought he would betray a friend, she thought he would do it for a rank bump. He wanted to crush her badge and then crush his too. Instead he flipped Allana's badge over so that she could see the number displayed. "Your rank isn't twelve hundred." He handed the badge back to her. "It's number one."

She stared at her badge, mouth open, breathless. "How did they . . . ? They shouldn't have. That's the mayor's rank."

Echo looked at the badge and shook his head. When Taylor had said rank was going down in a big way, she hadn't been speaking metaphorically. "The Dakine didn't do it," he said. "The rank program has a virus. I imagine everyone is number one now."

Allana's head snapped up. "No. Someone has to fix it." She gripped her badge harder, and her voice spiraled upward. "I have a great rank. A real one. Everyone can't have the top ranking."

Echo glanced back at his scanner. A lot of motion was rippling through the building. People were noticing their ranks, checking with other people, talking about it. The Dakine at the entrances hadn't moved. They wouldn't be distracted by rank. He wondered if Taylor had finished talking to Mendez yet, and if she had managed to convince him she needed his help.

Allana thrust her badge back into her pocket. "Taylor did this, didn't she? That's why she broke into the Scicenter." Allana's lips pinched together angrily. "Taylor will have to fix this. The Dakine will make her."

"Selfishness," Echo said, sliding his hands into his pockets. "Taylor told me you were motivated by power, but she was wrong. It's selfishness. It overpowers anything else that might have redeemed you."

Allana flushed, stiffened, and then nearly as suddenly relaxed again. She tossed her head so that her silver hair gleamed around her shoulders. "Echo, you have to be reasonable about this. You belong here, with us." She reached her hand out to him. "You're coming with me, aren't you?"

Echo shook his head, still didn't take his hands from his pockets. "I saved your life because I thought I could change the past. I should have realized—some things can't be brought back from the dead."

She stepped away from him, chin raised defiantly, and pulled a laser box from the underside of her belt. "Then I'll give you to the Dakine too." She took another step backward, making sure she was out of his reach. "Sorry, darling." She gave him a rueful smile. "Don't make me shoot you. People take nasty falls when they're stunned. I'd hate to leave you here with a concussion."

He returned her stare calmly. "Go ahead and shoot me."

Her eyes narrowed into slits. She aimed at his face, where he had no protection from laser fire. "Fine."

She pushed the button. The box gave off a faint clicking sound. Nothing else happened. She pushed the button again. And again.

Echo pulled the laser disrupter from his pocket and held it up for her to see. "Joseph invented this while we were gone. I have to admit, his mobile disrupter turned out to be more useful than the stationary one I invented for the government. But then, Joseph always was the smarter one, wasn't he?" While Echo put the ruined disrupter back in his pocket, he glanced at the scanner, checking it. Then he pushed a few buttons on his comlink. "So, have fun with the Dakine."

Allana gripped her useless laser box not knowing what to do with it. "Echo, wait, you can't leave like this. . . ." She gulped. Her voice went high. "The Dakine are at all the entrances—you won't get away. I won't. We have to give them Taylor."

"Don't worry," Echo said. "The disabler took care of the Dakines' laser boxes too. You've got a good chance of getting by them. Of course, they may wonder why you called them here, disabled their laser boxes, and then called the Enforcers."

Her face grew pale. The laser box slipped from her fingers onto the floor. "I didn't call the Enforcers."

"Yeah, I know, but I just did." He put his comlink back on his belt. "Good-bye, Allana." He opened the door, stepped into the room, and locked the door behind him.

Taylor was standing by the hole. She hadn't changed. They both knew Allana could have put a tracking device on the clothing. Taylor would go barefoot, and they had to hope she didn't draw too much attention to herself.

Echo picked up Xavier's medkit from the couch and fastened the pack around his waist. "Let's go," he said, and without further conversation they went through the hole. It would take the Dakine a while to realize they weren't in the building anymore. With luck, he and Taylor would be gone before then.

The only people around were ones milling in the courtyard between buildings. No one close by. No one had seen them emerge from a wall.

They headed around the side of the building. Taylor's limp was barely noticeable now, and she kept up with Echo's quick pace.

"Did you convince Mendez?" Echo asked her. "Are the DW sending someone?" If a car wasn't coming for them, they needed to find a place to hide. They could make it to one of the nearby apartment buildings, but the Dakine would search those first. The Dakine would know Taylor couldn't walk far on her injured ankle.

"I think Mendez is sending someone," Taylor said. "At

least, he didn't say he wouldn't."

It wasn't the most reassuring answer. "What exactly did he say?"

"He said he would check my story." She paused. "Okay, actually he said he would check with meds to see if they'd lost a neurocrashed patient, but I'm pretty sure that was code for checking my story."

They reached the side of the building. Should they head to the street and wait, or go to the next building and hide? Echo looked at the clock on his comlink. It had been a little over five minutes since Taylor's call to Mendez. Probably not enough time for anyone to come. How long could they wait on the street before the Dakine made their way there?

Echo's gaze switched between the two directions. The looming pale-blue apartment building across the courtyard or the distant street. "How sure are you he believed you?"

Taylor swallowed hard. She seemed exhausted already. "Sure enough that now I'm worried Ren and Lee won't rescue Sheridan. I told Mendez I destroyed the QGPs."

This again. Echo took hold of Taylor's hand and led her toward the street. "Ren and Lee don't know about the QGPs."

"Yeah, but when Mendez finds out who our contact is, he'll tell the contact, and the first thing that contact will do is check in on Ren and Lee."

Echo surveyed the area around them, watching for anyone who hurried their way. "And they'll still do their best to rescue Sheridan."

Taylor frowned. "You don't know that. You're too trusting—

and the last person you trusted was Allana."

"Yes, and she cured me of bad judgment."

Neither spoke again until they were nearly to the street. It wasn't busy at this time of day. A few people sat on benches waiting for cars. A few more were walking in either direction. Every once in a while a car swooshed by on the rails. Echo didn't see a car waiting anywhere nearby. He didn't see anyone standing around looking for them. He glanced at the clock. It had been about ten minutes now. How far away was the nearest DW agent? "Do you see anyone you recognize?" he asked her.

"No."

Maybe someone would approach them. Echo didn't let go of Taylor's hand. They paced down the walkway a bit. A minute went by, then two. How long should they wait before they went somewhere else to hide?

Echo glanced over his shoulder and cursed. "We have a problem." He and Taylor had been seen. Two men were running toward them from the direction of the building. They both wore overcoats that flapped out behind them like racing flags.

"Can you run?" Echo asked Taylor.

In answer she dropped his hand and took off in a sprint down the walkway. He ran beside her, weaving around a woman whose dress flashed so many colors, she seemed to be wearing nothing but lights. Taylor made it only a minute before she slowed to a limping jog. "My ankle," she breathed out. The words were edged with pain.

The ligament-repair shot he'd given her must be breaking down under the strain of running. He slowed to keep pace with her. "Go as fast as you can."

Echo looked up and down the street. This would be a good time for a car to pull up to them. Unfortunately the only car in sight was gliding to a stop in front of a waiting woman a few meters down the street. Her frothy white dress blew bubbles all around her. By himself he could have made it to the car in time, but not carrying Taylor. Besides, if the woman realized people were trying to force their way into her car, she would probably call the Enforcers.

Echo checked over his shoulder again. The men were still there, gaining on them now. He could make out the black Enforcers' armor underneath their overcoats. The Dakine had been prepared for a shoot-out. He scanned the other people strolling on the walkways, searching for anyone who could be Taylor's contact. A couple across the street were kissing, oblivious to anything else. A man up ahead was talking into his comlink and eyeing them suspiciously. Probably not a DW agent.

Taylor glanced behind her, and her eyes widened in fear. "We need weapons."

The men were close enough now that Echo could see their red-faced, determined expressions. They would catch up with Taylor and him in another minute. Echo reached into the med-kit and handed Taylor the scalpel. "It's like a knife from your time period. You know how to use it, right?"

She gripped it tightly. "Actually, I've never stabbed anyone before, but I get the general idea."

"If you can keep the men away from you, I'll take care of them."

She slowed to a stagger. "Both of them?"

"There's only going to be one of them in a minute."

Echo took Xavier's zip-line shooter from his belt. Ordinary citizens weren't allowed to use this sort of equipment. Echo had spliced into VR military training programs enough times over the years to learn how to work them.

A little ways up ahead, the woman with the bubble dress was climbing into a car. In a few moments, it would be gliding down the street at forty kilometers an hour.

Echo aimed the zip-line shooter at the closest man and fired. The cord zinged through the air and hit his armor. The man stumbled a couple steps in surprise, then saw that Echo had only shot a hook into his armor. The man swatted at it and kept running. The hook held. Zip lines were built to withstand a lot of pressure.

Echo sprinted toward the slowly moving car until he caught up with it. He bent down and wound the zip-line cord around one of the claws that was used to turn the vehicle on the rails. He barely had time to finish before the car hummed off down the street, quickly picking up speed.

The man on the other end of the hook took only two more steps toward Echo before he was yanked after the car. He had been running fast, but now he ran faster, yelling as he went.

His companion kept charging toward Echo and Taylor. As he got closer, Echo recognized him. The man wore multicolored checkers on his face that partially hid his identity, and his long, shaggy gray hair had the same effect, but it was definitely Lobo.

Echo pulled out a sleeping vial from Xavier's pack. While Taylor caught up to Echo, he attached the biggest needle in the pack. It wasn't much of a weapon. Lobo had a ring with a long built-in switchblade. He used to brag he could cut someone's wrist while he shook their hand.

Lobo saw that Echo and Taylor weren't running anymore and slowed to a walk, breathing deep, angry breaths as he strode toward them.

"Do you see your contact?" Echo asked Taylor without taking his eyes from Lobo.

"No," Taylor said.

"Do you trust me?" Echo asked.

"Yes," she said, and then added, "Wait, you're going to ask me to do something no sane person would do, aren't you?"

Probably. "Stay behind me—wherever I go. When I yell, 'Now,' leap backward."

"Okay," she said.

In another moment Lobo reached them. He seemed taller than Echo remembered, more menacing. The name Lobo was fitting. Something wild and wolf-like stirred in his eyes. He had a way of moving that let you know he would lunge at you, teeth bared, going for your throat.

Lobo flicked his wrist, and a long metal blade appeared in his right hand. "You're a fool," he told Echo. "No one disobeys me this many times and lives."

Echo stepped backward into the street, noting in his peripheral vision that Taylor followed him. She held the scalpel firmly out in front of her. "You won't kill us here," Echo said. "Not with witnesses."

Lobo stepped into the street after them. He made a sweeping motion with his hands. "Look around. None of your witnesses are coming to help you. They're all scurrying away."

Echo didn't look. He held the needle higher and took a couple of cautious steps backward. "The streetcams are running."

"Those can be erased if you have the right connections. And believe me, I have the right connections." Lobo took two quick steps forward and made a slashing motion that nearly cut across Echo's cheek. Echo stepped back, then made a jab with his needle, aiming for Lobo's face.

The needle wasn't long enough to hit its mark, but it stopped Lobo from advancing.

Lobo shifted one way and then the other, legs slightly bent and ready to spring forward. "I'll kill you and the girl too if she fights me. Do you know what it's like to die, Echo?"

"Actually, yes. I admit it wasn't my favorite moment."

Lobo made another swipe at Echo, close enough that Echo heard the blade swish through the air as it went by. Lobo came at him again, this time underhand toward Echo's throat. Taylor screamed in alarm. Echo jerked his head back to avoid the blow and swung the needle around to plunge it into Lobo's arm. The needle hit but didn't manage to pierce Lobo's Enforcer armor. All Echo could do was take another step backward out of range.

Lobo grinned. He enjoyed this. "More Dakine are on the way," he said. "It's only a matter of minutes before you're outnumbered. One of us will get you." He made a jabbing slash at Echo's arm.

Echo dodged to avoid it. "Maybe. But it won't be you."

Lobo advanced another step. "I've killed harder men than you."

"Which is why you have enemies in the Enforcement

Department. Even with the streetcam footage erased, one of them will notice your crystal was here."

Lobo shook his head, laughing now, triumphant. "Dakine block their crystals while they work. Have you forgotten that already?"

"No," Echo said. "My crystal is blocked too." He couldn't see Taylor anymore and only hoped she was where he'd told her to be. "Now!" he yelled, and jumped backward.

Lobo was still wearing the look of triumph when the car smashed into him. He tumbled over its roof and flew into the air like a loose piece of litter. Then he dropped to the ground with a crack—the sound of armor hitting pavement.

Echo strode over to him. Lobo was alive but unmoving. He stared blankly upward, blinking.

Echo knelt down. "People without signals should be careful in the street." He plunged the needle into Lobo's neck. The sleeping drug slid in, immediately doing its work.

Lobo had been thrown out of the way of the rails, so Echo didn't bother dragging him anywhere. He turned to Taylor. She stood not far away, the scalpel still gripped in her hand. "There are more coming," she said.

He looked back toward the building. Four men were hurrying toward them. Four. How could he hold off four?

"I meant *there*," Taylor said.

He turned and saw her pointing to a car that had stopped not far down the street. Men were getting out. And none of them looked friendly. Echo didn't know why they hadn't already started firing.

And then the answer drove up. An Enforcer on a rail-jumper.

The Dakine were waiting for him to move on before they pulled out their laser boxes. Only the Enforcer didn't move on. He drove right up to Taylor. "Get on," he told her, then motioned to Echo. "You too."

"Mendez," Taylor breathed out, and was already on the bike before the man had finished speaking. She ignored the handles at the side of the bike, and wrapped her arms around Mendez's waist. Echo joined her, just able to grip his handles before the bike jolted down the rails.

The Dakine got off a few shots in their direction, but none that hit them. The bike was too far away. "You believed me," Taylor called to Mendez happily.

"When my rank went to number one," he said, "I became a believer."

The Dakine might have tried to pursue them. Echo couldn't tell. He kept his eyes forward, watching the bike overtake cars as though they were standing still. Each time the bike jumped a car, Echo was lifted, weightless, into air. It was a feeling like flying—the feeling of freedom.

chapter hapter
35

When Sheridan woke up, Tariq was gone. The Tough One stood over her. "Get up," he grumbled. "I don't want to have to carry you to the medroom."

She propped herself up on one elbow. Someone had changed her clothes while she was unconscious. Instead of the tan prison overalls, she wore crisp white ones. She hoped The Tough One hadn't been the one to change her clothes. "Egyptian queens used to have their slaves carry them around," she told him. "Funny how civilization hasn't changed all that much."

"Get up," he said again, this time pointing the laser box for emphasis.

Slowly, she got to her feet.

Was this real life or another VR program? She had no way to tell.

The Tough One used his crystal to open the cell door. Keeping his laser box trained on her, he motioned for her to go out.

Sheridan took unhurried steps toward the door. "You're bringing me somewhere to get a memory wash?"

He didn't answer, just waved for her to go through the door.

"It's a pity I'll forget our heartfelt talks about your family."

He grabbed her arm and yanked her through the door into the hallway. She had expected him to let her go after that, but he kept hold of her, squeezing her arm tightly. As he pulled her down the hallway, he leaned over to speak into her ear. His voice sounded as harsh as churning gravel. "My daughter is dead. Killed by Dakine scum. The scum you refuse to help the government fight."

Even then, while he squeezed her arm, Sheridan felt a jolt of sympathy for him. She wanted to make him understand her refusal—Taylor's refusal. "It's not just the Dakine the government will kill. They'll kill anyone they don't like for any reason. Do you want that?"

"I don't care about the rest," The Tough One hissed. "I want the Dakine dead. All of them."

"Then you're in prison too," she said. "One made of anger."

She should have known better than to say anything. He twisted her arm until she cried out. She fell forward and he yanked her to her feet again, wrenching pain throughout her arm and shoulder. "You shouldn't fight guards," he said. "I have no choice but to subdue you."

She'd grown stupid in prison, because she couldn't stop herself from speaking. "Does my pity torture you? How ironic."

He shoved her against the wall hard. Her back and head hit

it with a snap, then he pulled her forward again, nearly dragging her down the hallway. Stupid VR programs. Why did they have to be so accurate when it came to pain? The Tough One didn't speak again. Neither did she. They went through three more metallic hallways and took an elevator down two floors. Another hallway. Then The Tough One led her into a room.

It was large and so brightly lit that she had to squint to let her eyes adjust. Bare white walls surrounded her. Everything looked sterile and blank, smelled that way too. Three Enforcers stood against the back wall. It seemed like a large number to guard one unarmed teenage girl.

Reilly was at the far end of the room talking to a woman dressed in a red pantsuit. Her hair was pulled away from her face and shoved into a long red cap. The cap reminded Sheridan of something the Seven Dwarves would wear . . . if they were taller, women, and really liked the color red.

A desk covered with unrecognizable equipment sat along one wall. A medical table stood directly behind Reilly and the woman. Hand and leg cuffs connected to the top of the table with thin ropes, and two metal clamps lay open at the head of the table—the place where her head would be strapped down. The side of the table had a computer screen with glowing buttons and charts. The sight of it made Sheridan's stomach lurch. Even worse, a large, cave-like machine sat a few feet away from the table. She could tell by the rails on the floor that the table rolled into the machine.

Sheridan's heart pounded against her rib cage. Her ears rang with sudden fear. *It's just another VR program*, she told herself. *One designed to freak you out*. If they thought a fear of sharks would make her give them information, right now she would be floating on an inner tube in the middle of the Pacific Ocean covered in steak sauce.

The Tough One marched Sheridan over to Reilly. Reilly turned, smiled casually at Sheridan, and gestured to the woman in red. "This is Emile, the med who'll oversee your memory wash."

Emile was a thin woman, with pronounced features that might have been pretty when she was younger but looked sharp and birdlike now. The woman met Sheridan's eyes and nodded as though they were being introduced at a cocktail party. More proof this wasn't real. You wouldn't look a person in the eyes before you shut down part of her brain.

"It's a simple procedure," Reilly went on, eager in his explanation. "We strap you onto the table, push this button"—he tapped his finger on a square light in the control panel—"and send you into the erasing chamber. I could do it myself—in fact, I will—but regulations insist a med is present. If your head isn't in the right position when you enter the chamber, you could lose things besides your memory: your hearing or sight, your ability to recognize faces or identify patterns. So many things could accidentally be destroyed." Reilly leaned toward her, his eyes gleaming with angry satisfaction. "We wouldn't want any of your intelligence to be affected. You see, even after all the problems you've insisted on causing, we're still looking out for you." He straightened and glanced around the room. "Where is my coffee?"

The Tough One, and the row of Enforcers along the back wall, all stared blankly at Reilly, unanswering. Reilly grumbled something under his breath and unclipped his comlink. Before Reilly called anyone, the medroom door slid open and Tariq walked in carrying a mug.

That made five men here to guard her. Or, Sheridan thought with a flutter of hope, maybe Tariq had come to help her. He might have changed his mind about this. Could he do anything to fight off four other guards? She searched his face for some clue. He didn't look at her, just strolled over to Reilly and handed him the mug. Steam curled from its top.

Reilly brought the cup to his lips, took a sip, and sighed happily. "Exactly the way I like it, with a hint of caramel and vanilla." Keeping his gaze on Sheridan, Reilly motioned to Tariq. "I believe you've already met my personal assistant."

It was only then that Tariq turned his attention to Sheridan. "Yes, we've . . ." He looked as though he was about to say something intimate, then settled for the word, "met."

The amusement in Tariq's voice made Sheridan's cheeks flush in anger. She had known Tariq worked for Reilly—but his personal assistant? Was that true or just a new twist in the VR program? It could be true, and that thought alone made the memory of their kisses burn painfully on Sheridan's lips. She hated the smiling, smug version of Tariq standing before her, hated him worse than Reilly. That was the thing about betrayal. It stung even when you saw it coming.

The Tough One walked to the back of the room and stood beside the row of Enforcers. They all watched her, a still and silent group of grim reapers. Reilly swirled his coffee, then motioned to Tariq.

Tariq sauntered over to Sheridan and took hold of her arm.

"I'm sorry," he said softly.

"Not sorry enough to help me." She knew Reilly overheard everything they said. She didn't care.

"I tried to help you." Tariq pulled her toward the table. "I tried so many times."

She planted her feet and resisted, didn't make those few steps easy for him. "Your help was never real. I always knew that."

"Did you?" He yanked her forward, then pushed her into the table so hard, its edge bit into her hips. She knocked into one of the cuffs and it jangled as it slid across the table. She turned, trying to get away. Tariq grabbed hold of her arm to keep her in place. He picked up the closest cuff and snapped it onto her wrist. As soon as the cuff closed, the rope retracted into the table, pulling her hand until it was pinned down. She had to bend over to stay standing.

"I'm sorry you won't remember our time together." Tariq's smile returned, arrogant and punishing. It had been a blow to his ego, she realized, that he couldn't get her to cooperate. "I'll always remember it, though. How sweet you were. How eager and trusting."

He reached for her other hand. She moved it away. "That's not a memory. That's a fantasy. Apparently you've lost track of the difference."

Tariq's expression darkened and he drew back his hand to slap her. As he did, Reilly snapped his fingers. Tariq at once dropped his hand and stepped away so that Reilly could see her.

"He's trained you well," Sheridan told Tariq. "I couldn't get my dog to obey that quickly."

Tariq's eyes narrowed. A muscle in his cheek twitched in annoyance.

The door to the room slid open again. Three more Enforcers walked in and took their place against the back wall. It seemed almost laughable to see them lined up like that. Had her resistance really merited three more guards?

Reilly took a sip of his coffee and slowly stepped toward Sheridan. He was close enough now that she could have hit him with her free hand. She supposed he didn't worry about that with eight guards around.

"This is your last chance," Reilly said. "Will you work with me or will you lose your memories? Your life, your sister—it will all be gone."

"I know this is one of your VR programs," Sheridan said. "You're overlooking the details again."

"Am I?" he said, with genuine surprise. "And what would those details be?"

"Your program is getting the faces wrong now." She couldn't have failed to notice, after all, that one of the Enforcers who had just come in was Echo. Their helmets didn't completely obscure their faces, and she'd gotten good at seeing through the helmets' glare. His face was rounder than it should have been, his nose a little too big.

She glanced at the row of Enforcers again. The one who looked like Echo gave an almost imperceptible shake of his head, warning her not to speak.

Reilly glanced over his shoulder, scanning the row of Enforcers lined up and standing at attention.

The nice thing about knowing you were in a VR program,

Sheridan decided, was that you didn't have to overthink what you were doing. It was like playing a computer game in which you could shoot people without compunction. She didn't think twice about leaning her weight against the table and kicking Reilly as hard as she could. Her foot connected below his waist with satisfying force. He gave a small groan, a sound like the lid being popped off a bottle, then crumpled and fell to his knees. The mug flew from his hands, spraying coffee on Tariq as it clanked to the floor.

Sheridan pulled at her wrist, tried to free herself from the cuff. It didn't budge.

Tariq strode toward Sheridan, wiping at the coffee dribbling down his thigh. His mouth was a tight line of fury. She lifted her leg again, aiming. Tariq's armor would absorb most of the impact, but if she kicked him in the knee, she might still manage to knock him down.

Before he reached her, the Enforcer who looked like Echo pulled a box from his belt, pointed it at Tariq, and fired. She heard a whiz, a small *thunk*, and then Tariq jerked backward like a sprinting dog who had reached the end of his leash. He fell to the ground, yelling, and was dragged away from Sheridan.

After that, all the Enforcers along the wall moved, erupting into action. Half of them turned their laser boxes on the Echo-like Enforcer. Nothing happened, though. No ripping sound that laser boxes made when they fired. Must be another VR program malfunction.

It didn't matter. If Reilly wanted to learn something from her, he could learn she wouldn't give up. She would always fight him, even when she knew it wasn't real.

Sheridan didn't have time to watch the Enforcers or to see what happened. She needed to get free from the table. A dozen buttons lay on the side panel. One of them must release the cuff, but another would send the table into the erasing chamber. Which one was it? In her panic, she couldn't remember which button Reilly had pointed to. Some had symbols, others showed letters or numbers. Sheridan didn't understand any of it.

Reilly staggered to his feet, his eyes blazing with rage. He didn't straighten all the way. "You'll regret that," he rasped out.

Sheridan's gaze bounced between him and the controls on the table. None of the symbols resembled a cuff being released. "Isn't this what you want?" she asked. "Isn't this part of your plan to break me? You must want me to fight, or you wouldn't keep putting me in these programs."

"I will break you," he said. "I'll break every bone in your body."

Sheridan hadn't noticed the club hanging from Reilly's belt before. Now he reached for it, yanked it loose. As he did, he turned and saw the Enforcers fighting behind him.

He stared for a moment in confusion. "What are you doing?" he called to them. "What's going on?"

Emile lay on the ground, an unconscious red heap of jutting limbs. The Enforcers had abandoned their useless laser boxes and were fighting with other weapons, grunting and shouting as they did. Some swung long, thin chain saws. They spit sparks as they whirred around, buzzing hungrily. Other Enforcers used canisters that shot out black ooze. Patches of it were splattered on the Enforcers, the walls, and the floor, making the whole room look like it had been dabbed with shadows. Apparently the ooze stuck things together. The Tough One was cemented to the wall like a black butterfly pinned in someone's collection. Another guard fell onto a patch on the ground and couldn't get up. He kicked uselessly at the floor.

Sheridan returned her attention to the table. She pressed the button with the most likely-looking symbol.

Instead of her cuff releasing, the bands at the top of the bed snapped shut. No good. She pressed another. The bed lowered a couple of inches.

Reilly pulled his comlink from his belt. He checked its screen, then shook the device in aggravation. "What's happened? Someone go for backup!"

The Enforcers were too busy fighting each other to comply. In the surges of swinging chain saws and moving bodies, Sheridan couldn't tell which Enforcer was Tariq and which was Echo. It was all thrusts, dodges, kicks, and grunts—a violent dance set to the music of the buzzing saws.

"Computer malfunction?" Sheridan asked Reilly. "I just hate those." She pushed another button. That one seemed to do nothing at all.

An Enforcer called out, "Brothers!" It was such an unexpected yell that it drew Sheridan's attention back to the fight. Were there brothers here? No, even as the thought crossed her mind, she knew the call had been a plea, or perhaps a reminder. There were unspoken words behind that word, ones that bound people together.

Black ooze covered one Enforcer's helmet, blocking his sight. He held a chain saw but could only wave it wildly in front of him. Another Enforcer came toward him, chain saw lifted to slash him.

"Left thrust now!" a third Enforcer yelled. The blinded man lunged forward, striking to the left. His blow hit his opponent's shoulder and made a sharp grinding sound.

The third Enforcer drove his chain saw at the man he fought, making him back up so quickly that he tripped over one of the downed Enforcers. Before the man even hit the ground, the third Enforcer was on his way to help his blinded friend.

Sheridan pushed another button. Again, nothing. The Tough One was screaming out threats, even though he was still stuck to the wall. Over by the door, two Enforcers—Echo and Tariq; she recognized them now—circled each other, both holding sparking chain saws like fencers in a duel. Tariq swung his chain saw at Echo. Echo blocked the blow with his own.

Sheridan pushed another button on the side of the table. This one rotated the bed a couple of inches. Reilly looked over and saw what she was doing. He flung his comlink to the ground so hard, it bounced before skidding under the desk. "No!" he yelled, and marched toward her, the club gripped in his hand. His eyes had gone glassy, feverish with hatred.

He paused when he got close to her. She faced him and waited, perfectly still. Perhaps he thought she was compliant, that she would accept whatever blow he gave her. She wasn't compliant though; she was focused. The cuff around her wrist kept her manacled to the table, but it also provided her with leverage. The table was low enough now that she could put all her weight on it.

He came toward her, slicing a blow aimed at her head. She leaned back and kicked him squarely in the chest. The impact made a gratifying thudding noise.

He stumbled backward, arms floundering, and he hit the floor with another thud. Just as gratifying. This was probably why people had played violent video games: pent-up anger. It felt good to take it out on someone even if he wasn't real.

Sheridan didn't wait to see how long it would take Reilly to get up. She pushed another button. The table rose a few inches. She looked at the gaping mouth of the erasing chamber. How long could she push buttons without pushing the wrong one? But what other choice did she have?

She looked back at the Enforcers. Tariq swung his chain saw at Echo's face, barely missing his helmet. As Tariq's arm continued in its downward arc, Echo brought his chain saw down on his arm. The grinding sound of saw hitting armor screeched from the blade. Tariq fell forward, pushed by the momentum of Echo's blow. Before he could get back on his feet, Echo kicked him in the side, toppling him into a patch of the black ooze. Tariq jerked left and then right, but he was held tight.

So this was how the program would go. Reilly knew she didn't trust Tariq anymore, so the program brought in Echo to rescue her. He would help her escape and then tell her he needed information about the QGP. It would be the same thing she'd already done with Tariq all over again. But worse. She cared about Echo, missed him. It would be hard not to fall apart in his arms.

She felt another rush of anger toward Reilly. He wanted to see an escape scene? She would give it to him. She would fight, and she would laugh when this ended, not cry. Even if she had to force the laughter.

Reilly pulled himself to his feet, his face red and blotchy with fury. "I won't let them rescue you," he spit, and limped over to the desk beside the bed.

Sheridan pushed another button. A lamp above the table flicked on and flooded the area with light. It was too bright. She could barely see anything now. Stupid program. It wouldn't let her win.

Reilly picked up a long needle from the desk. It glinted in his hand, clinical and dangerous. He came back toward her.

She pressed another button. This time the pressure on her wrist released. The computer must think Reilly was so close that she couldn't get away from him. She didn't look at her wrist. Her eyes were trained on Reilly and the shot in his hand. He was nearly to her.

His eyes pulsed with a blunt sort of rage and his words were no more than a guttural growl. "You will die!"

He lunged toward her, trying to stab her chained arm. If the light hadn't been so bright, he might have seen that she had released the cuff. Or maybe not. The cuff hadn't completely come off. When she jerked her arm away from the table, the cuff stayed on her wrist for several seconds, pulling the rope loose.

What she did next, she did without thinking.

Reilly still leaned over the table. Sheridan took hold of the cuff and wound its rope around Reilly's neck. When that was done, she snapped the cuff shut on the rope.

"I've already died so many times," she told him as the rope

336

tightened and retreated into the table, "it doesn't bother me anymore. We'll see how you like it."

To Reilly's credit, he managed to get his hands in between his neck and the rope before it completely choked him. His head was pinned to the table, though, and his green hair flopped around as he jerked one way and then the other. He pulled at the rope with both hands, sputtering and gasping. "Help!" he coughed out.

Sheridan stepped away from the table. "Not brilliant last words, but fitting ones. You've always needed help, haven't you?"

Sheridan turned away from him and took in the room. Three Enforcers lay on the ground, one was stuck to the wall, and another was falling at the hands of two Enforcers. A third strode toward her. The light over the table shone so brightly that it cast a reflection on his visor. Instead of his face, all she saw was a distorted image of herself, staring wide-eyed at him.

Where was Echo? Was he one of the Enforcers who'd already fallen? She backed up until she bumped into the table, right next to Reilly's struggling form.

She didn't realize she'd hit the button that activated the memory wash sequence until the erasing chamber let out a low, vibrating hum. The table moved, sliding slowly along the floor toward the opening. Sheridan jerked away from the table, looking for a weapon, anything she could use against an Enforcer.

The shot Reilly had tried to use on her lay on the table. She grabbed it and held it out in front of her, brandishing it. The joints. Those were the Enforcers' only weak spots. It would be hard to get to them while the man kept moving.

"Stay away," she said, and took a step backward. The table

was gone now, swallowed up by the erasing chamber. She had only a few feet before she'd back up into the wall.

Reilly's yells from the chamber abruptly stopped. She didn't have time to think about him or what that meant. She edged to her left, farther away from the advancing Enforcer.

The man lifted his helmet visor, and some of her fear melted into relief. Echo's hair was no longer blue. He'd dyed it black and wore it slicked down. Two large black ovals surrounded his eyes—a tattoo version of a bandit's mask.

"Sheridan," he said. "It's me." He spoke in the twenty-first-century accent, as though she might not have understood him otherwise.

She kept a wary eye on the Enforcers behind him. "When did you start working in the detention center?"

"I'm rescuing you," Echo said. "That means you can put the shot down." He motioned to the other Enforcers. "These are my friends. We're going to get you out of here, but you'll need to cooperate with us."

One of the Enforcers took off his helmet and gripped it in one hand. No, not gripped it, Sheridan realized. It was stuck to his glove with the black goo. He was the Enforcer who had fought blind. His long dark hair was pulled back in a ponytail. Slashes marred his armor in a few places, black scars on his torso. He took off his glove and dropped it and the stuck helmet to the floor.

The second unfamiliar Enforcer peered around the room, still holding his sword chain saw. "Where's Reilly?"

The ponytailed Enforcer pointed to the erasing chamber.

It was humming even louder now. Lights raced up and down its computer screen. Reilly was no longer visible, but one of his shoes had been kicked off in his struggle. It lay halfway out of the chamber door, shivering from the machine's vibrations. "Is he dead?" the ponytailed Enforcer asked.

Echo held his hand out to Sheridan. "Put down the shot," he said soothingly. "We need to go."

Sheridan lowered her arm but didn't move. She was waiting for the answer to the Enforcer's question. Was Reilly dead? Was that something he would let a VR program do?

The second Enforcer walked over to the erasing chamber's control panel and read the data there. "In the ways that matter, yes. Which means I've decided to follow the council's guidelines of noninterference. We don't have time to wait around for this thing to finish, and I'm not going in there."

The conversation didn't make sense to Sheridan. While she watched the Enforcer read the chamber data, Echo had reached over and plucked the shot from her hand. He tossed it onto the floor. "Sheridan, we're going to pretend we're leading you to a cell. You'll need to wear these." He held up a pair of cuffs with the backs cut off. "Don't let anyone see they're not real."

Echo's friends went around to the downed Enforcers, giving each a shot in the joint that quieted him. The room seemed oddly silent without their stream of threats and curses, without their calls for backup.

"Hold out your hands," Echo told Sheridan. When she did, he put a metal band around her right wrist. "This will block your crystal's signal until we can take you someplace to remove it."

Well, that was a new twist. Every other time she'd escaped from the city, someone had taken her to a med center to have her crystal removed.

Where the ends of the metal band met, they grew warm, fusing together. Echo slipped the fake cuffs onto her wrists, then took her arm and turned her to the door. "That's Lee," he said, pointing to the man who still wore his helmet. "And that's Ren." He nodded at the man with the ponytail. "They're part of the DW."

Of course they were. They probably needed information about the QGPs that only she could provide. She didn't comment.

Ren reached Tariq. He was the last of the downed Enforcers still conscious and was calling out for help. Ren pulled off Tariq's helmet. "No one will come help you," Ren said with disgust, "because the guards here are used to ignoring screams." He plunged a needle into Tariq's neck. Tariq stared at Sheridan with an expression she couldn't identify. Was it frustration, regret, or just surprise? In another moment the emotion disappeared and his head lolled to the ground.

Ren put on Tariq's helmet and took one of his gloves as well. Echo led Sheridan to the door. She had been so full of adrenaline, so geared up to fight, but now her energy was fading into a numb acceptance of whatever came next. Don't hope, she told herself. This isn't real.

Echo's grip on her arm was gentle. "You'll need to be quiet until we're out of the detention center."

She glanced over her shoulder, half expecting Reilly to be standing by the erasing chamber watching her. Instead only his shoe was visible, vibrating on the floor like a dancer tapping out the rhythm to some morbid song.

"What about Taylor?" Sheridan asked. "Are you rescuing her too?"

"Taylor is safe," Echo said. "I don't have time to explain more right now."

He didn't have to. Safe was a good word, a word she didn't mind savoring until later.

As soon as they left the room, another Enforcer joined the group, a woman who had been standing guard by the door. She must have been one of Echo's friends, because no one seemed surprised to see her. She fell in line beside them and they marched down the hallway. "You'll need to hurry," the woman told Echo. "When the med doesn't issue a report on the memory wash, someone will check on her."

Sheridan wondered how long that would be. How much time did it take to wipe a life's worth of memories from a person's mind?

The group turned and strode down another hallway, this one mostly empty. No one spoke. They went up the elevator and then down another hall. When they reached the doors at the end, the woman Enforcer put her crystal to the door panel. The door slid open and they all went through. They walked down another hallway, and the woman opened the last door for them, one that led into a parking garage. Without any kind of good-bye, she turned and went back the way she'd come. Echo and the others hurried into the garage, propelling Sheridan along with them.

She was out of the building, one step closer to freedom.

Don't hope, she told herself. Nothing hurt quite as much as the shards of broken hope.

Lee took out a scanner, checked it, and said, "This way."

The group ignored the closest cars and went to one in a back row. Echo slid the cuffs off her wrists and helped her get inside. The others climbed in behind her. Instead of sitting down, they knelt on the floor and slid the top off the far seat. Ren reached down inside and pulled out a man's arm.

Sheridan jerked backward and let out a shriek. Two seconds later she realized the arm was connected to a man, which wasn't much more comforting. Who was he? Was he alive? What had they done to him? He lay limp and unmoving on the car floor.

Ren put the man's crystal to the control panel. "The Rico Estates building," he said, and then hefted the man back into the seat.

"It's all right, Sheridan." Echo knelt in front of her. He held his hands toward her in the same gesture she used to calm skittish horses. "They're not dead, just unconscious. We needed their crystals to get into the detention center."

"They?" Sheridan repeated.

Echo didn't need to explain because by that time Ren and Lee had removed the top off the other side of the seats. They hauled another man out and dumped him into the opening where the first man lay.

Echo moved toward the empty seat opening. "The guards at the checkpoint have to think Ren and Lee are the Enforcers in the car. You and I need to hide. Come on."

The empty compartment in the seat didn't look big enough for two people, but Ren and Lee had managed to put the seat top on the other side. Echo got in, lay down, and motioned for Sheridan to join him. She climbed in, feeling awkward, and lay down beside him. There wasn't any room between them. The stiff parts of his Enforcer uniform poked into her.

He took hold of her hand in his. "We're almost free."

Almost free. *Almost* didn't count. That was like being almost alive. It still left you mostly dead.

Ren and Lee leaned over them, sliding the seat top back into place. Ren said, "Be quiet until we tell you it's safe."

Then it went dark. She could only make out cracks of light above them where the seats were cut.

Echo squeezed her hand. "Are you all right?"

"I'm fine." It was a lie, of course. She was far from fine. She was surrounded by darkness even though her eyes were wide open.

"I'm sorry for everything you've been through," he whispered. "I'm so, so sorry."

She didn't answer. What could she have said? Besides, they were supposed to be quiet. She could feel Echo's breath near her ear, sense the motion of his chest moving up and down. They were so close, it might as well have been an embrace. And because he couldn't see, she let herself relax and pretended it was.

Lying where they were, they heard the rumbling of the car against the rail as loud. It muted everything. Which was probably why it still sounded like Echo was murmuring, "I'm sorry. I'm sorry," over and over again.

chapter~~hapter~~
36

Sheridan wasn't sure how long she lay in the dark with Echo, feeling him breathe and hearing the street rumble by. After a while, Ren and Lee pulled the tops off the seats. Sheridan blinked in the light, then let Ren help her out. Echo climbed out by himself, stretching his shoulders as he did. "Where are we?" he asked. His face was still wrong, too round. She had half expected the computer to realize its mistake and adjust him.

Lee picked up one side of the seat's top to put it back. "Fraternity Street."

Echo helped slide the seat into place, then took Sheridan's hand and sat down next to her. "The detention center might have realized there was a breakout by now," he told her. "We'll switch cars soon, in case someone decides to track the unconscious Enforcers."

Ren unclipped his comlink from his belt. "Ask her about pots and kettles."

Echo gently squeezed Sheridan's hand. His blue eyes were serious, intent. "I need to know the meaning of the phrase *That's the pot calling the kettle black.*"

An odd question. "Why?" she asked, automatically suspicious.

"It will take a while to explain everything. I need to know what the phrase means first."

Sheridan hesitated, trying to find the trap in the question. What did Reilly want? What information could answering reveal? She could think of nothing. Reilly must already know what the phrase meant.

"It means you're a hypocrite," Sheridan said.

Ren tapped something into his comlink. His lips were drawn in a firm, unhappy line. "If Taylor waited so long that she's been captured, I vow I'll—"

Sheridan didn't let him finish. "Taylor? Where's Taylor?"

"Hiding at the Scicenter," Lee said. "Hopefully undetected."

"At the Scicenter?" Sheridan repeated, with more than a little doubt. "Why is she there?"

"I'm sure Taylor is all right." Echo unclipped his comlink and checked its screen. "She probably ran her program and left long ago."

Ren's eyebrows drew together. "Why do you think that?"

"Because that's what I would have done."

Lee looked at Echo with evident confusion. "You would lie about your demands?"

Ren shook his head in disapproval. "We gave our oath that we would try to free her sister. That should have been enough."

Echo clipped his comlink back onto his belt. "Oaths can be broken more easily than threats."

"Not by men of honor," Ren said. Then he and Lee gave each other knowing looks and mumbled things about people who grew up in oath-breaking cities.

Sheridan didn't speak. She hadn't understood what the others were talking about, except that they weren't sure where Taylor was. This apparently would be a program in which the DW offered to help rescue Taylor in return for information.

Echo turned in his seat so that his full attention rested on Sheridan. His blue eyes were heavy with worry. "You're all right?" he asked for the second time.

"I'm hungry," she said.

Echo kept looking her over, frowning. "You've lost weight. We'll get you something to eat as soon as we're safe."

She imagined that wouldn't be for a while. They had to know she was judging the reality by her hunger.

Echo's gaze didn't break from hers. "Are you . . . did they . . . do you have any injuries?"

"Not yet," she said airily, "but it's still early in the day."

Her answer made him smile. It wasn't enough to rid his eyes of worry though.

The programs were so good at copying emotion, at using it to elicit responses from her. She wanted to both throw her arms around him and to yell at him to stop it. She turned sharply away from him and looked out the window. She saw tall buildings in different colors: blue, yellow, pink. One had something on its walls that made it sparkle like a disco ball. She hadn't been on this street before.

"I'm glad we're out of the building," she said. "Those are my favorite."

"Favorite what?" Echo asked.

"Don't get me wrong, the warden's VIP suites are nice too, and you can't beat the food there—what am I saying? An Enforcer can beat anything, right? That's why I keep hearing screaming down the hallway."

"What?" Echo asked. All the men were staring at her.

"Gallows humor," she said. "It's especially appropriate when people have just tried to kill you."

Lee's brows drew together. "She's not making any sense. Did Reilly inject her with something before we took her?"

"No," Echo said.

"He might have," Ren said. "We were too busy fighting to see what went on. We'll have Xavier scan her as soon as we meet up."

Echo leaned toward her, hands on his knees. "Are you feeling dizzy?"

"No." She relaxed against her seat, returning his steady stare. "I like the Zorro look. It works for you. That's the advantage of being a hot guy, isn't it? You can pull anything off."

"Pull what off?" Echo asked. "I understood the Zorro reference, but not anything else. I can't tell if you're speaking in twenty-first-century idioms or if something is wrong."

"Sorry," she said. "I only meant that I'm glad you're here. I was getting tired of Tariq. A guy can rescue a girl only so many times before it becomes passé."

Lee tilted his head, examining her. "It could be shock."

"Or," Sheridan said tightly, "it could be the chip Reilly put in my brain. That's always a possibility."

The color drained from Echo's face. "What?"

"Is it a tracking chip?" Ren asked.

Lee said, "Why would they put a tracking chip in her when they have one in her crystal?"

Ren sighed and gestured helplessly at Sheridan. "We don't know that anyone put anything into her brain. She might be suffering from some sort of neural failure. Who knows what they did to her?"

Echo moved closer to Sheridan. "I'm sorry," he said. "I'm so sorry. This is my fault. I was so stupid to risk everything." He ran his hand across her forehead and down the side of her face. She thought it was a comforting gesture, then realized he was looking for a scar, proof of the chip. She could have told him it was on her other temple but decided she liked the feel of his fingers brushing against her cheek. She had to enjoy the little pleasures while she could. She would let herself pretend this was real for a few moments.

"I rearranged the timestream," Echo said. "I didn't know it would hurt you." He lifted the hair at the side of her face, checking there.

Sheridan smiled lazily. "And you accuse me of not making sense."

He tilted her face toward him. "It's going to take a long time to explain everything." That was when he saw the scar on her temple, right below her hairline. "*Sangre*," he swore. "They *did* put something in her head."

Lee left his seat and sat on her other side, muttering about what a demon Reilly was. Sheridan tried to think of something cavalier to say but couldn't. All this sympathy was wearing down her barriers. Then she felt a prick at the base of her neck. She spun her head toward Lee and saw the needle in his hand.

"You're drugging me?" she asked indignantly.

"Until we know what they put in you," he said. "Otherwise you could harm yourself or someone else."

"'Someone else' has my vote," she said. Or at least meant to say. Before all the words came out, she went limp in Echo's arms.

chapter hapter
37

Riding the rail-jumper had been so noisy and intense, Taylor didn't notice any of Ren's calls until Mendez pulled into a parking garage. By that time, the smell of maple—Ren's signal—was so strong that it was making her crave pancakes.

Mendez drove into an empty car slot and turned off the bike.

Taylor scanned the rows of empty, waiting cars. "Why did we come here?"

"We've got to switch to a car now." Mendez dismounted by standing on the footrests and swinging one of his long legs over the front of the bike. Echo got off next.

As Taylor got off, she unclipped her comlink. She had four missed calls and a message.

Mendez pushed his car-call button. "People notice

rail-jumpers." The nearest car slid from its spot and obediently came toward them. "We've got to make sure no one tracks us."

Before Taylor could check her message from Ren, four men walked into the parking garage. They were dressed in the normal bright Traventon clothes. Not Enforcers, but maybe Dakine. They all held gadgets of some sort, things that resembled knives. One carried a large bag. They didn't speak, and their expressions were determined, fierce almost. The men headed straight toward Mendez, Echo, and Taylor with a fast, focused stride.

Echo immediately positioned himself between Taylor and the men. He was protecting her from laser fire, she realized. She didn't even have time to protest before Mendez called to the men, "*Ete sen.*" The men nodded at Mendez, and the one carrying the bag threw it to him. Mendez caught it and turned to the car without any signs of worry. These men were DW, apparently.

Taylor let the relief run over her, let her heart get back to its job of dutifully pumping. Mendez might have warned them they were about to meet up with some of his friends. But no, he wouldn't have. None of the DW were ever forthcoming with information that could be used against them.

Echo turned and went to the car without saying anything to her. She followed him, amazed that he had put himself between her and danger. Again. She hadn't given him any reason to make that sort of sacrifice.

Mendez climbed into the car and handed her the bag. "Clothes and hats. You'll need to change."

Through the window, Taylor could see that the men had

made their way to the rail-jumper. They bent over the bike, putting their gadgets on the wheels and handlebars. By the time the car glided out of the garage, the men had disassembled the rail-jumper and were carrying its pieces into a nearby car.

The smell of maple wafted over Taylor again. She'd been so startled to see the men in the garage, she'd forgotten about Ren's message. She opened it. *You're a hypocrite*, it read.

Well, that was nice.

And you're a tactless troglodyte, she wrote back. *Do you have news for me or not?*

A moment later, Ren called her. His voice was full of frustration. "Did you destroy the QGPs? We have Sheridan. That's what the pot calling the kettle black means—you're a hypocrite."

"You have her?" Taylor nearly came off her seat in excitement.

"I just said we did, didn't I? The QGPs?"

"I destroyed them already, and you're not a troglodyte after all. Let me speak to her."

A pause. "You can't. She's unconscious right now." Ren said this in the same tone a person would use when saying, "She's busy," or "She stepped out." *She's unconscious right now.*

"What?" Taylor asked.

"Just a precaution," Ren said. "Reilly put some sort of chip into her. It will need to be taken out."

"What sort of chip? Who's going to take it? Where are you?"

Ren gave her a brief rundown of their escape from the detention center and the things that Sheridan had said. "We're at the Recreation Center now," he finished up. "Joseph went to the restaurant to talk to someone about Sheridan."

Taylor turned to Mendez and passed that information on to him. "Call your people at the restaurant," she told him. "Vouch for Joseph."

Ren was about to end the call when Taylor said, "Wait, I have something else to tell you. It's bad news. About Xavier." She swallowed hard. Her throat felt like she'd eaten nails. "He was shot while we were coming out of the courthouse." She somehow got the rest of the story out. She told him, in faltering sentences, how Xavier had stepped in front of her and how they'd had to leave his body in the car. She added, almost as a footnote, that Allana had betrayed them to the Dakine.

Ren listened without comment, and his silence felt like— what? Judgment? Sympathy? Accusation, maybe? When she finished, the only thing he said was "I'm sorry about Xavier. I'll contact the council as soon as I can and let them know." Then he ended the call. More silence. Only it wasn't really silent, because she could hear the sounds from the courthouse lobby. The gasbots whirring. Shots being fired. Xavier's voice calling her name.

Echo's gaze was on her. He'd been watching her for most of her conversation. "Xavier's death—it wasn't your fault."

"It feels like my fault."

"It wasn't," Echo said. "I know the difference."

She paused, realizing what he meant. When Lobo had ordered Joseph's and Allana's deaths, it had been because Echo had told Lobo that Allana had broken a Dakine law. The weight of that—no wonder Echo had done everything he could to save them both.

"The Dakine assassinations weren't your fault," Taylor told

Echo. "You didn't order Joseph's and Allana's executions."

"It was my fault because I joined the Dakine," he said.

Taylor knew she couldn't say anything that would change his mind about that, so she just put her hand on his and gave it a squeeze.

A HALF HOUR LATER, Taylor, Echo, and Mendez made their way across the Traventon Plaza Recreation Center courtyard to the employees' entrance at the back of the Fisherman's Feast. Mendez walked a few paces ahead of them so that they wouldn't look like they were together.

Taylor allowed herself to feel relieved. The hard part of the mission was over. Echo was quiet as he walked. His gaze swept around the area, checking for anyone who might recognize them. The people they saw were all busy in conversations about the rank badges, either on their comlinks or with friends who were with them. Taylor saw more than one group of teenagers taking pictures of themselves with their rank badges proudly displayed.

Even if anyone had given Echo and her a second look, it would have been hard to recognize them under their wide-brimmed hats. They were both dressed like cowboys who'd been in a paint fight. Echo's shirt was a kaleidoscope of blues that made his eyes stand out. Such a pretty blue, one that reminded Taylor of the missing sky.

She and Echo would be safe soon and on their way to Santa Fe. What would happen when they reached the city? Would Echo want to see her again? Would they be friends?

Echo caught her staring.

She cleared her throat. "I never really thanked you for pulling me from the rail, or carrying me to the building, or fixing my ankle. I sort of stink at thank-yous."

"You're welcome," he said.

The smell of fried food wafted out from the back of the restaurant. The building looked like a huge tin tackle box: made of metal and a little beat-up on the edges. "You were amazing fighting the Dakine," she added. "Thanks for that too."

"Don't thank me for that one." His stride was tense and quick. "I'm the reason the Dakine found us. I brought Allana from the past. It was stupid of me."

Taylor reached out and put her hand on Echo's arm. "You wanted to save her life even though she'd hurt you. That's not stupid, Echo. That's noble."

Echo let out a grunt of disagreement. "Yeah, you can tell Joseph that when he starts yelling at me."

They reached the restaurant door, and Mendez led them inside. Taylor barely noticed her surroundings. The yellow stripes on the wall that hid the secret door, the cement steps that led downstairs, the narrow hallway that opened up to a large room—it was a blur. She was too eager to see Sheridan to care about anything else.

A dozen people who were dressed in camouflage bustled around the windowless room, putting things into backpacks. Taylor saw Sheridan right off. She lay on a gurney, unconscious, a blanket covering everything but her head. Her face was painted in browns and greens, and her hair had been put in a camouflage cap. Joseph, his pack already on his shoulders, stood by the gurney talking to another man.

Taylor ran the distance to them and knelt down by her sister. It was hard to tell much about her while she slept. Taylor brushed her hand across Sheridan's forehead. "Is she all right? She's not injured?" Ren had told Taylor that Sheridan was fine, but she wanted to hear it from Joseph, needed the reassurance.

"Her stats are all good," he said. "The meds at the DW center will be able to take out the chip when they take out her crystal. We're about to leave for the clinic right now."

"Okay," Taylor said. "I'm ready to go."

Joseph eyed her. "No, you're not. You're not in camouflage and you're limping. You need to have a med take care of your ankle before you make the hike."

"I can be ready soon," Taylor said. She looked around the room for a med. With everyone dressed in camouflage, she didn't recognize anybody, couldn't even tell who was in charge.

Joseph didn't say more to her because Echo walked up. Joseph pointed a finger at him. "I can't believe you strained Allana, someone you knew was—"

Echo lifted his hands. "I know."

"If anything had happened to Taylor—"

"I know," Echo said, more firmly.

"You don't know," Joseph snapped. "You don't know how hard it would be for me to tell Dad that I brought you back to life and then killed you myself."

Taylor stood up. "It's okay, Joseph. Echo had to save Allana. He saved my life too—more than once. Now let's concentrate on saving Sheridan." She looked around the room again. "Where's some camouflage stuff? I need to change so I can go with you."

Four men came over to the group, packs secured on their

backs. They had an air of efficiency about them, an unspoken authority. Each picked up an end of Sheridan's gurney. "It's time to leave," one of them told Joseph.

Joseph adjusted his pack and turned to go with them. "I'll see you when you reach the clinic," he told Taylor and Echo.

Taylor followed after him, doing her best to hide her limp. "I have to go with Sheridan. I need to make sure she's okay."

"I'll make sure she's okay," Joseph said patiently. "Trust me, all right?"

Trust him. She supposed it was time she did that. She stopped, sighed, and watched as he walked away beside Sheridan.

chapter 38

When Sheridan woke up, the first thing she noticed was a skylight over her bed. A cottony cloud sprawled across a blue patch of sky. That was new. Some fern fronds dangled on top of the window, shifting in the wind. She wasn't in her cell. She was underground somewhere, looking up.

She blinked and took in her surroundings, remembering what had happened: Reilly, the memory wash room, Echo rescuing her, Lee drugging her in the car. The room she was now in was medium sized and, judging from the computer screen above her bed, was some sort of hospital room.

Echo sat on a chair beside the bed. His face was normal again—that effortless sort of handsome that made her feel self-conscious. His hair was still black, but the Zorro dye was gone. His eyes looked tired and worn, like blue glass that had been chipped.

"How do you feel?" he asked.

She sat up, and a sharp pain flashed through the side of her head, momentarily making her dizzy. "Where am I?" She touched her temple. The skin was numb and had a coating on it that felt like plastic. "What did they do to me?"

"You're in a DW center," Echo said. His voice was low, soothing, and tinged with an apology. Even when he didn't say it, the "I'm sorry" was still there, lingering in between his other words. "A med removed your crystal and the VR chip from your brain." He leaned closer to her. "Reilly ran programs on you— made you experience things that weren't real. Did you know that already—that some of the things that happened to you in the detention cell were computer generated?"

"Yes," she said, eyeing him warily. Chances were, none of this was real. She looked around the room hoping to see some food. None was around. "Where is Taylor?"

"She'll be here soon. We left the city before she did. We thought it was important to get the chip out of you as soon as possible."

He was promising Taylor but not delivering her. Typical of Reilly's programs. She gazed around the room again. The door didn't look like the sort that locked people in. She checked those sorts of things automatically now, the same way she searched for items to use as weapons. In this room, the best weapon was probably the chair Echo sat on. It looked light enough to throw. "Can I have something to eat?" she asked.

Echo glanced at the time on his comlink. "Not yet. The med said you need to wait until the anesthesia is out of your system or the food will make you sick."

No food either. She narrowed her eyes in suspicion, already angry. Reilly was dangling hope in front of her, dangling freedom, just to snatch it away from her again. "You're not really Echo," she said.

He startled, and his eyes widened in surprise. "How did you know?"

"Because it's never real." She threw off the blanket, wanting to run, to fight, to do anything besides let this happen again. The sudden movement made her vision spin and tilt. She put her feet on the floor anyway.

She hadn't seen him leave the chair, but Echo stood in front of her. She wobbled, and he took hold of her arm. "Wait, Sheridan; you don't understand."

"It's not ever real!" She tried to wrench her arm away from him, and when she couldn't, she pushed at him, hitting him almost. "It's never real. Just leave me alone." Her voice cracked, and she took deep breaths to regain her control. She couldn't break down. She wouldn't let them do that to her.

"This is real," Echo told her. "I'm real. Let me explain."

She kept pulling away from him.

"You and I had a secret," he said. "I gave you a picture of Santa Claus when we were at the city walls. Do you remember?"

Of course she remembered. She'd had enough free time in her cell to think about every moment she'd spent with Echo. She stopped struggling and looked at him, still suspicious.

"I helped you dye your hair," he said. "You wanted red so you could be a real redhead. I said you should do red and gold stripes because plain red was no longer in fashion."

Sheridan stared at him without speaking. Could Reilly know those things?

"I'm not Echo," he went on. "You thought I was—everyone thought I was–but I'm Joseph. Echo was part of the Dakine, and when they ordered my death, he switched places with me to save my life. I had to pretend to be him so the Dakine wouldn't kill me."

Sheridan thought of the things about Echo that hadn't made sense—how he knew things about the DW that only Joseph had known. How he wouldn't tell her why he wanted to leave the city. This new information snapped together in Sheridan's mind like an unexpected puzzle piece. "Joseph," she said, testing the word. "You were Joseph all along?"

He nodded—*Joseph* nodded. "You understand why one twin would pretend to be another to save their twin's life?"

Yes, she understood. She had done it for Taylor. Maybe Reilly had finally realized this. Maybe he wanted a confession from her. She edged away from Joseph. "What did we eat for breakfast the first day Taylor and I came to the Wordlab?"

Joseph gave her an incredulous shrug. "I barely remember what I had for breakfast yesterday. That was a month and a half ago."

"What was something else we talked about then?"

"You told me about your horses in Tennessee," he said. "Breeze and Bolt."

A chill spread down Sheridan's back and lodged deep inside her. She shook her head and took another step away from him. "I never told you about my horses. How do you know about them?"

He shut his eyes, wincing, then opened them again. "You're right. You told me that later, in Santa Fe, but when I changed the timestream, it hadn't happened." He went on then, telling her a story of how they had escaped and gone with the DW to Santa Fe. He and Taylor had come back to Traventon to destroy the QGPs. Only Joseph didn't destroy them. He had used them to bring Echo back and by doing so had inadvertently changed time.

If it was a hoax, it was a creative one. Sheridan couldn't think of any reason Reilly would come up with this story. Unless he was using it to explain away the problems and inconsistencies in the program that he knew would crop up. If a character accidentally gave information he shouldn't have known—hey, blame it on the change in the timestream.

Joseph took Sheridan's hand, gently running his thumb across the back of it. "I don't expect you to forgive me for what I've done, for what I've put you through. I shouldn't have risked your life." His gaze dropped to her hand. He held on to it more tightly. "I'm sorry for all the pain you've suffered, and for every single memory you've lost."

Sheridan had a sudden desire to put her arms around Joseph, to relax into a hug and tell him it was all right. She wanted to believe him, to believe this. But she wouldn't let hope seep through her. Not yet. "What did we do after you gave me the picture of Santa Claus?"

He ought to remember that event.

"This," Joseph said, and pulled her closer. He slid one arm around her back. He ran his other hand through her hair, tangling his fingers in it. Then he leaned down and kissed her. At first it was gentle, his lips brushing across hers as though whispering something precious. More *I'm sorry*s.

She leaned in to him, let his arms envelop her. His lips were urgent now. This kiss had gone beyond *I'm sorry* and had turned into *I need you.*

It was proof he was real, that all of this was real. Then again, Taylor had known about the kiss. She could have told Reilly. She could have told Reilly any of the things Joseph had just said. Sheridan pulled away from Joseph. "Um . . . yes. I don't recall our kiss being quite that intense."

He took hold of her hand again. "That came later in Santa Fe too."

"Sounds like an interesting place."

"They have horses there. You volunteer at the stables. Or at least you did." He gave her a rueful smile. "I guess none of them will remember you when we go back."

Horses. Another piercing ray of hope.

The door slid open and Sheridan turned, expecting to see a med of some sort. Instead, Taylor came in. Her hair was forest green, her face a patchwork of browns and greens. A guy followed her into the room. He had to be Echo; he looked like Joseph in camouflage.

Taylor let out a sound that was half gasp, half cry, and hurried across the room. She flung her arms around Sheridan and hugged her.

"Are you okay?" Taylor asked, holding Sheridan away for a moment. "You're skinny. They starved you, didn't they?"

"No," Sheridan said. "They just put me through supermodel training." She never took anything anyone said during a

VR program too seriously. It helped her keep her emotions from becoming involved.

Taylor kept staring at her and then burst into tears. Taylor didn't cry easily. Which meant she was either really emotional or Reilly had gotten her personality wrong again.

Sheridan watched her sister carefully. "What were our brothers' names?"

Taylor let out a gasp and turned to Joseph. "You told me they didn't give her a memory wash."

"*I* know their names," Sheridan said. "I'm seeing if *you* do."

"Of course, I do," Taylor said. "Justin and Jake."

Joseph let out a sigh. "You still don't believe this is real, do you?"

Sheridan took a step sideways so that she could see everyone better. "I've spent most of the last month escaping. I've already had the chip removed half a dozen times, and I've seen all of you more than once. Well," she said, gesturing at Echo, "you're new."

Echo gave her a half smile. "I would have been around earlier, but apparently I was dead."

"We've all been busy," Sheridan said.

Taylor put her hand to her chest. "I can prove I'm your sister. Ask me anything."

Sheridan thought for a moment. "What was the color of my bedspread?"

"White with little pink flowers."

"Our fourth-grade teacher's name?"

"We weren't in fourth grade together."

"Why did I sprain my ankle last year?"

"Okay," Taylor said, drawing out the word, "that wasn't my fault. The other skier distracted me. You should have noticed I was talking to him and not paying attention to you."

"You ran over me, Taylor."

"He was really cute."

Sheridan smiled, then let the smile fall away. "Reilly captured you too. You could have told him all this."

"Yeah," Taylor said, tilting her chin in exasperation, "because that's the sort of thing he asked me about—disastrous flirting experiences while skiing."

And then the big test. The one that almost hurt to say because it could mean her hope would pop like a bubble. "Are you going to ask me anything about the QGP design?"

"It wouldn't do me much good," Taylor said, "since I'm the one who invented it."

This wasn't a bubble. This was real. Sheridan let the relief pour over her, let it saturate ever dry corner of her mind. She hugged Taylor, holding on to her with trembling arms. She didn't want to ever let go.

NOT LONG AFTERWARD, ONE of the nurses brought in tomato soup and sesame-seed crackers for Sheridan. She sat on her bed, taking slow sips while she told Taylor, Joseph, and Echo everything that had happened to her.

"So," Taylor said, when Sheridan finished with her story. "I was worried you were being tortured, but mostly you were running around with a hot guard?"

Sheridan took another sip of her soup. "Mostly I was stuck in a cell listening to government propaganda. The hot guard was only there some of the time."

Taylor let out an offending-sounded sniff. "Reilly hit me thirty seconds after he started questioning me and didn't stop until you told him you invented the QGP. But you—you got wined and dined by some male model?"

Sheridan shrugged. "I can't help it. You tick people off quickly."

Taylor normally wouldn't have left that sort of statement alone, but she didn't argue it this time. She just let out a long breath. "It's amazing they can put a chip in your brain that makes you experience a different reality."

"It's amazingly awful," Sheridan said.

Echo was sitting on a chair next to Taylor's. "People go to VR centers for fun—to explore places, be characters in stories—fly, if you want to. We'll take you to do a recreation program sometime. You'll see it isn't all bad."

Sheridan shook her head. "I don't ever want to leave reality again."

"When you say Tariq kissed you," Joseph said, still clearly stuck on that part of her story, "what exactly do you mean? Do you mean you kissed him back—that you were"—he rolled his hand, searching for the right phrase—"that you actually liked him?"

"Well, he wasn't bad as far as guards went," Sheridan said. "He did give me chocolate."

"I gave you chocolate too," Joseph said.

She glanced at him over her spoon. "When?"

"All right, not in this timestream, but I gave you some in the last one."

Sheridan took a sip of soup. "It doesn't count if it's not in this timestream."

"I'll give you more as soon as we get to Santa Fe."

Echo shook his head at his brother and made disappointed *tsk*ing sounds.

"What?" Joseph asked him.

"All my lessons on the art of flirting have been completely wasted on you." Echo waved his hand in Joseph's direction. "You're trying to buy her affection like it was a store item. What are you going to do next, offer her jewelry if she agrees to kiss you?"

Joseph raised an eyebrow at Sheridan. "Would that work?"

Sheridan took another sip of her soup. "What sort of jewelry?"

"I'll let you pick it out," Joseph said.

Echo looked upward. "Absolutely pathetic."

Taylor checked the time on her comlink. "Are the meds discharging Sheridan soon?"

Echo and Joseph gave her identical looks of perplexity. "Discharge?" Echo asked. "You mean the nasty stuff that comes out of an infected wound? Sheridan doesn't have any of that, does she?"

"No," Joseph said. "In the twenty-first century, *discharge* meant firing a gun."

"Well, that's obviously not it," Echo said. "Taylor wouldn't ask if the meds were shooting her sister."

Taylor leaned toward Sheridan. "This is the sort of scintillating conversation you've missed in the last month and a half." Then to Echo and Joseph she said, "I meant when can we leave?"

"As soon as Sheridan is ready," Joseph said. He leaned over to see the progress she'd made on her soup. "Are you still hungry?"

"No." Sheridan couldn't help it that her voice wavered with emotion. She didn't do anything to stop the tears forming in her eyes. "I'm full."

chapter 39

Taylor hadn't realized how much stress she was under until she felt it silently slip away. She sat watching her sister eat soup and couldn't think of anything she'd ever seen that was quite as wonderful. Sheridan was safe. She was going to be all right. Not the same, Taylor knew—a person couldn't go through a month and a half in a detention center and be the same—but Sheridan was going to be all right. And judging from the glances she kept sending Joseph's way, the new timestream would probably end up at the same place the old one had gone.

While Sheridan finished up her meal, Taylor volunteered to go get the backpacks. Then she volunteered Echo to come with her. Joseph absently said, "I'll help too."

He stood, but Taylor waved for him to sit back down. "We can do it," she said. "Someone should stay with Sheridan."

Joseph sat back down without further encouragement.

Taylor walked out the door and Echo followed her. After the door slid shut behind them, she stopped in the hallway. She had meant to say something. Instead she found herself just standing there, staring at Echo's torso.

If Echo thought this was strange, he didn't comment about it. He put his hands in his pockets, a casual gesture. "She seems nice, your sister. She reminds me of you."

Taylor looked at his face to see if he was serious. He smirked at her.

"Sheridan reminds a lot of people of me. It's part of that whole identical-twin thing."

"I know," he said, chuckling. "I finally got to use that line on someone else. You don't know how many times I've heard it."

Taylor tilted her head. "Does Sheridan really remind you of me?"

"No," he said. "She seems naturally kind, charitable, and tenderhearted—qualities you're clearly lacking."

He was laughing again, so Taylor gave him a playful push. "I never should have told you about that."

Echo grabbed hold of her hand. "Yes, you should have." He pulled her a step closer. "Because I want to know everything about you."

Taylor smiled, wrapped her arms around his neck, and kissed him. It occurred to her, as he kissed her back, that she should have given him a choice in the matter. It had been presumptuous to assume he still wanted to kiss her. But he didn't appear to mind. He wound his arms around her waist and pulled her closer. He was warm and strong and made her feel happy.

When he finally lifted his head, he kept his arms around her. "So does this mean you've forgiven Joseph for bringing me back?"

Taylor let her fingertips brush through the ends of Echo's hair. "Who could blame Joseph for wanting to save his brother? It was a moving, generous thing to do."

Echo laughed, then bent down and kissed her again.

chapter hapter
40

Sheridan loved being out in the forest, loved seeing the sunshine lighting up the leaves, making everything glow around her. Birds chattered in the trees, and the earth smelled alive and welcoming.

They rode horses single file, and no one talked because their guide didn't want them to draw the attention of vikers. They didn't reach the next base—another underground one—until the forest had grown cool and shadows dimmed everything.

At dinner they were finally able to talk again. They sat at a table eating a rehydrated pasta dish that wasn't half bad considering it had looked like beige Styrofoam until they'd poured hot water onto it. Ren and Lee mostly talked to each other, discussing things they were going to say to the council when they returned. While they ate, Taylor and Joseph told Sheridan and

Echo the things that had happened in the first timestream.

"I figured out how to contact the DW?" Sheridan asked when they were done. "Not my genius sister?" She speared a forkful of pasta. "I'm not going to let you forget that, even if I don't remember it."

"Great," Taylor said.

"I saw the city wreckage," Sheridan added, suddenly remembering this fact. "I went that way in a VR program once. I thought I recognized it. Is that why—because I really had been there?"

Taylor, Joseph, and Echo all sat for a moment pondering the question, their food forgotten. Sheridan could nearly see the physics equations running through their minds.

"It doesn't seem possible," Taylor said, "but then, who knows why people have déjà vu or what happens to experiences when a timestream is switched. Perhaps people can experience ghost memories, just like people who've lost limbs can still feel ghost limbs."

"Memories may be made of a type of matter," Echo agreed. "Perhaps they leave an imprint in the time continuum—like light that still travels after a star is destroyed. Perhaps you experienced an echo in there."

"Time has a curve to it," Joseph added. "Perhaps . . ." He didn't say more. He just looked hopeful. "Was there anything else that seemed like a memory?"

Sheridan flushed and poked at her food. "I dreamed once that I was sitting with you on a green couch. We were, um, talking."

"Bright green?" Joseph asked. "Sort of ugly?"

"Yes," Sheridan said.

"That's my couch," Joseph said happily. "Anything else?"

She shook her head. "Do you think more memories might come back?"

"I hope they will," he said.

After that, Echo and Taylor related the things that had happened to them while they were in Traventon. Taylor grew somber when she talked about Xavier and angry when she talked about Allana. Joseph, Sheridan noticed, clenched his teeth when anyone mentioned Allana's name. Although when the story was done, all he said about her was "I hope she has better luck with the Dakine this time around."

"The Prometheus Project worked great," Echo told Joseph, changing the subject. "Granted, it worked against us, but it still worked great."

Joseph finished off a bite of pasta. "You should have made it mobile. My model saved you from the Dakine."

"I admit your model is better," Echo said. "If you only need to use it once. The problem is, if you're running from the government or the Dakine—yeah, you're going to need it more than once."

Joseph took a sip of water and leaned back in his chair. "You just don't want to admit mine works better."

"*Better* is a subjective term," Echo said.

Taylor's gaze bounced between the two of them. "Are you always this competitive?"

"No," Echo said. "Sometimes we're worse."

Joseph laughed, a sound of happiness without any

competitiveness. He smiled at his brother, watching him for a moment. "Don't ever die on me again."

Echo grinned back. "I hadn't planned on making it a habit."

They were all so happy that it was easy for Sheridan to relax, to shed any dark thoughts that pressed in on her. She was safe. She was free. But that night, Sheridan couldn't sleep. She couldn't even try.

She and Taylor unfolded their thermo-blankets onto some gel mattresses in the room that they shared. Taylor lay down on her bed and adjusted her pillow. Sheridan wrapped her blanket around herself and sat on her mattress with her back resting against the wall.

"We've got a long day ahead of us tomorrow," Taylor told her. "You need your sleep."

"I'll be fine." How could Sheridan explain to her that she never knew when she woke up whether she was in a VR program or not? It wasn't rational. She had already proved to herself that this was real. She'd eaten. Taylor knew the truth about the QGP. But Sheridan was still afraid that if she went to sleep, when she woke up this would be over. She would be back in her cell. She couldn't face it, so she couldn't sleep. She didn't even want to lie down.

Taylor watched her from her gel mattress. "Do you want me to stay up with you?"

"No," Sheridan said.

Taylor didn't hit the controls for the light. She eyed Sheridan with concern, waiting for her to say more. A minute went by. Taylor kept waiting.

"I killed Reilly," Sheridan said. "I killed someone."

Taylor shifted her blanket. "It was self-defense. And you didn't *actually* kill him. He's probably still alive. In the technical sense. Besides," she went on, because Sheridan hadn't spoken, "it was his own fault for putting you through all those VR programs. You didn't know it was real."

"But if I had known it was real," Sheridan said, "I would have done the same thing. I just would have felt worse while I did it."

"It was self-defense," Taylor said again. "You can't feel guilty about that. Everyone has the right to—" She paused, reconsidering. "You know, you actually *saved* Reilly's life. Lee had orders to kill him. And Lee would have, if you hadn't sent Reilly into the erasing chamber. I'm sure if Reilly still had the ability to speak and remember it, he'd want to thank you."

"I'm not so sure he'd thank me," Sheridan said, but she smiled at her sister's attempt to make her feel better.

"You saved his life," Taylor emphasized. "Think of it that way." She watched Sheridan for another moment. "I can stay up with you if you want."

Sheridan shook her head. "Get some sleep. I'll be fine."

Taylor turned off the light and settled into her bed. Sheridan stared out the window at the night sky, at the darkness that was now pierced and glowing with stars. Countless stars. Ones she couldn't even see. Suns as bright as the one that gave Earth life.

The darkness wasn't so bad as long as you could see the stars.

Sheridan pulled the blanket around her, tucking its edges

in. Eventually she would be all right. Eventually she would feel like she was really free. She tilted her face upward and let a million points of light shine down on her.

Sometime during the middle of the night she fell asleep.

chapter hapter
41

On the last day of the trek, Echo grew nervous. Lee and Ren had called the leaders of Santa Fe to report on the mission and had told them everything from Xavier's death to Reilly's demise. The leaders knew that Echo was coming. Which meant his father knew too.

Jeth also knew that Echo had joined the Dakine, and that this bad decision had led to an assassination attempt against Joseph. When Echo got to Santa Fe, he would have to see the disappointment in Jeth's eyes, the accusation, a coldness where love used to be.

Several times during the trip, Joseph had reassured Echo that Jeth would be happy to see him. But that was the thing about having a twin brother—Echo could tell when Joseph was shining up unpleasant facts. Joseph wasn't any more sure what

Jeth's reception would be than Echo was.

As they flew the last distance on their airbikes, Echo began to sort out expectations, to quantify them. It was fine if Jeth was angry at him and yelled a lot. Echo deserved it. He hadn't just made a bad decision; he'd crashed all their lives. Anger was fine. Just so long as Jeth still talked to him. Jeth might, after all, refuse to see him.

It would be all right if Jeth said he didn't want Echo to live in the same apartment with him. Echo was twenty years old. Most children lived on their own at that age. Joseph only lived in Jeth's apartment because they were both new to the city and it was crowded. Echo wouldn't mind rooming with someone else. Just so long as it was near to Jeth and Joseph. He still wanted to spend time with them.

And then there was work. Originally Echo hadn't even wanted to be a historian. He'd only gone along with it because he'd wanted to work with Joseph. But now the thought of Jeth not wanting Echo around, of him not sharing his theories and asking for Echo's opinions . . . Echo's chest felt tight every time he thought about it. What if he had to find a new profession, had to start over and apprentice at something else? Jeth might completely delete Echo from his life.

And that was the worst thought of all.

When Santa Fe was looming ahead of them, so large that they could no longer see the top of the dome, Lee and Ren landed their bikes and Joseph followed. As Lee dismounted, he told Echo, "We've got to wait here for the security team. They need to make sure we're legitimate before they open any city gates." Lee looked at his comlink. "We called in. It shouldn't take them long to get here."

It didn't. Almost as soon as Lee finished speaking, Echo heard the rumble of vehicles coming their way. Moments later two large covered trucks pulled to a stop in front of them. Armed men hung from the back, scanning glasses on their eyes as they surveyed the area. "They're alone," one man called.

A ramp lowered, making room for the group to roll their air-bikes onto the truck. Before the ramp even touched the ground, a man jumped down from the back of one of the trucks. Echo immediately recognized him. It was his father. Jeth's maroon hair was shorter, and he no longer wore any sort of face dye. It made him look older somehow. Or perhaps the stress had done that—having a son killed, and knowing that the son had brought it on himself.

Echo stared at Jeth in surprised silence, searching for something to say. All he could do was swallow.

Jeth's gaze ricocheted between Joseph and Echo. "Echo!" he called. In their camouflage dye, Jeth couldn't tell who was who.

Echo stepped forward. There was no more putting it off, no way to deny any of it. His mistakes hung off him, raw and visible for his father to see.

Jeth came toward him, staring as though he still didn't quite believe it. When he got within arm's reach, he stopped and his face crumpled with emotion.

"I'm sorry," Echo said. It was the only thing he could get out before Jeth broke into tears. Echo hadn't ever seen his father cry before. This was going to be bad.

"I'm sorry," Echo said again, feeling how inadequate the

phrase was. His words tumbled from his mouth, too fast, disjointed. "I didn't realize what would happen—I didn't want—I never would have joined if I—"

"I know," Jeth said, putting his hands on Echo's shoulders. "I know you wouldn't have."

"Then why are you crying?"

Jeth wrapped his arms around him like he'd done when Echo was a little boy. "Because you were dead and now you're alive."

chapter hapter
42

Taylor wanted to go back to her apartment and rest. Instead the entire group went into council chambers, where they had to tell about their experiences all over again. Taylor told what had happened up until her group reached the courthouse lobby; then she couldn't speak, couldn't even look at the councilmen and councilwomen who watched her with heavy gazes. They already knew what had happened to Xavier. Lee and Ren had given Santa Fe a report when they'd reached the first base. But she still couldn't speak. Her throat felt as though someone had tightened a knot around it.

Taylor remembered the day the team had left for Traventon. She had told President Mason, "Freedom means paying off your debts. After this is over, we're even." She would never be even now. Xavier had died for her. How did a person pay back that sort of debt?

Echo finished their story while Taylor looked at the table, watching the wood grain go in and out of focus. As he concluded, she managed to say, "Tell Xavier's family he was a hero. Tell them I'm sorry we couldn't bring home his body. . . . Tell them I . . ." But then the words seemed to lodge in her throat and she couldn't get anything else out.

She didn't ever want to meet Xavier's family. She didn't want to know if he was married or whether he had children. She didn't want to see them weighing the value of his life against hers.

Lee and Ren spoke next. They were surprisingly complimentary of each other during their report. That was something Taylor hadn't expected. It was the first time she'd noticed, though she should have seen it on the trip home, that their earlier distrust of each other had gone.

President Mason thanked them for their efforts on Santa Fe's behalf, but the words had a hard time finding purchase in Taylor's mind. She was still back in the Traventon courthouse lobby, endlessly reliving those last minutes and trying to redo them. If only she hadn't fallen down and delayed herself. If only . . .

Taylor didn't realize that the president had excused the team, and given the council a recess, until everyone got up from the table and made their way to the door. Then she stood up and followed the others outside.

Joseph paused a little ways away from the building's doors.

"I was thinking," he told Taylor, "that after we get Sheridan and Echo situated, we could take them on a tour of the city." He turned his attention to Sheridan. "You'd like that, wouldn't you?" The corners of his mouth lifted into a smile. "I've got a lot of credits now. We could look at jewelry. . . ."

Sheridan blushed and laughed.

Echo took Joseph by the arm and began leading him away. "Don't worry," he told Sheridan with exaggerated concern. "While we're gone, I'll have a talk with Joseph on the art of being subtle." Echo gave Taylor a wink. "Message us when you're ready."

And despite what he'd just said to Sheridan, the smile Echo sent Taylor wasn't subtle at all.

Taylor would have started off with Sheridan to their apartment, but President Mason walked up to them. His expression during the council meeting had been stern. Now it held different emotions: sadness and concern. It softened him, made him seem more human.

"I wanted to let you know," he told Taylor, "that Xavier's family doesn't blame you for what happened."

The phrase didn't give her much comfort. It sounded like the polite sort of thing people in Santa Fe said to each other when they weren't arguing. "How do you know that?" Taylor asked. She blamed herself. How could they not?

"Because I'm his father," President Mason said.

Taylor heard Sheridan's sharp intake of breath, but she didn't say anything. Taylor didn't either. Her worst fear had come true, was standing here looking her in the eyes. Eyes, she could see, that were tinged with the deep pain of loss.

"It was Xavier's choice to give his life for yours," President Mason went on, perhaps because she was still staring at him, horrified and mute. "It was always in his nature to help others. It's why he became a surgeon. He wanted to save lives. . . ."

This only made Taylor feel worse. It had never been in her nature to help others. She felt the debt of Xavier's life weighing down on her, heavy, impossible. A flash of fury ran through her at all of it. "You knew it was a dangerous mission," she said, "and you knew what your son was like. How could you have let him go? Why didn't you stop him?"

President Mason should have gotten angry at her. He had come over to comfort her, and she had turned around and blamed him for his son's death. President Mason's eyes were still kind though. "I knew the importance of the mission. Who would I have sent instead?"

The tears that had threatened Taylor throughout the meeting came now. She couldn't stop them. She wiped at her face and didn't say anything else. She was horribly bad at giving condolences and apparently just as bad at accepting them. What she should have said was *thank you*. She wanted to say it, needed to say it, but somehow she could only stand there and cry.

President Mason turned to Sheridan as though this was any other conversation and it wasn't awkward for Taylor to be silent and weeping. "Ren and Lee said you couldn't sleep on the trip home. Would you like an appointment at the MedCenter? They could help find the problem."

Sheridan shook her head. "I already know what the problem is. I just don't know how to deal with it. How does a person forget being held captive for a month and a half?" She forced a smile. "Do they have memory washes that work in small increments?"

Sheridan was joking. Well, at least mostly joking. President Mason answered her seriously. "We don't erase memories in Santa Fe. We learn from them. Remember your captivity in order to better cherish your freedom."

He turned back to Taylor, putting his hand on her arm. "If you want to honor my son's sacrifice, then this is what you need to do: live well." He dropped his hand away from her arm. "I'd better go back to the council chamber now. We're hearing the last arguments before we decide the issue of populating the new cities." He glanced back at the building's doors. "Ren and Lee are both urging the council to vote for keeping our diversity intact. I was surprised by that."

President Mason turned to leave, had already taken a couple of steps away, before Taylor found her voice. "Thank you," she called to him.

He looked over his shoulder at her, nodded, then went back into the council building.

Taylor and Sheridan headed down the walkway toward their apartment. Neither of them spoke. Finally Taylor told her what the apartment was like. "It will be odd," she added, "to walk in and not see your stuff everywhere. But on the bright side, I already know where to find the things you're going to want, so it shouldn't take much time to rebuy all of them." She reached for her comlink. "I can order your clothes right now if you'd like."

"That's okay," Sheridan said. "Choosing things is half the fun. Besides," she said with a curving smile, "I'm going to want some clothes that match whatever jewelry Joseph buys me."

Taylor looked upward past the outlines of buildings. Traventon and Santa Fe had a lot of similarities: cars that ran on rails; tall, clean buildings; domes that covered the city. Santa Fe's dome was clear, though, so that you could see the sky. She couldn't believe what a difference that made—seeing the sky. Blue today with fat, bunchy clouds.

Taylor turned to her sister. "You're not really going to make Joseph buy you jewelry, are you?"

Sheridan laughed and didn't answer. Trees lined the walkway, and she kept reaching out and touching the leaves on the lower branches, fluttering them with her fingertips. She was enjoying them, Taylor knew, because she'd lived for a month and a half without them.

"Joseph feels so guilty," Taylor said, "he's probably already scrolling through settings with sapphires and emeralds."

Sheridan smiled. "Eventually I'll tell him just to live well, but maybe I'll let him buy me some earrings first."

Taylor smiled back at her. It was okay to smile. It was okay to look up and think that the clouds looked like piles of white pearls spilled into the sky. Happiness was part of living well.

C. J. Hill is the mother of twins. They aren't identical, but this doesn't mean she always calls them by the right name. In fact, she occasionally calls all her children by the wrong names (she has five) and has even been known to throw the dog's name into the mix. Laugh now, but you'll do the same thing when you have kids.

If C.J. had a time machine and could visit another century, she would probably go to the Regency era instead of the future. According to all the novels she's read, the past was filled with a multitude of dashing lords and viscounts who were always on the lookout for damsels in distress, whereas the future is populated by scary dystopian societies.

Visit C. J. Hill online at www.cjhillbooks.com.